It was only seconds after Catti left that Mary heard the voice and, going to the window, looked into the hate-filled face of Mag Cronin. The window was open and she clearly heard Mag's voice, hoarse with rage, spit out the words.

'That the malediction of God may fall on you and yours. That your children and theirs writhe in the agony mine did. That you cattle sicken and die and your crops wither. That you nor he may never prosper, know happiness or a contented mind. That every ill may befall you and yours. Your children and theirs and them that come after them. From the bottom of my heart, that's my curse on you and this house for all eternity.'

… Catti put the tumbler in Mary's trembling hand. She sipped a little before asking, 'D'ye believe in curses, Catti?'

'That I do not, Mrs Mac,' said Catti, turning her back on Mary for she couldn't meet her eyes while she lied. Instead she busied herself rearranging sheets that were airing on the clothes horse, wondering as she did so where had Mrs Mac been all her life? Wasn't she born and reared here? Didn't she know well that some have the power? More so them that had been sorely wronged. And if anyone was ever sorely wronged 'twas poor Mag Cronin.

Elaine Crowley was born in Dublin, and has also lived in England, Egypt and Germany. She has had a variety of occupations, including apprentice tailor, a stint in the ATS, Avon lady, and in the personnel department of British Steel. In addition to numerous articles, she has written four successful novels and a collection of short stories. Elaine Crowley is married and lives in Port Talbot.

A FAMILY CURSED

Elaine Crowley

ORION

An Orion paperback
First published in Great Britain by Orion in 1996
This paperback edition published in 1997 by Orion Books Ltd,
Orion House, 5 Upper St Martin's Lane, London WC2H 9EA

A CIP catalogue record for this book
is available from the British Library

ISBN 0 75280 409 X

Typeset by Deltatype Ltd, Birkenhead, Merseyside
Printed and bound in Great Britain by
Clays Ltd, St Ives plc

Acknowledgments

I would like to thank the following people for their help in the writing of this book:

Dr H. Darling, Master Of The Rotunda Hospital, Dublin; Mr Stephens, Iveagh Trust, Dublin; John Spender, Solicitor, Port Talbot; Mr Waller, Military Historian, Aldershot; Rose McNeill, St John the Evangelist R.C. Church, Horsham; the staff at Kings Inn, Dublin; Canon Sean Kearney; The London Times and Dublin Office; and last but by no means least, Christina Newcombe, Southwick, Brighton, whose letter to *The Times* on events in army married quarters over seventy years ago helped me enormously.

PART ONE

Chapter One

1850

THERE were only two prosperous men in the small town of Ballydurkin: Michael McCarthy and Daniel O'Brien. Michael was a provisions merchant and Daniel a publican. During the recent famine both men had increased their fortunes. Michael had done so by charging the highest penny to anyone who during the terrible years could afford food, and buying from men and women in desperate circumstances whatever they had to sell: garden implements, spades and slanes, holy pictures, even the women's wedding rings or their bedding such as it was, anything at all which he could get at the lowest price and sell on to dealers at a profit.

This business he conducted in a shed away from the shop where he catered for the local clergymen, a Protestant minister and the Catholic priest, and for the gentry who farmed in the area, supplying them with their hams and wines, sugar and tea, and all manner of delicacies brought down from Dublin. He sold snuff, white and brown, wax candles, dried and candied fruits, coffee and spices, cheese and chocolate. Anyone who entered the shop would remember its aroma for always.

Daniel O'Brien sold porter, stout and hard liquor. Even in the famine time he always had customers. Farmers on Fair Days, tinkers, destitute men who had earned a few shillings building on the relief schemes, putting up walls that guarded nothing, roads that went nowhere, all the schemes supposed to relieve their starvation. Once the money was in their hands their first port of call was the public house

3

though their wives waited at home demented with worry as to where the next slice of bread was coming from.

Both men had a common ambition. They wanted to own land. They believed that once their families had owned great farms, before the English came to Ireland. So they made a match between Michael's son, Peter, and Daniel's daughter, Mary. With what Michael could put up and the dowry Mary would bring they knew how to get the land they so desired.

Living outside the town was a man called Nicholas Ashleigh, a Protestant landowner whose family had come over from England during the time of Cromwell, his ancestor being one of the General's officers who, like many of his troops, was rewarded with a generous grant of land. Originally the first Ashleigh had had nearly a thousand acres. But poor management, profligate sons and his own generosity to tenants during the famine had reduced his fine farm to less than four hundred acres. But four hundred acres to an Irishman, whose ancestors may have owned much land in the long distant past but in the preceding centuries were lucky to be able to rent an acre on which to grow potatoes for their sole sustenance and enough grain to sell for rent, was considered a vast amount.

Besides the farm there was a fine stone Georgian house and good outbuildings. It would make an ideal home for the newlyweds.

'He'll sell it for a song,' Michael told Daniel one evening as the two men sat in the room behind the public house bar.

'How can you be sure of that?' Daniel asked.

'For one thing he hasn't settled his bill this long time and that was never a habit of the Ashleighs. Though the same can't be said for many a member of the gentry. For another, didn't he let the rents run in the bad years? Not one tenant of Nicholas Ashleigh's lost the roof over his head. The man is desperate. He wants rid of the place.'

'Where will he go, so?'

'That's no concern of mine. So long as my son has the land he can go to Timbuctoo for all I care.'

' 'Twill be grand all right,' said Daniel O'Brien. 'And a great catch my Mary is.'

'To be sure,' agreed Michael. 'A fine, lovely girl. A well-built girl who, please God, will give Peter fine sons to carry on when he and I and you have gone to our long rest.'

Michael's wife came in to ask if there was anything the men wanted. A few sandwiches? Another bottle of whiskey? She was devoured with curiosity as to how things were going and hoping a careless word might be dropped. 'Yerra, woman,' said her husband, 'if we want anything, haven't we tongues in our head? Away out and mind the customers.' Matchmaking and the buying of land wasn't a woman's business, he said after she closed the door.

They drank more whiskey, smoked their pipes and gazed at the fire. Then Daniel said, 'Apart from the Cronins there's no tenants to bother about on the land.'

'All gone to America or the famine pit, thanks be to God.' Michael took the pipe from his mouth, hawked his throat and spat into the fire. 'That Mag Cronin will create a fuss for sure.'

'She will that. Would you never consider letting her and John see out their time where they are? The field is no size at all. They've had a hard road. Four of their children died of the fever, and after their eldest girl disgraced herself it broke their hearts. A beautiful young girl she was, barely sixteen years. I do be often wondering who the man was.' As he spoke he was studying Michael's face, for rumour had it he was the father of the child. The girl Bridgid used to clean the rooms above the provisions shop, and someone had put up the money to pack her off to America. The priest had arranged the passage but where would he have laid hands on the money?

If Michael McCarthy was the child's father his face betrayed no hint of it as he said, 'Sure it could have been

anyone. A fella passing through, a soldier from the barracks, any one of a dozen or more. As you say, I'm sorry for the Cronins but sorrow never buttered a cut of bread and it's business we're talking. They'll have to go.'

'We'll be thought bad of. 'Tis one thing for the English landlords to evict, but for Irishmen to do it to Irishmen – I don't like it, Michael. She's crippled with the rheumatics and Johnny took paralysis after Bridgid disgraced herself. I'm telling you, they're not long for this world. Couldn't we wait them out?' Daniel said.

'We will not. The field has grown wild. They can't see to it nor themselves. They'll be looked after in the Workhouse. They'll have food and shelter and medical attention. And besides, I don't want anyone on that land except a McCarthy. Mag Cronin is a mad oul' bitch. I remember Ashleigh once telling me she walked as many fields as she could every day of her life.'

'What in God's name would she do that for?'

'Laying claim to them. Ashleigh told me himself. He had asked one day when he came upon her and she said to him: "These fields were the Cronins' when your father's people were ploughboys beyond in England. They were wrenched from us, the rightful owners."'

'Is that a fact? I never heard that before. How did Ashleigh take it?'

'Sure he only smiled. Hadn't her mother-in-law done the same thing in his father's time, and going back beyond that? He knew well the answer he would get. But being a gentleman he could not pass her by in the field without a word of conversation. Well, she'll not walk them any more. I'll see to that.'

Mary O'Brien was a gentle dreamy girl, an only child adored by her mother who as she approached marriageable age felt many a pang of sadness, knowing well how her daughter's head was filled with dreams of romance. Of

meeting a man to fall in love with. A man like those Mary read of in her books of poetry.

Mary, unaware of her mother's unease, continued to sew and work her bobbins, and if she wasn't recalling the poetry she was thinking of romance and love. Of meeting a man of her choice, and the wonderful, romantic courtship that would follow. Of love and kisses, whispers, secret meetings. Standing against her parents' wishes until finally all objections and resistance were overcome and with her mother's and father's blessing she and the handsome man were married and lived happily ever after.

Such things did happen. At least the poets wrote that they did, and there were stories told of such happenings and songs sung about them. And she used to dream when she was younger that they would also happen to her. But lately it had been brought home to her that real life was seldom how the songs or poems portrayed it. The man you married was chosen for you. Money and or stock changed hands. The money she brought to the McCarthys would buy land. In other cases the dowry was the means of the bridegroom's sister finding a husband. The husband's family used it to marry off one of their daughters. It was how the system worked. A way of ensuring that women could marry.

And because she was a biddable girl Mary accepted it as she would accept Peter McCarthy. Consoling herself that at least he wasn't an old man as many bridegrooms were. Some old enough to be their bride's father.

She would have chosen a dark-haired man, one with dash, one who could set her heart racing. Not that she knew such a one except in her dreams. And now she was grown up and such dreams must be cast aside and she be thankful that it wasn't an old, bent man, with no hair and spindly legs, a widower with children older than herself, whom she was to marry.

The girl who had disgraced herself was Bridgid Cronin, a

girl with wild, black curly hair and startlingly vivid blue eyes. After Bridgid's complaining of feeling ill it took her mother Mag very little time and few questions to find out the cause. 'Who was it?' she screamed, and brandishing a stick, beat her daughter round the arms, shoulders, back and legs. 'You hoor, who was it? Was it Michael McCarthy and you above doing the rooms over the shop? Answer me, you hoor's melt, or I'll kill you!'

Bridgid evaded as many blows as she could and remained silent. Her father John, hearing the commotion, came in from outside, a thin man bent double, able only to walk with difficulty because of arthritis. He tried to protect his daughter, so that the blows from the stick rained also on his frail body. 'Leave the child alone,' he implored his wife. 'You'll be the cause of killing her.'

'Kill her I will if she doesn't name the name. And a good riddance she'd be. Why was she spared and my other lovely innocent girls above in the famine pit? Lord have mercy on them.'

Not until Bridgid collapsed on the floor did her mother put down the stick, throw a basin of cold water over her and order her to stand up. 'Get up,' she ordered. 'You're coming to the priest, and if you won't tell him Hell is staring you in the face.'

Father Clancy was no more successful than Mag Cronin had been in finding out the man's name. He shook his head sorrowfully and told Mag not to worry, he would see to things. The girl wouldn't stay in the parish to sully the Cronins' good name.

'Keep her in the house until you hear from me. Say nothing to no one. There's homes run for fallen women by the nuns in Cork and Dublin, and further afield. I'll fix it.'

'It's signed and sealed,' the priest said when next he spoke to Mag Cronin. 'There's a convent across in New York. I've sent a letter to the Mother Superior explaining the

predicament. I knew her well when I was a boy, there'll be no bother at all, and a generous benefactor in the parish will pay Bridgid's passage to America.'

The dirt bird, Michael McCarthy, Mag thought to herself. 'Tis him that's the guilty party. Destroying my child and now sending her to the ends of the earth. But sure what can I do to the likes of him? And there's no fear that the priest would offend him by making him do the decent thing and lose the money that McCarthy greases his paw with. God's curse be on the pair of them! I'll hold my tongue and live out the rest of my days in sorrow with neither chick nor child in my old age.

Bridgid was never let across the door except to relieve herself not far from the cottage where a clump of bushes grew. And it was to there that her cousin, Patty Cronin, crossed the fields from the next village, having heard as one heard everything that went on in the vicinity that Bridgid was leaving the next day. No one was sure exactly where she was going though there was a strong rumour as to why and who was the cause of her downfall.

It was early in the morning when Patty came and hid herself in a ditch to watch for Bridgid come to relieve herself. And when she did and was out of view of the cottage, Patty hissed, 'Bridgid, 'tis me. I've come to say goodbye.' And she rose from the ditch and, approaching the cousin she loved, threw her arms round her. 'I'm that sorry for your trouble and I couldn't let you go without taking my leave of you.' The two girls wept in each other's arms. And then Patty asked, 'Where is it they're sending you?'

'To America.'

'America! I'd get myself into trouble to go to America. Sure you're made for life. What's here in Ballydurkin, or Ireland for that matter? Dry your tears, girl. In America you'll find a grand husband. I only wish I was in your shoes. Relieve yourself now and get back before your mother comes looking for you and takes a stick to both of us.'

'I'll send for you, Patty. I'll send you the passage money when I'm on my feet,' Bridgid promised as she rearranged her clothes and they embraced in farewell. 'And I'll tell you who the man was. Let me whisper it in your ear. But first you'll have to promise never to let the secret cross your lips for I'd find out and not send the money.'

Patty promised and Bridgid whispered. Patty's face paled when she heard. 'May God love you,' she said, 'and I'll never breathe a word of what you've told me.'

'And I'll send the passage money.'

Bridgid left the next morning before it was light. She had few possessions, so few that they made only a small bundle wrapped in her threadbare shawl. Along with them she took her baptismal lines and a sealed letter from Father Clancy to be handed to the Mother Superior when she arrived in New York. Tears washed her father's face as he said his goodbyes. Her mother kept her back turned and not until Bridgid was walking away down the boreen did she go to the door and look after her. Her slip of a girl. Her beauty still with the marks of the famine hunger about her thin arms, legs, shoulders and immature breasts. Hatred for Michael McCarthy surged in Mag's heart. Hatred and an overwhelming desire to avenge her daughter. And she knew there were ways and means of visiting vengeance on him. She would call upon her power to do it.

After a five-week voyage Bridgid arrived in New York on a roasting hot day. Momentarily she forgot why she was here, caught up in the excitement of the strange place. The smells from the warehouses that lined the quays. The sky with not a cloud in its brilliant blue. The burning dry heat. The crowds. Men with black faces. Men and women speaking in languages she didn't understand.

But soon she came to her senses and found her way to the waiting nuns who held above their heads a banner with the name of the convent lettered on it. Here she was to wait

until all passengers had disembarked. When they had and more girls and women had joined the group they set off in a straggly line with two nuns leading the column and two bringing up the rear to a tall forbidding-looking building behind the waterfront.

There the Mother Superior interviewed each arrival, read the letters they had brought from their parish priest and told the girls what their duties would be. They would work in the laundry until their babies were born. The children would be taken from them at the moment of birth, given to wet-nurses and afterwards put up for adoption.

Bridgid's baby was born early in January 1850. The infant was a boy. She haemorrhaged and died without ever looking on the face of her son. He was baptized John Patrick, and when he was adopted his mother's baptismal lines and his birth certificate were his only possessions.

Preparations for Peter and Mary's wedding were made. Father Clancy would officiate. Months beforehand Mary and her mother went to Cork City to buy material for the wedding dress. They chose an expensive heavy oyster-coloured silk and a hat with ostrich plumes. The local dressmaker made the gown. Neither it nor the hat was the height of fashion but both were attractive. The wide-brimmed hat framed Mary's face. The dress showed her tiny waist and was comfortable to walk in. Her only ornament was a gold cross and chain.

Two months before the wedding the Ashleighs' land and house became Peter's property and he set the eviction of Mag Cronin and her husband in process, having arranged that they should move into the Workhouse. On the morning that the cottage was to be vacated he arrived with the local sergeant of police and executed the order. John went quietly, but Mag stood her ground and cursed him and all belonging to him then went at a hare's pace away over the fields, where she found shelter with relations.

The church was of recent origin and despite the luridly coloured statues and flowers placed in it by Mary's mother there was a raw feel to it.

A girl from Limerick with whom Mary had gone to school was her bridesmaid and an acquaintance of Peter's his best man. The guests for the most part were other strong farmers and publican friends of Mary's father. Local people come to see a wedding filled the back seats.

Resignedly Mary went to the chapel and offered up her prayers that she would be a good wife to Peter, a good mother when God blessed her with children.

Her own mother wept openly, knowing that her gentle Mary should have married a man she was greatly in love with, and she prayed that Peter would be a considerate husband, go to his wedding bed reasonably sober and treat her daughter with consideration.

After the wedding breakfast, which finished in the late afternoon, the serious drinking began. Mrs O'Brien was relieved to see that Peter wasn't amongst the drinkers, and that when the bridal couple left for their new home he was sober.

Mary had no idea what to expect when he came from an adjoining small room where he had undressed and shyly got into the bed beside her. They were both virgins and on their first night the marriage wasn't properly consummated, Peter apologizing in an embarrassed voice that he was afraid of hurting her and saying things would improve with time. Eventually they did, but never to any great extent. But having nothing to compare their lovemaking with Mary enjoyed the kissing and accepted the rest as part of married life.

The next morning Peter was up early and out about the farm. Catti, who had worked for the Ashleighs, stayed on to work for Mary and another two young girls had been employed to work under her supervision. Catti was the same age as Mary, unmarried, from a big family, warm-

hearted and good-natured. She and Mary had gone to the same infant school, the same chapel, and until Mary went away to school were always on good terms. Mary knew that they would get on well together.

When she came down to the kitchen, a very big room with an enormous table left by the Ashleighs, a dresser the length of a wall, many kitchen chairs and two wooden armchairs, one each side of the range, on which Catti had placed brightly coloured crocheted cushions she had made as a wedding present, Mary felt at home and that it was a good room in which she would be happy. And that Peter was right in deciding they wouldn't for a long time use the cold dining-room and drawing-room. He had said when they looked over the house: 'I wouldn't feel that comfortable in them yet. But our children will, please God. Like the Ashleighs, they'll be born to such a way of living.'

Catti put two new-laid boiled eggs and a plate of freshly baked soda bread in front of Mary and brought her the tea pot. The kitchen got the sun in the morning, dazzlingly bright, and Catti advised Mary to change places and sit with her back to it. 'You've got all your wants now, Mrs Mac, so I'll see what the two young girls are up to. You have to start them off on the right foot. I'll only be a minute.'

It was only seconds after Catti left that Mary heard the voice and, going to the window, looked into the hate-filled face of Mag Cronin. The window was open and she clearly heard Mag's voice, hoarse with rage, spit out the words.

'That the malediction of God may fall on you and yours. That your children and theirs writhe in the agony mine did. That your cattle sicken and die and your crops wither. That you nor he may never prosper, know happiness or a contented mind. That every ill may befall you and yours. Your children and theirs and them that come after them. From the bottom of my heart, that's my curse on you and this house for all eternity.'

Mary screamed and screamed and screamed. Catti came

13

running followed by the servant girls. Streams of abuse still came from Mag's foam-flecked lips and her arms waved wildly. Catti sent the girls to find Peter, told Mary to shut the window and herself went outside. When coaxing didn't work, she dragged Mag away out of sight.

Peter and two of the hired hands arrived, bundling Mag into the pony and trap where one of the hired men restrained her. She was driven first to the Presbytery and from there, accompanied by Father Clancy, to the Workhouse where she was admitted.

'The poor creature, she's lost her mind,' Catti said after the trap had driven away. Mary was still too shocked to say anything and Catti suggested she should have a little sup of whiskey or brandy to revive her. 'Just a few teaspoons. I'll sugar it and put in hot water, 'twill do you a power of good.'

'Maybe just a drop then,' said Mary, and while Catti was preparing the drink, asked, 'Did you hear the things she said?'

'How could I and me outta the room?'

'She cursed us. The most terrible things she wished on us. Terrible, terrible things.'

Catti put the tumbler in Mary's trembling hand. She sipped a little before asking, 'D'ye believe in curses, Catti?'

'That I do not, Mrs Mac,' said Catti, turning her back on Mary for she couldn't meet her eyes while she lied. Instead she busied herself rearranging sheets that were airing on the clothes horse, wondering as she did so where had Mrs Mac been all her life? Wasn't she born and reared here? Didn't she know well that some have the power? More so them that had been sorely wronged. And if anyone was ever sorely wronged 'twas poor Mag Cronin.

'That was grand,' Mary said, getting up from her chair and placing the glass on the table. 'I used to believe in curses and fairies, leprechauns and fairy forts, before I went away to school. But the nuns taught us sense. Old pishogues the

lot of them, they told us. Not a word of truth in any of them, and moreover a sin for a Catholic to believe. Mag Cronin is only a poor old demented woman as you say. Amn't I right, Catti?'

' 'Deed an' you are, not a word of truth in any of them, Mrs Mac. They'll be back any minute. I'd say Father Clancy will drop in to see how you are. Will I get out the whiskey again?'

'Do,' said Mary, 'and I'll go and tidy myself up.'

Peter and the priest had a drink and Catti made tea. Mary asked about Mag Cronin and the Workhouse. 'There wasn't a hig out of her. Went in like a lamb. She'll be taken care of. Plenty to eat and drink and medical attention, which God knows she needs. The pity is she didn't go in on the day John did instead of hiding in one place and another. Brooding over her imaginary wrongs, letting them fester, and coming here to blackguard you this morning. But you're all right now?' the priest said.

Peter went back to what he'd been doing when Mag caused the commotion. Catti poured another whiskey for Father Clancy and Mary began to cry. 'What ails you?' asked Catti.

'I've tried and the whiskey helped at first but I can still hear the terrible things she said. I'll never be able to forget them.'

The priest motioned to Catti to leave the kitchen and close the door, and when she had he pulled his chair closer to Mary. 'Now you listen to me, child. That woman is a lunatic. Driven mad by the years of the hunger, the children who died . . .'

'And,' interrupted Mary, 'being evicted.'

'Ah, not at all. She was deranged long before that.'

'And her daughter being destroyed by a man and sent to America.'

'Before that as well her mind was gone. You mustn't dwell on such things. And as for the eviction, wasn't that an

act of charity? Neither John nor Mag could look after theirselves, the cottage was gone to wrack and ruin. Sure John couldn't dig a bed for the potatoes. No more could she. Nor bring in the turf from the bog. An act of charity, that's what the eviction was. Left to their own devices, one day they'd have been found dead or set fire to theirselves trying to get a sod of damp turf going.'

Father Clancy drained his third glass of whiskey, wiped his florid fleshy face with a snow white handkerchief and lit a cigar. 'Now, Mary, have I put your mind at rest?'

'Supposing it's true? Supposing what she wished on us happens?'

'Well, well, I am surprised at you. I credited you with more sense. There's no such things as curses. As a good Catholic you should know that. Didn't the nuns drum that into you? The only danger in a curse is if you dwell on it. If you believe in it as the unfortunate savages do.

'Of course,' continued Father Clancy, 'you're not a savage. You've got your faith in God and His blessed mother. They are always watching over and protecting you. Promise me now you'll put what happened this morning out of your mind, and I'll bless the house again before I go.'

It took several days before the vision of Mag Cronin and the words she had spoken to fade a little from Mary's memory. But gradually they diminished as she became involved in setting up house in her new home.

Still, once a week she sent Catti to the Workhouse with sweets and snuff for Mag Cronin and her husband and when, a few weeks later, John Cronin died, went to his funeral although terrified that Mag might be there and scream her curse again. But Mag wasn't considered fit enough to attend. Mary found herself praying that God might call Mag, let her be reunited in Heaven with John and the children she had buried. But Mag lingered, clinging to life.

Chapter Two

ONE day Peter came into the kitchen and announced that the first cow to be impregnated by Bennet's bull was in calf. Mary thought how boyish he looked, his fair-skinned face flushed, his fine light hair tousled and his blue eyes shining. He was rarely demonstrative but today he came and slipped an arm round her. And she knew the thought in his mind. When will I hear news from you that we are to have a child?

She smiled at him, as much as to say: be patient for a little while longer. God will send us a child, many children.

Three months after the cow Mary knew that she too had conceived. She let several months pass before telling her mother, then Catti, and finally Peter.

He looked at her with great pride, his little lithe Mary with her cloud of dark hair, now doubly precious since she was carrying his child, but shyness and awkwardness and it not being the custom prevented him from gathering her into his arms, kissing her and dancing her round the kitchen. All he said was, 'God has been good to us. Mind yourself now.' And he was back to his cattle, almost all now in calf.

Mary was almost six months pregnant and the cow who had conceived first not far off her time. She was dozing by the fire when she heard a tapping on the window. Looking to it, she saw the hate-filled face of Mag Cronin, and though the window was only open a few inches, heard her screech

out her curse again. Mary screamed and Catti came running in from the yard where she had been feeding the hens.

'Oh, Mrs Mac, have your pains started and you not due for many a month yet?'

'No, not my pains. Mag Cronin! She was here at the window. She cursed us again.' Mary's hands enfolded her belly, subconsciously protecting her baby which moved and kicked and made its presence felt.

'Asthoir,' crooned Catti to the distraught Mary. 'You were dozing and had a dream. Sure how could Mag be in two places at once? Isn't she in the Workhouse at death's door? A dream, 'twas all it was. My mother used to get them when she was carrying.'

'But I heard the tapping on the window and when I looked up Mag was there.'

'You heard that ould tree's long boughs tapping. The sound woke you with your mind still dreaming and you thought you saw what you saw. This time of the year the Ashleighs always had that tree cut back for the very same reason. I'll get one of the men to see to it.'

'Maybe you're right. Maybe 'twas only a dream. Already it's fading from my mind,' Mary lied.

Halfway to the byre Peter saw the herd running towards him calling, 'Come quick, Mr McCarthy, something's wrong with the cow. I think she's gone.'

'You fool!' cried Peter, pushing the man out of his way. 'How could she be dead? Wasn't she grand when I left you?'

The cow was stretched on the floor, her great rough tongue lolling from her mouth. Peter knelt in the manure-sodden straw and looked at the staring eyes, heard no breath and felt no movement of the calf when he ran his hands over the cow's belly. He laid his head down on the brown and cream hide to listen. She was still warm but not a

murmur of either heart could he hear. He rose and vented his anger on the cowman.

'What did you do to her? Why did you leave her? What happened? You bloody fool, you've been the cause of killing her, the best cow in the herd!'

The herd defended himself. 'I never stirred until she was gone for sure. And gone she was in a minute. She was moaning the way they do, but otherwise great. We knew the calf was big, that maybe we'd have to give her a bit of assistance. There seemed time enough so I waited and then she took this fit, you might say as if she was choking. Like that it came on her,' he said, snapping his two fingers together. 'And then she died. Maybe we could go in after the calf. Sometimes you can. I've seen it done.'

'The calf is dead, too,' Peter said, wiping his hands on a bunch of straw. And as he did so the face of Mag Cronin on the day he had evicted her flashed across his mind and he remembered her words. He shivered, then reminded himself that cows did sometimes die when they were calving, and that although she was the best there were many, many more cows about to calve in the prize herd he was building up.

'Get word to the butcher. She died in the whole of her health. We'll eat her.' The herd said he'd see to it.

In the kitchen, drinking his whiskey, his fee secure in his pocket, the butcher said, 'Never in all my days slaughtering animals did I see such a thing. Choked she did. Choked on a potato an elephant nor one of them hippopotamuses that you read about could swallow. But what I'd like to know, is where in the name of God would she have come across such an item?'

Out of his and Peter's sight Catti crossed herself.

'From many a begrudging hand,' said Peter. 'The herd for all I know. One of a dozen who wishes ill to befall me.'

'That's possible. But what possessed the cow to attempt swallowing such a monster of a potato?'

'Maybe,' said Mary, 'that poor cow was like women when they are carrying – had odd fancies. Sure how would you know?'

'Because,' replied Peter scornfully, 'cows have better sense.'

Finishing his drink and preparing to go, the butcher said, ' 'Twas a great pity all the same. She was carrying one of the grandest bull calves I've ever seen. You'd have had a champion in him.'

Chapter Three

SHORTLY after Peter lost the cow Mag Cronin died. Mary experienced a great sense of relief. Poor Mag's troubles were no more and after her time spent in Purgatory she would be with God in Heaven. To speed her passage through Purgatory Mary sent a large donation to Father Clancy so that Masses should be said for Mag's soul, then settled down in peaceful expectation for the birth of her baby which was born with little pain and in a relatively short time considering it was a first baby.

She had a son. When he came to see Mary and the baby, after a perfunctory kiss on her cheek, Peter devoted all his attention to the child. What a fine baby he was! Maybe he would lose the dark head of hair as he grew and come to resemble the McCarthys. 'He's a grand child, God bless and spare him. I'll call him Michael after my father.'

Tired though she was after the birth and wanting nothing except sleep, Mary immediately, and for the first time since she married, asserted herself. 'No,' she said. 'Not Michael.'

Peter was so taken aback that for a few minutes he didn't know what to say. But once having regained his composure he had plenty. 'Every first son of a McCarthy is called Michael. My father, his before him, my brother that died. The child will be christened Michael and that's an end to it.'

'He won't,' declared Mary, raising herself in the bed. 'I'm not fond of your father, nor my own for that matter. They're not men to whom I'm proud to say I belong, and

I'll not puff your father's pride by naming my first son for him. That's an end to it.'

She called him Justin and for fourteen days lay in bed cosseted by her mother and Catti, getting to know and love her little son.

By 1855 Mary had three sons, Justin, Fintan and Michael, born in that year, and a daughter, Ellen, born in 1854. Justin and Fintan had dark hair and resembled their mother. Ellen was also dark and considered by everyone to be a beauty. Michael was hailed from the minute he was born to be a McCarthy. ' 'Tis a pity,' said Peter, 'his grandfather didn't live to see him, and he his namesake, too.'

'A great pity, Lord have mercy on him, and on my father as well,' said Mary. Knowing that her words were false. She didn't grieve for either of the old men and doubted that if her father-in-law still lived she would have given his name to her third son.

During the next five years she gave birth to six more children: Honora, Laetitia, twin boys, Bernard and Brendan, Kathleen, then her last child, Dermot.

She took her pregnancies as the natural outcome of being a married woman. Adored her babies, oversaw the running of her home, worked in the dairy with Catti and the two girls making the butter, went to her religious duties, had Masses said for the dead and submitted very regularly to Peter's lovemaking. Occasionally she read a favourite poem about a man who said his sweetheart had a honey mouth that smelled of thyme, and wondered what life would be like married to him. Surely not like hers and Peter's? Surely a man like him would sometimes talk to you? Talk about things other than the next field he hoped to buy, the price of beef cattle or how the milk yield might be improved. And surely after taking her body he might have something to say? A word of tenderness, a caress. A hand that would smoothe her hair.

Not that Peter wasn't a good husband. He seldom said a harsh word to her, and anyone could see that he loved and was proud of his children. And she wasn't deprived of someone to talk to. There was her mother, Catti and the neighbours. Men, she would conclude, weren't the great talkers where women were concerned. But let them get together and there was no stopping them. Half joking, wholly in earnest, she'd heard them say, 'Leave it to the women. They'd talk the leg off a jackass!'

From the first day in school Michael made his mark, and as the years passed great reports of him came home. 'That child,' the master said, 'could be anything.' And from an early age Peter began planning that when he was old enough Michael would be sent away to school.

He was a lovable child but never as boisterous as his brothers, though able to run as fast, jump as high, handle his hurley stick and kick a ball with the best of them.

Sometimes Mary wondered if he might become a priest. It was a great honour to have a priest in a family. Once she mentioned this to Peter who agreed that having a son who was a priest was a great honour. 'But we have plenty of sons who can take the cloth. I have different plans for Michael.' What they were he didn't say.

The farm prospered. Peter purchased more acres as impoverished landlords left Ireland and more peasants were evicted and went in droves to England and America. He was proud of all he achieved. His spread of land. His six sons and four daughters. Fine bright healthy children and Michael the star in his crown. Michael who one day would move the McCarthy name into the professional classes. Mary was a grand woman, a wife for any man to treasure.

His health was good, for which he thanked God. He attended to his religious duties, had Masses said for his dead relatives and for the soul of Father Clancy who'd been more

than the McCarthys' spiritual adviser, a family friend as well. Not a transaction had ever taken place in his father's time that the priest wasn't party to. Peter missed him sorely. The pleasure it would have given him to go of an evening and talk about Michael. Relate how well he was doing in school. How in no time he would be off to Clongowes College.

Occasionally as he rode to markets and fairs Peter would pass Patty Cronin whose wild-looking dark hair and vivid blue eyes reminded him of her relatives, and for a while his mind would slip back into the past. To the acquisition of his farm, the eviction of the Cronins and the pregnant Bridgid. To the rumours that had circulated that his father had been her seducer, and one or two that he himself was responsible for the girl's condition. Lies. All lies. He had never laid a finger on her. And as for his father, he was a God-fearing man who had never looked at another woman after his wife died.

Peter was aware that he wasn't popular yet he was a fair master. Hard but paying an honest wage for an honest day's work. Never asking a man to tackle a job he wasn't capable of tackling himself. Not interested in politics or secret societies. Thrift and hard work could achieve anything a man desired, he believed. His father, Mary's, and Peter himself were the proof of that.

He knew that the eviction of the Cronins hadn't endeared him to the local people. The event was as fresh in their minds as if it had happened yesterday. That daily they waited for him, his family and his farm, to have Mag's vengeance take its toll of them. He could imagine them gathering in their cabins at night, telling and retelling the story of the Cronins. Adding to it as the years passed and it went down the generations. Time meant nothing to them. The curse could fall on him at any minute, and what difference did it make if it took a year or scores of years? Fall it would upon them. They'd puff on their clay pipes,

spit in the fire, nod their heads and murmur their agreement as the storyteller finished his or her tale.

Poor fools, Peter would think. Would they never learn? Always ready to believe anything. Always living in the past while the present passed them by. Was it any wonder they seldom prospered?

Every night Catti knelt by the side of her bed and said her prayers. She prayed for God to spare her parents and her brothers and sisters. She prayed for all those belonging to her who were dead. She prayed that if it was pleasing to His will that one day she might find a husband. And then she prayed for the McCarthys. That they would be spared from the curse that Mag Cronin had laid upon them. She prayed for Justin, Fintan, for the twins, Brendan and Bernard, for Ellen, Michael, Honora, Laetitia, Kathleen and Dermot, and for their mother, Mary. For all of them that she loved and worshipped. And because he was their father, though she had no regard for him, she added Peter to her list of those in need of protection. Lastly she had a word with Mag. 'I know the heart scald you suffered. But sure, Mag, you wouldn't want to harm a hair of the innocent children nor their mother either. Sure didn't she have to marry him? Wasn't the match made for her? What say no more than any woman did she have in it?'

'She didn't want you evicted. I heard her plead for you. In the name of God, don't you be doing anything up there that would harm one of them and displease Our Lord. Until the day I die I'll remember you in my prayers.'

And as the years passed without mishap she would tell herself that Mag had maybe listened and taken pity on Mary and her children. And then, for all that, fear and anxiety would possess her again and for days she'd go round the place with a long sad face.

Chapter Four

In 1867 when Michael was almost twelve he went to Clongowes College, a school run by the Jesuits in Clane, a village in County Kildare. With his father and mother he travelled from Cork to Dublin by train and from there to the college by a hired carriage. The excitement of travelling by train for the first time overcame his grief at leaving home and his apprehension of life in the college.

His father, who had made the train journey several times previously, pointed out places of interest that they passed. Mary spoke very little, her heart full of sorrow at the thought of parting from Michael, her clever son who delighted and sometimes irritated her with his showing off the knowledge he was acquiring from all his reading and special attention from his master.

As the train approached Kingsbridge she wondered how he would fare amongst his new surroundings. Would his showing off make him disliked by the other boys? Would they think of him dismissively as a 'fella from the country'? Would they make mock of his country accent? Would he be well fed and minded if he were sick? He was tall and strong and nearly twelve but to her who knew his vulnerability he was still one of her little boys.

'He's a grand little man,' Peter said when they had left him. 'He'll do well for himself.' And he seemed to grow by inches and his chest expand with pride that his son was taking his place with the cream of Catholic Ireland. 'If only,' he said, 'my father had lived to see this day, Lord have mercy on him.' After echoing the prayer for his father,

silently Mary added one of her own for family and friends and for Mag Cronin to have been granted Eternal Rest.

For a while Michael missed home, disliked sleeping in a dormitory, the darkness of the chapel, and was scared by tales of ghosts rumoured to haunt the college. Ghosts from long ago when the castle had been owned by others stretching way down the centuries.

His height and presence prevented bullying. He was good at games and clever at his school subjects. Clever also in a way that prevented his showing off as he had at home. For here he was surrounded by boys with equal intelligence and knowledge. He also had much of his mother's sensitivity and early in his first term took another new boy, a small shy boy, under his wing. By the end of his first term he was well settled in and he and James Farrell had become firm friends.

He wrote home regularly. From his letters Mary learned about James: that he lived in Dublin, that his father was a barrister, and that James had invited her son home. On hearing this Peter rubbed his hands. Watching, Mary was reminded of farmers at a fair after making a good sale. She waited to see him spit on them and congratulate himself on the bargain as was the custom. However, he desisted, saying instead, 'Wasn't I right sending him to Clongowes? Isn't he already making the right connections? And that's as important as the education.'

All the girls got measles at the same time. 'A blessing,' Catti said to Mary. 'With the lads we were tormented. For no sooner was one clear when the next went down.' Mary agreed that it was as well to have the thing over and done with, and wasn't it as well it was summertime and no school?

The curtains were kept drawn to protect the children's eyes. They were fed light diets and given draughts of saffron, and although the weather was warm their chests

were kept well covered for fear of pneumonia. Their ears were watched for discharge or pain for it was well known that many a child was left deaf after the measles.

Once the fever went they became well enough to leave their bedrooms, all except Ellen who had a relapse, causing her terrible pain in her head. Pain which made her scream aloud. The doctor said, 'It sometimes happens after measles. Keep her in bed for a while longer. Wet cloths on her forehead will bring down the fever and I'll send up a bottle for the headaches.'

The pain and fever left her but Ellen became listless and the doctor said that sometimes happened, too, and prescribed a tonic. Her fine features blurred as she put on weight. An unnatural amount, more of a bloating than fat. 'That'll go, Mrs Mac,' Catti assured Mary when she expressed her concern. 'Once she's up and about, haring here and there, it'll melt from her.'

But when Ellen was up she showed no inclination to hare about. Not much inclination for anything but lolling in a chair or on a sofa. She was no longer interested in the cats and dogs. Once or twice the thought flitted through Mary's mind that the fairies had taken away her lively little girl and left a changeling in her place. She kept such thoughts to herself. But as Ellen became worse, slurring her speech, either not able to hear what was said to her, or unable to understand, another fear took hold of Mary's heart: Mag Cronin's curse. Mag wasn't in Heaven under God's command, surrounded by His love. She was a lost soul, wandering the world and fulfilling the curse she had placed on the McCarthys.

Mary resolved to rid herself of the worm which had burrowed into her brain and prayed more fervently than she ever had before. To the parish priest she gave a large sum of money, enough to pay for six months of daily Masses for the soul of Mag Cronin. And she arranged to take Ellen to

Dublin, asking Peter before she went had he noticed anything amiss with their daughter?

'Why?' he wanted to know.

'I was beginning to think there is a want in her. You know, sometimes I have found myself wondering if . . .'

'If what? What are you on about, woman?'

'It crossed my mind that she might be a bit simple.'

'One of my children – a bit simple? I've never noticed her any different to the others. But I'll tell you this, God forbidding all harm. If she is, it isn't from my side of the family!'

The specialist gave Ellen a thorough examination of which she seemed oblivious. Afterwards he sat Mary down and talked to her. 'Mrs McCarthy, the measles didn't affect Ellen's hearing. That something ails her I am in no doubt, but I can't give a name to her condition. It may be a complication of the measles, though I have never come across such a case. Her relapse, the high fever and headaches, may have been a symptom of something affecting her brain. I have to admit I don't know. We've still a lot to learn about the brain. And sure, who's to say the affliction might not leave her as quickly as it came? I'll remember her in my prayers.'

With great sorrow mixed with fear, Catti and Mary's mother noticed daily the change in Ellen. Saw her once lively eyes take on a vacant stare. The limbs that not so long ago danced and ran and jumped grow daily heavier until she could walk only a short distance. They missed the merry prattling of her voice. Neither mentioned their fears to each other, nor to Mary. Between the three of them they nursed her and in the evenings the older boys carried her up to bed. At first her sisters were attentive, bringing her bunches of wild flowers, reading her stories, telling her of happenings in school. But as daily she responded less and less, they left her alone except for a passing touch of her hair and a smile.

Mary now pinned her hopes on the doctor's parting words: the affliction might leave her as quickly as it came. To this end she went on pilgrimages to local holy shrines and travelled the country to others where she fasted and walked barefoot over sharp flints. She bought relics from her places of pilgrimage and set out for home, hoping for a miracle. And found Ellen as she had left her.

In her letters to Michael his mother told him that his sister wasn't well. It was, she wrote, something to do with the measles, but with the help of God she would get better. And she asked him to remember her in his morning and evening prayers. On his first visit home he was surprised that Ellen didn't make the same fuss of him that his other brothers and sisters did, but not alarmed or distressed for her deterioration was as yet not discernible to a young boy. But on future homecomings, when it became apparent, he was in turns horrified, terrified, and felt a sense of revulsion as he looked at the shapeless slobbering figure on the couch. He suffered moments of panic, fearing that whatever ailed Ellen could also strike him down. That he too would become gross, insensible, helpless, and he was reluctant to touch her.

But in time a great pity replaced the fear and horror. He stroked her face and brought her wild flowers, little gifts bought with his pocket money, and though he doubted if she could hear or understand, he talked to her: telling her about Clongowes, James, the train journeys he made, and recalling all the adventures she and he had once had.

As time passed, like his brothers and sisters, he came to regard her less and less. She was just there. Someone to touch in passing, say a few words to and prop up. Someone to include in his morning and evening prayers.

Chapter Five

IN 1872 Michael went to Trinity College to read law. His friend James Farrell also entered the college to read the same subject. James lived in Merrion Square where many times during his schooldays Michael had spent weekends. In the beginning he didn't pay too much attention to the house in the beautiful square but as he grew older it made a great impression on him, as did Dublin which he came to love, and he made a vow that when he qualified he'd live in Dublin and have a house like the Farrells'.

Often as he walked through Sackville Street, the widest street he had ever seen, crossed the bridge over the Liffey, pausing to look down the river at Gandon's magnificent Custom House, and continued his walk to College Green where Trinity College faced the Bank of Ireland, he felt an overwhelming sense of relief at his escape from the country and the farm. Comparing his life now with that of his brothers who remained at home. Thinking of their pastimes. The games of hurling and football, an occasional escape to the races, handball and throwing the leaden ball along the country lanes.

Always under the eye of their father. Treated no better than the hired men. He wondered what they would make of the Dublin theatre, the music halls, all the attractions and amusements that were to hand. And each time his thoughts followed these lines he reaffirmed his vow to settle in the city, have a house like James and marry a lovely girl.

Not long after Michael went to University his mother met

31

Bridgid Cronin's cousin Patty at a fair. It was years since she had last seen her, before she was married to Peter. Occasionally then the girl would be in Ballydurkin visiting Bridgid. All the same Mary recognized her for she had a strong resemblance to the other Cronins, the same startlingly blue eyes.

Mary went to her. 'Patty,' she said, 'is it yourself? How are you this long time?' Patty was cool with her. Remembering how it was she and her husband who'd been the cause of hastening her uncle's death by sending him and Aunt Mag to the Workhouse.

'Grand, thanks,' she replied, and asked with little enthusiasm, 'And yourself?'

'Not too bad, thanks be to God. You're the image of Bridgid. The living spit of her.'

'That one,' said Patty, the coolness gone, her face becoming animated. 'Don't mention her name!'

'What happened? I always thought you were very close.'

'We were that. Closer than many sisters. And then off she went to America after promising to send me a passage. No more than I'd have done for her. No more than many a relation does for one of their own. And never a word, never mind the passage! Not one word in all the years. And don't give me the excuse she couldn't write. How many of us can? And isn't it a well-known fact that there's plenty in America who can and will for a small amount? Aren't there letters arriving every day of the week from them that never knew A from a bull's foot?'

'I'm sorry to hear that,' said Mary, 'very sorry indeed. Maybe she had a setback. Sure any day you could get a letter.'

'If I do, you'll be the first to know,' said Patty, her face closing. 'I'll leave you now for I've things to do.' And she turned her back on Mary and moved through the fair.

The meeting, the woman's hostility, and the word about Bridgid sent Mary's mind back to the past. Patty's animosity

was understandable. Given the time over again Mary realized it would have been better to have passed by without a word, for the memories she would have awakened in the woman must have been painful. Mary was a McCarthy and the McCarthys had wrecked the lives of Patty's people. In more ways than one if the rumour was true that Michael McCarthy had fathered Bridgid's child.

Still and all, Mary told herself as she began to drive home, Patty had found a husband and had her children. One of the lucky few. But what had become of Bridgid? She'd be round the forty mark, the same as herself and Patty, and the child, if it had lived, older than Mary's eldest. It was strange that she had never sent the passage. Stranger still that no word of her had come. Turning in through the farm gates another thought came to Mary. For all those who sent the money she supposed there were as many who hadn't. After all, thousands and thousands had gone to America and she only knew about those from her own locality. All over Ireland there would be women like Patty, still hoping. And all over America the ones who couldn't or wouldn't send the passage, Bridgid no doubt amongst them.

The miracle which Mary prayed for never transpired. Ellen lay on the sofa, slept and ate, and Catti, Mary and her mother continued to nurse her. Michael, in his second year in Trinity College, came home during the holidays and sometimes James Farrell accompanied him. James was now a handsome young man with auburn curly hair and eyes near enough the same amber shade. James was good company. The girls liked him. Mary often wondered if Honora wasn't a little smitten. But already a match was being arranged for her, to the son of a wealthy farmer from Kildare. The wedding would take place when she was eighteen.

If the young men stayed down until September they went out on the boat when the mackerel were running.

Justin and Fintan were keen fishermen, as was their father. They seldom missed the fishing.

In 1874, the year in which Honora was to be married, Mary's mother had a stroke which left her speech unaffected but paralyzed her legs. Mary accepted this as the will of God, something to be expected, for her mother was a good age. A devoted servant looked after her and every afternoon, leaving Ellen in Catti's care, Mary visited her mother.

Always her first question was, 'How is she today?'

And Mary's answer seldom varied. 'As usual, God love her. Eating and sleeping. It's like having a baby that never grows up.'

Then the servant would bring tea and the talk turn to other things. Lately it was about Honora's coming wedding and the bridegroom. 'I took a liking to him straight away,' Mrs O'Brien said one afternoon. 'He has a lovely open face. Though at one time I had hopes for her and Michael's friend, James. D'ye think they had notions of each other?'

'They might have had but she was already spoken for since she was sixteen. Tell me this, Mother. Did you have notions of anyone other than my father?'

'I did that,' her mother said. 'And he was a gorgeous man. A tall man with dark hair and the loveliest smile you ever saw.' Her eyes filled with tears. 'A daft old woman, that's what I am. Talking about things that happened nearly fifty years ago. Wipe my eyes, there's a good girl. I'd be better employed saying my Rosary,' she said, and smiled.

Not long after that visit Mrs O'Brien died in her sleep, and so did Ellen the following month. Mary missed them grievously. At her mother's wake the neighbours gave their sympathy, said what a kind good woman she was, that her life had been a long one and that soon she would be in Heaven. At Ellen's they said, ''Tis a happy release,' and Mary replied that it was. Knowing that the kind women were also saying, 'You carried a heavy cross for all the years,

'tis time it was lifted.' And she thought, little d'ye know how light it had become. How, as her children had grown up and distanced theirselves, Ellen had filled her life. The satisfying thing it was to make her clean and comfortable. Brush her hair, stroke her face, sing to her.

A selfish satisfaction, of that she was aware. Poor Ellen had become a substitute for all the love and affection that had gone out of her life. Poor Ellen had needed her when no one else did. Honora's mind was occupied with thoughts of her coming wedding. Impatient to be away to Kildare with Fergus, for, made match though it was, she was madly in love with her husband to be. And who could blame her? It was natural that she had less inclination to talk and gossip or put an arm round her mother as once had been her habit.

Laetitia had grown into a stolid, surly young girl.

Not a word to throw to a dog. She'd never settled away at school so that in the long run the nuns advised she might be happier at home. But it made no difference.

Mary felt sorry for her and hoped that when a husband was found for her she might improve. She prayed that he would be a tolerant man for Letty could try the patience of a saint. She found fault with her food, with her brothers and sisters. She disagreed for the sake of disagreeing.

Kathleen, on the other hand, was as happy as the day was long in her school. Only lately she was forever being invited to spend holidays and weekends in one of her many friends' homes. Mary could have stopped her but didn't for what enjoyment was there for her in her own home? With mopy Laetitia, Honora in a dream world, poor Ellen as she had been and the boys – well, the boys were of an age when females didn't concern them. Even Dermot, her youngest, shying like a startled colt if her arms reached out to touch him. There was of course still Peter. Always eager in the bed. He needed her. He would, she was sure, if he

was eighty. Only nowadays it wouldn't trouble her if he never laid a hand on her again.

The kitchen was still used as a living- and dining-room except on the occasions when a guest Peter wished to impress was invited. He wanted to impress Fergus's family, and so the drawing-room was refurnished. The beautiful threadbare silk hangings replaced by heavier coarse bright fabric. The fragile rosewood chairs, occasional tables and cabinet, dismissed as old-fashioned and put in the attic. In their place Peter chose heavy sturdy replacements of beech and oak. 'A man,' he said when the changes were made, 'wants to be proud of his home. Not have it filled with bits of things you'd be afraid to look at in case they collapsed.'

Honora whispered to Mary, well out of her father's hearing, ' 'Tisn't far from the cabbage patch he's come for all his money.'

'Nor the bacon slicer,' added Mary.

The girls used the drawing-room for their piano playing and painted their pretty water colours there and did their embroidery. Mary had seen the puffed up pride on Peter's face when he came upon them at their hobbies, and knew he'd be thinking: Born to it, like the Ashleighs before them. Though since the refurbishing she often wondered what the Ashleighs would think of the changes to their once elegant drawing-room.

Hams were boiled, geese and turkeys roasted, salmon poached. Crates of whiskey, sherry and brandy were bought in, and minerals for teetotallers. Mary, Catti and the two servant girls worked from morning till night. Everyone prayed that the fine June weather would hold. Honora's intended mother-in-law enquired if there was lace in the family. Mary sent word that there wasn't. And word came back that if Honora agreed she would send the veil of Brussels lace she and her mother had worn on their wedding day. Honora was delighted.

36

Michael brought James Farrell down for the wedding and Mary smiled to herself, remembering how her mother had once thought that Honora was smitten with him. And thought, maybe she was too, before she laid eyes on Fergus. Tears filled her own eyes as she thought about her mother and Ellen. Then she felt afraid. Afraid that life was being too kind to them. Afraid that Mag might be about to strike again. And she prayed, asking God to protect them all.

The weather held. The sun shone in through the open door while in the hall the family awaited Honora's descent from her bedroom. Peter and Mary were standing close together. When their daughter appeared at the top of the stairs, dazzlingly beautiful, Peter took hold of Mary's hand, squeezed it and whispered, 'It's like seeing you again on the day we were married. I turned round in the chapel to see you come up the aisle. You were that beautiful, I thought my heart would burst.'

She looked at his face and saw tears in his eyes. The only time ever in their life together she was to see them. Then he let go of her hand, blew his nose, and took over the organizing of the carriages.

After Honora left to live in Kildare, Mary increased her efforts to improve her relationship with Laetitia, hoping that now she was the only daughter at home, Kathleen being away at school, they might become close. Mary loved her as she did all of her children but sadly admitted to herself that Laetitia wasn't easy to like. Why it was difficult to put a finger on lately for she wasn't argumentative. Would help around the house, drive the pony and trap into the village if called on to do so. But never, not for a minute, did anything seem to touch her. Whether the skies were spilling rain or the sun scorching, the garden a riot of flowers, the rhododendrons dazzling to anyone with eyes to see — Laetitia appeared to feel neither heat nor cold, not to

distinguish between a beautiful Godsent day or one with leaden skies, damp and dreary. Nothing appeared to touch her. She expressed no preferences about what she wore. Not like a young girl at all, Mary would think when it came to choosing dresses for her and Kathleen, or materials for the making of them.

And when Honora came for a visit and whispered to her mother that she was expecting a baby, and later Mary told Laetitia, there were no squeals of joy or exclamations of delight. No extolling the fact as Kathleen had with: 'Now I'm going to be an aunt.'

'I'll say a prayer for her,' was Laetitia's only response.

And I for you, Mary said to herself. A prayer that you'll change your ways. Or that God may open my eyes as to how I can get close, even if only a little, to you. For though you never complain I feel that something is always on your mind. Something troubling you. Something that, if only you could bring it out into the open, would ease the crippling of your youth.

The news of the expected baby was a great boost to Mary's spirits. A new baby in the family, please God! A baby to hold, to lavish her love on, to watch, please God, grow up.

'You'll come up, won't you, Mother?' Honora asked after Mary had cried and laughed and hugged and kissed her.

'Nothing would keep me away,' she said. 'I'll come a couple of weeks beforehand.'

Chapter Six

MICHAEL graduated from Trinity College in June 1875. Peter and Mary were invited to stay with the Farrells on the night before the degree ceremony. They spent a pleasant evening, Mary and Lucy Farrell talking mostly about their children while Peter and James's father Edward discussed farming. Talking about the latest methods of agriculture. 'I wouldn't have thought a man like yourself would have been abreast of the changes?' Peter said.

'It's a hobby of mine. Relaxing after the courts. And maybe one day it's to a farm I'll retire. My grandfather was a small farmer in Clare. I used to go there in the summer. I remember it well.'

After that admission the men got on like a house on fire.

Sitting in the imposing hall the next day, waiting for the degrees to be conferred, Mary noticed that few of the men were dressed like Peter. He wore what a wealthy farmer wore. A heavy suit of thick cloth which emphasized his girth, a double-breasted waistcoat and a black high-crowned hat. Edward Farrell and the majority of other fathers were grandly dressed in black frock coats cut from fine cloth and their hats, resting on their knees, were black, like velvet or silk, she thought, with a bloom on them.

Though Peter had refurbished the house to impress Fergus's parents, he hadn't felt it necessary to make an effort on this occasion. He had no need to impress anyone. Wasn't his son having his degree, a first-class one at that, conferred on him? What more impression would he want to make?

Later, at dinner in the Farrells' house, their daughter Lizzie, home from her Paris convent, made her appearance. She was a pretty girl with a warm-hearted manner. Mary took an instant liking to her and Peter excelled himself, laying on the charm. Mary could guess the thoughts going through his mind. Here was a suitable match for Michael.

And on the way home the following day, thinking about the Farrell family, their hospitality and what a lovely child Lizzie was, she found herself in agreement with her husband's unspoken thoughts of the night before.

A few months later Mary was on her way to Honora's house in time for the baby's birth. Fergus was waiting when the train pulled in. At their first meeting she had taken an instant liking to him and had had no reason since to change her opinion. He shook her hand and asked how had the journey been. Told her she was looking grand. Bowling along in the pony and trap, Mary saw the rolling fields of grassland. She saw too a troop of soldiers riding by. They were near the Curragh, she recalled, where there was training for the military. She mentioned this to Fergus.

He had never been a talkative man but today he was less so than usual. She remarked on the lovely day. All his replies were monosyllabic. It wasn't that she wasn't welcome. And shy though she knew him to be, it wasn't reticence that made him ill-mannered. So she enquired: 'Are you not well, Fergus?'

'No, I'm well. At least, I'm not sick.'

'I wondered. You're so quiet.'

'I'm sorry,' he said. 'You must think badly of me. Don't. It's nothing to do with you. I'm delighted and relieved you've arrived. It's Honora . . . I'm worried about her.'

Mary's heart somersaulted in her breast. 'Is she sick? She was fine in the last letter. What ails her?' The questions came without pause for breath.

'Ah, no nothing like that. She's well really, and the

doctor keeps an eye on her. But she has something on her mind. Something worrying her. Only of late. It comes and goes. I'm hoping she'll confide in you.'

Mary was so worried it was a relief to see Honora with the bloom about her of a woman happily married and late in pregnancy. There were a great many hugs and kisses before her daughter said, 'You must be tired and parched with the thirst. Come in out of the hall. Take off your things. Throw them over the banister for the time being. The tea is only waiting to be wet.'

They went into the drawing-room and sat facing each other at a small table set with tea things. While Honora poured, Mary studied the face she knew like the back of her hand for any signs of distress. There were none. Honora looked radiant. And Mary wondered if Fergus wasn't over anxious. There would be days when Honora would be tired. Mornings perhaps after nights spent tossing and turning, trying to accommodate the size of her changed body. And she was a fine size. Carrying a big child, please God.

The next morning Fergus's mother called and the time passed pleasantly. After tea Honora went to rest on her bed. 'Don't let me stay there too long. I'll fall asleep, and if it's for too long I won't sleep tonight.'

'No more than an hour or two,' Mary promised.

When she came up Honora was still sleeping. With only her arms and face visible, she looked like a small girl in the big bed. Mary was loath to disturb her. But remembering from her own experience when pregnant how sleeping too long in the afternoon could mean being awake in the small hours, Mary touched her daughter's cheek gently.

She opened her eyes and smiled. 'Oh, Mother,' she said, 'I've missed you so much.' And Honora started crying.

'Love, what ails you?' Mary put her arms around her daughter. 'Tell me, aghillie. What is it at all?'

'I keep thinking about Mag – Mag Cronin and the curse.

I never believed in it. I used to laugh about it. We all did except Laetitia. I never gave it a second thought until lately when the child became more real to me with all the kicking and heaving.'

Despite the heat of the July day and the closeness of the bedroom Mary went suddenly cold. Ripples of it running up her backbone and beads of icy perspiration breaking out on her forehead. Her head spun so that for a minute she thought she might fall down, and all the while in her spinning head questions clamoured. Mag? The curse? How did Honora know about it? Who told her? Why would anyone tell a woman carrying a child such a thing?

She continued to rock Honora in her arms and make soothing noises while attempting to regain control of her mind. Breathing deeply to calm herself. Telling herself that it didn't matter who had told the story. What she had to do was decide how best to lay Honora's fears to rest. Not tell her the whole truth. Not admit to the terror that had haunted her down the years. And so, taking another deep breath, she spoke.

'Well, I am surprised. You, a sensible, educated, God-fearing girl believing in such a thing. Next you'll be telling me you heard the banshee last night, and for me not to displease the little people. All old pishogues, every one of them! You never heard of such things at home. Take this and wipe your eyes.'

'You don't believe in any of them?' asked Honora as she dried her tears.

'I do not,' said Mary, in what she hoped was a convincing manner. 'Not a single one.'

'Neither do I. Though I liked hearing the stories. I liked being frightened for a minute or so when I was warm in bed. It was exciting and we'd all scream and . . .'

'Who's we?' asked Mary.

'All of us, all the girls, and poor Ellen too, Lord have mercy on her soul.'

'Where? Where did you hear such things? Who told you?'

'Everywhere, Mother,' Honora replied as if surprised that Mary didn't already know how such information was passed on. 'In school, in the fields, playing in the village. But mostly from Catti. And 'twas she who told us about Mag Cronin.'

Under my own roof, where I thought they were safe! Mary was appalled but in a level voice managed to say, 'Sure you'd not want to mind Catti. Her heart's in the right place but there's not much above in her head. How did she come to tell you about Mag Cronin?'

'At night she used to come up to see we blew out the candles. We'd coax her to tell us stories. She knows great stories. All the usual ones and more. Real things that happened to people she knew. About her cousin who drank and was a terrible man for the cards and one night at a whist drive he won a leg of mutton and when he was walking home . . .'

'. . . he looked around and there was a big black dog following him,' Mary cut in. 'And doesn't everyone in Ireland know the Devil sometimes takes the form of a black dog? I know the story well, and what's more I knew Catti's cousin. Never sober a day or night in his life! And by the time he got home, with the dog still behind him, the mutton was gone and a white glistening bone in its place. Ask yourself what truth is in that story except for a poor starving beast with the smell of raw flesh tantalizing him? What else would any dog do but eat it?'

'But that wasn't all. Her cousin got such a fright he took to his bed and died in a few weeks.'

'Six months, and it was the drink and consumption that killed him. All his family were consumptive.'

'Maybe so,' said Honora. 'But Catti was very convincing. She told us Mag killed a cow and its prize calf. And when Ellen got sick after the measles, she said that was Mag's

43

doing as well. Catti said she knew the curse off by heart. She must have made it all up!

'I'm so relieved I told you. Fergus might have thought I was a fool. You've put my mind at ease. I'll never give Mag Cronin or her so-called curse another thought. But, Mother, you'll have to do the same for Letty. She does believe. She's terrified. That's why she seldom leaves the house. Seldom talks much.

'I'm the only one Letty confides in. She told me the real reason why she had to leave school. She couldn't do her work, she couldn't do anything for thinking about the so-called curse. The nuns didn't understand, they thought she was just bold and stubborn. So talk to her. Put her mind at ease like you have mine.'

Oh dear God, what sort of a mother am I? Mary reproached herself. Wouldn't you think I'd know my own child? See that something ailed her? How she must be suffering! She won't be easy to handle. She's not like Honora. We could always talk. Not so with poor Letty. And no matter how many excuses Honora makes for her, she was never an easy child, not from the minute she drew breath . . .

'Tell me this, how old were you when Catti told you the story?' she asked.

'All around about the five year mark. I remember I was in school.'

'As long ago as that? And the boys, did they hear the story?'

'They did, let on to listen, all the time making a laugh of Catti when she wasn't looking. I wouldn't worry about them. You talk to Letty, and after the baby is born let her come here for a spell. Between us we'll put her right. I'm going to get up now. I feel as if a ton weight had been lifted off me. No one should ever bottle their worries up, should they, Mother?'

'No,' said Mary, 'it does no good.'

She left Honora then and went to her own room where she lay on the bed and thought: My poor lovely trusting daughter. How easy it was for me to fob her off with lies. How long will it be when on a visit to Ballydurkin she'll one day get the bang of the eviction and the curse come back to haunt her for the rest of her life? Like me she'll try to make sense of happenings in her life. The crosses that like everyone she'll have to bear. And she'll be wondering and asking herself: Is this the Will Of God or Mag Cronin's hand on me and mine? And how, like myself, will she ever know the answer?

Chapter Seven

Michael was introduced to James's sister's friend, Nicole Demart, on the day before a birthday party was held for Lizzie. Nicole was, he thought, the most beautiful girl he had ever seen in his life. Feelings he had never experienced before assailed his senses as he shook her hand and heard her delightful voice. He could feel his heart beating rapidly, his colour rising, and when he spoke, he, who had never done so before, stuttered slightly. Was this what falling in love was? And was there such a thing as falling in love at first sight?

As the day progressed, while they ate lunch then sat in the garden where Nicole's aunt told of their dreadful crossing, her headache and the pain in her side, he became convinced that falling in love at first sight was a reality. Certainly in his case. This girl was going to be his wife.

Lizzie, who had been in love with Michael for several years without ever betraying her feelings, felt as if her heart was breaking as she sensed what was happening to him. Saw him hang on every word Nicole spoke in her spellbinding French accent, saw adoration shine from Michael's eyes. How like a Jack-in-the-box he was, up and down to offer her more lemonade, to adjust her sunshade, to chase and kill a wasp that threatened her.

Aunt Monique went to lie down and Mrs Farrell suggested that the young people should stroll as far as Saint Stephen's Green. James escorted Nicole, and Michael and Lizzie walked behind. Inwardly Lizzie fumed with rage. The visit wasn't working out as she had imagined. She and

Michael should have been so happy, he enthralled by her company and what she had to say. Instead he walked beside her mostly in silence, and when he did say anything it was of a general nature.

But she was a determined girl, not easily quashed, and told herself that Nicole was only in Dublin for a few days after which she and Michael would never see each other again. So she linked her arm in his and attempted to engage him in amusing conversation, racking her brains for anecdotes that would make him smile. Stop him staring forward to overhear the trilling of Nicole's voice, punctuated now and then by peals of silvery laughter.

But her efforts were to no avail. For all the attention Michael paid her she might as well have been a wax doll hanging on his arm. And she found herself bitterly resenting her friend. Wishing she had never come to Ireland.

'Already I adore Dublin,' Nicole said when they were seated by the circular flower beds with a fountain playing in the centre. 'Yesterday I passed through London in a cab and saw only glimpses of it. And for years I was in school in Paris but saw little of that. Like London, it is so big. I think you would have to live in these cities for many years before knowing them, is that not so?'

'Here,' said James, 'that is definitely not so. Dublin has all the delights of a capital city and yet because of its size you can get to know it fairly well in a day. From almost every vantage point the mountains are visible. The sea is only a stone's throw away. There are beautiful buildings, marvellous shops, wide streets and narrow ones, elegant ladies, even here in the Green.'

'I have already noticed them,' said Nicole.

James continued, 'And cheek by jowl with all that splendour, the poor, the beggars, the slums – supposedly the worst in Europe. And the people! The marvellous Dublin people. The friendliest in the world. The funniest. And gifted with a repartee I'm sure you'd find nowhere else.

47

Notice how often you see people stopping to talk to each other. How long they remain in conversation, how often they laugh.

'You'll see it all, I promise. Before you go home, you'll know the city inside out.'

While Nicole and James were talking Michael was marvelling at her beauty. Her face so animated yet with not a hint of coquetry in her eyes which were surely more black than brown. Wonderful eyes, teeth, skin, hair. Everything about her was enchantment.

'Ah, but maybe not,' said Nicole. 'I am only here for one week. Aunt Monique has many letters of introduction, many people to see, and an invitation to the French Embassy. A distant relative is an attaché there.'

Listening to her plans, Michael despaired of ever having a moment alone with her, and Lizzie imagined her heart to be broken and nursed it in sullen silence.

The doors between the front and back drawing-rooms were folded back to accommodate the dancers. The ceiling-to-floor sash windows were pushed up and the top section pulled down for the night was sultry and oppressive. Nicole wore a turquoise silk gown and a pendant with a matching blue stone. The proximity of her as Michael marked her card made his heart beat so rapidly he felt faint. He wanted to mark every dance on the gold-embossed programme. It hung from her waist, fastened there by a silken cord, the tiniest waist he had ever seen. His hands itched to enfold it, his arms wanted to enfold her, his lips to press themselves to hers. In a voice coarse with emotion, he remarked on the heat and wrote his name by two waltzes.

He sought out Lizzie, Mrs Farrell and various girls, other friends of Lizzie's, and claimed dances. He danced with them, smiled and talked, but over their shoulders his eyes sought Nicole's. Sometimes their glances met. Sometimes he thought that he saw her aunt watching him watching

Nicole. When his turn came to dance with her he was so nervous that he danced badly. He apologized and she smiled into his eyes and said she hadn't noticed. At supper he sat between her and Lizzie. Good manners forced him to be as attentive to one as the other. He raged inside himself that soon the party would end without his being able to have a moment alone with Nicole. He despaired that he ever would before she went back to France.

It wasn't until the evening before her return that an opportunity presented itself, and then only for the briefest time. The family, Nicole, her aunt and Michael, were sitting in the long walled garden after dinner when Nicole's aunt complained of feeling unwell. 'The beginning of a migraine,' she explained. 'My head is going round and round. I must go indoors and lie down.'

Mr and Mrs Farrell helped her from her chair and assisted her into the house. Soon afterwards Lizzie let out a little shriek and slapped the side of her face. 'Ugh, I've been bitten! I hate them. Gnat bites swell on me. I'll be a dreadful sight tomorrow if I don't put something on it. James, run and get that salve. It's on my dressing table. Run, quick! Be up and down the stairs by the time I get to the hall.'

'You are the limit, Liz. Don't order me to do things.'

'Oh, shut up and get the salve. You know how I react to bites.'

'All right, all right, bossy boots,' James said, and went.

Michael rose. 'I suppose we had better go in.'

'I suppose so,' Nicole replied.

'I hope your aunt isn't seriously ill. It would be inconvenient and you leaving in the morning.'

'I'd be delighted. No, I didn't mean that! Not that she should be seriously ill. But to be delayed, that I would like. I would love to stay in Dublin for ever and ever.'

'And I would love you to also.' He took hold of her hands, lifted them to her chest then bent and kissed them.

'Sisters,' they heard James grumbling as he came back into the garden. Michael let go of Nicole's hands. 'May I write to you?' he asked as they walked to meet James.

'I would like that very much.' Then she asked, 'Did you attend to Lizzie, James?'

'I wouldn't dare do otherwise. God help the man she marries!'

Michael walked back to his rooms in Trinity, the thought going round and round in his head that Nicole had given him permission to write.

Chapter Eight

As the expected date of Honora's confinement drew near, Mary slept badly so that the slightest noise woke her. The creak of wood as the old house settled after the heat of the day, a rise in the wind, a shower of rain beginning. And always she woke when the bells of the morning Angelus chimed. For the hour between that and seven o'clock she lay with thoughts racing through her mind of the ordeal that lay in front of her daughter. For no matter how quick or easy her labour might be, it was still an ordeal.

On one of the mornings, when she had begun to console herself and was just about to go down for a cup of tea, Honora came to her room with a smile on her slightly flushed face. Excitedly she said, 'I've started, Mother, at least I think I have. I've funny little niggly pains in my back like nothing I've had before.'

Honora's mother-in-law came to see her. 'You'll be grand,' she assured her. 'Everyone's praying for you and the child.' A tray was sent up. Mary had no appetite. The nurse devoured sandwich after sandwich and gorged herself on cake. Honora, on the doctor's advice, although she said she was starving, drank only water.

Fergus came to see his wife for the third time since her labour had started. Shyly he kissed her on the cheek, asked how she was. He was ill at ease in such an unfamiliar situation and made an excuse to leave the bedroom.

The doctor came in. 'I slipped over before my dinner. How often are you having the pains now?'

'Every six minutes near enough,' said the nurse, not waiting for Honora to answer.

'Good, very good. I'll leave the dinner for a bit. You could speed up. I'll go below and have a bite with Fergus.'

By midnight the pains came quicker and stronger. 'You've been very good,' Mary crooned to her daughter as she laid vinegar-soaked cloths on her forehead. 'It won't be long now.'

The doctor confirmed this. 'I'll be telling you to push soon, and then please God it'll be all over. You're doing fine for a first baby.'

She pushed when she was told, and pushed again and again, and screamed and called on her mother and the Blessed Virgin, asking for help. 'And again now. A big strong push,' the doctor urged. The contraction peaked, subsided, and Mary thought she saw concern on his face. He made a sign to the nurse who knew every move of his and handed him a little trumpet-like instrument which he placed on Honora's belly and put his ear to.

Mary's heart constricted with fear for she knew things were going wrong. Honora's contractions were coming without pause. She writhed and screamed and her mother thought of Fergus below, hearing the piercing screams, and felt sorry for him. But nothing like the emotions she was feeling for her child.

'Honora, listen, child. I'm going to give you a little whiff of ether. You'll fall asleep and when you wake up it'll be all over.'

'I don't care,' she said. 'I don't care what you do. Only make the pain stop or I'll die!'

Silently Mary prayed. Honora lay exhausted, her face pale, lips bitten, hair saturated with sweat. The nurse was busy by the bedside table laying out a brown ribbed bottle and a pad of wadding. At the foot of the bed the doctor took from his bag a large narrow bundle wrapped in white linen.

With great care, after uncorking the bottle, the nurse began to drip chloroform on to the pad. The smell of the anaesthetic permeated the room. Mary felt her stomach churn at the sickly-sweet smell. The pad was placed over Honora's nose and mouth. Above it her terrified eyes pleaded with her mother.

'Close your eyes, pet, there's a good girl. Let yourself fall asleep.'

Mary longed to run far away from the room, the stifling room with the cloying smell of chloroform and the curved blades of the forceps which the doctor was using on her daughter. But if Honora, even though unconscious, could endure such an ordeal, the least she could do was be by her side.

She saw the grimacing face of the doctor. The control with which he pulled. Babies, she had heard tell, brought into the world by this method, came sometimes without a head. Torn off by an inexperienced man with the forceps. 'Sacred Heart of Jesus, aid his efforts! Let him not be too hasty. Have pity on my child,' she prayed.

And then she heard a sound as if a hand had pulled a gigantic cork from a bottle and a baby lay on the bed. It didn't cry. It was a boy she saw as the doctor suspended him by his ankles and slapped his buttocks. She saw too that where his skin showed through the greasy white substance that covered it, it was blue.

The nurse was beginning to bring Honora round and Mary was willing the child to cry so she could bend over her daughter and say, 'Wake up, love, wake up. You've had a handsome son.'

The doctor, working on the child, laid him on the bed and puffed small breaths between his lips, fingering from his mouth strings of mucus.

Honora opened her eyes and smiled at Mary. She closed them and the nurse urged, 'Come on now, wake up.' Again Honora opened her eyes, for longer this time. 'Mama,' she

said. And reaching for Mary's hand she appeared to sleep again.

The nurse began her exhortations once more. From the foot of the bed the doctor said, 'Leave her, she's come round. Let her sleep for a while.' And to Mary, 'I did all I could.'

'I know that.' She felt great sorrow for him. And for the fat little baby, perfect in every way except that it was dead.

'Why?' asked Honora.

'I don't know,' Mary admitted. 'It's the way things are sometimes.'

'What was he like?'

'A beautiful boy. A fine lovely child.'

'Oh, Mother, Mother, Mother.'

Mary took Honora in her arms and together they cried. Neighbours, relations and friends came to offer their sympathy and condolences. Honora lay propped on her pillows, black shadows beneath her lovely pain-filled eyes. Her breasts and belly bound, her many stitches causing her pain, she received the visitors. It was God's will, they told her. There was a purpose behind everything he did. And with His help she would have many more children.

In a small white coffin, without any service or ceremony or his mother even seeing him, the baby was carried by Fergus to the graveyard. And there, in a small section called the Killeen, a place of unconsecrated ground kept for the burial of unbaptized infants, he was laid.

Mary stayed on for the two weeks that Honora was lying in. She packed away clothes and articles that had been prepared for the baby. There weren't many for it was considered unlucky to have more than the bare necessities before a child was born. She sat with her daughter in the afternoons and talked. They talked of many things, Mary dreading the time when Honora would raise again the name of Mag

Cronin and the curse. She did a few days before her mother was to go home.

'It isn't that I didn't believe all you told me about Mag Cronin and the curse. I did, really I did. And I suppose if the baby had lived I'd never have given it another thought. But he didn't and I can't help wondering . . .'

'I'd say that's natural enough. After the birth of a child you have the queerest thoughts come into your mind. And if you lose the child, well, they must be of a blacker kind. But every word I told you is the gospel truth. The poor woman was demented. Her gabbling meant nothing. You are one of the unfortunate many. Just think of all the women you've known and heard of whose babies are born dead. Ask your mother-in-law who's lived a great many years longer than you how many she has known. It happens, love, and God only knows why. It's a cruel, terrible thing, for a woman to carry for nine months, labour for hours, and at the end have nothing to show for it. But thanks be to God, you're a young woman with twenty years or more in front of you to have other children. Put Mag out of your mind. Pray to Our Lady. Will you promise me that?'

Honora made the promise – one her mother knew from her own experience she would have difficulty keeping. For like herself, once the seed had been sown in times of misfortune it would thrive and torment her. For a short time reason would smother its growth, until the next mishap befell the family.

Chapter Nine

MICHAEL found rooms in a pleasant Georgian terrace overlooking the Grand Canal. Walking from there to the Kings Inns, where he was reading for the Bar, his thoughts were almost constantly of Nicole. He had written to her shortly after she returned to France and waited each day for a reply to his letter. When it did arrive he read and reread it several times, now and then holding up the writing paper to inhale what he believed to be a trace of perfume. He kissed each sheet in turn, imagining as he did so that her fingers had held them. That as she wrote her hair may have escaped its pins and brushed the paper's surface. He conjured up an image of her on the night of the party, on the day they went to St Stephen's Green, seeing again her wondrous eyes, the tilt of her head, the shape of her lips. He saw in his imagination the dusk of that evening in the garden when they were alone for the first time. How the light from the french windows had seemed to cast a halo round her head. How he had raised her hands to his lips and asked for her permission to write to her. And then again he reread her letter in which she wrote that receiving his letters would arouse no suspicion. Her father didn't pry and her aunt assumed that letters from Ireland were sent by Lizzie.

The letters went to and fro. In the beginning they were both circumspect in what they wrote. He described his walks through the city. How he remembered her enthusing about certain buildings. The cafe where she, James, Lizzie and himself had stopped to drink coffee, and how passing it

and smelling the roasting beans evoked the time they had spent there. And always his remembrance of that kiss.

He told her how hard he was studying. How fearful he was of failure. That he saw less of James since they had left Trinity. James was now greatly interested in Parnell, a Member of Parliament, and another man, Michael Davitt, recently released from prison for his activities in the Fenian Brotherhood. Davitt, he went on to tell Nicole, was involved in the forming of a Land League for the protection of tenants likely to be evicted.

He would then apologize for boring her with such matters, and write: 'They aren't the things I want to say to you.' But for a while longer he continued to fill his letters with such facts and gossip when what he wanted to write about was how he was obsessed by thought of her. Wanting to propose to her, to go unannounced to France, arrive at her home. See the surprise and adoration on her face. Take her in his arms and kiss her until she begged for breath.

But eventually he became bolder, encouraged by Nicole's letters which now began to reveal her feelings for him.

A letter from her mentioned that Aunt Monique had raised the subject of marriage: 'Which means the old witch may have already found what she considers a suitable match. Actually she is very kind and I love her. She is only doing her duty. One day I must marry. She, of course, takes it for granted that it will be to a Frenchman.'

And he replied: 'I adore you. I want to marry you. I *will* marry you.'

Nicole wrote back: 'At last, a proposal! I thought you'd never ask. My darling, I accept. But not a word to anyone else. To James, Lizzie or the Farrells. First you must come here and ask Papa for my hand. He will be broken-hearted when he learns that marrying you means I will leave France. But he believes in love. His marriage to my mother was for love. Against the wishes of her family. Every first Friday he goes to the cemetery and puts flowers on her grave. He had

many opportunities to marry again but never did. After initially raising objections to our marriage he will give it his blessing, I am sure.'

Fearing that he had raised her hopes too high Michael wrote explaining that several years must pass before he could consider marriage. There were his Bar examinations to pass and then he would have to find chambers. But married they would be. The waiting time he knew was more difficult for her. He at least had his studies to occupy him, and when there was leisure time available, the pleasures of Dublin.

The following year Nicole wrote: 'My Darling, such a long time we've been writing! So many letters have passed between us and still Papa and Aunt Monique believe the letters coming from Ireland are from Lizzie. Though Aunt Monique did mention recently how strange it is that she hasn't come to visit since we both left school. Papa said I must write and invite her and her brother here . . .'

Michael was surprised that Lizzie no longer corresponded with Nicole. Nowadays he seldom saw her, seldom went to the Farrells' house, though he and James were still friends and would, he hoped, remain so. James had become more and more interested in politics and was an ardent supporter of Parnell and his fight for Home Rule for Ireland. Whereas Michael, like his father, was apolitical. He remembered having heard from James that Lizzie was being paid court to by an English Catholic officer in a Dragoon Regiment stationed in Dublin. It never crossed his mind that the reason she no longer wrote to Nicole was because of her involvement with Michael himself.

Over the years he wrote long letters to Nicole. Reassuring her of his love. Urging her to be patient. The time was approaching when he would arrive in France and claim her for his own: 'One more year at the latest. Mark the year 1879 on your calendar.'

In the spring of 1879 a frantic letter came from Nicole in which she urged Michael to come as soon as possible.

'Our postman Jacques has started to behave strangely. In the last few weeks he has become unpleasantly familiar. Sly grins on his face when he brings the mail from Ireland. Leering and winking if I am alone in the kitchen. I think he knows the truth. Each wink and grin seems to say: "Ah, my little one, I know your secret." Maybe it's only my imagination. Me being hysterical. But I think not. I'm sure he has opened our letters. And I know that if he continues in this way I will one day lose my temper, cause a scene, and then what? So please come quickly. Come and let our love out in the open.'

Without mentioning Nicole, Michael at once suggested to James that they should take a trip to France. 'Lizzie too,' he added hopefully.

'Might be fun, but I'm doubtful about Lizzie.'

'Oh?' Michael said. 'I thought she'd like to look up her French friend?'

'Nicole? Don't think so, they're not in touch.'

Michael pretended surprise. 'You mean they don't write?'

'Not so far as I know.'

'Why, I wonder?'

James shrugged. 'Lizzie doesn't confide in me.'

'A pity. Visiting someone we know would've been nice. Made us less like tourists.'

'I could always drop a line,' James said. 'When are you planning to go?'

'Sooner the better. Over the Easter holidays, I thought.'

'That's out. I've promised the parents to go to the West with them. Let's make it mid-September.'

'Have to do. Thanks, you're a brick. Why not drop a line to the Demarts? We should pay our respects.'

Michael wrote to Nicole: 'Another date for your calendar, 17 September. Mark it in red. The days will fly.

Soon we'll be together. I'll hold and kiss you. All our dreams and longings will come true.'

After making his travel arrangements for France, Michael went home to break the news of his marriage to his parents.

'French? Why in the name of God a French girl? Who is she? Who are her family? Where did you meet a girl from France?' Peter was puce in the face with annoyance. 'And what about Lizzie Farrell? Didn't you have an understanding with her? It was what your mother and I hoped for. A girl from a good family, and what's more an influential one. You'll not marry this foreigner except over my dead body!'

'Father,' Michael said, 'I didn't come to ask your permission. I came to tell you. You still have a hold over me. You can stop the money you allow me and cancel my fees. I'll manage without them. I am going to marry Nicole.'

'When were you thinking of it?' asked Mary.

'In a year or two, once I'm established.'

'That you'll never be if I have a hand in it.' His father spat out the words.

'I don't want to fight with you. I came to tell you about Nicole. About her family. Her father's a wealthy farmer. She was in school with Lizzie. I met her at the Farrells'. She's very beautiful. I love her and will marry her. And about Lizzie – I am very fond of her but there was never anything between us. I'm sorry I came. No, that's not true. I wanted to see you all. But after I've done that I'll go back to Dublin.'

Clinging to Michael, Mary asked, 'You'll come down in September when the mackerel are running? You and James like you used to? You will, won't you? We'll have a grand time. Honora will be here. Please God, by then she'll have a baby. Kathleen will be home from school, and you'll see a great improvement in Laetitia. I've been paying her a lot more attention. She's come out of herself, I think. Promise me you'll come?'

Peter began refilling his pipe with the flakes he had cut from his plug of tobacco while Mary talked to Michael. A visit in September would be a way round things. Out on the boat the matter could be patched up without either him or Michael losing face. Himself and the boys, just like old times. Like when they were young boys. The six of them and Tim-Pat helping. Yes, September would work the miracle. Then he heard Michael tell his mother: 'I can't. I'm going to France to meet Nicole's father, it's already arranged.'

Michael found Laetitia in the dairy skimming the milk. She greeted him warmly which was unusual for her. 'You're looking great,' he said. 'What have you been doing to yourself?'

'Praying,' she replied. 'Though Mama thinks it's all the new clothes she has bought me. That and her taking me out and about. We've been to Cork and Limerick a few times and she's planning a visit to Dublin.'

'Well, I suppose it all helped, Ballydurkin isn't the liveliest of places. But the praying – tell me about that? I wouldn't have thought that was anything new.'

'It all started when Mama came back after Honora's baby was born dead. D'ye remember when we were children and Catti told us about Mag Cronin's curse?'

Michael laughed. 'Will I ever forget it? Me and the boys used to be in fits trying to keep a straight face. Poor old Catti. What's she got to do with all of this?'

'I believed every word she told me. I was terrified. Afraid to go to sleep. Afraid of the dark. Afraid of walking in the fields on my own. Afraid in the dormitory when I went away to school. All the time I was waiting for Mag Cronin to appear before me and kill me, I suppose. Anyway, I was afraid of my own shadow.'

'Yes, go on, I'm listening.'

'Didn't Honora tell Mama about how I felt while she was

up in Kildare? And didn't she tackle me as soon as she came home? At first I wouldn't talk to her but did in the end and admitted my terrible fear. And she told me the truth. How Mag Cronin was a poor woman demented with the sorrow of losing her children during the Hunger and then her and her husband having to go to the Workhouse because they were old and crippled with no one to look after them. And how on the day they were going Mag came here to the house and ballyragged Mama, screaming and shouting. But the Lord have mercy on her, so demented was she that not a word of what she said could anyone understand. Except Catti who put her own interpretation on the babble. And being Catti, her version was the most terrible of curses.'

'That I can well believe,' said Michael. 'Leave it to the Irish. What they don't know they'll quickly invent, and in no time it becomes gospel.'

Laetitia finished the skimming, licked her fingers, then wiped her hands on her apron. 'Anyway, Mama made me see that I had been at an impressionable age when I heard the story. And a sensitive child though, as she said, it was the last thing anyone would have thought about me. A stolid little block was how I appeared, she said. And then she apologized for judging by appearances. God help her, as if with the streel of children she had there'd have been time for looking for the sensitive one!

'And that was it really. No doubt the shopping and the towns helped. But most of all it was because I knew the truth. Knew that there never had been any such thing as a curse. But to be on the safe side, I began to pray in earnest. Pray never to doubt in God and his goodness. His power to protect us all from evil. The peace of mind I've found you wouldn't believe. And this . . . but it's a secret for the time being . . . I think I have a vocation. Promise you'll say nothing until I tell Mama and Dada?'

'Of course I won't. Tell me about it?'

'It began forming in my mind when I first read about Father Damien. You've heard of him?'

'I think so. Yes, I have. Isn't he the priest who runs a hospital for lepers in South America or somewhere?'

'No, he's in the South Seas. On an island called Molokai. It's a leper colony. No one else on it except Father Damien and the lepers. Once it's discovered that they have the disease they are forced to go there. Some go alone, some whose families are brave and loving go with them. And there they stay until they die. All these sick, horribly disfigured people with only the priest to attend to them. He has done wonders single-handed and wages constant war with the authorities in Honolulu. The whites who run things are American Protestants and not sympathetic to him or his needs.'

'The poor man, he'll surely be canonized?'

'I hope so,' said Letty. 'That's where I'd like to go. Devote my life to helping him look after these poor forsaken creatures.'

'Well, it's an admirable ambition, but wouldn't it overtax you, seeing all the suffering, the appalling sights? Have you any idea what happens to lepers in the advanced stage of the disease?'

'I have. I've read all about it. God would give me the strength to cope.'

'If it is what you truly want, I'll pray that you get it.'

'Remember now, not a word to anyone. Promise?'

Michael promised again and went to find his brothers. They were walking the fields, wondering whether to start cutting the hay the next day. There was a change in the weather, they told him. The crop was good. 'If I had the say I'd start the cutting now,' Justin said, 'but himself will have the last word.'

Michael looked at the four of them with affection and pity. Four grown men. Justin and Fintan going on for thirty. The twins not far off it. And the baby as he still

thought of Dermot, whom he could see at the far edge of the field, six foot or more and twenty years of age. Men, and their father still held sway over them! The sense of power that must give my father, he thought as he listened to their comments. And as he frequently did, reminded himself how lucky he was to have escaped.

He told them about Nicole and the row with his father. They teased him good-naturedly about his French sweetheart. Asking when was the wedding? Would there be a journey for them to France? Saying what a great thing that would be.

'I hear tell it's the great place,' said Dermot who had now joined them. He was fair-haired and fine-skinned. Like all the McCarthys, like myself, Michael thought. Like my father we'll all run to flesh and our skins coarsen and redden.

He asked about local events. It was hard making conversation. Their interests were all centred in Ballydurkin and the farm. And for a moment it saddened him that they had so little in common but their looks.

'Will you be down in September?' Brendan enquired.

'No, I told you, he's forbidden me the house. In any case, I'll be in France.'

Dermot, who had missed out on the news of the marriage and the row, had to be told again.

'Ah,' he said, 'that's a bar that'll not last and you going to be a barrister. "My son the barrister." Can't you just hear him? "And his wife from Paris." You don't think for a minute he'd forgo that pleasure? I can see him outside the chapel introducing the two of you to anyone he'd think important enough.'

The brothers laughed. Justin clapped Dermot on the back. 'Begor', you're not as thick as I thought. Not as green as you're cabbage-looking.'

Michael felt a great surge of affection for these awkward, rowdy, kind brothers of his and for a second wished he

could be as close to them again as he once was. He took his leave of them amidst a barrage of advice on how to conduct his love affair, spend his time in France, and not grow too big for his boots.

Half a mind between them all, he thought on the way back to Dublin. His father was still in his prime, could live to be ninety, and they whistle till he died before they'd be their own masters. Half a mind, that was all they possessed — otherwise they'd pack their bags and head for America.

Chapter Ten

AFTER Michael left, Laetitia covered the bowl of cream with a muslin cloth, its edges weighted with beads, scoured the milk pans and placed them by the door for bringing to the kitchen for scalding. While she worked she listened to the voices speaking in her head. One she was sure was the voice of God. He had a gentle way of speaking, almost a whisper. He told her that she was holy. That he wanted her for his bride in Christ. That soon, very soon, she should go to the convent to be ordained a nun and then devote her life to Him.

She didn't like the other voice. It was strident. It tried to talk God down. Ridiculing the idea of her becoming a nun. It reminded her of someone and everyone. Everyone who had ever scolded her: her mother when she was impatient, her father when he was annoyed, the nuns in school who forever criticized her, her brothers and Kathleen when they tormented her. Sometimes the voice rose to a shriek inside her head, making such a din that she clapped her hands over her ears, trying to silence it. But it was inside her head. So that she knew even were she to cut off her ears or pour hot candle grease into them she would still hear it. When it shrieked she thought it might be the voice of Mag Cronin.

Honora's second baby, a daughter, lived only for a few days. After her initial grief she found some consolation in the fact that at least she had looked upon her child's face, nursed it at her breast, and most of all that the baby had been baptized, could be buried in sanctified ground and not

spend Eternity in Limbo. 'I know,' she said to her mother, 'that there is no suffering in Limbo, but for all that it isn't Heaven.'

And Mary, saddened at this second loss of her daughter's, agreed and said, 'With God's Holy help you'll have a family yet. I've known many a woman who lost several children and now has a houseful running around. And your little angel in Heaven will intercede for you with God and His Blessed Mother.'

One of Laetitia's voices told her to say nothing about the vocation she believed she had. It urged her to throw a few things in a bag and go. And when she attempted reasoning with it, it retorted spitefully: 'A lot they ever cared about you. Treated like dirt you were. Why tell them your business?' And she replied, 'Even if that was true, I couldn't do it. I wouldn't be accepted in the convent. My parents have to know, and the parish priest. His role is very important. And when you're professed, your family come to the celebration. I'm becoming a Bride of Christ. It's like a wedding.'

And the voice laughed scornfully. 'Is that what you think it is? And I suppose the honeymoon comes after. A fine honeymoon, washing the sores of lepers! Their fingers and toes fall off, and all the men's bits. Out in Hawaii, you and Father Damien, and all them brown bare girls . . . Not much of a look in you'll get! Honeymoon, my eye. You never did get much of a look in. No one likes you. No one ever did. They'd kill you in a minute.'

In the little space when the voice paused as if for breath, Laetitia prayed, imploring God to help her. To silence the voice for ever so that she didn't go mad. And her prayer was answered. The voice remained silent. For ever, she hoped. She spoke to the parish priest. Convinced him she had a vocation. She told her mother who embraced her and cried. For joy, she said, that Laetitia had been blessed with

'the call'. Arrangements were made for her to go to Dublin and meet a representative of Father Damien's Belgian Missionary Order, who, after much questioning, judged her to have a true vocation. She would begin her novitiate in June. During this trial period she would be watched closely for signs that her vocation was wavering. If it didn't, and if she appeared capable of the arduous tasks nursing lepers involved, she would be professed in September at the Mother House in Belgium.

'You'll come, won't you, Mama?' she asked her mother on her return to Ballydurkin.

'Nothing on earth would stop me,' Mary promised. 'Your father too, and Kathleen. And some of your brothers, them that can be spared from the farm.'

Mary smiled as each day towards the end of August Peter began complaining about the trip to Belgium. 'Why, like many a girl before her, couldn't Letty have joined an Irish Order and been professed in Dublin, Cork or Limerick? What does a man of my age want with foreign travel? The food is desperate in them places. My stomach will be out of order for months after it. Where's the tickets? I hope you got the right ones. I should have got them myself. You've booked us for the right date, I hope?'

She brought the travel documents for his inspection, a task that now occurred daily. And Mary watched and smiled her secret smile as he inspected them. Knowing well that he was as excited as herself at the prospect of a visit to the Continent. His first time to set foot outside Ireland! She could hear the boasts of him when they came back. The tales he would tell – all exaggerated. Every one with him emerging as a man whom no one, especially a foreigner, could cod with their tricks. And as for his stomach – he had one like an ox, capable of digesting food of any description.

One day he said, 'Wouldn't you have thought Michael would make certain he was there on Letty's big day?'

'He may still. She has heard from him. And now that she knows she'll be professed on September the twentieth, she feels sure he'll be there.'

Mary knew what he was thinking. Why couldn't Michael's trip to France be put off? Why couldn't he have travelled with them? Why didn't he write and say he'd be down for a few days fishing before they set out for Belgium.

'Michael's a good boy, with a great regard for family. And I have this feeling, you could call it a premonition, that come September he will be home.'

'You and your premonitions! You're every bit as daft as Catti.' His face had a glowering expression on it. One it assumed to convey mock annoyance. To convince the onlooker he had no faith in their pronouncements. Knowing him as well as she did, Mary was aware that in his heart, though he'd die rather than admit it, he was hoping her premonition would come true. And if Michael did insist on marrying the French girl, that would be accepted, she knew.

10 September 1897
Issoudon

My darling,

Only ten more days. I ask myself can it be true? After almost four years we are to meet again. I know that courtships last for many years, but usually the boy and girl see each other often. And so I am in a feverish state, longing to see you but at the same time frightened. Afraid that you may find me changed, not so attractive, and you may not love me. Then I would surely die. But if it is so and you can no longer love me, don't pretend. For I love you so much I couldn't bear the thought of your feeling you must honour a promise, marry me and spend the rest of your life unhappy.

But, please God, this is me being hysterical again. It will

be as it was in the beginning. The magic will attend us again and stay for the rest of our lives.

My calendar is hidden. Aunt Monique would want to know why the days in September have been crossed off. Tomorrow the eleventh will go. I love you. Soon I will start counting the hours, and from the sixteenth the minutes. Goodnight, my darling.

Your
Nicole

The morning after Michael received that letter another came from Nicole. The envelope was blotched as if drops of water had spilled on it, and when he took out the pages they were marked in the same way.

Darling,

We have been discovered! I can't see for crying. My hands are shaking. For a long time I avoided Jacques, but this morning I was so happy thinking of your arrival I was careless. I wanted to be alone. Away from Monique who talks such a lot. I went for a walk. I forgot that along the track there is one cottage, and there I met Jacques after he had delivered the post.

It was quiet and lonely there. He stood close to me and leered. 'My little one,' he said, 'you have been avoiding me. Avoiding your old friend Jacques.' And he took hold of me and tried to kiss me. I was so frightened but angry also and slapped him hard across the face. Then I ran away down the track and sat by the water for a long time.

When I came home Papa and Aunt Monique were in the kitchen. I could tell by the atmosphere something was wrong. She did the questioning, telling me that Jacques was convinced the letters that came from Ireland were not from Lizzie. That he had suspected this for some time, but being only the postman didn't like to interfere.

I lied, swearing the letters were from Lizzie. 'I think not,'

said my aunt. 'Jacques reminded us that for years she has written here and that he knows her writing as if it were his own. Please bring them here.' I refused and appealed to Papa, betraying my guilt by doing so. He supported her, but promised the letters wouldn't be read, only the signature looked at. I had to fetch them.

They have forbidden me to write to you. Letters from you or James will be returned and the invitation for you and him to visit is cancelled.

I am distraught. I will kill myself. This letter I have bribed a servant going to Issoudon to post, but Marie-Claire will take no more for fear of losing her job. I shall stop eating. Starve myself to death, then they'll be sorry. Or I'll run away. But I have no money. I never needed money. Mama left me lots of money but that is in a bank.

If only Lizzie would write or even address the letter, I think they would let me have it. You could send me money, lots of money, so that I could come to you. Beg her to. Give the money to Lizzie. Beg her to help us. Tell her to say the money is a donation for the African Missions to which we subscribed in school. Send enough money for passage from France to England and on to Ireland.

I have hidden your letters in a place where no one will find them. In a tin box in the cave beneath the house. My eyes are blinded with tears. I cannot write any more. If I cannot be with you, I will die. I love you.

Nicole

Michael's first thought was to go to France immediately, find Nicole and take her away. He believed her life to be in danger. She had threatened not to eat. Said she didn't want to live. His love. His life. And he was responsible for her being in such a position! He paced his room, now and then rereading her letter. Cursing the prying postman. Feeling a loathing for the aunt. His little girl. His precious darling made to suffer so. He had to go to her rescue. What he

must do was go to the Farrells immediately and ask for advice and help.

It was a sunny Saturday morning as he cut through Cumberland Lane and out into Fitzwilliam Street. A beautiful street, some said the most beautiful in Dublin, with houses similar to those in Merrion Square. It was the street in which he intended to live when he and Nicole were married. In no time he was outside the Farrells' house.

To his consternation the maid showed him into the drawing-room. He, who was like a member of the family.

He was even more surprised when instead of James, his mother came into the drawing-room. He stood at her entrance and she said, 'Sit down, Michael.' Her lovely, soft, friendly face, which he had only ever seen wreathed in smiles of welcome, had a severe expression on it.

'Michael,' she said, 'you've been coming here since you were a child. It saddens me to receive you in this fashion. But you have displeased me greatly. This morning I had a letter from Nicole's aunt. The unfortunate woman is distraught and I feel responsible for what has taken place. Nicole was a guest in my home, as were you, and you abused that privilege.'

Michael sat with bowed head, one hand clapsed in the other. He wanted to beg forgiveness for having caused this woman he loved an iota of distress.

'What on earth were you thinking of? Proposing to a child you had only met for a brief moment. It's beyond belief. Haven't you anything to say for yourself?'

'I love her. We love each other. We wrote letters and we planned to marry.'

'Ah, Michael,' Mrs Farrell said, and raising her eyes, he saw that her expression had softened. 'Aren't you aware of the ways of the world? Did you not consider how such affairs were arranged in your own family? As far as I know in everyone's family. Life isn't a romantic story. There are rules to be followed.'

'I did. Not in the beginning. I was carried away. When I came to my senses I tried putting things in order, but it wasn't to be.'

'Only because the postman drew Monique's attention to the strange handwriting. And you planned such a deception. A deception involving my family.'

'Nicole has been forbidden to write to me and isn't allowed to receive letters from me. Mrs Farrell, she is desperate. She has threatened to stop eating. I fear for her life. She begs that Lizzie should help her . . .'

'She is a young, hysterical girl. You mustn't worry. It is all talk. People rarely die for love. In what way does she want help from Lizzie?'

He told her, seeing as he did so her mouth set in grim lines, and knew without being told that no help would be forthcoming.

Chapter Eleven

AFTER the discovery of her deception Nicole took to her bed and stayed there where she refused solid food, living on water and milk, and waited for a letter to come from Lizzie. Lizzie wouldn't let her down. They loved each other. Monique came regularly, coaxing and scolding by turn. Telling her she would destroy her looks, go into a decline, lose the gloss from her hair, sicken and die if she kept refusing food.

On the third day, awakening from a troubled sleep, a terrible awareness struck her. She would never receive a letter from Lizzie. Her father and Aunt Monique would suspect all letters from Ireland. She and Michael were doomed. They would never see each other again. From that moment she wanted only to die. Milk brought by the servant and her aunt was refused. She left her bed only when it was necessary, stopped washing herself and combing her hair.

When on the fourth day she still lay listlessly, refusing nourishment, Monique became frightened. Disguising her fear as anger, she rounded on her brother-in-law. 'Never have I known such wilfulness. Like a mule! Such a stubborn nature. A good shaking or a slap across the cheek would bring her to her senses. You should go and talk to her, make her see sense.'

'Perhaps,' Nicole's father said, 'we were too harsh. They were only letters after all. This young man was only coming to visit. I don't think Lisette would have handled the situation this way.'

Monique's face became scarlet and she blustered, 'Are you telling me my sister would have welcomed this young man as a suitor for Nicole? Someone we know nothing about. A deceitful, conniving person who has taken advantage of her youth and innocence. Are you telling me, who has reared her since she was an infant, that I don't know what is best for her?'

'No, of course I'm not. You have been a wonderful mother to her. Only sometimes you can be, with the best intentions, I know, a bit of a martinet.'

'Yes, I am strict and make no excuses for it. I am not only Nicole's aunt, I am her godmother and responsible for her spiritual welfare. She is more precious to me than my own life. How could I be party to throwing her into the arms of a stranger? A handsome stranger as I remember. A man who might have ruined her.

'But in the long run she is your daughter. Your responsibility. So go and see her. Talk sense to her. Let the man come. Let us be the talk of the village. Compromise Nicole's reputation. I wash my hands of the business!' So saying she walked from the room.

Pierre Demart was an awkward man with women, even with the daughter he adored. Unable to find the right word, to make a natural-seeming gesture. Unable willingly to witness sickness or discomfort in those he loved. Which was why, in the four days since Jacques's disclosure, he had not gone to look in on Nicole.

Now he did and was terrified at what he saw, so vividly did her sunken eyes and hollow cheeks remind him of his wife in her decline. Nicole stirred restlessly then opened her eyes.

'Papa,' she whispered.

He smoothed the tangled hair from her forehead. He had brought with him a glass of lemon cordial. 'My little one,' he said, 'will you take a sip for me?' And to please him she sat up and sipped. The acidic drink reaching her empty

stomach made her retch. He held her head until it stopped then laid her back on the pillows. 'Rest for a minute and then some water, eh?' He sat and held her hand, neither of them speaking until she fell asleep. Then he went and found Monique. 'First thing in the morning, have Maurice call. My child is very sick. What have we done to her?'

The next morning, tense and apprehensive, Nicole's father and aunt heard the doctor's footsteps in the flagged passage.

'You can stop worrying, she isn't in decline. She has a broken heart and the beginnings of malnutrition. The latter can be cured but the former rests with you.'

'I've heard the term bandied about, mostly by women. Does such a condition really exist?' Pierre Demart asked.

'It most certainly does. Not, of course, in the literal sense. An all-consuming grief would be a more accurate term. An awful sense of loss so great that the afflicted person wants to die rather than suffer the anguish. Doesn't eat. Loses interest in their person, in their surroundings, their instinct for survival, and so dies. Very seldom does it affect the young. Most recover quite quickly from their spurned or unrequited love, even the death of a sweetheart. I see it more often in the bereaved elderly. But there are exceptions to every rule and Nicole is one.'

The doctor sat at the table. Monique poured him a glass of wine and offered one to Pierre. He waved it away and poured from the cognac bottle.

'Nicole is one of the exceptions. Gone beyond interest in food. Short of force feeding her, she will continue to refuse it unless . . .'

'Unless what, man? For God's sake, tell me. I'll do anything.'

'Allow her to write to the Irishman and receive his letters. What harm can there be in that?'

A letter arrived from Michael addressed to his mother. He

wrote that there was a change of plan about his trip to France, so instead of meeting them in Brussels for Laetitia's ceremony he would be on the night boat to Holyhead on the eighteenth and meet up with them there.

'The pup!' his father said when Mary read him the letter. 'Not an inch of give in him. Meet us on the boat! Well, you can do as you like but I'll not recognize him. What's the weather like?'

'There was a nip in the air earlier on. A reminder that the summer's gone. But it'll be a fine day with not a breath of wind. A grand day for the fishing. Eat your breakfast before it goes cold.'

He said no more about Michael and appeared to be in good humour as the boys and Kathleen came to the table. Though Mary knew it was a pretence. Knew that he was every bit as disappointed as herself. Then she took consolation from the fact that they'd meet on the boat and travel together. Even so, she was puzzled as to why she'd had such a strong premonition that Michael would have been down in September.

Justin, Fintan, the twins, their father, and Tim-Pat the handyman were going out in the boats. Tim-Pat reported that the sea was flat; not even far out was there sight of a white-crested wave. Peter gave his orders as to what they'd have to eat. Meat and no sweet cake. Meat and well-buttered bread, white not wheatmeal. Throw in a dozen hard boiled eggs and don't forget the twist of salt.

'And you, Fintan, see to the porter, fishing's thirsty work.'

The boys teased their youngest brother Dermot. He was a bad sailor and didn't go fishing. The breakfast was almost finished, Catti and Mary putting the finishing touches to the packed lunch, when Kathleen got up from the table and moved to stand by her father's chair. There, in a coaxing, wheedling voice, she asked to be allowed to go with them.

A silence fell in the kitchen. Each one thinking: A

woman in the boat? Such a thing was unlucky. Her father asked, 'Are you mad or what? Girls nor women don't.'

'They do so,' she contradicted. 'How else would they get to the islands?'

'That's different. That's a necessity.'

'They're still in a boat. And look at the gentry, aren't their women out from morning till night on the lakes dapping?' Kathleen retorted.

'The gentry are different. They have queer ways.'

'It's not only the gentry or the island women – there's plenty of girls in school who go in the boats and fish.'

'That's what's wrong with educating girls.'

'Please, Dada. Please let me come. I'll be no trouble. I won't move from where you put me to sit.'

Fintan then pleaded for her. 'With Letty gone it's lonely for her. She goes nowhere.' Justin seconded him, and the twins, but less forcefully. Catti showed her disapproval by keeping her back turned to the table and not uttering a word. Mary couldn't see the harm in Kathleen's going but said nothing, knowing that Peter was still fuming because of Michael. Only Tim-Pat dissented. 'Women don't go out in the boats. It's bad luck to have them with you. The sea has an objection to them. Anyone will tell you that.'

'Is that a fact now?' Peter asked.

'Well known passed down the generations by wise men,' replied Tim-Pat, not aware that his interference had raised Peter's hackles. No hired man was going to tell him who could and could not go out in his boat. 'When I want your opinion, I'll ask for it. Though it's unlikely I ever will. You're like the rest of the amadhauns, believing anything you hear round your fire of a night. Put something warm on you once away from the land. The air off the sea is cold,' he said to Kathleen, who threw her arms round his neck and thanked him profusely.

They went down the narrow sandy path that led to the shore in single file, Peter leading and Tim-Pat lagging

behind them, puffing on his dudeen. Now and then taking the clay pipe from his mouth to spit into the blackberry bushes. The fruit was over ripe. No one picked a berry for fear of its being maggoty. Spider's webs glistened amongst the brambles. They came to the beach where the boats lay on the sand. The sea was blue and calm and, as Tim-Pat had said, not a white seahorse in sight.

In Dublin a letter from Nicole came by the afternoon post. Michael's hand shook as he picked it up. What terrible news did it bring? For a moment he hesitated about opening it. Then his common sense asserted itself. She had written it, hadn't she? Addressed it in a steady hand and the envelope wasn't stained and crumpled like the last one. The letters he had sent had somehow got through. What a wise friend James was, advising him to keep on writing. Before taking out the letter a smile crossed his face as he thought: Maybe the postman broke his leg or died. Maybe after all God was on the side of lovers.

Tears of joy ran down his face as he read her news. How the doctor had intervened and her father and Aunt Monique relented. They would even permit his visit to go ahead. She knew the letter had come too late for him to arrive on the seventeenth, but after his visit to Brussels she would be waiting for him.

'They've had a grand day for the fishing,' Catti said as she finished rolling a ball of wool from the skein Mary had been holding on her outstretched wrists. 'The weather held, and not a breath of wind rose, though you can feel the chill in the air now that the sun is going down. They'll have powerful appetites on them.'

'They will to be sure. The meats are cooked, the blackberry tart will only want warming and I've a jug of cream brought from the dairy. The minute I hear them I'll put the potatoes on to boil,' said Catti.

The sun was sinking fast. Roses and Michaelmas daisies still bloomed in the garden where the two women were sitting. The scent of the roses came to them, and now and then agitated wasps flew around their heads. Catti becoming as agitated as the insects, flapping her hands above and around her face and head while Mary advised her to keep still and they wouldn't bother her.

'Whisht,' said Catti, 'that's a peculiar sound. Earlier I thought it was a curlew. Listen.'

The sound was coming nearer. Not the call of a bird. More like a human voice keening. Catti made the Sign of the Cross. 'Someone has died, the Lord have mercy on them.'

They left the garden seat, dropping the wool, steel needles and the stockings they had been knitting, went to the gate and outside it from where they saw the tall, thin figure of Tim-Pat's wife, Annie, coming along the path to the gate, beating her breast, her voice rending the still September evening. Behind her old men, women and children were following.

'God between us and all harm, what's up? Something terrible must have happened,' Mary said with a terrible sense of foreboding.

Annie's words were audible. 'My husband! My lovely man! Lord have mercy on his soul. A man that never harmed anyone, snatched by the cruel sea.'

Racing like a runaway horse a young boy came pushing his way through the men, women and children. Passing Annie, arriving in front of Mary and Catti, where on the verge of collapse, he gasped: 'I saw it happen! I was on the headland watching the two boats. One minute they were there – and then gone! I ran to O'Learys' and raised the alarm. I left them racing to the strand to launch their boats. The O'Learys will get them. The O'Learys will, never fear.'

Tim-Pat was the only one to return. Tim-Pat in his old

breeches and coat pasted to his body, water dripping from it. Tim-Pat with his head as bald as a sea-washed pebble, visible for the first time anyone could remember. Except perhaps his wife, Annie, though some said he slept with his cap on. Behind him entered two other village men. Mary's eyes were fixed on the open door but no one else came through it.

'Where are they?' she asked, speaking for the first time since the boy Martin had brought the news. 'Where are Kathleen, the boys, himself?' she asked distractedly. 'Are they coming? Did they stop off on the way?'

'Oh, Mrs Mac,' said Tim-Pat, and tears ran down his stubbled face. 'Mrs Mac, they're gone. The sea took them, God have mercy on their souls. The sea took them, every one.'

His wife ran to him and showered his face and bald head with kisses, pausing now and then to thank God for having spared his life.

The two men who had come with Tim-Pat took it in turns to explain how, hearing from the O'Learys about the missing boats, they had followed them down to the strand where they found Tim-Pat. 'Flat on his back. I thought he was gone. Then he gave a stir.'

'He did so,' the other man said. 'He gave a stir and sat up. "He's alive," I shouted to the O'Learys who were pushing their boat into the sea. "He might be able to tell you something about the happening." But they were away. No time to lose. And in any case it was many a long minute before Tim-Pat said a word. And then divil a bit of sense what he did say made.'

' 'Twas the truth!' Tim-Pat protested, pushing Annie from him. 'It was a terrible thing, Mrs Mac. There we were about to come in and over went the boats. And down I went, thinking my last hour had come. Down and down and the fish swimming all round me and no more than the

others I couldn't swim a stroke. I was going to be drownded.

'I don't think there was a thought in my head. Terror that was all, and the feeling that my lungs would burst. And the next thing I knew, wasn't I on top of the water and being rushed to the shore? Swishing through the water as if a powerful fish had me in tow. I don't remember another thing until I opened my eyes and Johnny and Dessie were standing over me. I'm that sorry, Mrs Mac. Why couldn't God have spared your lovely sons and daughter and man and taken me? Amn't I an old man?'

Mary sat hugging herself and rocking backwards and forwards on the chair, never speaking a word.

Dessie, the older of the two men, took Tim-Pat by the elbow and steered him to stand beside his wife. 'Don't, Mrs Mac, be paying too much attention to what Tim-Pat has to say. There's a smell of porter on him. He could have fallen overboard, not been missed, and the boats sailed round the headland. You've the right men on the job. The O'Learys know this coast, every inch of it. Sailors every one of them. They'll find them.'

The people in the room murmured their agreement, all except Annie who was offended with the accusation that her husband was drunk and an unreliable witness. 'Tim-Pat,' she said, 'I know when I'm being insulted. The water running off you, in danger of getting pneumonia, and no one asked if you had a mouth on you? If a glass of whiskey would stave off the chill that's on you? Come home with me this minute and I'll mind you.'

No one tried to stop them leaving. A woman went to fetch the priest. Catti sat by Mary, holding her hand.

Dermot came in from the fields, unaware until he entered the kitchen that anything were amiss. Catti told him as much as they knew, adding a prayer that the O'Learys would find his father, sister and brothers. He knelt

on the floor beside his mother's chair, laid his head in her lap and cried.

By the time the priest arrived the people who had followed Annie to the house had left, talking to each other in low voices as they made their way home. Recalling other tragedies. Boats that had been lost. Bodies washed up miles from where they went down. Reminding each other how treacherous the sea was.

To the priest Dessie related all he knew about the incident. Dermot stood up and wiped his eyes. Mary looked blankly at the priest and listened uncomprehendingly to the words of hope he spoke. Catti left Mary's side, poured whiskey for the men and pulled the kettle to the centre of the range. She made tea and cut bread and buttered it. All the while the priest continued talking to Mary who didn't respond. He then motioned to Dermot to step outside with him where he said, 'God forbidding all harm, Dermot, but in case some terrible thing did happen out there, wouldn't you be as well to send for Michael? Or maybe first to his good friend James – he can break the news.'

Michael spent a leisurely morning pottering about his flat. As the Angelus bell rang out, he thought about lunch. He'd stroll through the Green, maybe see James on a similar mission. They were friends again even though Michael was no longer welcome at the Farrells' home. About to leave his flat, he glanced out of the window and was surprised and delighted to see James climbing the steps. He raced down the stairs, reaching the hall door as his friend knocked.

'I was just thinking about you. Wondering if I'd bump into you. Now you're here we can get a bit of lunch together. I'm starving. Come in. Come up. What brought you?'

'I'll tell you in a minute,' James replied.

Something about the tone of his voice alarmed Michael.

Nicole! Had the Farrells received bad news from France? Had she had a relapse?

In the flat James told Michael about the letter from Ballydurkin. 'Oh, my God!' Michael exclaimed. 'Poor Mama. All of them missing. Oh God, James, d'ye think it's as bad as it seems?'

'I don't know. And it's no good raising false hopes. There's a train from Kingsbridge at two o'clock. I'll come down with you. Only there will we know the truth.'

It was late evening when they arrived. The priest was there to meet them and before they could ask, he said, 'I'm afraid the news isn't good. The O'Learys scoured the coast and not a sign of man or boat. It's a great mystery what could have happened. And Tim-Pat's experience makes it more mysterious still.' He related what had happened to the handyman. 'He swears his story is true. But I've long had my doubts that Tim-Pat isn't the full shilling.'

The pony and trap rolled along through the familiar lanes. People at farmhouse gates saluted them and Michael thought how everything was the same and yet nothing was for him and his family.

The priest continued talking. 'I'm worried about your mother. Everyone else is still clinging to a hope, feeble though it may be. But not her. Catti tells me she had hopes until Tim-Pat came in the door. After that she drew into herself. Not a word, not a tear, not a prayer, not so you could hear anyway. In all my years of comforting the bereaved, of them waiting for news that could be bad, I've never seen the like before. With the help of God, Michael, she'll respond to you.'

Catti broke down when she saw him. 'Asthoir,' she said, 'I'm that concerned for your poor mother. She hasn't shed a tear nor uttered a word since Tim-Pat told the tale of his escape. We're all praying for a miracle. Every family with a

boat is out searching but with every hour that passes so does the chance of finding them alive.'

'Oh, Michael, Michael!' Dermot said, hugging his brother. 'I'm that glad to see you. It's that lonely with them not here and poor Mama in a world of her own. I keep waiting to hear a roar behind me and Dada giving me a roasting. He's a hard man but what wouldn't I give to see him walk in the door or hear that roar of his?'

His mother sat like a graven image. His embrace and kisses, his whispered words ignored, as if indeed she was a statue fixed in a sitting position by the range. The hands that he always remembered being occupied with the steel knitting needles, a sock she was darning, a dress or petticoat she was hemming, or deep in a bowl of flour making bread, lay motionless in her lap.

'Mama,' he pleaded, 'd'ye not know me. D'ye not know your own Michael? You do, sure you do. Remember the night we went to the music hall in Dublin? The songs and the yarns and the smell of pig's feet. Ah, you do. Tell me you do?'

In years to come he recalled that moment when his mother failed to recognize him as the saddest in his life, far outweighing the grief for his lost family. His mother not to know him. That was a terrible thing.

Word was sent to Honora and to Laetitia. To Laetitia Michael wrote about his mother's condition and asked for her prayers:

> I don't know what the convent rules are, I mean whether or not you would be allowed to visit. But I would suggest that you didn't. Mama appears not to recognize anyone nor speaks a word. If it wasn't for Catti spoonfeeding her she'd starve. I think it would break your heart to see such a change in her.
>
> I don't know what to do about the farm now there is

only Dermot left. In the middle of the night I think I should come down here, forget about the law and take it over. Not that I know anything about farming. But sure, neither does Dermot. In the cold light of day I know that I won't come back. We will wait for the reading of Dada's will and decide then. I expect a manager will have to be brought in. I'll keep you informed of all that happens. God bless you, my dear sister.

Michael

He posted the letter, and one to Nicole telling her of the tragedy, that he loved her and would come to France as soon as possible.

Honora and her husband came on the day before Michael went back to Dublin. She knelt before the chair where Mary sat motionless. 'Mama,' she said, 'it's me. Say you know me? Nod your head. Oh, Mama, I'm so sorry. Dada and Kathleen and the boys. What'll you do without them? You can come and live with me and Fergus. I love you. Don't look at me as if you don't know who I am. Don't look through me. Don't do that, Mama, please! Not that. I can't bear it. I need you, Mama. Come back to us. Don't leave us all alone.'

She pleaded and cried but all to no avail. Eventually Fergus helped her to her feet and led her from the room.

'What ails her, Catti? I expected her to be broken-hearted but not like this. What ails her?' Michael begged.

'She's gone far away. She can't fight it any more. All her life she has. A human being can only take so much and no more. Your mother has reached the end of her road, and who can blame her?'

From the day Tim-Pat had come through the door with the sea dripping from him, and Peter, the boys and Kathleen weren't behind, Mary knew the sea had had them. And

gave up the struggle with which she had lived since entering this house as a bride. It was over. All over.

Now, for the first time in years, peace had enfolded her. A genuine one that wrapped her like a soft warm cloak. A peace she was convinced would remain with her for the rest of her life. For in her heart she believed that 'it' was over.

Chapter Twelve

NEIGHBOURS and the parish priest came to the house daily. They stood before the silent figure of Mary. They spoke to her and said they were praying for her family, for their souls be granted eternal rest. The priest told her they were in Heaven, prayed for her, touched her hands affectionately and took his leave.

The next day Michael too took his leave of his mother. Kissing and hugging her, tears streaming down his cheeks as he recalled the once animated face, now as expressionless as a death mask. He looked into those blank eyes. His mother, his lovely merry mother, gone from him as surely as if she lay in her coffin. While Catti, spry and wrinkled but with her mind as alert and bright as ever, fussed round her.

Catti came to the door to see him into the pony and trap and, taking hold of his elbow as he was about to mount the step, drew him out of the driver's hearing and began again to relate what happened on the day of the tragedy.

'Tim-Pat said 'twas a day without a ripple on the sea. The fish like rainbows in the water. You could have reached in and picked out handfuls. And your father, poor Kathleen and your brothers, God rest them, in great humour, about to turn for the shore . . .'

'Catti, you've told me all this before, not once but three or four times.'

'Not this part I haven't, for Tim-Pat didn't mention it in your mother's hearing. It was afterwards he told me as I'm telling you. There wasn't a stir in the water except for the fish, not a cloud in the sky – and then over went the boats.

Tim-Pat said 'twas as if a pair of giant hands reached up from the depths, took hold of them, tipped them over the way you would a basin and dragged them down to the bottom of the ocean. Those boats as sound as a pair of bells. Yet up they never came nor the poor crathurs either. And doesn't everyone know a drowning man comes up three times?

'God between us and all harm, as Tim-Pat says it was the queer happening all right. Himself that no more than the others couldn't swim a stroke transported on a wave that came from nowhere and landed him safe and sound.'

'Catti,' Michael said, 'I love you as if you were my own flesh and blood. I've known you all my life. But I swear to God, if you tell that story to my mother I'll have you in the Workhouse quicker than you know!' He was still, as he had been when a child, a little afraid of her. He knew that if she was suddenly to raise her hand his reflexes would make him duck.

She didn't raise a hand, only looked steadfastly at him with her little black button eyes. 'The Workhouse, is it? And me with a home in my mother's. That's an empty threat if ever I heard one. And as for your poor mother, she knows well the truth of what happened. For years and years she has tried putting it from her mind. Sometimes she'd convince herself she had. Sometimes she'd have me almost believing it was only an old pishogue – Mag and her curse. And then something would happen. And 'twas as if Mag had thought: I'll show them. I'll show the McCarthys it wasn't idle words I spoke.

'God look down on your mother. She can take no more. Not here at all, only her poor body by the fire. Her mind's gone astray and can never find its way back, for she'll never let it.'

For a moment her story struck fear into Michael's heart then his common sense, his education and lawyer's training, rebelled against such lack of reason, and forgetting that once

he had feared Catti, he took hold of her thin narrow shoulders, wanting to shake her until her big yellow tombstone-like teeth rattled in her mouth. But affection overcame his anger and, loosening his grip, he said, 'Catti, every word of that tale is nonsense. You weren't there. It was a freak wave. They come and go in an instant. It was such a one that carried Tim-Pat to the shore. Such a one that tipped over the boats. My father, Kathleen and the boys got entangled in the ropes and the boats holed on rocks on the sea bed. That's why they didn't come up. That's the truth and you must believe it.'

'Oh, aren't you the clever boyo? The great scholar. But you forget one thing. How did Tim-Pat come to be saved? Tell me that now?'

Losing his patience, Michael spoke crossly to her. 'I told you, a freak wave. And I'm warning you, you're to say no more about it. You may have a home with your mother but if I hear another word of this story, you'll not have a situation in this house.'

'Poor Michael. You're a good boy. You always were a nice child. But you haven't an ounce of sense in that fine brain of yours. D'ye want to know why Tim-Pat was saved? Why the freak wave carried him and not one of the others to safety?'

Michael turned towards the pony and trap, walking away from Catti. Her voice followed him. 'He wasn't a McCarthy, that's why! Not a drop's blood to them or your mother's people. Mag wouldn't harm him,' she crowed triumphantly as he got into the trap and the driver touched the horse with his whip and they moved off.

Catti walked round the outbuildings dabbing at the tears that fell from her eyes with a corner of her apron. Crooning to herself, 'My poor lovely boy, 'twasn't lashing you with my tongue. I was only trying to warn you. May God protect you and yours.

'A silly old woman, that's all I am. Warning him indeed!

As if it would make a ha'porth of difference. Maybe somewhere, some day, it will change. Maybe there's a way to lift a curse. I've heard tell of such things, but long ago, so the story went. Long, long ago when the little people were more to be seen. Nowadays you'd hardly ever catch a glimpse of them. It's all the newfangled machinery and them trains that race across the countryside. It's driven the fairies nearly out of our world altogether.

'I'll pray for Michael and Dermot and Honora and Laetitia, out amongst the savages. And for herself. Morning, noon and night, I'll pray for the curse to be lifted.'

For the first half-hour of the train journey thoughts of Catti and her story chased each other through Michael's brain. Gradually he dismissed them and concentrated on Dublin. James was meeting him from the train, having returned to town before him. The Farrells had forgiven Michael, shocked by the tragedy. He had been invited for dinner and to talk over his career. First he would stop off at his flat where he hoped to find letters from Nicole.

For the rest of the journey she occupied his mind. He wondered how she was physically and thought of her sadness, mixed naturally with disappointment, that his trip to see her was postponed. He too had experienced those dual feelings and was plagued by guilt that anything but the loss of his father, brothers, sister, and his mother's condition, should concern him. He thought himself a callous person. Surely someone with more heart would not have had room in his mind for feelings of anything but terrible grief?

Mrs Farrell must have been watching for his arrival for as soon as the maid opened the hall door she appeared to receive him, her arms outstretched. She embraced and kissed him and told him how sorry she was for him and his family's loss. 'And your poor mother, how is she?'

Michael played down her condition. 'It was a terrible

shock. So sudden. She seems stunned. Not able to take it in yet.'

'That's only natural. Please God, in time she'll be over it. I'll remember her in my prayers. And what about poor Laetitia? Any news from her?'

'Not so far.'

'The poor child, having no one belonging to her on the big day. I will drop her a line.'

'And Nicole? I heard from her aunt that things had been sorted out. I was very sorry to have been so hard on you, Michael. I did what I thought was right in the circumstances but I spoke harshly to you. I hope you forgive me?'

'Of course I do.' He wanted to tell her how much he loved her and admired her. Almost as much as he loved his own mother. But he couldn't trust himself to speak in case emotion overcame him.

Had he wanted to, Michael, as the eldest living son, could have claimed the farm. Dermot, before the will went to probate, reminded him of this. ' 'Tis yours by right now,' he said, and Michael wondered what his brother's reaction would be if he were to claim the land. Would he go off to America, or accept as he always had that as the youngest son he would never have much say in anything? All his life he had obeyed his father, played second fiddle to his brothers, and in their place now there would be Michael. He imagined he could see these thoughts expressed on Dermot's face, in his manner of speech, belying the words he spoke. 'No argument about it. Sure aren't you the eldest and isn't that how things are – the farm to the eldest? I wouldn't begrudge it to you. We'd get on fine. No more than me you aren't a farmer at heart, but I'd bet you'd make the better one.'

'Put your mind at rest. I'm not a farmer. And don't play down your own experience. You've been working the land since you could walk. Frighting the crows, picking up the

stones, and then on to all the other aspects of farming. You'll be surprised when you're put to the test how much you do know. I'll lay no claim to it. My life is in Dublin. I'm a lawyer by training and inclination. You'll make a great job of it.

'But to start off I think you should look for a good manager. You're taking on a great responsibility. For a start you'll be four men short. Four reliable men, your brothers, who had the interest of the farm at heart. You'll have no trouble hiring men, and you may be lucky and get trustworthy ones. On the other hand, you may not. There's always the ones who'll try to take advantage of your age. So my advice would be to find a good manager.'

'I wouldn't have thought of that, but you're right. Would you help me pick a fella?'

'I would, though I'd advise you to have a word with Mr Bennet. He'd be well up in these things and willing to help, I've no doubt.'

'I'll do that. I'll get a manager. I'll make a success of it, never fear. Dada would be proud of me.'

Dermot appeared to grow in stature as he spoke. His intentions, Michael knew, would be of the best and he wished him well, though in his heart he grieved that this young man, scarcely more than a boy, should have such a heavy yoke thrust upon him.

Chapter Thirteen

At last another date had been set for Michael's visit to France. He was caught up in the excitement of again seeing Nicole and all his thoughts were optimistic as he went from shop to shop in Dublin buying presents. For Aunt Monique he chose an Irish linen table cloth and set of napkins. For Nicole he spotted what to him seemed an exquisite and suitable gift. It was a tiny silver locket set with turquoise stones around its edges. She had worn turquoise the night they fell in love so he thought the locket was very appropriate. For her father there was a bottle of best Irish whiskey.

The crossing to England was rough but he was scarcely aware of the screeching wind buffeting the ship, its rolling and lurching. Not that he slept much but his mind was so occupied with happy expectations of his reunion with Nicole that the hours flew. He travelled first-class and so wasn't aware until he was disembarking of the steerage passengers, poorly dressed, clutching bundles, the women carrying children, the look of want and weariness about them. Again at Euston he watched them as they left the train. Wondered where they were headed for, hoped they would find work, welcome and shelter.

He anticipated that the crossing from Dover to Calais would be calm. It was and he stayed on deck watching for the first sight of France where he would travel by train to Paris, then change for Issoudon where Nicole would be waiting.

*

Michael's heart raced as the platform of Issoudon station appeared and in his excitement and impatience to open the door, he cut his hand. Leaning out of the window, he saw her: a young woman accompanied by two men. Perhaps he had been mistaken. Maybe it wasn't her. The train stopped and he was down the step and the group of three were walking quickly towards him. It was Nicole. He presumed one of the men was her father and the other the doctor with whom he was to stay. The men were short, not much taller than Nicole who was now waving to him, hurrying to meet him, leaving the others slightly behind. His mind was registering everything. How cold it was. How beautiful she looked. How welcoming.

Then they were face to face. Nicole introduced him to her father and Maurice. She offered her cheek for his formal kisses, then noticed his bleeding hand. It gave her an excuse to hold it, exclaim over it and attempt to bind the graze with her scrap of a lace handkerchief.

Pierre Demart welcomed him to France and Issoudon in a French that Michael had difficulty understanding. The local dialect, he supposed. But his smile and wrinkled, weather-beaten face radiated warmth and genuine welcome. In a pony and trap similar to the one in Ballydurkin they set off, Nicole still fussing over Michael's hand until Maurice intervened.

'It is not so serious. Some iodine at the house. This girl hasn't let me greet you properly with all her chattering. I hope your stay will be enjoyable and that you find my house as comfortable as Pierre's.'

There was no difficulty understanding what he said. Michael thanked him and said he was grateful for his hospitality. Maurice congratulated him on his French and then Nicole again took over the conversation. Enquiring about his journey. About Dublin and the Farrells. Complaining that Lizzie still hadn't written. Wanting to know how Laetitia liked Hawaii? Never waiting for answers. Like

him she was beside herself with excitement and disbelief that at last they were together again.

'Almost there,' Maurice said as they entered the village. There was a tiny square where the local cafe stood. A little further on, Michael saw a baker's shop, closed until later in the day, Nicole explained, when the second baking would be on sale. He also saw that the minutest of cottages had shutters on the outside, and every house, to the back or a side visible from the road, had a plot of land, well tended, with winter vegetables growing.

And then they were through the village and approaching the farmhouse. Before the turn, as far ahead as he could see, which was a long way, there were fields on either side of a road fringed with poplars. A boring vista, he thought, and so unlike the one at home with trees in abundance, cottages scattered here and there, and soft hills. They turned down a narrow rutted track and he saw the house. It seemed half as tall again as his home in Ireland because of the height of its red-tiled roof. Never had he seen such a steeply pitched roof.

The hall was stone-flagged and commodious, and though the walls were several feet thick it felt cold and damp in there. Michael shivered. Pierre noticed and hurried him into the kitchen where a fire blazed as it consumed logs he judged to be a yard long. The window was small yet the room was anything but dismal for the flames danced high up into the chimney and every utensil, whether brass, copper or steel, was burnished and glowed. The ceiling, as were all those in the house, was beamed: roughly hewn, massive oak beams. The table and benches to either side of it appeared to have been fashioned by the same hands that had made the beams and a great low table like a living thing rooted in the kitchen floor.

Smoked hams hung from the beams, herbs hung to dry, and an enormous bunch of bay leaves. In corners of the

room were several dusty-topped barrels, and all the air was permeated with the smell of cooking.

Monique bustled in from another room, grown stouter and older-looking than Michael remembered. Immediately she scolded Nicole and the men for not having given Michael a glass of wine, for not having seen to it that he removed his outdoor clothes. Only then did she greet him personally. Smiling from the teeth out, as they say at home, he thought, noticing her eyes were hostile.

'And tell me, how is your poor mother?' she asked.

'Still grief-stricken. We are hoping and praying. Time and all that, you know.' He felt tonguetied in her presence.

The daube was delicious and he was glad to see that dipping bread in the juices and wiping the plate clean with it was in order. Rough red wine was being poured into his glass at an alarming rate. He must refuse the next glass or risk falling off the bench. He ate cheese such as he had never tasted before, and then tart with apple slices arranged on the pastry, the apples caramelized a golden brown.

By the end of the meal he loved everyone, even Monique, and was head over heels in love with Nicole. And he believed that if he had the signs right, the blushes, the glances, the expression in her eyes, she loved him in return.

Monique had also mellowed as the meal progressed. Her smile now reached her eyes and he believed she was even flirting a little with him. He forgave her her earlier coolness. If his wish was granted he would be taking Nicole away from her. Monique adored her, and for her the parting would be heartbreaking.

The hours flew as they continued to eat and laugh. Now pleasantly intoxicated, Michael believed he had no difficulty understanding what Pierre said although he had lapsed more into the local dialect. From time to time his misunderstandings and the responses he made gave rise to peals of laughter from Nicole for which Maurice gently rebuked her. But in

his euphoric state Michael didn't take offence. How could he, with Nicole sitting opposite him, dazzlingly beautiful? Each smile, gesture, even her teasing, he interpreted as proof of her love. Gone from his mind was the misery of being so near and yet divided by convention, unable to hold or kiss her. The uncertainty of how the visit would end. How many more might have to be made before talk of an engagement and marriage would be raised?

Monique was making plans for the following day. 'If it is fine you must go out. Perhaps a walk or a drive in the pony and trap. And on Saturday see the market in Issoudon and the castle which Richard the Lion Heart did battle for. I will come on the walk and Pierre or Maurice can go with you to Issoudon.'

'I shall be delighted,' said Maurice. 'You must also see the hospital, very historic and picturesque, close by the river. Crusaders on their way south to slaughter the infidel in the name of Christianity availed themselves of its hospitality.'

Pierre, quaffing glass after glass of rough brandy, warned that tomorrow was unlikely to be fine. 'According to the sky it will be bitterly cold and windy. Stay by the fire. You must have plenty to talk about.'

Reminded of the time, Maurice apologized for breaking up the party. Michael and Nicole must part. Leave with no more than the touch of her lips on his cheek. Her eyes were luminous with unshed tears as she bade him goodnight, begging him to come early the next morning.

The walk to Maurice's house wasn't a great distance. On the way he mentioned the drownings, expressing his sympathy, complimenting Michael on how well he was conducting himself despite his sorrow. 'Pierre noticed also. We talked about it when we left the kitchen for that little while. There was nothing to show me outside. He wanted my opinion of you and if I thought your interest in Nicole

and hers in you was more than a childish interlude. "I think so," I told him. "In fact, I'm almost sure." '

'Thank you, sir! Thank you very much indeed,' Michael said warmly.

He was back at the farmhouse before nine o'clock in the morning. Monique greeted him pleasantly. She made him excellent coffee. By the minute, he thought, France becomes more enjoyable.

'Nicole slept late, too much wine last night, but she will be down presently.'

Pierre's prediction was correct. The weather was bitterly cold and windy. Nevertheless Michael's spirits soared when Monique announced she would be out until lunchtime. His face showed his high hopes: they would be alone for several hours.

Nicole, recognizing the look for what it was, said when her aunt left the kitchen, 'Don't count your chickens before they're hatched. It won't be all you hope for.'

Monique returned and then took ages to leave on her visit. So that Michael would like to have shouted, 'For God's sake, go if you're going,' each time she was on the threshold then remembered something she had forgotten and came back into the kitchen.

Finally she went and Nicole laughed. 'Wasn't I right?'

'She has gone now. We are alone.'

'Wait and see.' Hardly were the words out of her mouth when Veronique, an elderly servant, came in, grumbling. 'Madame has asked me to tidy the presses. So many presses, stuffed with so much, I'll be here till lunchtime!'

During the following days the wind dropped and the weather felt less cold. Michael and Nicole went for walks, but always there was someone not far behind them. Now and then Nicole excused herself from the outings and on these occasions Pierre accompanied him and talked about Ireland. Asking what Michael thought of Parnell? Could

Home Rule be achieved by political means? Michael admitted his ignorance about such matters but promised to send him Irish newspapers. On another day Pierre asked how big was the farm in Ballydurkin? The size of the herds, the crops they grew? As the eldest living son, had he inherited the farm?

Michael explained the position. That Dermot now had the farm. That he had chosen as his father wished to pursue a career in the law, having been offered a pupillage in the chambers of a good friend of Edward Farrell's.

'As a Catholic will you come up against much discrimination? Do the professions in general?'

'Not any more, though the ratio of Catholics to Protestants, considering we are in the majority, is abysmal. But once you're in – and, as in my case, with an eminent chambers – there is no problem.'

One day during the questioning Michael realized that his prospects were being sounded out. He was heartened and thought: He is considering me as Nicole's husband. He hoped that before the day was out he and Nicole might sneak a few moments alone so that he could tell her the good news. But it wasn't to be.

He would just have to be patient, though God knows it wasn't easy. In some ways he would be glad to return to Dublin. It would be less frustrating and tantalizing. They could write freely and plan his next visit, by which time there would surely be some relaxation of the rigid rules?

All morning Nicole was restless, her cheeks flushed, her eyes dancing with excitement. The same mood seemed to be affecting Monique though now and then she hurriedly left the kitchen and when she returned her eyes appeared red.

'What ails her?' Michael asked Nicole after another hurried exit.

'She has a cold coming. It is how it affects her. She is feverish.'

'You seem feverish too. Have you a cold as well?'

'No, I am very well.' She smiled mysteriously.

Risking Monique's or a servant's sudden appearance, he caught hold of her and kissed her on the lips. Then he too felt decidedly feverish. His head reeled, his heart pounded, and an exquisite sensation, thousands of them, went coursing through his body. He bent to repeat the perform- ance but the sound of heavy shoes in the hall parted them. 'I love you,' Nicole whispered, and turned to look out of the window.

Marie-Claire of the clattering shoes came in. Michael spoke in English to Nicole. 'What's got into you? You're all keyed up. Tell me the reason?'

She raised her shoulders in a shrug. 'Nothing,' she said, then turned to face him. 'I can't. It's a surprise. You mustn't make me,' she pouted.

'You mean, you'll never tell me?'

'Perhaps not me. But someone will. Very soon someone will. And now, before you torment me any more, I'm going to rest in my room.'

'But you've only been up a few hours.'

'Maybe after all I have a cold coming on.' She smiled again with the same air of mystery, tossed her head and was gone.

Not long after Monique came to tell him Pierre would like to see him in the parlour. It smelled of disuse. There were many stiffly upholstered chairs, several arrangements of wax fruit, flowers and stuffed birds under bell jars, and sombre embroidered pictures on the wall.

'Come in, sit down. I think we have something to celebrate.' Pierre too had the excited feverish look about him. He poured a glass of cognac for Michael.

'You are going back to Ireland in a few days, is that not so?'

Michael said it was.

'I have watched you and Nicole since you arrived. I have thought of nothing else except asking myself the question, "Are they right for each other?" I have talked over the same question with Maurice and Monique. When I felt doubts setting in I was careful to examine my conscience so that Nicole's leaving France wasn't influencing my judgement. One by one the doubts went. I think you are a fine young man, and so I will gladly give her to you.' Pierre smiled mischievously, his weathered face wrinkling into many lines around his eyes. 'That is, of course, if you still want her?'

'Oh, sir, I don't know what to say. Except yes, of course I want her for my wife. I'll cherish her all my life. How happy you have made me! And Nicole, she knows this?'

Pierre said she did.

'So that's what all the performance was about. I don't know whether I'm on my head or my heels.' Michael drained his glass.

Marie-Claire and Veronique were told the news and expressed their delight. And Michael told Marie-Claire he would remember always how it was she who had smuggled out and posted Nicole's frantic letter and how grateful he was. Monique then dispatched the maids to begin preparations for the special dinner they would eat that evening. To which Maurice came with his congratulations and wine he had kept for such an occasion.

A date was discussed for the wedding. Different months suggested by each one until Pierre intervened. Michael and Nicole must make that decision. 'Go to the parlour and talk about it alone.'

In between kisses they agreed on the middle of June the next year.

It was early on Friday that Michael arrived in Dublin. After going to his flat for a change of clothes and collecting his

mail, he went to Ballydurkin. He read the letters on the train. Amongst them was one from Brussels in reply to his enquiry about Laetitia.

Dear Mr McCarthy,

I am sorry you had to wait so long for news of Sister Marie-Elène. She was taken ill on the voyage out and on arrival worsened. The sea journey and the reality of seeing the plight of the lepers for the first time sometimes has this effect. The nervous system cannot cope with the shock. However, her Mother Superior assures me that she will make a full recovery and has promised to keep you informed.

Yours in God,
Mother Superior Benedict

PART TWO

Chapter Fourteen

1880

NICOLE wore her mother's dress and veil. On her father's arm she walked through the village to the church. In gardens, window boxes and the grass verges summer flowers bloomed. Bystanders lined the way as she passed then took short cuts, the young racing ahead to the chapel followed by the elderly.

The ancient church of pale sandstone was decked in every available space with greenery and blossoms brought and arranged by the village women. Michael stood before the altar next to a young Frenchman, a stranger to him until the night he arrived without Dermot who was to have been his best man. But Dermot, having recently broken his ankle in a riding accident, rumoured to have happened when he was the worse for drink, did not show up despite all his promises. James, who had seen Michael at the harbour, had kept repeating, 'If only you had asked me. Even now, at the last minute, I'd come in what I stand up in. But all this week I'm in court.'

'It's not your fault. Stop reproaching yourself. I'll kill that fella the next time I lay hands on him. I had my doubts about relying on him. It was you I wanted but felt I should have the only one of my own. What am I going to do?' Michael asked, looking out of the window, which he had been doing off and on for the last hour, hoping for a miracle, the sight of Dermot arriving. And thinking how sad that his mother couldn't share his great day.

'The Demarts must know other young men. Anyone

would do it. I know it's not the same as having a relative or close friend, but you've no choice.'

The day before the church wedding, after the legal ceremony, Monique wagged a finger. 'For Catholics,' she said, 'this has no real significance. A legal thing not a sacrament so no thinking tonight you are married, eh?'

Now the real marriage was about to take place. Like a hive of bees a buzz of excitement and whispered words could be heard. Then the ancient organ wheezed, notes sounded, heads turned – Michael's with them – and he saw Nicole entering the church in a cloud of creamy old lace, carrying a bouquet of cream and pink rosebuds. He was so overcome with emotion he thought it possible he might faint. In a little while she would be his wife. She who looked so ethereal, angel-like, dazzlingly beautiful.

Through his mind flashed old thoughts, advice from the lechers, the ones who went to Dublin's notorious night town: 'A man owes it to his wife. He should have experience before attempting anything on the wedding night. Not fair on the woman otherwise.' And a pang of uncertainty and fear assailed Michael.

She was by his side now and smiling at him. All his fears vanished. With love, patience and tenderness their wedding night would be sublime.

Long before the sun set Michael curtailed his drinking. Alcohol, he had heard from his Dublin acquaintances, was a killer on a wedding night. When it was time for them to go to bed he and Nicole came in for a barrage of innuendoes but finally they were alone in the big bedroom to which her mother had come as a bride with its great bed, plump pillows, lace-trimmed valances and vases of sweet-smelling flowers which Monique had insisted must be removed before they went to sleep. Nicole disappeared behind a papier mâché screen and after a little while emerged in ankle-length fine cambric trimmed with blue ribbons. Through the fine stuff he could see the outline of her body,

her breasts pushing at the nightgown, the dark shadow at the parting of her legs.

She walked slowly towards him then stopped and began raising her nightdress, above her knees, her belly, exposing the thick dark hair he had seen the shadow of. Then dropping it to the floor, she stood before him naked. 'My love, my little wife,' he said in awe before taking her in his arms. His hands began tracing the contours of her body, the texture of her skin, leaving go of her so he could gaze again on this marvel of a naked woman, the first live one he had ever seen. Not a cold unyielding piece of sculpture, not a painting hanging in a gallery, a warm, soft, yielding body that moved as one with his towards the bed.

In each other's arms, to the sound of drunken revelry, they fell asleep. Michael woke and before opening his eyes thought he was back in Dublin during the long wait and had been dreaming. Then he realized that wasn't possible for in Dublin he hadn't know the reality, hadn't known what it was to lie with a woman.

He opened his eyes and saw her hair spread on the pillow, her lashes curling back from her cheeks, her lips slightly parted. He kissed her and she woke, smiled at him and moved into his embrace.

They kissed and Nicole, taking the initiative, began to make love to him. Afterwards laughing and saying: 'I'm a bold, immodest girl but God will forgive me for I love you so much. And love is good and beautiful, and we're married and it can't be a sin.' And then, clapping a hand over her mouth, she looked alarmed. 'We forgot the flowers. Quickly, put them outside before Monique discovers them. You must never sleep in a room with flowers, they suck up all the air.'

'Forget about the flowers, I've more important things to do.' They made love again and she whispered into his neck, 'Imagine, I never knew such a wonderful, marvellous thing

existed. Will it always be so? For all of our lives? Tell me that it will. Until the day we die, promise me?'

'Always,' Michael told her. 'Always. For ever and ever.'

Though wearied and dishevelled, the guests threw themselves back into the festivities the next day, pausing only to cheer and wave and call advice to Nicole and Michael as they set out on the first stage of their journey to Dublin. Monique, not trusting Paris hotels or restaurants to feed them properly, insisted they take a hamper which she had prepared. There were only two seats on opposite sides of a compartment free on the train. They sat without speaking, their eyes never leaving each other's face, and each knew what the other was thinking: This has only happened to us. No one else in the whole world has ever experienced anything like it. It is our secret.

In Dublin Nicole didn't see Michael from early morning until late in the evening for there were meetings late in chambers discussing briefs, sometimes continued with clients in the convivial atmosphere of their clubs, Law Society dinners, and numerous other things. So she filled her time going to house agents with Lucy Farrell, who had kindly befriended her, to auction rooms where antiques were on sale, to shops in Grafton Street to view damasks and serges for curtains, bring home swatches of fabric to show to Michael.

And in between times she and Lucy went to Switzers and Brown Thomas to look at the latest fashions, drank tea and ate cakes in the window of Mitchell's cafe in Grafton Street, drove in the Farrells' carriage with its matched pair of silver high-stepping horses out to the Phoenix Park. On the way Lucy pointed out sights of interest, such as College Green with the Bank of Ireland, and facing it Trinity College where she said so many famous men had studied: Swift and Goldsmith and Oscar Wilde, who was now being talked

about. Passing Dublin Castle, she explained that it was the seat of power in the city.

Then one day Nicole found the house. And Michael, during a court adjournment, dashed across the city to view. It was a four-storey over basement built from pale yellow bricks. It was part of a square in the middle of which stood a small park to which only the residents had keys. The agent showing them the house added that sometimes, in the summer, military bands played there at the invitation of the residents.

'D'ye like it, Michael?' Nicole asked hopefully.

'I do. It's great. I like it very much.'

'And,' said Lucy, 'it's in excellent condition. Very well and tastefully maintained. Unless the colour scheme offends you, I'd leave it.'

'I will, but the horse will have to go.'

'But there isn't any horse,' Nicole said.

'Oh yes there is,' said Michael, preparing for a dash back to court. 'A white horse.'

'Where? I haven't seen a horse and I've been down to the mews cottage and stables.'

Lucy laughed. 'Michael means the white one above the fanlight.'

'I liked it. It's a pretty ornament.'

'It's King Billy's horse on which he won the Battle of the Boyne. No room or tolerance for such a creature in a Catholic home. I have to fly. We'll take it. Tell your man to contact my solicitor.'

'You never asked the price.'

'The price is right. I want it. We're buying it all except the horse.' He kissed her quickly and left.

'Oh, and by the way,' he said, half in and half out the door, 'the decor suits me. We'll leave it. Get settled in quicker.'

Nicole and Lucy hugged each other, had a last look round and went to the Shelbourne for lunch over which

they lingered for ages making lists: linen, silver, Limoges ware, French pots and pans and personal things, mementoes of Nicole's childhood, to be shipped to her new home.

It was two months before the transaction of the house was completed. On that day Nicole and Michael went to look at it, by which time she believed she was pregnant.

'The shutters are so well made, fit so snugly, you wouldn't have noticed them now except the man who came to repair the sash cords left one slightly undone.' Michael pulled a shutter out to its full width. 'See how neatly they fold back,' he said, delighted.

'And,' said Nicole, 'with strong iron bars to close them.'

Then she told him about the baby and expected him to be as overjoyed as she was.

'So soon?' he said. 'I have to share you? So soon another will have a claim on you? You'll never again be mine alone.'

Her face became crestfallen. 'Don't you want a baby, our baby?'

'Oh, my darling, you silly little goose! Don't look like that.' He took her in his arms, held her tenderly and kissed her. 'Of course I want a baby. I want, please God, lots and lots of babies. I'm just a little bit jealous. I've had you such a short while. I'd planned to take you to Italy, to Venice, to Paris. To have the honeymoon we never had.'

'We haven't stopped honeymooning since we got married.' She stroked his face.

'Nor shall we. Did you know, there's a custom in Ireland?' He was inventing one there and then. 'When a man and a woman mad about each other go to see their first permanent home, and if that coincides with news of an expected baby, they make love.'

'But where, Michael, when the beds haven't arrived yet?'

'The custom predates beds. Back to the time of finding a new cave. Back into primitive times.'

'Michael, you are telling me lies.'

'Honest to God, I am not. And it's supposed to be very unlucky not to honour the custom. In the olden times the man would have thrown a wolf skin or a bear's on the ground, anything to cushion it a bit. That rug left by the previous tenant would do grand. Decent people – maybe they have the second sight. Had a presentiment that the woman coming in was carrying a child.' With each lie he was manoeuvring her towards the rug. And she, pretending to be unwilling, was breathlessly saying, 'I can't. How could I?'

And he replying, 'Don't you worry. I know how to do it. I'll show you.'

They lay on the rug, her bonnet thrown one place, her drawers another, their breathing subsiding. The afternoon sun showed dust motes in the light about them. Raising himself, resting on an elbow, he looked down at her and said: 'Whenever we use this drawing-room I'll remember today. When there's a ball and it's filled with beautiful women, dancing, music, I'll see one more beautiful than all the rest and hear above the strains of waltzes and polkas her voice whispering, "I love you. Oh, my darling, I love you." And when we're old and our dancing days are over and we're sitting side by side watching our grandchildren dance, I'll still remember this day.

'And now, madam, get up and get your hat and your drawers!'

'I don't know whether to laugh or cry,' she said, and did both at the same time.

'I should have taken you down home,' Michael said after dinner one night. 'I meant to but somehow the time flew and now Lucy advises against it. Travelling from the seventh month isn't sensible, she tells me.'

Will I, wondered Nicole before replying, ever know as much as Lucy does about everything?

'Well, she is invariably right,' Nicole replied a little coldly.

'Are you beginning to find her trying?'

'A little.'

'Bear with her. You fell into her lap after Lizzie left with her husband. And you'll be glad of her in the months ahead, no matter how many nurse maids you have. Sure most of them – in fact, I'd say all – have never had a child of their own. So be patient a little while longer. You'll find that gradually and naturally you'll be seeing less of each other. Now shall I repeat what I was saying earlier?'

'I'm sorry, yes, do tell me again.'

He did and she replied that it was a pity. 'But it wasn't your fault. First there was the house. Then I had to rest for several weeks. And you've been working so hard. Do all barristers spend so much time at their work?'

'The ambitious ones. And you chose one of them for a husband. Whatever job I'd done, I'd have wanted to be the best.'

'Not like poor Dermot.'

'Don't waste any sympathy on him! He should have been born in the last century. The son of a lord with an enormous fortune to squander. Though God knows he's making a good fist of it now. Drinking and gambling, piling up the debts. Into his second farm manager in less than a year. No self-respecting one will work for him.'

'I liked him. He was kind and made me laugh. And he did come to Dublin to meet me.'

'Will you ever get sense? Didn't he let us down for the wedding? His ankle giving out at the last minute! All my eye, as I suspected. Like a lot of liars he hasn't the best memory. Didn't he let the cat out of the bag while he was here? About the surplus of drink the night before he was to go to France. And another thing . . . he didn't come up to see you only. It was to find another solicitor. The other one's been reading him the riot act for his extravagance.'

'Dermot told you this?'

'Of course he didn't.'

'Then how do you know?'

'I'm in the business of the law, amn't I? We're tight-lipped about clients to outsiders but not to each other.'

'Don't you feel sorry for him?'

'Ah, damn it, he's my brother, isn't he? He's living in that terrible house with its ghosts. Of course I feel sorry for him. But it's the thought of the farm being destroyed that kills me.'

'He's still young. He could turn over a new leaf. We'll go to Ballydurkin after the baby is born, please God. I want so much to meet your mother and Catti.'

'That'll be the sorry sight – my mother and her grandchild. Her first grandchild, and her not able to recognize it.'

Chapter Fifteen

WHEN in the early afternoon of 15 May Nicole went into labour, and Lucy sent word to Michael, he panicked. 'Calm down,' she wrote to him. 'Everything is fine. The doctor's been, he'll call again. But first babies are seldom in a hurry to arrive so there's no need to dash home immediately.'

When he did come several hours later Nicole appeared so distressed he feared the worst. This showed on his face as, almost in tears, he stroked Nicole's forehead and murmured words of comfort. Finally he was led down from the room while the doctor and nurse helped Nicole give birth to the child, a beautiful daughter weighing nine pounds.

Afterwards he expected to find her lying prostrate on the bed, evidence of suffering on her face. To his amazement she was propped on her pillows, wearing one of her prettiest nightgowns, her hair hanging silkily round her shoulders and her face joyous. On the bed beside her lay a swaddled bundle making grunting sounds. Nicole held out her arms. 'Isn't it wonderful? I can't believe it.' He kissed and held her carefully, himself unable to believe she was whole.

'I'm not going to fall apart – you can kiss and hug me properly. Oh, darling, I love you! And wait until you see our daughter. Hand her to me.'

'I'd be afraid of my life to touch her,' he said.

'I was giving you the excuse,' said Nicole, reaching for the baby. She loosened the outer wrap. 'Isn't she beautiful? The image of you.'

She had a fat, round face, no hair, and was a pinky-puce colour. 'She's gorgeous,' he said, gingerly reaching a finger to touch a fat cheek. Her head turned and her mouth made searching movements.

'She's looking for my breast,' Nicole explained.

'Already?'

'As a farmer's son you should know that. All creatures, calves, kittens, pups, everything including babies, it's the first thing they do, look for food.'

She opened the front of her nightgown and placed the baby at her breast. Before this moment, Michael thought, I was the only one ever to touch them, to lay my lips on them, take them in my mouth. He felt a stab of jealousy.

Nicole patted the bed. 'Sit here. Or lie beside me. Wasn't I lucky? It wasn't nearly as bad as I imagined.'

'From what I heard it sounded as if you were being killed.' He kissed her, lingering over her mouth until he desired her so much that he moved away. 'I wouldn't like to think of you having to go through that ordeal again.'

'If I don't, you know what that means.'

'I know, I know,' he said. 'Would I have that much willpower, I wonder?'

'I don't think I would,' said Nicole. 'I was thinking what we should call her. And I've decided that I shall choose her name and the name of any other little girls. When we have sons, you'll do the naming.'

'That sounds fair enough, what will you name her?'

'Marianne. You know how happy I am in Dublin. How much I love you and would never want to live in France again. But sometimes I miss it. Very seldom, but there are days when it comes vividly to mind. Papa, Monique, Maurice, the servants, the smell of the house, the sound of the language. You're very good about speaking in French to me, and when you forget or respond to me in English I understand it's because you're too tired to be switching to another language. But Marianne will be brought up to

understand and speak French. Then I can gossip away to my heart's content.'

At that moment the nurse hired to look after Nicole came back in. 'Your face is highly flushed, madam. You've become overexcited. That will never do. Say goodnight, Mr McCarthy, this young lady must get some sleep.'

'Goodnight, darling, and thank you,' he said, and did the nurse's bidding.

As he was about to leave the room Nicole called to him, 'You forgot to kiss Marianne.' He came back to the cradle and kissed the baby, thinking as he did so how much he liked the smell of her and the softness of her cheek.

He bought a turquoise locket for the child the next day. It was almost identical to the one he'd given Nicole.

'Each time I have a daughter, you must buy the same lockets for them. I'll have miniatures of them painted to go inside, and week by week, I will wear the lockets in turn. When they are twenty-one, the lockets will become theirs. Isn't that a good idea?'

'Grand. And so what shall I buy you when, please God, we have sons?'

'Like their names, you can choose. Isn't that fair?'

'Fair and wise like Solomon,' said Michael. 'I could jump into bed with you this minute.'

'I'm tempted to let you.'

'You brazen whipster. You'll wait your time like any decent respectable woman.'

Marianne was showered with gold and silver gifts at her christening. Mugs and inscribed plates. Teething rings with chased silver handles to hold and ivory to chew on. Honora had made the gown from Mellick lace and crocheted a shawl almost as fine as a spider's web. The baby's bonnet was satin and swansdown-trimmed. Her face had paled from puce-pink to a pale shade of rose and Nicole insisted she wasn't bald, only exceedingly fair, and held her this way

and that to display the almost white hair which lay so close to her scalp that only those with keen eyesight could spot it.

When Marianne was six months old, by which time her hair was obvious for all to see and Michael's secret fear that he had fathered a daughter destined to go through life bald was allayed, she was taken to visit Ballydurkin.

She was dressed in her best. Her blonde curls peeped out from her bonnet and she smiled and gurgled at anyone, who made much of her, remarked on her wide-set blue eyes, her ready smile and good humour, and held out their arms asking her to come to them.

Marianne was placed on Mary's lap with Nicole and Michael hovering each side to prevent a mishap. But her arms went round the child and held her close. Hope surged in Michael, as it had on previous occasions. The baby might have touched a chord in her heart or mind. A chord that would draw her back from wherever she had gone after the drownings. Watching her, he willed it to happen. But though she held Marianne securely, she didn't make a move to look at the child's face, or at Michael's, and only for a few seconds regarded Nicole when she was introduced.

Dermot arrived as Catti was ready to serve the dinner and told her to delay it for a while as he wanted to pay attention to his niece. 'Isn't she the gorgeous child?' he said, lifting Marianne from her grandmother's lap. 'Cut down off the McCarthy's.' He began hooshing her up in the air but keeping hold of her. He smelled of whiskey and when recklessly he began to let go of her for seconds at a time Nicole became terrified.

'She's not long been fed. She may get sick.'

'You won't get sick on your Uncle Dermot, sure you won't, you little dote.' And he threw and let go of her again.

'Dermot, you heard the child's mother, give her back,' Catti ordered. He did so without a protest. 'And the lot of you, sit over to the table or the food will be destroyed.'

It was bacon, cabbage and boiled potatoes, the vegetables having been cooked in the bacon water. 'Good wholesome ingredients served in a rough and ready way,' Michael said as he began to eat.

After the meal they continued to sit round the table drinking tea and eating a variety of Catti's soda breads, she relating happenings in the village to people Nicole had never heard of and Dermot and Michael starting on the topic of Honora and how her health wasn't good. Michael said that so far Laetitia hadn't written, but her Mother Superior in Hawaii had and that she was making slow but steady progress. Then Michael enquired about the farm.

Dermot told him about the bulling, calving, the ploughing, sowing, reaping and harvesting, exaggerating the success of each cycle, evading pertinent questions. Why the barn roof hadn't been repaired, evidence of crops that had been left to rot in the fields, the appearance of the house with its paint peeling and slates off the roof. When still Michael pressed for explanations he blamed the manager, the third in two years.

'Amn't I owed a fortune in arrears of rent? Farming's finished,' he said defensively.

'Certainly this one seems to be heading that way.'

Dermot flared: 'Don't you come down here from Dublin to criticize me. You could have had it. I offered it to you. But you wanted to be the gentleman. Live the life of Reilley above in Dublin. You were right too. Who'd want to be a farmer? Who in his right mind would want to live here? But I am and doing my best, so don't you come quizzing me as if I was still a child. All my life that's how I was treated. Any time you want it, it's yours. Live here, work it. Look on your mother, day in, day out.'

'That's enough out of you, Dermot McCarthy,' said Catti. 'If only your father was alive, there'd be a different story to tell, Lord rest him.'

Dermot's head drooped. He fell asleep. Catti shook him.

'Away to bed now like a good boy.' She led him to the door. 'Go careful on them stairs.

'Poor Dermot was stripped of everything he cared about,' she said. 'Drink never passed his lips beforehand and now he's at it like a fish.'

'What about this girl Sheila Crowley? Any move there?' asked Michael, having heard in a letter that his brother was sweet on a local girl.

'I'd say she'd be interested all right. He has a nice nature. And I don't think she'd object to me and your mother in her home.'

'She couldn't,' said Michael.

'That's not what's stopping any progress,' Catti said. ' 'Tis himself. He can't make a decision. Can't take responsibility for anything. And it's not in his power to alter a thing. It was laid out for him before he saw the light of day.'

Michael knew that despite his previous warnings Catti was preparing herself to tell the tale of Mag Cronin. In her element with Nicole as a new audience. Well, he'd best her.

'Nicole,' he said, 'you've had a long day, you look jaded and the child's asleep. Go up to bed, I'll carry Marianne. We've an early start in the morning.'

'You're not leaving so soon? You're hardly here yet,' said Catti.

'I'm sorry, but I am a working man.'

'Well,' she said, 'that was short and sweet. In the door and up the stairs. I don't know why you bother coming at all.'

'Work,' he said. 'The pity is we live so far away.' Even as he thought, thank God we do.

In the bedroom Nicole cried, 'It is such a sad, lonely house. What will become of them?'

'Catti is in her element, two helpless beings needing her. My mother removed from everything. Dermot is the one

to be pitied. The farm should be sold, and the land. Let the house remain for the women's lifetimes. With the millstone from round his neck he might marry Sheila, find a small place, go to America, anything. But he won't. He's trying to live up to what my father would have expected of him, or what Dermot thinks he would have. Honest to God, love, I just don't know.'

Before leaving Ballydurkin Nicole went to the Crowleys' farmhouse with Catti who introduced her to Sheila Crowley's sister Julia who was looking for a nursemaid's position. Nicole immediately took a liking to the pleasant-faced young girl. There were several children in the house and she noticed how well Julia coped with them, showing no impatience or annoyance at their boisterous behaviour but, as if she had eyes in the back of her head, noticing if they approached the fire or attempted climbing on chairs. Then her soft voice became firm and the children obeyed her. Nicole judged her to be just the person she would like to have in charge of Marianne and any other children she would have.

'Would you be willing to consider working for me?' she asked after describing the house, the nursery, and saying that Aggie the maid of all work would help.

'I'd be delighted, ma'am. I'd feel as if it was a child of my own family I'd be minding for haven't I known the McCarthys all my life?'

Chapter Sixteen

WHEN Nicole told Michael of the second baby she was expecting his face showed all the enthusiasm and pleasure he knew she would expect, displaying nothing of the sadness he really felt that Marianne so soon, too soon, would have to share his and her mother's love with another. He was constantly amazed by the depths of his feelings for his daughter. She who on her first day had been bald and red in the face and had elicited from him little emotion except a vague pride in being a father. But the more he saw of her, held her, became aware of the softness and fragility of her, the scent of her like nothing else he had ever inhaled, he grew to love her. And on the day she first made eye contact with him and smiled a crooked smile, he knew that until the day he died no other child would mean as much to him.

Julia was a great success, took on all the nursery duties, was good-humoured and easygoing, immediately accepted by the other servants and Aggie in particular so that Nicole knew there would be no problems when the new baby came and they would have to work together.

The friends Lucy had introduced her to called, and she in turn visited them. Women near her own age with young children, expecting others. They were the wives of doctors, solicitors, barristers and businessmen. They gossiped, drank tea, complained about their servants, enthused over the latest fashions and regretted how their figures had never been quite the same since giving birth.

They took it in turns to give small dinner parties, card

parties, and musical evenings where if they hadn't engaged a professional singer or musician, which mostly they hadn't, they themselves sang ballads and played the piano.

On the days, though they were seldom, when she had an overwhelming longing for France, Nicole wrote long letters to Monique and her father and occasionally to Maurice, telling them how sorry she was that she hadn't been back yet. Describing how she longed for them to see Marianne. That had she not become pregnant again so quickly she had planned to visit, and how now that Marianne was starting to talk, she was teaching her French. There was besides nothing to stop them coming to Dublin.

Monique wrote letters in reply and her father added a few lines to a page. Reading Monique's letters was like being in the room listening to her as she flew from one subject to another. Who had died, who had gone to live in Paris. Plumbers and carpenters were like gold. Everyone going to the towns to earn big money. And what would she call the new baby? They had always kept names in the family.

Nicole smiled as she read that. Poor old Monique. She'd never have a namesake. Hers was a horrible name, but her mother's name . . . Lisette? Yes, maybe Nicole would think about that.

She had another girl, a thin, wiry, dark-haired baby. A French baby, Nicole thought, looking at her new daughter. I can see myself in her.

Michael, Lucy, the servants, everyone who came to see her, all agreed that she was the image of her mother. And Annie, the cook, said, 'She's been here before.' Nicole asked what that meant. 'She's that knowing. See how she's taking in everything. Turning her head when someone talks. I declare to God, she's listening and taking notice already.'

Nicole named her Françoise Lisette, and Michael duly

bought her a turquoise locket to match her mother's and sister's.

'No one believes they're sisters,' Aggie was forever reporting when she and Julia returned from airing the babies in Saint Stephen's Green. Looking at her daughters, each in her high-wheeled, boat-shaped perambulator, Nicole agreed that they were unalike. Even allowing for the difference in their ages, Marianne nearly two and Françoise only seven months, though able to sit up, there wasn't the slightest resemblance between them. Marianne was all golden curls, dimples, rose-flushed skin, smiles and waves, kisses for the asking. Françoise had thick pale creamy skin in which colour rarely showed unless she was feverish or very angry, which she often was. Her pallor was highlighted by the darkness of her hair, lashes and brows, and her eyes whose colour was hard to ascertain. But whether the shade appeared to be hazel, green, or a mixture of both, the overall impression was that they were dark and soon after birth they fixed on one person at a time as if she was studying them.

Marianne's face was broad; Françoise's a long perfect oval. Marianne was pretty; Françoise was beautiful. One afternoon on their return from their outing, when Aggie made her usual comment, Nicole, who had just had her third pregnancy confirmed, wondered what the next baby would look like. Maybe it would be a boy? Michael would like that. He'd call him Peter, after his father. And if I have another girl she'll be christened Hélène, Nicole decided. Aggie would need coaching in how to give it the French pronunciation, though why she should find it more difficult than Julia or the other servants Nicole couldn't understand. A few times she had heard her call Marianne 'Marion'. Aggie was a law unto herself. Perhaps it was something to do with her upbringing in the orphanage from which Nicole had taken her to be their general maid.

'Yes, ma'am,' she'd say, looking you straight in the eye. 'I'll do it that way, surely,' she'd agree whenever Nicole had to correct her, then go her own sweet way.

But the names were important to Nicole. She didn't want a Marion or a Molly, a Frances or a Fanny. Marianne and Françoise they would be called, and nothing else.

While it was still early enough in her third pregnancy to travel they took the children to Ballydurkin and had a great surprise. Dermot was busy and sent his apologies for not meeting them by the hired hand who drove the pony and trap. That there was a change about the farm was immediately noticeable. The sagging roof of the barn had been repaired and doors and windows painted. Catti was watching for their arrival and ran spryly to meet them, calling as she came, 'There's been a miracle! Dermot's taken the Pledge. Not a drop's passed his lips this six weeks. He's up at the crack of dawn and works like a trooper. And, what's more, sees to it that so do the men. No more standing round breastfeeding their shovels! God has answered my prayers – though Sheila Crowley may have had a hand in it as well. It's my belief she put her foot down. Said he would take the Pledge or she was off to America.'

'That's marvellous news,' said Michael. 'And how's he getting on with the manager?'

'Like a house on fire. Sure without the drink he's not contrary at all. I wish I had the same good news about your mother. She drinks, eats and sleeps, that's her life. Never even fingers her Rosary. I hear tell, Nicole, there's to be a new addition. When, please God?'

'In four months, December.'

'Isn't that grand? And look at herself. Give Catti a kiss, darling.' Marianne deposited kisses on various parts of Catti's face. 'And you, Françoise, have you a kiss for me?'

Françoise was choosy whom she kissed and Catti wasn't favoured. 'How old are they now, I do forget?'

'Marianne was two in May and Françoise one in September.'

'God bless and spare them, they're fine children. Julia wrote and told Sheila she went with you to France at Easter. She was mad about the place.'

'Poor Julia's easily pleased,' said Michael, who had come in from a short inspection of the outbuildings.

'We didn't stop over in Paris and there's little to see or do in Issoudon.'

'Julia wouldn't mind that, wasn't she reared in the country? Tell me, how were your father and aunt?'

'So happy to see us all, especially the babies. But they've aged. Aunt Monique's legs are bad, ulcers and her circulation. She has high blood pressure also. She tells me Papa drinks too much, more cognac than wine. And though not in so many words hints that it's my fault for leaving him. Perhaps it is the truth. But I have to be with my husband.'

'Of course you do, child! Dermot will be in any minute. Put something under their chins or they'll destroy their clothes. Ah, here he is.'

Dermot looked a different man. Slighter, sprucer, and altogether a more relaxed, confident person. He greeted Nicole warmly, and his nieces, and Françoise, without being asked, offered her face for kissing.

' 'Tis you has the way with women, she had ne'er a kiss for me,' Catti said.

'She likes you obviously,' said Nicole. 'She's very sparing with her kisses.'

'So everything and everyone is well?' Michael said as they began the meal. 'Three letters there's been from Letty and so far she's made a great recovery.'

In a mournful voice Catti said, 'Aye, everyone except

your poor mother and that unfortunate child, Honora. Year in, year out, carrying her little babies, only to lose them.'

'She's a wonderful person. We go up to see her. Kildare's not too far from Dublin. There's never a complaint out of her. She has wonderful faith and looks in the best of health, so don't worry too much, Catti.'

'Nicole's right, she looks in the pink,' Michael agreed.

'That may be so, but who's to know what goes on in her heart? Never be done thanking God for your good fortune and praying for it to continue.' Catti's voice became more mournful as she continued, 'We never know the hour or the minute . . .'

Michael had a shrewd idea of what would come next and changed the conversation to a subject he knew she wouldn't be able to resist.

'Is it right what I've been hearing? That you and Sheila have an understanding, Dermot? That you might be considering . . .' he was about to say, 'Buying a double plot', a joke often made. He caught himself on in time and said instead, 'Wedding bells?'

Dermot blushed and laughed but looked pleased at the teasing. 'I'm saying nothing. You can all wait,' he said. Catti cheered up and joined in the codding and teasing. Michael relaxed and ate his dinner.

'It might well be a Christmas baby,' Nicole's doctor said as he finished examining her.

'That would be wonderful. A Christmas baby!'

'However, don't pin your hopes on it. Babies aren't concerned with when they arrive, but you might be lucky.'

Christmas Day came and went, and Saint Stephen's Day. Hélène arrived on 28 December: another fat, round, bald infant, looking like all the McCarthys.

She was a placid baby, suckling and sleeping by turns. Nicole's friends came to visit and admire her. Sweets and chocolates and hothouse flowers were showered on her

mother, and suitable gifts on her, along with presents for Marianne and Françoise so, as the visitors said, 'They don't feel their noses have been knocked out of joint.'

Michael bought a fourth identical locket and had her name inscribed. Marianne tried to kill her with kindness and eventually Françoise reluctantly bestowed kisses on her but was more interested still in attempting to pry open her fingers and open her eyes when she fell asleep.

Three months after her birth Julia came one morning to see Nicole. 'Ma'am,' she said, 'there's something the matter with Aggie. A couple of times recently I've come upon her when she wasn't expecting me and the girl was in floods of tears. I tried coaxing her to tell me what ailed her, but she wouldn't. Today, though, she says she'll tell you.'

'Send her along then, Julia. I wonder what can be the matter? I'd say it's most unusual for Aggie to be crying. Very high-spirited she always seems.'

'That's right enough, ma'am, but not this last week. I'll send her up.'

Aggie's face was without its usual pert monkeyish grin. 'Sit down, Aggie, and tell me all about what's worrying you. Tell me, and if I can I'll put it right,' Nicole promised.

'Oh, ma'am, if only you could! But it's too late. I done a terrible thing. The same thing my mother did before me. I'm going to have a baby.'

'That can't be true. You're only a child yourself. In the beginning your courses can be irregular, and you do know you can't have a baby because you might have kissed a boy? Though who he was or where you kissed him I can't imagine for you go nowhere except to the park with Julia and the children.'

'And the chapel. And I've had my courses this long time. The time does fly. I was twelve when I came to you and that's three years gone.'

'As long as that? Time *does* fly. About the chapel . . . you could hardly have been kissing anyone before or after Mass.'

'You forgot about the Novena. The Nine Fridays. Though I did ask if I could go and you said yes. Back in the summer, d'ye not remember?'

'Vaguely,' said Nicole. 'You go to the chapel the night before the first Friday of the month, and on the Friday morning receive communion. I remember it from school. The Novena lasts for nine months.'

'The same as having a baby, ma'am. That's how I got it. D'ye see, one night, coming back, the nights had got dark by then, didn't this soldier from Beggar's Bush Barracks get into talk with me? He was nice, and he walked part of the way from Haddington Road with me. He liked Dublin, he said, came from a country part of England himself. He asked me where I was going and where I'd been and I explained about the Novena and that I went every week. He let on to know what I was talking about but sure how could he, and he a Protestant? We said goodnight.

'I was hoping he might be there the next week. He was and I was delighted. And then I saw him every week. He used to bring me sweets and sometimes we'd go in a dairy and have a glass of milk. Then one night it happened. Only a few minutes it was and only the once. He was going foreign the next week. I never saw him again. Oh, what'll I do? I never meant to have a poor little baby that'll finish up like me in the Foundling Hospital. Don't tell the others, sure you won't?'

'Don't cry any more, Aggie. Here, take this hankie and dry your eyes. Crying won't solve anything, only upset you more. Are you having any sickness?'

'No, ma'am, in myself I'm grand when I forget about my trouble.' Aggie dabbed at her eyes, sniffed and sobbed, and Nicole pursued her own thoughts. The poor unfortunate child. No man to be proud and pleased at her news. No money or home. No doting relatives. No gold and silver christening gifts. Nothing facing her except a home or the Foundling Hospital.

And it's all my fault! Not paying enough attention when she mentioned the Novena. I took her from the Union. I should have been more caring. Asked who would go with her. Remembered that the summer evenings wouldn't last for ever.

'Now listen to me, I'll say nothing to anyone for the present. Eventually they'll have to know but not yet awhile. I have a good friend, a wise kind one. I'll ask her advice. We'll work something out between us.' Still not fully accepting that Aggie was pregnant, Nicole asked, 'How often have you missed?'

'Twice, ma'am. I've just missed for the second time.'

'Don't lose heart yet, it could still be a false alarm.'

'Thanks very much. You're that good to me, thanks again.'

'Say nothing to no one and I'll make an excuse to Julia who'll be curious as to what's been upsetting you. You go on back to the nursery and I'll have a word with my friend and let you know.'

Lucy Farrell had several suggestions. 'There are homes run by the nuns for girls in Aggie's predicament. In and around Dublin and down the country. The girls stay there until their confinement.'

'And their babies?'

'They're not encouraged to keep them. Many finish up in the Foundling Hospital.'

'The Foundling Hospital! The place where Aggie was reared, from where I took her!'

'Well, yes, but there wouldn't be any other choice really.'

'That idea appalls her.'

'I suppose it would. A pity about the whole thing. You'll miss her. She was so good with the children. Let's hope it may be a false alarm. What is the latest about Letty? Poor girl, she has been unfortunate.'

'She has had another relapse, a more serious one this time. Michael had a letter from a doctor there who is looking after her. He is going to recommend that she is sent back to Europe. But as he said, by the time the letter reached Michael she could have recovered again.'

Nicole let another week pass during which she prayed and hoped that Aggie's pregnancy would prove to be a false alarm for she dreaded making the proposition she had in mind to Michael. And yet, she could see no other course to follow.

He wasn't particularly interested when she did tell him that Aggie was probably going to have a baby and the circumstances in which it was conceived. That was until she announced that she intended to keep Aggie on.

'Keeping her? Keeping her here, you mean?' he asked, laying down the newspaper he had been leafing through.

'Where else?'

'And the baby?'

'Naturally.'

'Definitely not. You cannot do that. It would be a scandal. Many would consider it so.'

'Who would?'

'The church, our friends, the neighbours.'

Nicole made a dismissive gesture and said, 'I'm only interested in what's best for Aggie. She's little more than a child. I'm partly to blame for what happened. I should have . . .'

'Don't be ridiculous! How are you involved, for God's sake?'

'She lives in my home. I took her in. I should have checked she didn't go out alone at night.'

'You knew she was?'

'Vaguely.' And she explained how at the time the nights were light and she had forgotten that the Novena went on for months. 'I'm not very good with the servants. So long as

things are running smoothly, I tend not to pry. And I was expecting Hélène.'

Impatiently he said, 'All right, all right. Now tell me how you intend keeping her here?'

'There's nothing to tell. Just carry on as normal.'

'The situation is anything but normal. What are your plans for the child?'

'Aggie keeps her with her.'

Michael rose from the chair and said, 'Oh, no, definitely not.'

'But that's the purpose of Aggie's staying on here. Otherwise the baby's life will be a repetition of what happened to her. What difference will one more baby make to us?'

'You're not suggesting it should be brought up with our children?'

'That wouldn't interfere with or harm them.'

'Oh, Nicole, you're sweet and innocent. But even you must see it's not a desirable thing to do?'

'I didn't mean we should privately educate the child, send it to dancing lessons, but while they're little it wouldn't matter.'

'Let's compromise. No home, and no nuns for Aggie. She can stay here until her confinement, despite the scandal it will cause. When her time comes she'll go into hospital, have the baby, have it adopted, then come back to her job. I'm not happy about that solution but because you are so concerned I'll go along with it.'

'That's not a solution. How will Aggie feel? Who's to know what sort of people will take the child, how they'll care for it?'

'Aggie should have thought of that on the night she spent with her soldier.'

'I don't believe you said that! I don't want to hear any more remarks like that. I'm going to bed.'

'Well, hear this before you go. I've changed my mind.

You are to let Aggie go, the sooner the better. And I don't want to hear another word about her or her bastard!'

Nicole clapped her hands over her ears and ran from the room. From the following day she stopped eating with Michael, didn't utter a word in his hearing, and repelled his advances in bed.

He told James about Aggie and the situation at home and asked his advice. His friend thought Nicole was being a true Christian. 'Let them stay, at least for a year or two. Anything might happen. She might find a situation where she could live in and the child not be objected to.'

'Hardly likely,' said Michael.

'Perhaps a husband?'

'Even less likely.'

'Have a word with Mama,' James suggested.

Michael did. And Lucy said, 'I'm afraid Nicole's heart rules her head. But you must not allow her to keep either Aggie or the child in your home. What's to stop the same thing happening again? Aggie's mother was obviously a weak character. I'm afraid such traits run in families. Tell Nicole firmly that you will not countenance such a thing.'

That was his intention. He would show her that he was the head of the household. He decided on the important issues. All her silences, tantrums, whatever weapon she employed, would not alter his mind. That was until the night he had the dream.

He dreamt he was walking along a road in Ballydurkin. Ahead of him he saw, standing by the side of the road, an old woman dressed in black rags. No one he recognized. This surprised him for he knew all the people of the parish and she appeared too old and frail to have walked any distance.

It had been a fine evening. Now the sun was about to set. And although all day and until this moment the sky had been cloudless, now, except where the sun was disappearing in a blaze of colour, the light went, leaving above and

around the old woman just sufficient brightness to make her visible.

Michael came nearer. She raised an arm, pointed a finger, and when he was within earshot screamed: 'Did you think you had escaped, Michael McCarthy? That you'd sail through life untouched in your gown, your poll covered with a curly wig? You and the girl from over the sea. In your fine house in Dublin. With your carriage and pair and lackeys galore at your beck and call and your pretty babies. Never knowing a care in the world.'

She cackled, a sound that sent a shiver through him. 'You thought it was finished and done with it. Sure for you and yours it hasn't started yet! But it's coming. Slowly but surely, it's coming.'

He was abreast of her now, and afraid to look upon her face, turned and began running back the way he had come. Behind him he heard her chasing him while the thought registered that such a thing wasn't possible for she was too old. Yet he could hear her gaining on him. And the slight wind brought her foetid smell wafting about him. He breathed it in, his stomach heaved, sweat saturated him and his heart beat so rapidly he felt that at any minute he would collapse. He tripped on an exposed root and fell on his face. Then, like a wild beast she was upon him, her hands fastened around his neck. He wanted to scream, cry out for help, but his breath was choked and no sound came. He woke with his hands frantically clawing at his nightshirt collar, the dream still vivid in his mind.

Why, he wondered, wasn't Nicole awake also? Why wasn't she concerned? Hadn't he struggled and threshed about in the nightmare? He listened to see if she was feigning sleep. But he knew her so well, her every movement, how she breathed, awake or asleep. She hadn't been disturbed. He knew from other dreams that very soon this one would begin to slip away. Before it did he wanted to try and make sense of it. Who was the old woman? Of

what or who was she warning him, with what threatening him? A face he did not know! Perhaps he had glimpsed such a face, a beggar on the streets or someone who had looked in his carriage window when it stopped at a crossing? When he was alone in it? When he and Nicole and the children were riding with him? How did she know Nicole was foreign? If she was only a beggar he had seen in passing, how did she know so much about him?

Far down in the depths of his mind a memory stirred. One from when he went to school in Ballydurkin. A memory of walking home from school followed by the poorer, rougher boys and the things they shouted after him. About his grandfather, an eviction, a girl and a bastard child. A girl who was sent to America and never heard of again. The taunts had annoyed him but he'd known had he shown this they would have continued. He ignored them and eventually they stopped, another victim was found to bully.

He had never told his mother about the boys and what they said. Asked if it was true. You didn't talk to your mother about such things. And as the years passed he thought he had forgotten the incident completely. The dream was fast fading.

Memories of Catti that weren't so deeply buried, of her stories, surfaced . . . was there the slightest grain of truth in them? In the light of day they were easy to dismiss. Unlike now, with his heart still not calm, in the dark amongst the noises that all old houses make in the night. It would be easy to believe them. And that way lay the loss of his reason. It was a bad dream, that was all. He was upset at how things were between him and Nicole. He missed her pleasing, inconsequential chatter. Her company at the table. And most of all the joy and sweetness of their passion when they lay together. All these things had weighed on his mind. And the cause of them: Aggie and her child.

He got up and went to the bathroom, drank cold water, splashed his face with it and felt better. Returning to the

bedroom he looked at the sleeping face of Nicole, becoming visible as dawn came through the tiny chink in the curtains.

He bent and kissed her cheek. She stirred, opened her eyes and looked at him, forgetting in her first moments of wakening that there was trouble between them. Before she did and turned from him, he whispered, 'Darling, I was wrong. I'm sorry. Aggie and her child can stay.' She held out her arms to him and he lay down beside her.

After they had made love and she had drifted back to sleep, a sadness came over him as it often did, no matter how passionate or joyful their lovemaking had been, and with it a worrying thought. When the old woman had said: 'Sure you thought it was finished and done with it. Sure for you and yours it hasn't started yet. But it's coming! Slowly but surely, it's coming,' what did she mean? What was coming and to whom? What could an infant do to cause trouble, except what it had already between him and Nicole? And that was now remedied. Was it something the child could do to his beloved Marianne? Give her one of the lethal diseases that thrived in Dublin, infect his beautiful Françoise, make Hélène, his baby, sicken with something the bastard child picked up?

Nonsense, nonsense, he told himself. It was only a dream. A nightmare. It has almost vanished from your mind. By breakfast-time you won't be able to remember an iota of it.

The next morning he explained there were conditions attached to Aggie's remaining. 'You must make it clear to her that there can be no second chance.'

'Yes,' Nicole said, 'I agree with that.'

'And secondly, you'll have to talk to the servants. Some may not want to stay because of Aggie's fall from grace.' She also agreed to do that. 'I love you,' she said, hugging

him. 'I knew your heart couldn't be so cruel as to make Aggie leave.'

'I hope I won't live to regret it.'

'Why should you? How could a little baby give you cause for regret? You'll hardly ever lay eyes on it.'

'No, I suppose you're right.'

Nicole called the servants together and told them of Aggie's condition and the arrangments for her and the child.

'God help her, sure doesn't it happen to many a girl? I've no objection,' was Julia's answer.

The cook and the parlourmaid felt it was the business of Nicole and Michael, their only condition being that the child shouldn't interfere with their duties. But the general maid, not much above Aggie in the hierarchy of the domestic staff, was scandalized. Her plain pale face blanched further, her coarse stubby-fingered hand covered her open mouth at the shock and astonishment of hearing such a suggestion and remained there until she recovered enough to say her piece. 'I'll work the week out. I'd be afraid to stay longer in a house where there's no fear of God or respect for His Son, Jesus, and His Holy Mother. For luck couldn't attend a house where such goings on is encouraged.'

Nicole thanked the others.

Chapter Seventeen

AGGIE's baby was a girl who looked like her. She called her Phyllis. 'Philip was her father's name,' she told Nicole when she visited her in hospital. Once out of hospital she organized a routine for the baby that didn't interfere with her caring for the other children, or only very seldom.

She had sworn to Nicole that there would never be a second time. 'Your mind can rest easy on that score, ma'am.' And except for Mass on Sundays and Holy Days, times when she had to go on an errand, and airing her baby, she went nowhere alone. A cot was moved into her basement room which before the child's birth she had cleaned thoroughly and given a fresh coat of whitewash. Nicole supplied the baby's bedding and passed on Hélène's clothes. The servants, including the groom, bought gifts for Phyllis and made her very welcome.

Marianne was besotted by her, treating her like a doll. Wanting to dress and undress her, brushing the black hair of which she had a headful and reciting nursery rhymes long before Phyllis could understand a word of them. After weaning she had her meals in the nursery. Françoise paid her little attention except when Phyllis began to crawl and knocked down intricate buildings she was attempting to erect from her coloured bricks. Then she screamed with rage. She reacted in the same way if Hélène was the culprit. 'That child's fiercely independent,' Julia said one day to Nicole. 'She loves her own things. Hates the others to touch them. Very possessive about what's hers. Very

curious. Wants to know the ins and outs of everything. Why, why, why is it so? What makes it do that? She does have my head spinning with her questions, most of which I can't answer. Oh, she has the head on her, all right. She'd annoy you, but I've never seen her give Marianne a poke or a pinch. She's kind and fair so long as you leave her alone.'

'You've weighed her up all right,' said Nicole. She had a soft spot for this beautiful independent daughter. Whereas sometimes Marianne's constant smiles and preening affection with her father, with James, with any man who came to the house, irritated her. Never for long, though. Marianne was hard to resist when her arms were wrapped round your neck and kisses being planted all over your face.

Phyllis was a good baby and the house continued to run smoothly. Michael rarely saw her. He saw almost as little of his own children, so busy was he always. For which from time to time Nicole scolded him, and as quickly forgave him. That was how he was: work took precedence over all else.

Always she was thankful for the nights. Then he was hers. They made love as frequently and with as much passion as they always had. And now there was a new dimension added to it. It was a more leisurely act, had more of a lingering quality. This they talked about. Remembering their wondrous wedding night, believing then that for no one else in the whole world could there be such an experience as theirs. 'I thought,' said Michael, 'during that first week we had reached the ultimate. And had that been so I would still have considered myself so lucky. But it's better now than it ever was. D'ye think that's right?'

'I do, but I couldn't have put it as well as you. I could die happily like this,' Nicole whispered against his chest.

Despite the frequency and quality of their lovemaking, month after month passed without Nicole conceiving. At first this amazed and vaguely worried her. Then she rejoiced and hoped the situation would continue. The bliss

of no more morning sickness. The freedom to sleep through the night. Being able to stay the length of an evening at a function without leaking breasts, her bodice padded with wadding to absorb the milk, her mind uneasy in case the baby at home was cranky, sucking a bottle. And her body . . . She loved her body again. Slight and shapely, the stretch marks daily becoming less noticeable. And the joy of her new gowns! Her dressmaker able to create fashionable modes whose lines didn't have to be altered and so slightly spoiled by making allowances for a thickened waist and a belly still bulged despite tight lacing.

Friends, intimate ones, asked what was her secret and wouldn't she share it? Shaking her head, Nicole told them, 'There's no secret. Everything between me and Michael is normal.' Wanting to add, 'Wonderful, magical, breathtakingly beautiful.' But they weren't thoughts for sharing.

In 1885, two years after Hélène was born, Julia came one day to talk with Nicole. Her face was flushed with excitement and she carried a letter in her hand. 'What d'ye think, Mrs McCarthy? Dermot and Sheila have named the day. They're putting in the Banns. Isn't that grand? I'm so happy for them.'

'I'm delighted, Julia, but wouldn't you think Dermot would have dropped a line to Michael?'

'Sheila sends his apologies. He's terrible for the writing. And apart from that has no time for anything except the farm. Between that and the hunting, letter writing gets put on the long finger. It'll be before Christmas, a good bit.'

'So the wedding will be at the end of November?' Nicole said, and looked through the window at the dreary damp day. 'I wished they'd planned it for the spring or summer.'

' 'Twould have been better so but once the humour was on them they couldn't wait that long.'

'Apparently not,' said Nicole, gloomy at the prospect of

another visit to Ballydurkin. She had come to hate the house, dreaded being in the presence of Michael's mother and knew that so did he. He was depressed before, after and during the visit. Whatever the weather was like he went out soon after breakfast, walking through the fields, the lanes, climbing the little hills, not returning until late in the evening, morose and silent. And without fail, before leaving, he warned his wife that Catti was losing her mind and to pay no attention to anything out of ordinary she might say.

She doubted that anything ailed Catti's mind, but reassured him that she would heed his warning. If the weather was at all reasonable she wouldn't be long after him in escaping from the house: taking the children on short walks in the woods, to a little cove nearby or to visit Julia's big, noisy, good-humoured family. She would have gone anywhere to escape from the kitchen where one old woman sat mute and motionless, and the other couldn't still her body or tongue.

Marianne had been in school for two months when word of the wedding came.

Before she started Nicole asked Michael's advice as to where she should send her. 'I'm sure you've already decided,' he replied, 'and I wouldn't be at all surprised to hear it's the one in Lesson Street belonging to the Order you went to yourself.'

'Aren't you clever? Psychic even. But you're right, it was one of the deciding factors. Not for sentimental reasons. It specializes in languages, especially French. I don't want her to lose her French and she is in danger of just that. You hardly ever use it, the servants haven't got it, and now Phyllis and Hélène are beginning to prattle in English, my influence is sadly weakening.'

Marianne, with her dimples, curls, ready smiles and excellent French, was in no time the school pet. Nuns, teachers and pupils alike made much of her. And when

Nicole told her that they were going to Ballydurkin for a few days and she would have to miss school, she cried and didn't want to go. But as always, not for long. She was so easy to persuade, Michael thought, watching her wipe away her tears. And as he often did he feared for her future.

Sheila and Dermot married in the last week of November on a miserable day.

' 'Twas now or wait until Advent was over – no weddings in between,' Sheila told Nicole when they were talking after the ceremony. 'There'd be little difference in the weather and Dermot was impatient. Frightened, maybe, that I'd change my mind.'

'And why would you do that?' asked Nicole.

'Of course I wouldn't but he knows I've found out about his debts and the gambling.'

Not wanting to pry Nicole tried changing the subject by saying, 'I wish you both all the happiness and prosperity you deserve,' and she kissed her new sister-in-law.

'Happy we'll be. We've a great love for each other. But as for the prosperity, that could be another thing altogether. There's a lot of show up front.'

'I don't understand,' said Nicole, deducing that Sheila wanted to confide in her.

'More show than substance. That fella took the Pledge but there's no Pledge for gamblers.'

'Serious gambling? Big money?' asked Nicole.

'Big money. He started in with the hunting lot, one thing led to another, then it was the racing crowd. Don't you mention it to Michael. He'd have a fit if he knew the sums owed. To pay them off, some of them, Dermot'll have to start letting go of the fields. God knows, things are hard enough for farmers in any case since Gladstone was coerced into Parnell's Rent Act. And soon enough tenants'll have the right to buy.'

'Did you know about his gambling before you decided to marry?'

'I had my suspicions, all right. But, d'ye see how it is, I love him. And a woman can only wait so long. The years do be against her. And like all fools of women, I have my hopes of changing him. After all, he did give up the drink. Maybe he will give up the gambling too.'

'I'm so sorry, Sheila. Maybe you should tell Michael? He could and would help.'

'No, it would do no good, and for all that I keep hoping, I know my own know. Throwing good money after bad, that's all he'd be doing. I sometimes think poor unfortunate Dermot is cursed never to succeed. And in any case, Michael is the last one he'd want to know. Dermot's pride would crucify him. It's Michael and his dead father he wants to prove himself to.'

The Crowleys' farmhouse by local standards was big but still it overflowed with family and guests.

Nichole thought of her wedding day and felt a great nostalgia. She saw her lovely old house, so solid and safe, so comfortable. She could smell the kitchen, simmering herb-scented stews and soups, chickens roasting, her father's tobacco, Monique's lavender water made from the hedges that grew outside the door near the long herb trough.

Her father's face wrinkled with smiles, cognac on his breath. Monique with what she now described as a 'complication of complaints'. Nicole's eyes filled with tears. How thoughtless she was. How callous. They hadn't seen Hélène yet. And it was only France, not Africa where they lived.

How sad it was to leave your own country. Why couldn't Michael have been French or she Irish? Standing amongst the laughing, drinking, garrulous guests she knew that however much she loved Dublin, her life in it, in Ireland, she would always experience this intense longing for the place where she was born, and that as she grew older it would increase in its intensity.

★

She broke her promise to Sheila and told Michael. 'I had an idea,' he said, 'one hears whispers.'

'Your legal friends?'

'All kinds of friends, love.'

'Aren't you upset?'

'Sorry, not upset. He was set an impossible task.'

'Couldn't you buy the land he has to sell?'

'And do what with it? Give it back for him to sell again?'

'Then buy him out altogether.'

'I might if we had a son. For the sake of the name, for the sake of my father. But I'm not interested in farming, never was. Don't you be worrying — it's a big place, there are many fields.'

She took his remark about a son to heart. Lately he may have been hoping for a boy while she was congratulating herself on not conceiving.

Long ago she had ceased to wonder why. Delighted with her liberation from child bearing, and hoping it would continue. In any case, she told herself as Michael went back to reading some journal, what could she do about it? They made love almost as often as in their early years and with as much enjoyment. What else was there? Prayers and Novenas some would say. There were saints who specialized in cases such as hers. Many women she knew had great faith in them. She did not. And admitted that even if she had such faith, she wouldn't seek help. Not even if a son was guaranteed for Michael, the family name or the memory of his father.

In 1887 Françoise went to school where inevitably comparisons were made between her and Marianne. 'She's not as outgoing as her sister, hasn't the gift for singing nor for dancing, but she's the more intelligent. That child will go far, please God,' the Mother Superior told Nicole one day when she visited the convent. 'I have great hopes for Françoise. She's very beautiful, too, and no doubt will marry. But wouldn't it be grand if she was one of these girls

who have a career of her own first? It's happening more and more nowadays. Girls entering the professions. And not before time. In the world there are thousands of women, neglected by their husbands, kept short of money. And what are their alternatives to marriage?'

'You are right, Mother. It's only that I'm surprised you are so advanced in your thinking. Are many nuns? I don't remember ours being so.'

'Oh, indeed. Nuns have always believed in fostering women's gifts. For longer than any other group of women we've been managing our own affairs. Encourage that child. She will make her name one day.'

By 1888 Hélène had started school. Marianne still showed an aptitude for dancing and had a good singing voice. The nuns continued to forecast that Françoise was a brilliant pupil, and of Hélène said that she was a little dote. Marianne made her first communion that year and during the summer holidays Nicole took the three children to France, bringing with her the white dress and veil to show her father and Monique how she had looked on her great day.

Monique cried at the sight and Nicole knew her father had to fight back his tears. She was deeply saddened to see how much they had both aged. Monique seldom left her chair and when she walked could only do so with difficulty. Her father was not so spry as he used to be either. Though he never complained, in contrast to Monique who constantly said, 'Old age doesn't come alone.' Pierre's brown leathery face smiled easily and often and his eyes still had a sparkle to them. Nicole also noticed how often he had a glass of cognac in his hand.

The girls fell in love with the village and were out with the local children from early morning until the evening, running like wild things, seldom coming home for lunch, their mid-morning snack or afternoon one. Being fed by

one or other of the village families, fêted and petted as Nicole's children from Ireland.

Sometimes she felt as if she had never left home, so much the same did everything seem. And on other days she was all too aware of the changes. All those who had died, the ones of her own age gone to Paris and the big cities. Though, as her father explained, some only went to earn enough money to improve their house and land back home. But Maurice had gone for good to Bordeaux. She missed him.

Nicole took them to visit her mother's grave, picking wild flowers on the way. They dutifully knelt with her and went through the motions of praying, Marianne restlessly shifting about because her knees hurt, Françoise watching a bee enter the cup of a flower, totally engrossed, and Hélène staring about her. Nicole told herself she had expected too much of them, they were little more than babies. When they were grown up she would bring them again, and while they were growing up tell them all she had learnt over the years from Pierre and Monique about her mother.

Towards the end of the second week in France the weather changed and it rained every day, curtailing the girls' activities. They became bored and restless and talked about Dublin. Françoise said, 'I thought the weather was always hot and dry in France?'

'Not here,' Nicole said, explaining that they weren't far enough south.

'We might as well have stayed at home. At least there I'd have had Phyillis,' Marianne moaned.

'You'll see her in a couple of days and then the four of you will be off to Ballydurkin. Julia's taking you down to Aunty Sheila's.' They clapped and crowed excitedly. 'Don't show how eager you are to leave. That would hurt Grandpa and Monique,' Nicole remonstrated.

'It isn't that we don't love them. But when it rains here, what is there to do? It is a very desolate place, Mama.'

'I know, Françoise, I lived here until your father married me and took me away. I also miss Dublin and will be glad to go back. But I'll be sad as well, leaving those I love.'

'They should come to us.'

'Monique might if she was well enough, but not Grandpa. He has travelled very little and believes that the farm would go to wrack and ruin without his hand on it. But overall you did have a good time, didn't you?'

'While the weather was fine. There's nothing here belonging to us. No suitable books to read, none of our games. I'm glad we live in a city where what the weather is like doesn't matter.'

'And I miss my doll's house and all my dolls,' Hélène added.

'You won't have those in Ballydurkin either.'

'Ah, but down there it's different. Catti tells us grand stories when we can't go out to play. If it gets cold or is raining she builds up the fire, piles the sods of turf on until it's blazing, and we all sit round and listen to her stories. And besides, Phyillis will be there as well.' At the thought of being reunited with her best friend, Marianne's face was wreathed in smiles.

So much for the separate schools, Nicole thought. Phyillis also went to a convent. It was part of the same teaching order who taught the girls but not fee-paying, the education basic with no foreign languages taught, no dancing lessons, and no pretty uniform.

Michael had hoped that once Phyllis went to school Marianne's and her friendship would cool. That in her National School she would make friends with children of servants and labourers, her own kind. It hadn't worked like that even though she no longer had her meals in the nursery, for once she had finished eating with the servants, she was straight up the stairs seeking Marianne.

Every time he came across Phyllis about the house he remembered the vile old woman, the dream and her prophecy that soon his troubles would begin.

He brought his reason and logic to bear on his mind when it was in this state. But nothing worked to dispel the deep-seated feeling he had that Phyllis was a threat to his family. Why else had he only dreamed about that hag when she was expected?

From time to time he expressed his disapproval of Phyllis to Nicole. She, not knowing of the nightmare and how from time to time the old woman's threats returned to his mind, filling it with fear, assumed it was Phyllis's illegitimacy he found difficult to come to terms with. The poor little child – as if it was her fault! Nicole liked her. She was bright and cheerful and had her mother's mischievous grin. But in a few years it would sort itself out. After all, she was two years younger than Marianne. Soon, no doubt, their daughter would begin to find the younger child tiresome. Marianne's extra dancing and singing lessons and school friends of her own age would see to that. The pity was that she and Françoise weren't closer. Not having had a sister herself, Nicole had assumed they would be but it wasn't so.

Françoise was self-sufficient. She had little to do with either Marianne or Hélène. They quarrelled over their possessions, slapped and tugged each other's hair, sulked, and in a little while were as thick as thieves. Françoise stayed aloof, allowed neither of them to touch her books, the shells she collected from the seashore, or her scrapbook into which she pasted pictures of birds, insects and butterflies with great care.

Phyllis she treated with a detached affection. Once she said to Nicole, 'Phyllis is still a baby, younger than Hélène, why does Marianne bother with her?' Nicole admitted that she didn't know.

When she told Michael what Françoise had asked, he quickly retorted, 'She's never been a baby, she never

149

looked like a baby. She's a forward, knowing child. And the sooner she's grown up and out of here, the happier I'll feel.'

All these thoughts went through her mind as she packed for her return to Dublin. Aunt Monique cried and said she hoped God would spare her to see them all again, but doubted it. Nicole told her, 'Of course He will. You're as strong as a horse. You'll live to be a hundred.'

She hoped she spoke the truth and that Monique and her father would live for many, many years. And resolved to visit France oftener. 'The next time,' she said as she took leave of her father, 'Michael will come too and we'll stay longer, and maybe you'll travel back to Dublin with us? I would like to show you Ireland. Take you to Ballydurkin. Have you meet Dermot. You would love Ireland. The country people are like the French in many ways.'

'Yes,' he agreed, 'that would be lovely. Maybe we will do that.'

She leaned out of the train window waving, tears pouring down her face, until a turn in the track took her father and Monique out of her sight.

Chapter Eighteen

AFTER the travelling and her joyous, passionate reunion with Michael Nicole slept late on Sunday morning. She was still sleeping when he returned from Mass and came to the bedroom, bringing her coffee and toast. 'Don't go away again for a long time. I was lost without you,' he said, laying down the tray and kissing her.

'I missed you also.'

She told him about the changes in the village, how her father's and Monique's health had seemed to be failing, and how she had promised to visit oftener and bring him with her.

'Next year, perhaps?' he said, 'Why not? Maybe on our own. Stay in Paris, spend a few days there. A second honeymoon.'

'Oh, yes,' she said. 'That would be wonderful. Will you promise? The children can go down to Ballydurkin. Imagine how marvellous it would be. You and me completely alone. I'd adore that. Will you promise?'

'I'll tell you what,' he said, leaving his seat by the bed and walking about the room, 'let's leave it until Monday, until I see what's on the agenda.'

'But, darling, it's next year I'm talking about, not next week. You can't have briefs a year ahead.'

'No, but don't rush me into any commitment so far ahead. You know I don't like that. I hope you don't mind – I've asked James to lunch?' he said, changing the conversation.

'No, of course I don't. If he hasn't another engagement

he can stay to dinner.' She got out of bed, concealing her annoyance at having had her hopes raised and then as quickly dashed. Thinking how much she would love to throw something at him – nothing to injure him but to give him a shock. Water, cold water. She looked at the pitcher by her bed. Walk up behind him and pour it over him. And when he protested and asked why had she done such a thing, say, 'It's what you do to me so often. Pour cold water on my hopes and dreams. Get me excited with thoughts of a second honeymoon. You and me in Paris alone. And then when I'm aflame with the idea of such a thing – the cold water to extinguish my burning hopes.' She walked away from the tempting jug and sat before her dressing table, beginning to brush her hair, noticing that the three grey hairs had been joined by several others. I am growing old, she thought.

Soon I'll become stout like Aunt Monique and we'll never have a second honeymoon. Then, remembering the previous night, she smiled at her reflection in the mirror and her morbid thoughts fled.

But, she said to herself, I shall find a way of punishing you a little. And she hatched her plan. She tied up her hair and went to her wardrobe to decide what she would wear to Mass.

She chose a dress of lightweight cloth not too ostentatiously trimmed, a blue one. Blue was her most becoming colour; blue, turquoise and a certain shade of pink. At least the horrid crinoline was no longer in fashion, she thought. The bustle was neater, even though she sometimes imagined she could feel the horse hair padding prickle her backside.

She took out a pink feather boa, draped it round her neck and sashayed towards Michael.

'Like it?' she asked.

'You're so gorgeous, I could eat you.'

'Lace me into my stays instead. You can eat me later,

after Mass and before lunch. And about you and James . . . I was thinking, it's time the girls got to know their beautiful city and that the two of you might take them out this afternoon.'

'Why?' asked Michael.

'They know nothing of it. They've never been to the National Gallery, the Botanical Gardens, the Zoological Gardens. You could start with the Gallery, it's only a stone's throw from here. Françoise would be interested to know that once it was a Leper Hospital. And there's Marsh's Library, she'd like that too.'

'Have you gone mad or what?' said Michael. They're infants still, happier running round fields and going on swinging boats.'

'It's never too soon to start. And after all, it's your duty as their father.'

'Ah, Nicole, what pleasure would I get from going round those places? I spend all my life cooped up in elegant beautiful buildings: the Four Courts, the Law Library. And if I wasn't enjoying it, how could I make it pleasurable for them? Let Julia take them, or Aggie, they are their nurses.'

'Several reasons,' said Nicole. 'Neither of them knows anything about culture for a start.'

'Neither do I,' retorted Michael.

'But you can read. They're both semi-literate. And in any case, have you forgotten that Julia goes out walking with your coachman on Sunday afternoons? And were Aggie to take them, then Phyllis would have to go as well.'

He gave an exasperated sigh. 'I like my Sunday afternoons free, to read, to sleep, to take you to bed if you let me.'

'I seldom refuse you anything. Now will you lace me up?'

She knew he was sulking because he planted no kisses on her back. Let him, she thought. I love him but he is self-centred. He won't come to France next year. No more

than he goes to Ballydurkin, even when I do. He can at least take the children out this afternoon.

By comparison, she thought at lunch how sweet and agreeable was James, and for a moment toyed with the idea of what life would have been like had she married him. Surely he would never make her feel as Michael did, that she was becoming a nagging wife? That she never had anything interesting to say. That her only functions were to be dressed to the nines at social events, and above all in his bed. But handing him something he asked for, her eyes met Michael's and before their expression she became the girl she had been. As madly in love with him as ever she was.

'Sorry, James, you were saying?'

He smiled at her and she saw the friend, brother almost, she had known for so many years. The lovely handsome face, his dark red hair beginning to thin, and she felt affection and pity for this good man who maybe loved her.

Poor James, I wish you would find a nice girl, marry and have a family. Find a girl who could feel about you as I do about Michael, she thought. Then she told herself that was ridiculous, vanity on her part. For never had she, by look, gesture or word, known James to behave in a way that might suggest he pined for her.

'I,' she said, 'had a great idea this morning which included you and Michael doing something with the children.'

Michael groaned. 'I'd hoped you had forgotten about it.'

'Oh, no, and to make sure you wouldn't, I have already promised them.'

'You know what the great idea is, James?'

'No, how could I?'

'Nicole believes the time has come for our babies to be exposed to culture. You don't have to sing for your supper here, only escort three babies round the sights of Dublin.'

'They are not babies. Marianne has made her Communion, she's seven and reached the age of reason. If she can

154

tell right from wrong she can look at pictures in the Gallery, begin to appreciate buildings and such like. Françoise is streets ahead of her in intelligence, so no problem there. Maybe Hélène won't be too excited in galleries but the outing will be good for her. What do you think, James?'

'I think you're right. We underestimate what children are capable of appreciating. I'm all for it.'

'Good,' said Michael. 'Then you take them.'

'I'd be delighted,' said James.

'You can't foist your daughters off on James,' said Nicole, raging that her plan wasn't working as she had intended.

'Of course I can. James wouldn't object, would you?'

'I'd love to.'

'There,' said Michael, grinning at Nicole, 'I told you so. James and I are bosom pals. Do anything for each other.'

'It's awfully kind of you. I hope they'll be no trouble,' Nicole said, and glared at Michael. As usual he had had his way.

The girls wore miniature replicas of grown-up styles, tight and constricting, hems falling well below the knees, almost to the top of their buttoned boots. Hélène's head was covered with a bonnet and Françoise and Marianne wore a boater type of hat, a ribbon tied round the crown. Walking with them, James fantasized that they were his and Nicole's daughters. When this fantasy possessed him he tried to control it, knowing that it was sinful to covet another man's wife. He confessed it on many occasions, was contrite and promised not to commit the sin again. But only succeeded when he didn't come in contact with Nicole, for when he did a smile of hers could set his heart thundering and him stuttering and his imagination running riot.

And as Françoise grew more and more to look like her mother, the expression in her eyes, the turn of her head, he had to accept that unless he ceased all contact with the

McCarthys, he would go on and on committing the same sin.

'We'll go to the Gallery,' he told the girls. 'There are so many beautiful pictures to see. Far too many to look at in one afternoon. So today we'll only visit two rooms. That way you won't tire or become bored. And little by little we will see all the pictures and you'll get to know which are your favourites.'

Marianne and Françoise thought that was a good idea. Hélène complained of being tired, too tired to walk.

Marianne flitted from one picture to another. Hélène sucked her thumb and showed no interest in any of them. Françoise rewarded James's comments by asking questions. Where they had come from and how old were the paintings?

'On the way home,' he announced, 'we'll go to Stephen's Green where you can stretch your legs and see the ducks.' They welcomed this news with whoops of glee. He sat on a bench watching them play. Saw passers by look admiringly at the three little girls and hoped they would assume he was their father.

'Before we go home I'll show you Mercer's Hospital. It is more than a hundred years old. A woman called Mrs Mercer founded it, and when Handel, who was a famous musician, played *The Messiah* in Fishamble Street, the first time it was performed in public, some of the proceeds went to the hospital.'

Then he told them how once, a long, long time ago, the spot on which the hospital stood had been used for housing lepers. And to his surprise it was Hélène who announced that Aunt Letty had lepers.

'Does her hospital look like this one?' she asked.

'You're thick and stupid,' said Marianne. 'Aunty Letty's hospital isn't in a filthy dirty street like this one. It's in a beautiful place. The sun shines all the time, it's near a blue sea and there's flowers and palm trees. It's gorgeous there.'

Hélène began to sob. 'I am not stupid. You're stupid! Isn't she, Françoise?'

'A bit,' said Françoise.

'No, I am not. Papa told me all about the beautiful island.'

'D'ye know what a leper is? Did Papa tell you that as well?'

'I forget.' Marianne squirmed under Françoise's accusing stare, shrugged and said, 'I just forget.'

'I know,' Françoise told her.

'You know everything, clever boots! I bet you read it in a book, you've always got your nose stuck in one.' She made a face and stuck her tongue out at Françoise. James hadn't seen them behave like this before. 'Now, girls,' he said, 'that's very naughty. I'm sure your mama wouldn't be pleased to hear you screeching at each other in public.'

Ignoring him they carried on trying to score points, Françoise saying: 'And Aunt Letitia's island can't be that beautiful, no matter what Papa said.'

'It is, it is!' shouted Marianne, stamping her foot.

'It is packed with lepers, hundreds, maybe even thousands. When anyone gets leprosy round where the island is, they are sent there. Only lepers, Father Damien, the nuns and Aunt Letty live on that island.'

'Is that true?' asked James.

'Oh, yes,' replied Françoise. 'We have a pamphlet in school about Father Damien and his colony. Shall I tell Marianne what a leper is like, Uncle James?' she asked.

'I don't think so. Perhaps another time, but not now when we're about to have a delicious tea.'

By the time they reached the Shelbourne Hotel where he had promised them tea the quarrel was forgotten. Marianne and Françoise walked slightly ahead of James, by now carrying the dead weight of Hélène.

James looked forward to the Sunday invitations when he

could covertly watch Nicole. Listen to her delightful accent. See the occasional flush of annoyance on her face which enhanced her beauty, when the girls forgot her ban on their names being shortened and called each other Molly, Fanny and Nell. It was a sweet torture witnessing the family scene: the moments when Michael's and Nicole's eyes met and everyone else in the room was excluded.

Apart from all of that he enjoyed the outings for their own sake, and unless it was raining very heavily the four of them set out every Sunday afternoon. During the week he would plan where to take them. Making notes of things to see. Writing brief histories of the buildings and places in story form. And always finishing the expedition with a superb tea in the Shelbourne. Françoise, he knew, enjoyed the outings more than Marianne. She had an avid curiosity and an amazing knowledge for one so young.

He showed them the Customs House, Trinity College and the Bank of Ireland, telling them that once it had been the Old Houses of Parliament.

They saw the Zoological Gardens, the Botanical Gardens, watched the boats leave Portabello House for their sojourn along the Grand Canal. On one of their walks along the Quays he stopped at Church Street Bridge and, holding each in turn to look over the quay walls, at the brown-green Liffey flowing to the sea, told them this spot was where the first bridge in Dublin had been. 'It's from here that we get the name Dublin which means 'The Black Pool'.

Marianne and Françoise vied with each other for his attention. His head often began to ache from their endless questions, their wrangling, and Hélène's tired whimpering. On one afternoon when the girls had bickered more than usually he gave up and hailed a passing cab.

'The Shelbourne, please.'

'Right y'are,' said the driver, touching his hat with his whip. The cab crossed the river at Winetavern Street

Bridge. Françoise and Marianne called out the names of buildings they recognized. 'That's where I'll go to be a doctor,' said Françoise as the cab slowed in Dame Street by Crow Street, at the bottom of which, facing up its short length, stood the Medical School.

'She's mad,' said Marianne.

'I am not,' Françoise responded, digging her in the ribs.

Marianne began to cry. 'I wasn't saying *you* were mad. I meant Aunt Letitia. I heard Papa tell Mama. He said, "Poor Letty's mad, I don't suppose we'll ever see her again." '

'You great big fibber! Papa wouldn't talk like that in front of you.'

'He didn't know I was there. I was standing behind the curtain when they came into the room. Don't say I told you, sure you won't, Françoise. And you, Uncle James?'

'I am not a tell-tale.'

James had learned his lesson and didn't intervene.

Within minutes the girls' arms were round each other and they were whispering what he supposed were their secrets. While he pondered on what Marianne had said about Letty.

Chapter Nineteen

JULIA married the coachman, and went to live in the mews house at the bottom of the garden. In the first two years she had two babies, a boy and then a girl. At first Marianne was greatly enamoured of them and went each afternoon after school with Phyllis to play with, kiss and cuddle them. Phyllis helped Julia to clean, wash and iron the babies' clothes. She now had special friends in her National School, as Marianne had in hers. Marianne soon lost interest in Julia's babies, playing tennis instead or attending rehearsals for the many concerts at school in which she always had a leading part.

Still her father's favourite, he indulged her love of all things theatrical by taking her once a month to a variety show. 'You're too young still,' he consoled Hélène, and explained to Françoise. 'And I know you wouldn't like this sort of thing, it's noisy and bawdy. I'll take you to the opera or a ballet the next time there's a company over from London.'

Françoise concealed her hurt and disappointment. She loved and admired her father and to be taken out with him would have been wonderful. Sometimes she hated Marianne. She was noisy, untidy, quarrelsome when the mood took her. Thought nothing of poking Hélène or pinching her hard enough to make her cry. And then, with a face of innocence, would deny that she had touched her. But Françoise loved her too. Marianne was very generous. Never minded if you rooted through her things, borrowed a brooch or hair ribbon. Of course she wasn't very bright,

but she could sing and dance, and make everyone laugh, and her hair was magnificent, so long and so thick — heavy in your hand when you picked it up. But why, despite having friends who came to tea, to whose homes she was invited, played tennis with and went for rides in their fathers' carriages, she still had as her special friend Phyllis, Françoise couldn't understand.

She thought that Phyllis looked like a monkey. She smelled like one sometimes. Remarking on this once to her mother, Nicole said, 'Yes, dear, I have noticed it. You must never comment on it. It isn't Phyllis's fault. Servants don't change their underclothes as often as we do. They don't have as many as we do. I'll mention it discreetly to Aggie and at the same time pass on some of your things. I haven't for a long time.'

Marianne didn't notice the smell from Phyllis, or if she did wasn't bothered by it. They were constantly huddled together, arms round each other, and always whispering. 'Secrets,' Marianne replied any time Françoise asked her what they had been talking about. 'Secrets. You're too young to know.'

'But I'm older than Phyllis, she's younger than Hélène.'

'She knows things. She tells me. But I have to say: "Honest to God, I won't tell anyone else." '

Dermot's wife, Sheila, had a baby just when everyone was thinking that she would be another Honora. And then, to the delight of all, so did Honora herself. The family went to Kildare for the christening. Honora, in the midst of the celebration and her personal joy, said to Nicole, 'Only one thing mars the day — the thought that Mama isn't here. That so often Catti will tell her news she won't understand.' The two women shed tears, then Honora wiped hers away and said, 'I must be grateful. This was my last chance. I'm growing old, too old to have babies.' He was christened Peter after her father.

Fortune, Michael said to himself, looking at the beautiful

infant, was smiling on them. Two new McCarthys and good news of Letty. Her health seemed to be restored and without having had to leave the leper colony. Looking at Nicole, he marvelled at how little the years had changed her. And as he did on many occasions, wondered why she had never had another baby. A son would have been the grand thing to have. Now, he remonstrated with himself silently, no regrets, no giving room in that head of yours to gloomy thoughts. And so saying he went to the drinks table and poured himself a generous glass of whiskey.

Nicole wrote regularly to her father and Monique and in each letter promised that soon she would visit them. Weeks and months passed and one thing and another prevented the visit. Law Society dinners, private parties, weddings, funerals, functions at the girls' school, minor illnesses. All of these, she admitted to herself, were excuses. The reason she kept postponing the visit was that she could never pin Michael down to agreeing when they would go. She desperately wanted to go away with him. Wanted to be alone with him. Know that days and days stretched in front of them with no legal functions for him to attend. No nights when he went out to dinner and came home in the small hours.

She wanted a new wardrobe, exquisite clothes and hats to wear to France and on to Italy where she intended they should also go. She coaxed and pleaded and he made half promises which, when the time drew near, he was unwilling or unable to keep. 'Why don't you take the girls?' he would say.

'The girls get bored in the village. They did when they were much younger. It would be worse now.'

'Not if you spent a week or so in Paris, either going or coming.'

'It isn't the girls I want to be with. I see and spend all my time with them. I love them but I also love you, and apart

from Kildare to see the new baby, and the one in Ballydurkin, we've been nowhere since we were married.'

He kissed her, said how sorry he was and that definitely next year he would take her to France.

And so five years slipped by. Five years in which she had admitted defeat in keeping in use the names with which her girls were christened. She saw it as a turning point in her life. Now they seldom talked French with her. Fanny seldom talked to her at all, seldom talked much to anyone, so absorbed was she in her studying. Nell was affectionate and clinging but hardly stimulating company, and Marianne had piano lessons, singing lessons, tennis parties, and any spare time she used to spend with Phyllis, either in the basement room where she lived with Aggie or in the separate bedroom Marianne had been given when she was twelve.

One evening Nicole left her room where she had been changing for dinner and was making her way to the back drawing-room where the girls usually were at this hour. Hearing the front door open she looked over the banister and was delighted to see Michael coming into the hall.

'You're home early,' she called down to him as he took off his coat and hat. 'I was just going along to see the girls. Come on up and we'll go together.'

The three of them were reading. 'Ah,' said Michael, 'it's a change to find you with a book, Moll, what is it?'

She became flustered, colour flushing her face. 'Only a book, Papa, just a book,' she said, attempting to push it underneath the cushion.

'No,' said her father, 'let me see it.' His voice was firm, but as always when he looked at Marianne, love shone from his eyes. She handed over the novelette. Its luridly coloured cover displayed a man and woman, he young, dark and handsome, she fair and pretty, with signs of disarray about her clothes.

'Where did you get this?' he asked.

She didn't answer. 'Fanny, what do you know about it?'

'Nothing, Papa.'

'Phyllis gave it to her. Phyllis is always giving them to her. She has a pile of them under her bed,' Nell said, smiling at her father with whom she was always trying to curry favour.

He ignored her and turned to Nicole. 'Did you know Marianne was reading this?' he asked, holding out the book.

She glanced at it, shook her head and said, 'No, I didn't.'

'You heard what Nell said. From your protégée. I warned you, didn't I? She is corrupting our daughter. Do you consider this suitable reading for a child?'

Nicole thought to herself, Oh God, Michael, you can be so tedious. I feel as if I'm in the dock. She snatched the novelette from his hand.

Wanting to goad him, she said, 'Without reading it, how can I answer your question? Girls, go to your rooms.' And when they'd gone she tried placating him. 'I'm sure it's a nonsensical bit of rubbish and of course I don't approve of Marianne's reading it, if for no other reason than it's a waste of time. But please don't create too much of a fuss. I'll have a word with Phyllis and Aggie.'

'I never wanted that child in my home, if child you can call her. I've always feared something like this. Felt in my bones that she'd be a bad influence on the children. On Marianne in particular, who is silly and impressionable.'

'That's ridiculous. Phyllis is only a child. They both are.'

'Her mother wasn't much more than a child when she met her soldier. That young one is years ahead of ours. She hasn't got their innocence. She never had. It's written on her face. A knowing look. You see children like her all over the city, with the same look. Children of her age who are already prostitutes.'

'You really hate her, don't you? You always have. She can't help how she looks. But to mention her in the same

164

breath as prostitutes is appalling. Not worthy of you. Who does she come in contact with except us?'

'Don't forget her mother.'

'Poor Aggie, who from the day she had her goes nowhere except to Mass and on errands for me. You should be ashamed of yourself!'

'No,' he retorted, 'you should, for bringing her under our roof.' And stormed from the room, slamming the door after him.

Nicole skimmed through the book. A love story. The girl from a wealthy family, the boy from a poor one, a ploughboy, handsome, strong and adoring. She tossed it in the fire and then went to Marianne's room where her daughter lay huddled on the bed, her eyes red from crying.

Nicole sat beside her. 'You silly girl. Here, take my hanky.' She smoothed back the golden hair that covered Marianne's face. 'What possessed you to read such rubbish when there are so many books in the house much more worthwhile?'

'They're all so boring! Boring and hard to read. I'm not like Françoise, she eats those sort of books, I can't get past the first few pages. I can fly through the others and I like the stories.'

'Have you read many of them?'

She didn't answer for a while then, still sobbing, admitted, 'Quite a few.'

'Where does Phyllis get them?'

'From Aggie. From girls in school. They swap.'

'You are not to read any more of them. They are rubbish. Nonsense. Things don't happen like that in real life.'

'Sometimes I expect they do, if people really love each other.'

'Oh, darling, turn round, look at me.' Nicole gazed down on the face of her child, her little girl as she still thought of her. Her eyes puffed from crying, her cheeks

wet with tears, her baby talking about love. 'Listen,' she said, 'in real life girls and boys marry other girls and boys from the same sort of families. As you will one day, please God. You're a beautiful, clever girl. Tomorrow we'll find books that won't bore you. Books with lovely stories. Not silly, sentimental, badly written rubbish.'

The tears which had almost stopped began again. 'And I'm not beautiful. Only Papa ever tells me that and now he won't any more. And Françoise says I'm like cream.'

'Like cream? What does that mean?'

'Rich and thick.'

Nicole concealed the smile, pretending her nose needed blowing. 'You know that's a silly thing to say. I expect she does it when you have a quarrel. And Papa will tell you you are beautiful again, but not perhaps for a few days. He's very angry but that will pass. Now get up and wash your face and let me have the pile of books Hélène says you have under the bed. I shall take them to Aggie and have a word with her.'

Was Phyllis being a bad influence on Marianne? she asked herself several times during the following days. Was she as precocious as Michael said? Who were her friends from school? What sort of homes did they come from?

After a while her vigilance ceased. Hélène never reported seeing any more of the books and Nicole knew she would keep a lookout and be quick to tell tales. She sometimes wished they were babies again, and she better able to protect them. But life wasn't like that. And the fact that Phyllis and Marianne still spent a lot of time together would have to be endured until Phyllis was twelve, left school, and found a situation elsewhere.

Chapter Twenty

O N New Year's Eve of 1894, Michael, for the first time ever, took them all to Christ's Church to hear the cathedral bells ring out the old year and the New Year in. There were crowds of all descriptions there: beggars, lords and ladies, Dublin men and women and their children. A marvellous atmosphere of excitement and expectancy was palpable in the air of the bright cold frosty night, lit by a sky filled with stars.

'No one knows for sure the origin of this,' he said. 'Pagan probably, going back long before the cathedral was built.' He held Nicole close. They had driven there in the carriage which Julia's husband had left a little distance away with a man he knew and could trust with the horses. He and Julia were keeping an eye on the girls. Molly had begged for Phyllis to be allowed to come with them. Michael had refused. 'I can't stop her coming to hear the bells, but not with us.' His favourite's tears and pleadings were in vain for once.

The crowd were singing and dancing, the drunken ones amongst them – and there were many drunken ones – starting fights. Michael kept Nicole at the edge of the crowd.

And then it was almost midnight and only the very drunk failed to become silent as the bells rang out. After the last stroke, shouts of 'Happy New Year' were heard and there was much kissing and embracing between husbands and wives, boys and their sweethearts, and boys and girls who had never until that night set eyes on each other.

Afterwards Nicole remembered how quickly that New Year and the following one showed what they held in store for the McCarthy family. In the first week of January Michael's mother died in her sleep. A sad happening but not unexpected, and in its own way a blessing everyone agreed. Though Michael took her death badly, not able to conceal his grief. Then Sheila began to show signs of consumption and her beautiful son, a fine big healthy infant, sickened also. Of what the local doctor couldn't be sure but suspected the same thing that ailed his mother. They were both dead before the summer was over.

There was always consumption in the Crowley family, Michael consoled himself. I often heard my mother say they were dawny. Even now that his mother was dead, Catti stayed on at the farm for Dermot needed her. He hardly knew one day from the next so constantly was he drunk.

Winter came and people talked about the cold frosty weather being healthy. But it wasn't so for Honora's baby who got a chest infection. Fearing he might kick off his covers during the night, he was taken into the bed with his mother and father where one morning, when they had thought the night before that he was improving, he was found lying blue and still between him.

In the kitchen the servants said, 'The poor creature, she overlaid him, smothered the life out of him.'

Honora herself feared this. 'Is it possible, Doctor? Could I have smothered my little child?'

'You could not, Honora. No mother could unless it was her intention. His slightest stir, his slightest whimper, and you'd have been awake. Infants are strong. They kick, twist, wriggle. Infants, like grown ups, struggle when their life is threatened in an unnatural manner. Your little son just died in his sleep. Had you been watching him, wide awake, the same thing would have happened. He isn't the first I've seen to go the way he did.'

And the servants said, 'She won't be long after him for

her heart is broken and her poor body worn out.' Their forecast proved right. Honora died like her little son, in her sleep, the following month. 'Her heart just gave out,' Nicole recalled the doctor telling Michael, who stood looking like a corpse himself.

The next New Year's Eve they didn't go to hear the bells. Long before midnight they were in bed, Michael stupefied with the amount of whiskey and claret he had drunk; Nicole lying beside him, imploring God to take pity on the family, to spare them for a while from any more deaths.

In the next following year Michael made an effort to drink less. Even amongst his hard-drinking colleagues he was getting the reputation of having the biggest swallow of anyone at the Bar, and he knew that soon this reputation would leak out and his career be affected.

With the coming of spring, new life appearing on the trees, in the earth, hope of better things to come returned to Nicole. Michael was drinking slightly less now. When she told him that Phyllis would soon be leaving school and had a job on the other side of the city, a live in job with one Sunday a week off, he was jubilant.

'At last! Thanks be to God she'll soon be out of my home, never to set foot in it again.'

'Except on her Sundays off,' Nicole reminded him.

'Never. Not at any time.'

'But where will she go?'

'That's her's and her mother's concern. And you make sure to make it known to them.'

'Oh God, how could I tell Aggie that? It's so cruel, so heartless. After all, this is her home. I can't do it. I won't.'

'Oh yes you can, and you will. You could torment me, deprive and neglect me when you fought for Aggie to stay and rear that child in my home. You lacked no courage then. My wishes weren't considered. You go down to that

basement and give her the news and I won't hear another word about it.'

And I went, a guilt-stricken Nicole told herself later. I went and told Aggie and saw the colour leave her face, knowing there was nothing she could do about it. Poor kind Aggie. But what could I do? Not fight Michael again for Phyllis's right to come on her Sundays off. Not after all he had gone through. Not in the state he was in. Having nightmares again, fighting his battle against drink.

Halfway through 1895 Dermot, out hunting, was thrown and broke his neck. The farm, mortgaged up to the hilt, had to be sold and Catti was sent to live with relations.

It was the beginning of another round of tragedies. Word soon came from Letty's Order that during a relapse she had walked into the sea, calling as she went, 'Kathleen, Dada, I'm coming, I'm coming! I heard your voices calling me and I'm coming.'

A leper without feet had witnessed this. Unable to help, he had crawled to get assistance. It took him a long time and there was no sign of Letty when rescuers arrived.

Nicole had grieved for Dermot, Honora, Sheila and the babies, and to a certain extent Michael's mother. She had known all of them. Letty she had never met. It was for Michael she grieved as she watched him sit night after night, drinking himself senseless, talking aloud to himself, not knowing she was listening by the door. Saying the strangest things. Talking not really to himself but as though there were someone else in the room. Asking as if of a person: 'Well, are you satisfied yet? You've taken them all except me. I'm the only one left now. Take me and finish it. Take me, but for the love of Jesus, don't touch my children. Haven't you had revenge enough? Didn't you make us pay a terrible price? Leave us alone now.'

And finally he took her to France. To Papa's and Monique's funeral. Their coffins there, one behind the other, in the little chapel. Closed, lids secured over the

heaps of whatever is left of burned bodies. Cinders, bones perhaps, debris just like the farmhouse. Charred pieces, unrecognizable as the remains of human beings or what had once been a home.

Nicole fell asleep one evening and returned to the awful scene of loss in her dreams. She didn't realize that she was crying and sobbing out loud until Nell came to her.

'Mama, Mama, what ails you? Are you sick, Mama? Fanny, Molly, come quick! Something is wrong with Mama.'

They all hovered round her, stroking her hair, offering handkerchiefs, asking if they should ring for tea or fetch her smelling salts?

'Darlings, no. I'm all right. I was dreaming, that's all. Dreaming about France. I felt so sad, but I'm fine now.'

Holly asked, 'Shall I fetch Papa?'

'No, he's resting, you mustn't disturb him. Honestly, I'm better now.'

Nell put her arms round Nicole, and laying her cheek against her mother's, said, 'It's all her fault and I hope she's burning in Hell.'

'Nell, that's an awful thing to wish on anyone. You mustn't say things like that. Tell me, who do you wish to be burning in Hell?'

'Mag Cronin, for putting the curse on the family.'

Nicole took Nell's arms from about her shoulders and turned her so that she could look into her face. 'Mag Cronin? Who is she and what's this nonsense about a curse? Don't look away from me, I want to know what you're talking about?'

'You know, Mama. Everyone knows about the curse Mag Cronin put on the family because Papa's grandfather was a wicked old man who robbed Mag Cronin of her field and evicted her from the cottage. Catti told me and Molly and Fanny, ages ago first. Amn't I telling the truth, amn't I?'

she appealed, turning to Fanny and Molly for their support. Neither of them said a word.

'Oh, Nell, that's such nonsense. Catti is an old woman. She rambles in her mind. She tells all sorts of stories. Of fairies, and changelings, and banshees. And you know there are no such things.'

'But there are, there really are. I've heard the banshee and seen fairies. I saw them dancing in a meadow. Catti showed them to me.'

'You heard the wind howling in the trees and saw flowers waving in the grass of the meadow. Lots of flowers grow in meadows, lots of pale flowers that on a moonlit night in a gentle breeze could look like tiny figures dancing.'

But Nell was adamant. 'I did see them and I did hear the banshee, only Catti said she doesn't follow our family so I didn't have to be frightened. And she said it's because of the curse that all our aunties and uncles and the babies died and the cow choked and Grandma went far away in the head. And I expect that's why our grandfather and Aunt Monique in France died as well.'

'No, no, Nell, that isn't so. My Papa liked to drink cognac, he liked to drink a lot of cognac, and he smoked a pipe. Maurice, an old friend of his, came back for the funeral. He's a very clever man, a doctor, and he told me that the reason the fire started was because Grandpa Demart had too much cognac, fell asleep and his pipe fell on to a paper or book he had been reading. That's the truth and there are no such things as curses. It's a sin to believe that there is for God wouldn't allow such things.'

'The Devil could though.'

'You really are thick,' said Fanny. 'One minute you're praying for Mag Cronin to roast in Hell and the next saying that the Devil's the one who makes her curse work. Don't you know that the Devil owns Hell and loves people doing bad things, so why would he roast Mag Cronin?'

'I hate you, you're horrible! You say things that make me all mixed up.' Nell began to cry again.

'Now, Nell, I want you to promise me that you'll put this so-called curse right out of your head because there is no such a thing,' her mother insisted.

'Then why did everyone die?'

'Because people die all the time, from all sorts of things. They get very sick, or old, have accidents like Uncle Dermot, your Grandfather McCarthy, your aunts. Every day people die.'

'Will you and Papa die?'

'Yes, but please God, not until we are very, very old.'

'I expect Catti will die soon. She's very, very old. I love Catti. I wish I could see her before she dies.'

'Perhaps,' Nicole lied, 'we'll go down to see her. Now you go to the kitchen and have a glass of milk. I want to talk to Molly and Fanny.'

'All right, Mama,' Nell said, and started for the door. Then she turned back. 'I forgot something else Catti said. She told me that Mag Cronin had a daughter called Bridgid. She had a baby and had to go to America, and that baby was Great-Grandfather McCarthy's.'

'I'm glad she told you that and glad you told me because it just proves what a fibber Catti is. Or maybe it's just that she's losing her mind. For don't you know well that girls cannot have a baby unless they are married? And this girl couldn't have been married to Grandfather McCarthy. Now you tell me why couldn't she have been married to him?'

Nicole, as she watched Nell puzzling at the answer, thought she heard Molly snigger. She wondered if the snigger was because of Nell's expression as she grappled for a reply or . . . but she dismissed that thought as highly unlikely. Molly could not possibly know about illegitimate children.

'Oh, I know, Mama. I'm such a dunderhead. She

173

couldn't have a baby because he was already married.' Nell beamed with pride. 'Aggie did but her husband died before Phyllis was born.'

'You clever girl, of course that's the reason. Now off you go and have your milk.'

As she passed her sisters Nicole saw Molly's hand sneak out and pinch Nell's arm and heard her whispered hiss: 'You horrible little telltale.'

When Nell had left the room, Nicole asked, 'Why did you do that, Molly? You're too old, too grown up, for such behaviour.'

'I did nothing,' she said, staring unflinchingly at her mother. 'Did I, Fanny?' Fanny didn't reply.

'You tell lies. How am I ever to trust you? I saw you pinch Nell and I want you to tell me why?'

Looking at her daughter, Nicole thought how from the time she could talk Molly had told lies.

In the last six months she had developed the figure of a woman, with the face of an innocent pretty child. Nicole felt a sense of despair. Molly was growing up so quickly. How was she to protect her when she so seldom told the truth? Sometimes she was late coming home from school, or her dancing and singing lessons. She always had ready excuses. 'Mother asked me to stay behind to talk about the concert.' 'Miss Lambert took a fit of coughing, I thought she'd choke, that's why the singing lesson was delayed.'

I could and should check on the answers she gives me except that if they aren't true I'd brand her as a liar, Nicole realized. I can't have her delivered and collected by carriage, it isn't always available, and no more can I meet her after school or send Aggie. It would make her a laughing stock. Nor should I put the responsibility on Fanny to see she comes straight home. In any case, Fanny doesn't have dancing and singing lessons. And in the long run, even if Fanny could see that she came home on time, it would make Molly hate her.

'Well, what have you got to say? I'm waiting,' said Nicole, staring fixedly at Molly, her voice severe, hoping that as on other occasions, though not many, this would elicit a truthful answer.

Molly looked away, shuffled her feet and mumbled.

'I can't hear you, speak up.'

'Because she tells tales. I was worried about you, about you and the curse. Nell promised she would never tell you. I didn't want you to be frightened.'

'Were you frightened when you heard about the curse?'

Molly looked back at her mother and laughed. 'No,' she said, 'I never believe anything Catti says. You know, about banshees and all that nonsense.'

'And what made you think I would believe any of it?'

Molly shrugged. 'I suppose because you're old you might. Isn't that what we thought, Fan?'

'Was that what you thought, Fanny?'

'Really, Mama, I don't remember but I suppose so. I never paid much attention to Catti anyway.'

'You never stick up for me. I hate you! You think you're so superior. You think you know everything just because you're going to be a doctor, but you won't because Papa won't let you,' Molly taunted her.

'That'll do,' Nicole said. 'But I'm warning you, Molly, if I ever see, or Nell tells me, that you have been tormenting her, I'll stop your dancing lessons, I mean that. Do you understand?'

'I'm sorry. I won't. Never again, I promise.'

'Make sure you keep the promise then. I'm going to rest now and I don't want any more squabbling.'

Hardly had the door closed when Molly put her arms round Fanny and begged, 'Don't tell on me, please. I'm sorry for what I said to you. I'm sure you will be a doctor, but promise you won't tell about Aggie, Phyllis and me?'

'I couldn't be bothered,' said Fanny with an air of disdain while brooding how unfair it was that Molly did what she

liked, told one lie after another, and still remained everyone's favourite, especially Papa's.

When Nicole had told Aggie that Phyllis would no longer be allowed to come to the house she had accepted the ban as she accepted all that had befallen her — with resignation. Then sorrow took over, sorrow that someone she loved and trusted had been capable of such cruelty, she tried making excuses for Nicole. Thinking, It was him, not her. She would never have done such a thing. Not barred my child from coming home again. I was never keen on him but I loved, worshipped and trusted her. She was kind and good to me. But she must have had an inkling this would happen. Known he had a down on my Phyllis. You couldn't live with a man for years and not be aware of such a thing.

She shouldn't have let it go on for years. Letting Phyllis up to play with the girls. Making much of her. Even taking her down the country on holidays with them. It would have been kinder to have kept her in her place long ago. I wouldn't have minded it then. I'd have expected it. But for twelve years to treat her almost as one of the family, and then bar her from coming home on her one afternoon off a week — that was an awful thing for her to do. She's a woman, a mother. Has she no feelings? Didn't she try putting herself in my place? Thinking how she would feel if one of her girls was no longer allowed home? He might have been at the back of it, but if he was, he had been there all along. He never, if he could help it, even smiled at Phyllis. You knew where you stood with him. But her, her Aggie would never forgive.

She sat in the gloomy basement and cried for hours. There Julia found her and was as incensed as Aggie when she heard the story. 'You wouldn't do such a thing to a cat or dog, indeed you wouldn't. Wait'll I tell Cook and the others. They'll be raging. What do they think we are? Stones, without flesh, blood or feelings? Don't you cry any

more, Aggie, we'll find a way round this. You won't be deprived of your child, we'll see to that.'

Around the kitchen table Julia and the other servants had a conflab, as Cook called it. They agreed that the McCarthys were good employers. But why shouldn't they be? They got value for their money and, up to the present, loyalty. But when all was said and done they were no better than they ought to be. What employer was? Being Irish and Catholic didn't make them more humane than the gentry. And what were they after all?

'A jumped up farmer's son,' said Julia, 'whose father before him wasn't known for charity. A man of driving ambition, never resting until he made a gentleman of his son.'

And wasn't it a known fact that they were often the worst when they got to the top, them that had not been born to it?

And they concluded that Mrs McCarthy had made a big mistake. They knew as much of the ways of the McCarthys as they themselves did. Where they went and when. If they went for carriage rides on Sunday or to bed in the afternoon. Between them they would see to it that most Sundays Phyllis would be with her mother.

'The only one I'm doubtful about,' said Cook, 'is your man, Julia. Isn't he very close to McCarthy?'

'He hasn't much fault to find with him, but less with me, and his heart is kind. Don't worry about him. He's a silent man. And sure wouldn't he be aware that if he opened his mouth, I'd be implicated? They'd have to let me go and he wouldn't stay without me.'

And so the secret meetings began. Phyllis returned to see her mother but there were meetings with Molly too. On the first of them, when Nicole, Nell and Michael had gone to Howth, Phyllis said, 'Let's go in the park and listen to the band.'

'I'm not allowed,' Molly protested.

'I know that, Moll, but they're on their way to Howth. Come on, they won't be back for hours.'

Arm in arm, giggling, they went amongst the people listening to the music. Pushing their way through those not seated. The nursemaids with their high perambulators, women in leg o' mutton-sleeved dresses, twirling parasols and holding on to the arms of their husbands. The girls pushed their way up near the bandstand. 'See him?' Phyllis said, pointing.

'The one playing the trumpet?'

'No, the one on the black horse, one of the band's escorts. Well, he's a Lancer and he's going out with the maid who works in the house next to where I work. Isn't he gorgeous? But Maggie says he's very fast.'

'What d'ye mean, fast?'

Phyllis whispered in Molly's ear. She laughed, then blushed, then laughed again and looked nervously around to see if they had been overheard. No one was paying them any attention. 'Is that what soldiers do to girls?'

'Not only soldiers, lots of fellas do.'

'And do the girls not mind?'

'Maybe some, I don't know, but Maggie loves it.'

Molly was agog with a mixture of curiosity, excitement and also a slight shame and sense of guilt. But mostly curiosity and excitement.

PART THREE

Chapter Twenty-one

1897

MOLLY and Fanny were now allowed to dine with the grown ups. It was seldom guests were invited for the McCarthys' dinners were no longer what they were. James, being considered family, came as often as he ever had. He lightened the atmosphere, but on the nights when he wasn't there Nicole found the girls' company a relief from hours of Michael's morose silence. She knew that drink was responsible for the drastic change in him. He had long passed the stage when alcohol made him merry, funny and garrulous.

Now he could, and mostly did, sit through dinner without uttering a word unless it had unpleasant connotations: was bitingly sarcastic, boorish or downright rude. The drink had also altered his appearance, ageing him before his time, coarsening his features, slackening his mouth, criss-crossing his fair skin with red and purple thread veins, and giving him a belly that even his expert tailor couldn't disguise. So that on the rare occasions when she saw him naked, he appeared gross.

Often, after an unsuccessful attempt at making love, when he fell asleep she cried for the man he had once been. The man in bed with her on their wedding night. The man who, while lacing her corsets, pressed little kisses on her neck and back. Whose eyes after the birth of Molly and Fanny had looked at her with such desire, arousing such an equal want in her, that had a nurse not always been in the vicinity of her room, she would have succumbed.

Now she was certain that were she to strip naked and dance on the dining-room table he wouldn't notice her. Oh God,

she would think, it isn't fair. We're not old. Not really old. Why did it have to change? When did it? What caused it? Is it just the drink or am I in some way to blame?

I loved him. I worshipped him. No matter what happened during the day, no matter what aggravations, disappointments, bouts of nostalgia or boredom, no matter what, there were the wondrous nights, the marvellous nights in Michael's arms.

Still unable to sleep while Michael's infuriating snoring and the smell of whiskey dinned her ears and nauseated her, she would search for a reason why a man who had been a moderate drinker should change to one who drank morning, noon and night.

Was it because of all the sudden deaths coming one after the other? Though they were not all unexpected. His mother was old, Honora never in good health, and poor Letty – no one knew the full story about her. Dermot died suddenly and unexpectedly. Of course there had been the drownings just before they married but that hadn't driven him to drink. It didn't happen until years after that. It wasn't disappointment with how his career had gone. He had taken Silk and was tipped to become one of the youngest Judges in Ireland. She doubted now that he would achieve it. People weren't fools. He was no longer in such great demand as a QC.

If only he would talk to her. If their marriage had been as good as she believed it was, why hadn't he turned to her? Trouble, she believed, should draw two people closer, not drive a wedge between them.

Eventually she would drop off to sleep and in the morning waken with a sense of depression hanging over her. If it was before Michael was awake, she would sometimes put an arm round him which was always shrugged off.

On the majority of the mornings when Nicole reached for Michael he had been awake for hours. These days his sleep was fitful. And in the early morning, the middle of the night

and during the day, his mind was obsessed by thoughts of Mag Cronin's curse.

For many years, even after the nightmare, he had succeeded in banishing it from his mind for periods of time. Now, until alcohol had fogged his brain, it was there all the time. Consuming him with fear for his daughters. Of what lay in store for them. Of when, where and in what manner the malediction would fall on his girls. He knew and didn't care that his career was ruined. That behind his back his colleagues ridiculed him. He saw the contempt in Nicole's face. Her beautiful eyes regarding him as less than a man. And that crucified him. He loved her so much, wanted her so much. To be one with her again.

Occasionally he gathered his courage and attempted to make love to her. But almost before he began, fear of failure overwhelmed him. Then he wanted her to take him in her arms, comfort him, tell him it didn't matter. Assure him that soon the trouble would rectify itself. That in any case it wasn't the most important thing in the world. If only, he would think, she would make the first move as she had the night we were married. I couldn't for I'd die if she rebuffed me.

Every time he looked at his daughters, saw Molly, now a young woman, and Fanny almost one, Nell not far behind, he thought: Soon they'll leave here. They'll get married. Their husbands won't know about Mag Cronin. Won't keep a constant watch to protect them. They are the only ones left in danger. There's me, too, but I wouldn't care if I died tomorrow.

One Sunday afternoon Molly said, 'The Lancer who goes out with your friend isn't here today.'

Phyllis laughed. 'He hit an officer. He's under arrest. He'll be court-martialled. It'll be the clink for him. Isn't the fella who's taken his place gorgeous? I'm mad about him already.'

Molly looked at the Lancer in his red coat with its silver trimmings. Beneath the helmet his hair didn't show but from

his moustache she guessed: it would be as fair as an egg. She too thought he was gorgeous and hoped that during the interval they might get into talk. But when the time came he didn't even dismount and never once looked in their direction.

From then on she lived from Sunday to Sunday and when the weather was very bad and the performance cancelled, was cast into the depths of despair. She and Phyllis spent Sunday afternoon in the basement instead, gossiping and reading novelettes, Aggie telling them which one was the best story. Enthusing over the hero and heroine. As foolish and romantic as the girls. Often she'd imagine herself in the role of the heroine with her lost lover coming to find her, Phyllis's father one day walking in the door, bowled over by the sight of his daughter. A sergeant at least by now who'd take her in his arms, tell her how sorry he was for all she had suffered but that now he would make amends. He'd marry her and the three of them would live happy ever after.

During the week Molly was bored and restless, sometimes thinking even school would be better than being stuck at home all the time. Nicole insisted she went shopping with her. Tried interesting her in clothes. Molly wouldn't have any her mother considered suitable. 'But that's so vulgar,' Nicole would protest at something she wanted. 'You couldn't wear that anywhere. Bright red and glaring blue. No, you can't have either of them.' Nicole would compromise on something reasonably suitable and on Sundays Molly would add her own touches to enliven the outfit and make the choice a bit more daring, slightly theatrical.

Fanny she found no company at all. When she wasn't at school she was studying for her matriculation. She couldn't talk to Fanny about the Lancer or her pash on him. She couldn't really talk to Fanny about anything.

Molly wanted information as to how she could get on the stage. Uncle James when he came to dinner talked often about the theatre. Forever going on about people called Yeats

and Synge and others including a Lady Gregory who hoped to form a company and have an Irish Theatre with the actors talking as Irish people really did. She wouldn't be interested in anything like that. It was the music halls and singing and dancing she wanted.

Just before Molly's seventeenth birthday, in May 1898, she got tonsillitis and had to miss her Sunday visit to the park. She was too sick even to sneak down to the drawing-room and gaze at the fair-haired Lancer through the window. Her fever was very high and just before it broke, when she was slightly delirious, she imagined that her Lancer, as she had begun to think of him, had killed an officer and was to be executed. She must have screamed so loudly that it was heard by the servants and Aggie came to see her.

Molly sobbed, telling Aggie her dream. ' 'Twas only a dream, pet, he's as right as rain. Didn't I walk up the area steps and see him having a conflab with Phyllis? So rest easy and before she goes I'll have her slip up and tell you all about it. But first I'll have to give you a spongeing and change your nightdress and the sheets, they're drenched with sweat.'

She made Molly comfortable and said Phyllis would come up in a minute and bring her a cup of tea cool enough to sip.

Phyllis soon came to the bedroom grinning all over her face. 'You won't believe it,' she said, 'wait'll you see what I've got for you.' And putting down the cup and saucer, took from her pocket a folded piece of paper. 'It's a note from him.'

'From who?' asked Molly, her voice a husky whisper.

'Your man, the Lancer, and it's for you.'

'Don't tell lies.'

'As true as I'm standing here. He got off his horse at the interval and beckoned to me. "Yeah," I said. "What d'ye want?" letting on I wasn't really interested. And he asked where you were.'

'As true as God?'

'As true as God,' replied Phyllis, 'so I told him you were

bad with your throat, and cheeky like said, "What's it to do with you anyway?"'

' "I've taken a shine to her. She's real pretty," he said.'

'You're making it up and it's not funny, especially when I'm sick.'

'I am not and this is the proof – a note from him to you.'

'Give it to me, give it to me! Oh my God, I can't believe it.'

'Will you read it for God's sake? I'm dying of curiosity and I've got to go in a minute before they're back.'

'I bet you already have,' said Molly, pulling herself up and leaning against a pillow.

'That's a terrible thing to accuse me of. I'm sorry now I brought it.'

'I'm sorry, I was only joking,' apologized Molly. She opened the folded sheet of paper, read it silently and then aloud to the eager Phyllis:

Dear Molly,

Your friend told me your name. I'm sorry you're sick. I missed you straight away in the crowd. My name's Herbert but everyone calls me Bert or Bertie. I look out for you every Sunday. I think you're lovely. And I was wondering if I could see you some time? If you're not better by next Sunday maybe you'd send word by Phyllis.

All the best,

Bertie Talbot

'He wrote to me, can you believe it? Never in my wildest dreams did I imagine he would. Well, of course I did. I imagined all sorts of things in my wildest dreams, but knew that's all they were. I never even thought he'd give me a second look. Oh, Phyllis, Phyllis, isn't it marvellous? Isn't it great? But how can I ever see him except in the park?'

Her cheeks, from which the flush of fever had subsided, became hot again as her heart beat madly with excitement.

Her golden hair was tossed about her shoulders and her eyes were shining.

'You look like one of them wax dolls – no wonder he fell for you. But you'd better drink a glass of water and lie down again. You have to be better for next week. Let me take away one of them pillows.'

Phyllis rearranged the pillows and Molly lay down, still holding the precious letter. 'I can't believe it,' she said. 'I've never had a letter from a boy before. Some of my friend's brothers make calf's eyes at me. Accidentally on purpose bump into me when we are playing tennis. I wouldn't bother with any of them. They get on my nerves. They're like little boys. These are the ones who'll be invited to my coming out party. You know, it's the beginning of finding me a suitable husband. Little do Mama or Papa know the sort of husband I'm looking for. He has to be big and strong and brave, a little bit wicked. Exciting . . . But to come back to what I was saying, how can I ever see Bert except in the park? That won't get us very far.'

'I'll ask my ma, she'll think of something. I'll have to go now. If I'm late back they'll stop me having next Sunday off. You mind yourself so that you're well enough for Sunday. And tear up the letter. If anyone finds it, the cat's out of the bag.'

The next Sunday, although her legs were still wobbly, Molly was well enough to go out and once her parents' carriage had left she went to the basement. Aggie said, 'I've worked it all out. You can meet the fella here.'

'Here in your room?'

'Of course you can,' said Phyllis. 'Now sit down while you hear all about it. We've time before the band comes.'

Aggie poured cups of dark brown tea which had been stewing on the hob for a half-hour or more. Molly had become used to it and drank from her cup. 'Now listen carefully. Julia and her husband and the two children go every

Sunday night to see his people in Stonybatter. Regular as clockwork they're out of here by seven and never come back before ten. But seven's too early to have your fella come. Thank God it's a Sunday and that the family have their dinner earlier than through the week. Even so you won't finish eating until seven and that'd be too early to pretend you were sleepy and had to go to bed. But eight o'clock would be gameball. You could let on the meal had made you sleepy, go to your room, and be down here just before eight.

'When you see him today, tell him to come through the back door and up the garden. To take off that helmet of his and keep close to the wall – the hedge will hide him. You'll have an hour or more together.'

'D'ye think I should tell Fanny? She's the only one likely to come into my bedroom.'

'In that case, do,' said Aggie. 'But not the whole truth. Say Phyllis's employees, being that pleased with her, are letting her sleep out of a Sunday night and it's her you're coming to see.'

'So far, so good,' said Phyllis. 'What about Cook and the other two? Any chance they might bump into Bert?'

Molly, still weak from her illness, the excitement, the planning and plotting, felt her head beginning to spin. She closed her eyes and took several deep breaths, repeating the question Phyllis had asked.

'As sure as you can ever be about anything,' Aggie said, and went on to explain how on Sunday evenings Cook and the other two servants had a big feed and drank stout till it came out of their ears, never stirring from the kitchen area until they collapsed into bed where the snores of them would deafen you. Her eyes shone with the exhilaration of the intrigue, the romance of the situation, and the idea of once again deceiving the McCarthys whom she had never forgiven for banishing her child from the house.

'Are you willing to take the chance, Molly?' she asked.

Without a moment's hesitation she said she was, and Phyllis added, 'I wish I had a fella to take a chance for.'

Aggie looked at the clock hanging on the wall and told the girls they had better go if they were going. 'And don't forget, tell him about taking off the helmet. If anything was to draw attention, that would.'

That afternoon Molly was nervous, and for the first time since getting Bert's note felt a twinge of fear as to what she was about to get involved in. But once she saw him and he winked at her, the fears flew away. The band played as usual a selection from Gilbert and Sullivan. Inside her head Molly sang along with 'Take a pair of sparkling eyes, take a pair of ruby lips', and wondered if Bert was thinking how her lips were ruby and her eyes sparkling.

He dismounted during the interval and stood by his horse, holding the reins in one hand while with the other he beckoned to Molly and Phyllis. She led the way and Molly followed on shaky legs, wondering as she did so what she could say to him. But Phyllis broke the ice, telling him the arrangements for seeing Molly. He listened and then asked was she better? She looked as if she was. She thought gazing at him, that he was indescribably handsome and so tall, towering above her. 'I'll see you next Sunday then,' he said as the bandmaster mounted the rostrum.

'Yes,' said Molly, her head beginning to spin again. 'Eight o'clock, don't forget.'

'I won't,' he said. 'Don't you worry, I'll be there.'

At dinner on the following Sunday night Molly kept an anxious eye on the clock, her thoughts on the meeting with Bert and how during the interval that afternoon he had held her hand. They had stood close to one other and she was intoxicated by the scent of him. The silkiness of his moustache . . . she longed to touch it. His smell reminded her of her father before he had started drinking heavily. But about Bert was also a whiff of leather and horse. She had an intense

longing to lay her head against his tunic, bury her face in it and inhale all the odours.

Her father pushed his food about his plate, eating little, a surly expression on his face. For a moment she remembered how he used to be. How much she had loved him. She still did but found him foolish and irritating nowadays. He pushed away his plate, saying he didn't want dessert, that he had work to do in his study, and left the room. Fanny and Molly exchanged glances, knowing exactly what the work was – serious undisturbed drinking.

When the meal was finished Nicole suggested they went to the drawing-room. 'It's only seven o'clock, we're lucky Papa is busy and has left us so early. Will you play for me, Molly? Something soothing until Nell goes to bed.'

She protested that she was going on fifteen and it wasn't fair being sent to bed so early. Her mother said: 'You were up until late last night. Tomorrow's Monday and school, so no arguments.'

When Nell was sent up Molly rose from her chair, hand over her mouth as she faked another yawn, and said she was going to bed also. She kissed her mother and bade her sisters goodnight. While she waited in her bedroom she brushed her hair and listened for sounds of her mother and Nell coming up and their doors closing. Fanny had probably stayed down to read for a while. It was five to eight and time to go. She dabbed a little scent on her wrists, had a last look in her glass, and cautiously opened the door. Everywhere was quiet.

Very careful not to make a sound, she went down the two flights of stairs and towards the back of the house. She passed her father's study on tiptoe and then went down into the basement and through the several passages that led to Aggie's room. She stood outside the door for several minutes before knocking, overcome again with fear of what she was about to do. But excited anticipation overcame the fear and she tapped on the door.

As if she had been standing behind it waiting for the knock,

Aggie opened the door and invited her in. Bert was sitting in the chair usually occupied by her. He stood up and smiled. His hair was glorious, Molly noticed, fair with a slight curl. Silky, she was sure, to the touch. He shook her hand, holding it for a long time before Aggie said, 'Sit over to the table.' Only then did Molly notice it was laid for a meal. Plates of the beef that had been served at dinner, beetroot, bread and butter, and a bowl of the same trifle she had not long ago eaten.

'You managed it all right then?' Aggie said when they were seated.

'I pretended to be very tired and it worked,' Molly replied.

Aggie told Bert to help himself. He complimented her on the spread. 'In barracks you're always hungry, nothing to eat after tea unless you go out to an eating house.' He offered the plate of beef to Molly. 'I've just eaten,' she said.

He tried coaxing her. 'A little bit. Go on, you need it after being sick.'

'I'd be sick again if I did, and no trifle, I ate two helpings, but I'll have a cup of tea, Aggie, please.' The tea pot was simmering on the hob, Aggie having wet it twenty minutes ago. She poured a cup. 'Sergeant Major's tea, hot and strong and sweet, that's how I like it,' said Bert.

'Why Sergeant Major's?' asked Molly.

'Theirs is special. Not like our gnat's . . .' He looked embarrassed, coughed to cover it and said, 'Not like our gnat's water.'

For a few moments they were all silent: Aggie beaming foolishly and Bert and Fanny desperately thinking of something to say. He broke the silence. 'Did you have far to come?' he asked Molly.

She smiled at him. 'Only down two flights of stairs.'

He looked puzzled. 'I live upstairs,' she explained. 'Didn't Phyllis tell you?'

'Me and Phyllis never spoke properly you might say, only

when I gave her the note. What d'ye mean, you live upstairs? That's where you sleep?'

'And eat and everything. I was even born up there.'

'Then you're not the same as Phyllis? I mean, you don't work with her?'

'No,' said Aggie, and explained who Molly was.

'Crikey!' said Bert. 'Your father may be down here after me in a minute. I've been in servants' quarters before. Nothing serious,' he said quickly, 'a maid I went out with once or twice, but never have I been in them with the daughter of the house. Are you sure there won't be any trouble? I know a bloke who was once found with a girl like you. Terrible commotion that caused. Her father up to the Commanding Officer the next day, and Charley who was a corporal demoted, his stripes ripped off.'

Bert laughed. 'The daughter of the house. Well, I never. I'm all for it. So long as you're sure there'll be no trouble then everything's gameball, as they say in Dublin.'

Both Aggie and Molly assured him that there would be no trouble. He appeared to relax after that and hardly stopped talking. Telling them how much he liked Ireland. Where he came from in England. How many brothers and sisters he had, sometimes looking at Aggie but mostly at Molly, thinking how beautiful she was and him a fool for not having noticed the difference between her and Phyllis. The way she spoke. Her clothes. Everything about her.

At a quarter to nine Aggie reminded him and Molly of the time Julia came home from visiting her husband's relations, adding that she'd go down to the back gate first and make sure the way was safe. Then she excused herself and left the room. Bert took Molly's hand in his. She blushed. 'You're the prettiest girl I've ever seen. Will you come down the stairs again next week?'

'I will,' she said in a voice he could hardly hear.

'And will you let me have a little kiss?'

She nodded her head. He leaned towards her and gently

kissed her lips. 'I'd better make a move. Better to be safe than sorry. Though I'm very sorry having to go. Still, lose five or ten minutes now. I'd rather do that than run into what's her name and give the game away, eh?'

Aggie came back. He shook her's and then Molly's hand, picked up his helmet, tucked it under his arm and when Aggie moved again to the door, he followed her, looking back longingly at Molly.

She returned upstairs as quietly as she had come. There wasn't a sound except the beating of her heart. In bed she went over and over again every minute she had spent with him. Remembering every word he had spoken. But most of all remembering the feel of his lips on hers. The first time ever she had kissed a man other than her father. She was in love with him, of that she was quite sure. She loved, adored . . . she fell asleep trying to think of other words to express her feelings for him.

They continued to meet in Aggie's room which after supper she left for longer periods each time. Did she walk round the square perhaps, sit in the garden or even the lavatory? Molly wondered. To let herself and Bert have half an hour alone.

Each Sunday he told her more about himself. He had four brothers and two sisters. The brothers were called Beaumont, Rafe, Nelson and Frith, which she considered peculiar Christian names. He was twenty years of age. One night, he said, 'The Talbots are a long-tailed family: cousins, aunts, uncles, nieces and nephews by the dozen, all over the place in Sussex. Farmers, butchers, cider makers, woodsmen, blacksmiths, all sorts. We came over with the Normans. I suppose we were Catholics then like you lot. Protestants now though we never go to church except for christenings, weddings and funerals. And me when there's Church Parade. You got to go then.'

In turn Molly told him of her sisters, her mother being French and her father a QC. That she wanted to go on the

stage and Fanny to be a doctor. Nell, she said, didn't have any ambitions.

When they weren't talking he was kissing her. Gentle kisses. He stroked her hair and told her she was the most beautiful girl he had ever seen and that he loved her. Sometimes, in between the kissing, Molly remembered what Phyllis had said the other Lancer had done to her friend and kept her knees tightly together. When he put his hand on her breast his kiss wasn't so gentle but thrilled her more. And all through her body were tingling, exciting, pleasant feelings. One night when the tingling was at its height and she was returning his kisses with a lot more feeling Aggie came back and they moved apart on the old sofa. 'I was thinking while I was out,' she said. 'It might be as well, Bert, if you didn't come for a few weeks.'

'Oh, but Aggie!' Molly protested. 'We're only getting to know each other.'

'Listen now, pet, this is the fourth Sunday you've let on to be so tired you had to go to bed early. Your mother will be worrying about your health or worse still begin to smell a rat.'

'Aggie's right, Moll, and in any case I'd have told you before I left – from next week I'm off for a fortnight on field exercises and then on furlough. I'll be gone all told for nearly a month.'

'Oh, no, that's terrible!' Molly said, her face crestfallen and tears filling her eyes.

'Don't cry, love. I'm not deserting you. I'll be back. Come on now, cheer up, give us a smile.'

While Aggie made the send off cup of tea, Molly sniffed a few times, dabbed her eyes, looking pitiful, but eventually agreed it was probably all for the best. 'But promise you'll write to me, Bert?'

'As often as I can.'

'Only don't send it here. I don't have letters from away. You don't have any letters, do you, Aggie?'

'Never one in my life,' she replied.

'My father handles the post when it comes in the morning and the afternoon one has to be kept until he comes home, except for letters for Mama. He'd ask questions. Where will I have yours sent to?'

'To Phyllis's place,' said Aggie. 'The doctor and his wife are easygoing, take what's addressed to them and leave everyone else's in separate piles. I'll give you her address.' She opened and rooted in the kitchen table drawer, found the stub of a pencil, a scrap of paper, and with her tongue slightly protruding, laboriously printed the name and address. 'Put that somewhere safe,' she instructed Bert who tucked it into a pocket.

Then it was time for him to leave. Molly didn't, as on previous occasions, go immediately. Throwing caution to the wind she waited for Aggie to come back. When she did, she said, 'He's mad about you. You can see it in his eyes, in the way he looks at you. And him handsome as a picture, and a real gentleman. It's like a story you'd read. Would you say you feel the same way about him?'

'I do, I do! I love him. I'll die if he doesn't write. I can't stop thinking about him.' Molly began to cry. 'Supposing I never hear from him? Supposing I never see him again?'

Aggie put her arms round Molly and comforted her as she had when a baby. Patting her, whispering soothing words, and calling her a little pet and a little dote, assuring her that he would come back and would write her grand love letters.

And as she spoke and stroked and comforted she was caught up in the cause of love every bit as much as Molly. All her lonely nights had been spent reading love stories. Now here was a real one, and however vicariously she was living through it. She imagined the kissing and embracing, the swooning sensations they induced, the fluttering heartbeat, the tears of joy – all of which she knew so well from the novelettes though not able to remember any of her own once only hurried experience on the banks of the canal.

'You'll marry him, love, you wait and see. You'll have a

gorgeous wedding. Be married in your mother's dress and veil, and the church will have that many flowers! It'll be the best wedding Dublin's ever seen and you'll go to some grand place for your honeymoon. I can just picture it.'

So could Molly and listened spellbound to poor foolish Aggie describe the wedding breakfast, her eyes shining as she elaborated on the food that would be served, the guests who would come, carried away by the fantasy, seeing Molly one minute as the bride, the next Phyllis, and then herself having the wedding she had never had. And never did it enter her mind that she was encouraging a girl, not much more than a child, to think seriously of a man she knew nothing about. A man who would be unacceptable to her parents. A man they would never consent to her marrying. A man Aggie had connived at bringing into their home to facilitate the romance, and have her own revenge on the McCarthys. That reason was completely forgotten. Now, if asked to explain why she had encouraged and allowed such a thing, she would answer, believing it to be the truth: 'They loved each other. I felt sorry for them. And they'd nowhere else to go.'

Bert wrote Molly four letters while on field exercises. She found the first two disappointing. Short letters with excuses about tiredness, lack of sleep, working from sunrise until it got dark. And only a couple of lines to say he missed and loved her. To get the letters she went on certain days into town and met Phyllis out on errands. Able to tell immediately by her face whether any more had arrived. The third letter was longer and full of his feelings for her. How he remembered her kisses, the feel of her soft skin, her beautiful hair, her lovely hands and shapely nails. That every night he'd dreamt about her and if he wasn't a man and a soldier, would have cried when he woke and found it had only been a dream.

She read and reread it, slept with it under her pillow and prayed to dream about him. In the fourth letter he asked her

to marry him and run away with him to England as he'd been posted back there.

Well, not with me. I'll have to go home first and break the news. But you could come the following week. Here's what we'll do. I'll be back from here on Sunday afternoon. I'll come to Aggie's on the Sunday night and you'll have to let on you're tired again. It won't matter what your mother thinks because you'll be gone soon. I'll bring money for your fare from Dublin to England and I'll meet you at Euston from the mail train. On Sunday we'll decide when it will be best for you to travel. That is if you really love and want to marry me?

I know all this is a bit sudden and that it wouldn't be the way you would have wanted to marry. But it's the only way. D'ye see, your father would never accept me. I'm an English soldier, no rank, and a Protestant as well. If we do it my way, once we're married he'll forgive you. Maybe not for a while but in the end he will. If you don't do it my way anything could happen. You never know from one minute to the next when the army might decide to send you to India or Africa. I could be there for years. But if you were my wife you could come too. I told you a lie about my age. I'm twenty-five not twenty. It's a lot older than you but it's not a bad thing. It means I'm on the 'the strength', I'm allowed to get married and entitled to an allowance for you and to an army house.

I know I'm not a Catholic but I promise I'll get married in the Catholic church. There's one in Horsham. That's near where I live. Please, my little love, be in Aggie's on Sunday night and then I know that you'll be mine for ever and ever.

She read the letter standing by Nelson's Pillar where she and Phyllis met. 'Phyllis,' said Molly, grabbing hold of her arm, 'we'll have to find somewhere and sit down, an ice cream shop, anywhere.'

'I can't. I'm late already. I'll be kilt if I'm much longer. I

had to get saffron in Findlaters and the cook is waiting to infuse it.'

'You have to. He wants to marry me. He wants me to run away with him. Next week he wants me to go to London and says he'll meet me.'

'You bloody, shaggin' liar, you're just trying to delay me!'

'As true as I'm standing here. That's why I want to sit down, my legs are shaking. I'll let you read it. Ah, please say you'll come?'

'Feck the cook and her saffron. I'll let on I took a weakness, fell outta my standing and had to be brought round. Come on then, there's a place in Talbot Street that sells coffee and ice cream.'

Linking arms, they crossed from Nelson's Pillar to the street directly opposite, found the cafe and sat down. Molly handed over the letter and watched Phyllis reading it. 'God, you were telling the truth. He's madly in love with you. I'm that jealous. It's just like a story. Will you do it?'

'I'm afraid of my life. I love him but I think I'd be afraid to run away. Would you if you were me?'

'Jump at the chance. You might never get another one. Fellas aren't ten a penny. And he's right about your father, he'd never let you marry Bert.'

'But it would break Mama's heart if I ran away.'

'She'd get over it.'

'D'ye think so?'

'Of course I do. Wouldn't she rather that than have you finish up an oul' maid? I wish it was me, I'd be over the moon. A fella that looks like him! Talk to my mother about it. She's very well up. A good judge of character. And she says he's a gentleman. D'ye not want the ice cream?'

Molly said she was too mixed up to be able to eat and Phyllis reached out and took the glass dish. While spooning out the ice cream she said, 'I'm going the minute I finish this. And don't be worryin'. You have a week to make up your mind. I'll complain on Sunday morning, letting on I've had

the scutters all night. That way I'll be in on whatever goes on between the two of you. I'm going now. Bye, bye.'

Molly sat for a while after Phyllis left, wondering what it would be like to be married. What it would be like to run away. She thought of her mother's grief when she discovered she was gone and of her father's anger. But not for long. Her thoughts soon returned to Bert: how she felt when his arms were about her, when he was kissing her. How the scent of his body acted on her. Making her wish he had no clothes on and neither did she and she could touch and smell his bare skin. When they were married she could do that.

A memory of her longing to go on the stage flashed into her mind. She quickly dismissed it for after all, what would singing and dancing be compared to living for ever with Bert? Sleeping in the same bed with him, wakening, and he being the first thing she would see.

By the time she had reached Brown Thomas in Grafton Street where she went in to buy the ribbon, her excuse for coming into town, she had made up her mind. She would be in Aggie's on Sunday night. She would go away to England and marry Bert. For as she told herself, apart from loving him and wanting to spend every minute with him, what was there to keep her at home?

Fanny, who could go for days without speaking. Nell – well, you never expected much from her. It used to be different before her father changed. He was gay and witty and made her laugh and paid her compliments. Her mother had always loved Fanny the best. Families like hers were hopeless. They thought they owned you and at the same time could be so cruel and inconsiderate.

She was lucky she had found Bert. Imagine staying in that house for years until she married, that's if she ever did. And then it would be to one of her friends' brothers, a doctor or solicitor. Boring boys. Nothing dashing about them like Bert. She knew no one as handsome, as broad or as tall as him. And

she was sure he was very brave. She could imagine him galloping his horse, charging at the enemy. All of that and so gentle as well. And able to kiss the way he did.

Aggie was ecstatic when Molly told her the news. Hugged and kissed her and said she was doing the right thing. Whether it was to be a wedding from the house or an elopement was all the same to her. The romance was all that mattered.

Molly let Aggie read the letter and after finishing it, she exclaimed, 'Didn't I tell you he was a gentleman? Look at him promising to marry you in the Catholic church. Don't forget to take your baptismal lines with you. Without them you can't get married. I'll make a lovely supper on Sunday. I think this is the weekend we have roast duck. Don't take too much with you. Whatever you leave can be sent on. Have you any money?'

'I never need money, only small change. We've accounts everywhere. Why?'

'It's always handy to have a few shillings by you. I'll see you right. It'll be my wedding present to you. Will you tell anyone? Fanny I was thinking of?'

'No. I'll leave her a letter in a place where she'll find it after I've gone.'

'That's your best course. You'd better go up now or your mother will be wondering where you are.'

At dinner that night, in a desperate attempt to get a conversation going, Nicole talked about how quickly the years went. That in 1889 Molly would be eighteen. 'I was thinking that perhaps I'd combine your coming out party with Fanny's. And soon after Christmas we must start thinking about your clothes. It's possible that next year we might be invited to a reception at the Vice Regal Lodge, wouldn't that be wonderful?'

From the other end of the table Michael glowered and said, 'I wouldn't go.'

'Why not, darling?'

'Bowing and scraping to that lot up in the Park. I'm no

Castle Catholic. I'm a McCarthy. I'm my own man and don't let anyone ever forget it.'

Nicole looked at the wreck of a man and thought how she had only been talking for the sake of it. And as for the Vice Regal Lodge, there was no fear of Michael going there for there would never be an invitation for the poor pathetic drunken man who was her husband.

Molly, to whom it didn't matter what was planned for 1889, agreed with her mother that a combined party was a good idea and that she couldn't wait to see next year's new fashions.

Fanny said she didn't want a coming out party this year, next year, ever. And again Michael spoke.

'We all know that. All you want is washing the sores of the poor. Going into the slums to deliver their babies. A nice job I must say for a girl brought up like you. But sure there's nothing stopping you so long as you have the money to pay for your medical education.'

Nicole wanted to scream, 'I have money, my own money, and I can pay for Fanny.' She remained silent. These days he was so unstable she feared to argue with him. Sometimes she thought he was deranged. That something other than drink ailed him.

He looked from one to the other of his family and saw their eyes. Contempt in Fanny's. Fear in Nell's. And for the first time in his beloved Molly's what was unmistakably hatred.

And inside his head Michael talked on. 'What am I doing to them? I love them. Why have I brought all this about? Oh, God, please help me. Free me from this terrible curse. Because of it I am destroying them.'

Chapter Twenty-two

Huddled in the corner of the smoky carriage Molly kept her eyes closed, her thoughts an excited jumble of all that had happened in the last two weeks. It had been frightening and thrilling at the same time, smuggling clothes and the small valise to Aggie's basement room. Keeping a guard on her tongue when talking to her mother of events she was planning for weeks and months ahead. Taking the turquoise locket engraved with her name and date of birth which she only wore on very special occasions, in between which it was kept in her mother's jewellery box until Molly became married. She had felt like a thief taking the key from its secret hiding place, opening the box, her ears strained for the sound of footsteps approaching the bedroom.

She couldn't have managed to leave without Aggie's help. She packed what few clothes she was taking. Ironed and folded them, sachets of lavender in between her underwear and the beautiful nightdress she had stolen from her mother's lingerie drawer. One she had never seen Nicole wear. It was wrapped in tissue paper. She knew it was the one her mother had worn on her wedding night.

Once or twice she felt a twinge of grief, thinking of how her mother would feel when she discovered her missing, but it was only fleeting. As Aggie had told her, her mother would soon get over the sorrow. She imagined her sister's shock when she found the letter in the front of a biology textbook – a book she knew Fanny wouldn't be using until a couple of days after she herself was gone. It was only a few

lines, telling her she was running away with Bert and that she would write with an address once she was settled. And not to worry — they were getting married and in a Catholic church. She pledged her sister to secrecy until she contacted her parents.

She remembered with such fondness the celebration when she had gone to the basement on the Sunday night with her answer for Bert. The whoop he had let out. How he had lifted her off her feet and danced round the room with her. Aggie and Phyllis laughing and crying at the same time.

Then Aggie taking her aside and whispering that she had hidden in her spare stays twenty pounds. 'Stitched in,' she said, 'between the layers of stuff.' How she had protested. 'But, Aggie, I don't need money. You shouldn't. You can't afford it. Bert is giving me money for the boat and train.'

'I know that, but all the same, keep it for a rainy day. Think of it as my wedding present.'

Everything had gone exactly as they planned. Except for when she last saw her father. Her father whom she had adored and recently come to detest. She couldn't fully understand why. It wasn't jealousy for he hadn't switched his affections to anyone else. She supposed it was the terrible change in him. How awful he looked, how awful he smelled. Her gorgeous, handsome, elegant father had let her down. Girls she knew made jokes about him, ones she wasn't supposed to hear, they'd maintain, though they made sure she was within earshot. All the same, she told herself, seeing him for what might be the last time, she couldn't even feel pity for him.

Yes, she thought, it all went well. Though it was a bit of a shock realizing that the money Bert had given her would only pay for a steerage passage and third-class ticket on the train. That was a shock, boarding the boat and being directed down and down into what she was sure was the hold. A vile gloomy space already jammed with men and

women drinking, some already drunk, and babies sprawled everywhere. Luckily it was still summertime and the crossing smooth. But it was vastly different from when she had travelled with Mama. Sleeping in cabins with a stewardess in attendance.

But always, overriding all the discomfort, was the prospect of Bert waiting for her in London. Of being in his arms, of his kisses. Then the meeting with his family. The visit to the priest to arrange their wedding. And then, after a while, the move to Aldershot, to their own home. She and Bert alone, she his wife with a gold ring and people calling her Mrs Talbot. And sleeping every night in his arms. She was a little scared about her wedding night. Not quite sure exactly what happened. Phyllis wasn't either. 'Stop worrying,' she had said. 'Everyone does it and I've never heard of it killing them.'

Huddled in her corner of the carriage, Molly dozed. She woke as the train jolted and swayed, changing points. Wiping the steamed up glass she looked out through the window. It was a fine night with a clear sky and a full moon. She could see the man's face and let herself believe he was smiling down on her. She slept again and woke when the train stopped at stations and saw mail bags being thrown on the platform. She saw the name Crewe and was amazed at so many people being about in the middle of the night, and so much activity. The mail bags again and porters pushing trolleys piled with packages and boxes.

Before arriving in London she dampened a handkerchief from her bottle of drinking water, packed by Aggie along with sandwiches, and wiped her face, first laying the wet piece of linen across her eyes which felt hot and dry and as if they were filled with grit. Her throat was parched. She drained the bottle. Dawn was breaking as the train began its run into Euston. She would have liked to undo her hair, brush and rearrange it. But even had there been room to

use a brush, you couldn't dress your hair in such a public place.

Tall houses now appeared on either side of the track. In some, faint lights showed. In a few minutes she'd be there. She'd be with Bert. Her heart raced as fast she was sure as the train itself. People were pulling bags and bundles from the overhead netting rack. The train was slowing down. A man opened the window. Smoke that smelled of cinders and soot blew into the carriage. The train slowed and stopped. Men and women pushed past her to leave. Molly waited. When she did get out she heard people greeting each other, saw them waving. She was stiff from sitting all night. At the end of the platform she saw a group of people. Bert would be amongst them. She forced herself to walk quicker, her eyes scanning the crowd.

She couldn't see him amongst the knot of people which had thinned considerably. Panic-stricken, wondering if she had come on the wrong day and would be stranded in this strange place, she contemplated finding a lavatory and with a hair or hat pin unpicking Aggie's money stitched in her stays. Then she heard his voice call her name.

For an instant she didn't recognize him and when she did felt a sense of disappointment. He wasn't as she remembered him. Not as handsome. Not as splendid. No brilliant red coat with its silver braid. No gleaming helmet. She had never seen him in mufti. In his civilian clothes, a dark suit and bowler hat, he looked quite ordinary. Then he was beside her and his eyes were still beautiful, his mouth and teeth and his moustache silky fair.

'Oh, Bert, I was so afraid when I couldn't see you. Afraid I'd come on the wrong day. Afraid you'd changed your mind.' She clung to him.

'As if I'd do that to the loveliest girl in the world. You're my little colleen. Don't you know how much I love you? How was the journey? I bet you're tired.'

'A bit,' she said.

'We'll have something to eat and then go to Victoria. I can't wait to show you off at home. And there'll be plenty there come to see "our Bertie's girl from Ireland", as they'll put it.'

Arm in arm they went to the station buffet where Bert ordered two teas, a pie for himself, and when asked, Molly said she would have bread and butter. They went by cab to Victoria and from there by train to Horsham. On the journey she sat with her head on his breast. His suit smelled of camphor, masking his body scent, but she didn't mind. They were together. He had an arm round her. On their way to his home to meet his family. And in a few weeks she'd be his wife.

'It's not far,' he told her, 'a mile or two, are you up to that?'

'Yes, I'm great now, a mile or two's nothing.'

She was surprised that Horsham was so small. Only a country town and almost everything built of redbrick. Not like the houses at home, not mellowed to soft lovely shades. As they left the town behind it became very countrified. Lots of beautiful tall trees. Here and there along the way she saw more redbrick cottages. She was very tired and uncomfortable as the sun rose higher and the morning became hotter.

After what seemed more like six than two miles they came to a cottage, a little bigger than those she had passed and set further back from the road. Two mongrel dogs came leaping and barking. 'Down, Floss. Down, Dandy,' Bert commanded, and Molly asked. 'Is this it? Is this where you live?'

'It is. This is my home. And yours until we're married and get an army place.'

'It's very nice, the flowers are gorgeous.' She felt she had to say something but not what she was thinking: It's not as big as our mews house.

They walked up the path. The front door opened and a

stout woman, dressed in a long black woollen skirt and blouse, stood smiling at them. 'So this is her, our Bertie's girl?'

'This is her, Mum. Isn't she nice?' Bert said, and gently propelled Molly forward.

'You're very welcome. Bertie must be keen on you. He's never brought a girl home before. Come in, there's plenty waiting to meet you and there'll be more later on.'

Molly followed her along the narrow red-tiled passage with Bert walking behind. On either side of the hall there were rooms, their doors open. Passing, she glanced in. One was a bedroom with a large bed taking up almost all the space. In the other she saw wooden armchairs with cushions on the seats, a picture of Queen Victoria over the mantelpiece, a table in the centre of the room, a sofa and a variety of other seats.

There was a kitchen at the end of the passage. The same tiles as in the passage covered the floor. A blazing fire had pots simmering on it, hobs and a kettle suspended on a hook and chain hanging close to the dancing flames. Molly felt a little faint from fatigue, the heat of the room, and the sea of strange faces all looking at her.

Mrs Talbot announced, 'Our Bertie's girl, all the way from Dublin,' and began introducing her. First to her husband, then to Bertie's brothers and two sisters. In turn they each smiled, the men shaking her hand, uttering words of greeting, the father saying, 'He knows how to pick a beauty, does our Bertie.' Molly felt ill at ease, tonguetied, and her replies were stilted. She had never given much thought to what Bertie's family or home would be like. Taking for granted they and it would be similar to people and houses at home.

They were welcoming and friendly, she could see and sense that, and trying in their own way to put her at the ease. Mrs Talbot, who along with Bertie seemed the most relaxed, invited her to sit by the fire. Molly thanked her but

said she was too hot. 'We weren't sure what time you'd get here. We should have sent the pony and trap, it's a long walk if you're not used to it. Sit there by the table and take off your jacket.'

She hadn't liked to do so and was too shy to have asked. Also she desperately wanted to go to the lavatory but couldn't bring herself to mention it. Bert's mother came to her aid. 'You must be tired. Bert said the train would take all night. You'll be hungry as well?'

'I am,' Molly admitted.

'Annie'll take you to freshen up and show you what's what. Then have something to eat and after that a lie down.'

Molly thanked Mrs Talbot and Annie stood up. 'It's this way,' she said, opening a door that led to the outside. 'Down there on the right-hand side. I'll wait for you.'

There was a garden with vegetables growing, fruit bushes, apple trees, hens, Floss and Dandy lying in the shade of a big wooden shed near the one to which Annie had directed her. The cauliflowers, cabbage and rows of peas and beans appeared well tended, but elsewhere there was long coarse grass, growing along the cinder path where she was carefully picking her way, grass and nettles and a profusion of weeds wherever the earth wasn't covered. Amongst the grass and weeds she saw what she guessed were rusted tools used for gardening, a few horse shoes and an enamel basin with a holed bottom.

The inside of the lavatory had a wooden seat from one side of the narrow space to the other and the pan was conical with no apparent bottom to it. From a nail in the whitewashed wall hung a bundle of torn squares of newspaper. It was all strange and quaint to her though not too unpleasant. It smelled faintly of urine and a dank green smell which she supposed was from being out in the garden and the creeper that grew round the shed, tendrils of it poking in through the little window high in the wall.

After peeing, crumpling a sheet of paper and carefully drying herself, she felt less tense, better able to face the scene in the kitchen. There was no chain to pull. She shrugged, reminding herself that in the Crowleys' they didn't even have a shed. There you relieved yourself behind a bush, carrying a piece of newspaper with you. As she left the shed she wondered what you did to flush away a motion. Annie, waiting for her, answered her unasked question.

'If you need it there's a bucket behind there.' She pointed to the back of the lavatory. 'Sometimes the rain fills it, or you take it to the pump, I'll show you where. Your skirt and blouse are very grand, and your boots. I expect people living in cities all wear such fine clothes?'

They walked back to the house and Molly warmed to this girl. Fair like Bertie, pretty and clean-looking, but careless, she thought, about her clothes and appearance.

'Most people in the city do wear clothes like mine. But not all. I suppose it depends on money.'

And for the first time since arriving and seeing Bert's cottage and then inside it she realized that maybe his family didn't have as much money as hers. And then she added, 'Of course, in the country you don't need such things. They'd get soiled easier for one thing.' She was trying to make amends for mentioning money. Though she soon realized that Annie hadn't been offended for she chatted away about Bertie. How pleased they were to have him home. How he was her favourite brother. And about all the relations Molly would meet later on.

'I boiled you two eggs laid this morning and there's cheese. We'll have a big meal this evening when the others come,' Mrs Talbot told Molly.

Bert sat beside her at the table, now and then saying to the others, 'I know how to pick them, don't I?' as he stroked her hair.

She was thinking of something to say, she didn't want to

seem unfriendly, knew that she had hardly spoken half a dozen words since she arrived. 'The eggs are gorgeous. I noticed the chickens in the garden. On my grandmother's farm they kept chickens. I used to go there for my holidays.' Now that she had started she couldn't stop talking. She knew she was always a great talker and more so when she was nervous. She told them about France, and her grandfather and aunt being burned to death. How Bertie had thought she was a maid servant like her friend Phyllis.

His brothers and sisters laughed at that. His father asked her questions about the farm in Ireland, and his mother about Nicole. Would they come over for the wedding, she and her father?

'They don't know, Mum. We eloped.' There were gasps of astonishment from his two sisters and concerned questions from Mrs Talbot. 'The poor dear, she'll be going frantic. I hope you at least left her a letter?'

'She did, Mum, a long letter,' Bert lied.

But his mother was not satisfied. 'If I'd known the truth, Bertie, I'd never have agreed. I thought it was all settled between Molly, you and her parents, and that's the truth. It was a wicked thing to do. Not that I blame you, Molly, you're only a child. But you, Bertie, should have known better, you're a grown man. I'll be worried until you hear from your mother. The state she must be in.'

Molly began to cry. Bert said, 'Now look what you've done, Mum.'

Molly, for the first time, thought about the state her mother would be in, and was simultaneously afraid that Mrs Talbot would send her home. So that when she said, 'Now what you'll have to do . . .' Molly's sobbing became uncontrollable, hiccuping through her, until raised above the sound she heard Bert's mother finish her sentence, '. . . is go and have a nice lie down. Annie will show you where.'

Nell discovered that Molly's bed hadn't been slept in and went running downstairs to the breakfast room to tell Nicole. 'Calm down, darling, Molly must have decided to make her own bed. She's about the house somewhere or in the garden, it's such a lovely morning. She'll be here in a minute.'

She wasn't but still Nicole didn't take that seriously and sent Fanny to see if she was in the park. 'No sign of her,' Fanny reported when she returned. 'I suppose she could have gone for a walk.'

'That's it, that's what she has done. Ready for more coffee, anyone?' Nicole asked.

When breakfast was finished and Molly still hadn't appeared, Nicole felt uneasy. 'Go and ask Aggie if she has seen her, and Julia.' They hadn't, and when Julia asked was anything wrong, Nell, obeying her mother's instruction, said no, there wasn't really. She ran up the basement steps and told her mother neither Aggie nor Julia had seen her.

By now Nicole was agitated, wondering if she should telephone Michael at his chambers.

'It would be the first morning for ages he left early. What'll I do?' she appealed to her daughters.

Fanny suggested they go and have a look in Molly's room. 'Her brushes and combs aren't on the dressing table, Mama. You don't think she's run away?' said Nell.

Letting her fear and worry get the better of her, Nicole snapped, 'Of course she hasn't. Don't talk such rubbish. Where could she run away to? Who could she run away to?'

In the meantime Fanny had opened Molly's wardrobe and was swishing through her clothes. 'Whatever she's done, she's done it in what she stood up in.'

'Darling, don't you start. Don't talk in riddles. What exactly do you mean, whatever she stood up in?'

'Only that all her clothes seem to be here.'

'Let me see,' said Nicole, pushing Fanny aside. 'Her grey

outfit isn't here, neither is the turquoise one.' She took a hat box from the shelf. 'And the matching hats are gone.'

'And her valise,' chimed in Nell, and began to cry.

'Oh my God, she has run away,' said Nicole, and went the colour of dirty snow. 'I'll have to ring Papa.' She sat on Molly's bed, Fanny and Nell on either side of her.

'Don't cry, Mama,' Fanny said. 'Maybe she went to spend the night with one of her friends. Maybe she'll be home by lunchtime. Is Papa in court this morning?'

'No, he's not.'

'That means he'll come home for lunch.'

'Maybe, Fanny, you can never be sure. What difference does it make?'

'Why not wait and see if he does? Molly will probably be home by then. In which case there'll be no need for him to know.'

'D'ye really think she might?'

'I do, I really do,' she lied, and said a silent prayer that Molly would turn up soon for it was breaking her heart to see her mother looking so terrified.

'I think you're probably right. And it would be silly to alarm Papa unnecessarily. We'll wait, though I can't think that any of Molly's friends' mothers would have agreed to her staying overnight without my permission.'

'Whoever it is could have sneaked her in for a lark.'

While her mother and sisters were agonizing as to where Molly was, she lay on a lumpy flock mattress recalling the shocks and surprises she had experienced since arriving in England. At Euston not recognizing Bert for several minutes; the little cottage that he lived in; having to share a bed with his sister who was a stranger really. And then the party in the evening. So many of his relations. How many hands she had shaken, big rough male hands, and the women's rough also. The number of times she was referred to as 'the little colleen' by the male relatives, or 'our Bertie's

girl' or 'sweetheart' by the women. They were almost too friendly. They had overwhelmed her. And the noise and everyone laughing at everything anyone said, most of which she didn't understand. She supposed it was the Sussex dialect or accent, not sure which. Bert's must have been toned down during his years in the army.

They were all kind and tried to make her feel at home, but she didn't try as hard as she might. Never in her life had she met people like these. They were country people, but so was everyone she knew in Ballydurkin and in Mama's village in France. But none of those was as boisterous as Bert's family. What they lacked, she supposed, was grace or charm. God knows the Irish country people could be boisterous when the drink was in them but in a different way. And the French in Issoudon, the farm labourers, old and young, took their time getting to know you. But not Bert's family.

Though perhaps it was because she was as they said 'our Bertie's girl', or 'our Bertie's sweetheart'. She was practically one of the family, and so they treated her as one. Or perhaps she was just being uppity. But all the same it was not very nice when one of the uncles asked: 'And how are the pigs in Ireland, Moll?' And she had replied, 'I don't really know, we don't keep pigs. My grandfather did but that's a long time ago.' And the room rocked with laughter. Only then had she remembered Uncle's James's fury at the *Punch* cartoons, the monkey-faced Irish always shown with long upper lips and with pigs in the kitchen. She had gone scarlet with annoyance and embarrassment. Bert noticed for it was then he asked her to go outside for a breath of air. He had kissed and cuddled her and told her to pay no attention. His relations liked her. They were trying to be funny. But they were, no matter how good-natured, still yokels. Sometimes he found them irritating, but you had to make allowances for them. Few had ever been further than Horsham. She would get used to them.

Pretending that she would, she gave herself up to his kisses and his gentle caressing of her breasts. She wouldn't have minded had he undone her blouse but he didn't. He wasn't at all like the Lancer who had gone out with Phyllis's friend. She was glad of that. It showed how much he loved and respected her. Maybe just before they married he might take more liberties, but that would be all right. Tomorrow they were going to see the priest about the wedding. Bert didn't think they'd have to wait too long before the army housed them. She was glad about that, knowing she could never get used to his family. Well, she could to Annie and his mother, and maybe a little bit to his father, but not to anyone else. And in any case, where could she and Bert sleep? There wasn't enough room. The big shed in the garden by the lavatory was where Bert and his brothers slept. Annie and the other sister, who was away in service, slept in the bed where she was now. That only left the small bedroom downstairs which his parents had. The army would have to find them somewhere soon. Tonight the other sister would sleep in the parlour.

Out in the garden, sitting underneath an apple tree with Floss and Dandy stretched beside him, Bert was thinking about Molly. She was a lovely little thing. The prettiest girl he had ever gone out with. In the park in Dublin she had looked like a pale pink rose amongst a bed of common flowers. Thinking she was a house maid like Phyllis he made up his mind to take her out. Use his charm and expertise on her. Get his way with her as he almost always did. But as for falling in love and marrying, no such thoughts were in his mind. He wasn't the marrying kind. Love 'em and leave 'em, that was his motto. Most soldiers' motto. That was until the Sunday he discovered she was the daughter of the house. And what a house! There was money there. Money that maybe he could get his hands on. He got really to like her. Maybe love her a bit. Well, she was beautiful. So innocent, he was careful not to frighten

her off. He'd never thought she'd agree to run away with him, but it was worth a try. And she had fallen into his lap. With a bit of help from that old fool Aggie and her daughter who would be anyone's for the price of a pease pudding. Married life with her wouldn't be too dusty. She'd work out all right. Passionate little thing. Once she got the hang of it, and he could teach her a thing or two.

In a month or so her parents would come round. All would be forgiven and the money come rolling in. They'd want her living in the circumstances to which she was accustomed. Like that those sort of people were. Only two more years to finish his service then set up in something cushy. Plenty of time to think what or where. And being married didn't mean tying a knot in it whenever you were away from home. But first things first. This vicar or padre had to be seen. Let him start the ball rolling. Get the nuptials over and then Molly's letter begging for forgiveness, including the marriage certificate signed by the Holy Roman.

Fanny, unable to sleep, wandered through the house. Each time she passed her parents' bedroom she heard her father snoring and her mother crying. Had Nicole been alone Fanny would have gone in to comfort her. She suspected that Molly might be sleeping in the house where Phyllis worked and if there was no word by tomorrow, knew she would have to break her promise for her mother's sake.

Dawn broke and she decided there was no point now in trying to sleep. She would catch up on her biology. Taking the textbook from a shelf, Molly's letter fell out.

'Oh my God,' she kept repeating as she read the letter, and asking herself where Molly was by now. Two days ago the letter was written. She could be a long, long distance from Dublin, or hiding out somewhere in the city. This was no lark. This was serious. Something Françoise couldn't handle.

Leaving her room she went to her mother's. If she heard her still crying she would open the door and beckon her out. She listened. Not a sound, not even her father's snores. It would be cruel to waken her mother out of her little sleep. She'd leave her in oblivion for a while longer.

Half-past five, quarter to six . . . the hands of the clock seemed to move slower and slower. She tried passing the time by studying the textbook. The words swam before her eyes, the diagrams a meaningless blur.

At a quarter past seven she could wait no longer and went on shaking legs to her parents' room, dreading her father's reaction, his accusations that she had known all along, had waited until now to give Molly time to go wherever she was going.

'Mama,' she whispered, gently shaking her mother's shoulder. Nicole came instantly awake with fear-filled eyes. 'Mama, I've just found a letter from Molly. She has run away. Here, read it.' Nicole pulled the cord which operated the gasolier and took her spectacles from the bedside table. Michael didn't stir until she screamed.

'What? What is it?' he asked, raising himself on an elbow. She gave him the letter. And as Fanny had feared, he rounded on her. 'You bloody little bitch! You've known all along. You were in on it with her. You saw your mother suffering and let her. You let me traipse round Dublin, out to Kingstown, up to Rathgar, Rathmines, Foxrock, making a holy show of myself.' He was out of the bed, standing berating her in his nightshirt. An arm raised as if to strike her. 'Of all the heartless little bitches . . .'

Fanny wouldn't cry. She stood her ground and defended herself. 'I found it this morning in a textbook. One Molly knew I would be taking to school today. I knew nothing about what she planned to do. You can believe it or not. I brought it the minute I found it. I brought it for Mama's sake, not yours. You have your own protection against suffering.'

He struck her hard across the face. Still she didn't cry. With a hand to her smarting cheek, she walked from the room.

'D'ye believe her?' he asked Nicole who was sitting on the side of the bed, her head bowed, rocking herself to and fro.

'Fanny isn't a liar and you are a blackguard. You struck her. I sometimes think you are losing your mind.'

His response was an order for her to get up, get dressed, and summon all the servants to his study within the next ten minutes which was how long it took him to throw cold water on his face, dress, and while doing so drink a tumbler of whiskey.

'Will I come with you?' Nicole asked as he started to leave the room.

'No, you make the breakfast, there'll be no one else to do it.'

They were waiting for him outside his study. Their clothes had the appearance of having been hastily thrown on. Cook's blouse was wrongly buttoned, two inches of it above the other side; the parlour maid's white frilly cap sat askew on her head, and hair straggled from buns put up in a hurry. Having no one to mind them, Julia had brought her two children along. The little girl whimpered and rubbed sleep from her eyes. Pat, Julia's husband, stood with a surly expression on his face for being summoned in such haste and with no explanation. They talked in hushed whispers as they did in the chapel before Mass started, becoming silent as Michael approached.

'Come in,' he ordered, and they followed him into the study. He let them stand shuffling their feet for several minutes, then announced, 'My daughter Molly has run away with a man some time the day before yesterday. Some or all of you knew of it, connived at it, and assisted.'

They gasped, looked at each other and then back at him. In a babble of voices they denied the accusations. Pat

pushed his way forward and said, 'Mr McCarthy, that's a terrible thing to say. It's out of order and I think you should take it back.'

Michael ignored him and questioned them one by one. They denied all or any knowledge of the affair, except Pat who refused to answer.

'Everyone except Cook go out and close the door. Wait in the hall. I'll call each of you in again.'

Without waiting for a question, Cook said, 'As true as God, sir, I know nothing about any of it.' She was old and had bladder trouble. Sometimes the water dribbled from her of its own volition at the wrong place. Or like this morning refused to come at all but might at any minute. She would drop dead of shame if it happened here and now, destroying the rug. She stood with her hands, thighs and knees tightly cramped together.

'Have you ever seen Molly with a man?'

'No, sir, never,' she truthfully replied.

'Or lately with anyone other than her sisters and friends?'

She hesitated, then concluding that Phyllis was a friend, replied, 'Never in my life, sir.'

The general maid, the parlour maid, and Aggie gave the same answers. Then it was Julia's turn. The maids took the children. Pat followed her into the room.

'I want to talk to Julia on her own,' Michael said.

'You can't. She's my wife. This isn't a court or police station.'

Michael began asking her the same questions. She felt sorry for him. She remembered the lovely man from Ballydurkin. The good happy times working for him and Nicole. How sore his heart must be. Maybe Phyllis was implicated with the runaway. She'd seen her and Molly in the park with soldiers, and regretted having been instrumental in getting Phyllis back to the house. But by then it was too late and she couldn't tell Nicole for that would get the others into trouble and her the name of informer.

But this was more serious than girls tricking with soldiers in the park. She imagined the heartbreak Nicole and he were going through. From outside the door she heard her little girl cry. In her mind's eye she saw Molly at the same age. All smiles, dimples and golden curls. Easygoing Molly. Molly who'd believe anyone or anything. Soldiers had bad reputations. The fella could ruin or even murder her. It was her duty before God to tell Michael what she knew.

'I do know something, but before I tell you, you have to believe this – Pat had no part in it. 'Twas of a Sunday and he'd be out driving the carriage. And if it was a day when you were up in bed because the weather was bad, he would be in his, sleeping his senses away.'

'What are you talking about, girl?' Pat asked, taking hold of Julia's elbow.

'Whisht, will you, and let me finish.' Michael listened to the unfolding story of how Julia and the other servants had conspired to smuggle Phyllis into the house, and all the rest of it. Phyllis and Aggie . . . Phyllis and Aggie . . . the names hammered inside his brain and a film of cold sweat enveloped him. In his bones he had always felt those two would bring danger and corruption into his home. In the depths of his heart he had always known they were evil. As if from far away he heard Julia explain what had led the servants to aid and abet Aggie and Phyllis and how it seemed only natural that Molly and her friend would get together.

'But about a man, never that. We knew nothing about it. And Pat knew nothing about nothing.'

And while he got the gist of what she was saying with a part of his brain, another part was thinking: Aggie and Phyllis have a connection with Mag Cronin. Reincarnations of her. I understand it now, the nightmare, I understand it. She came to terrify me when Aggie and the bastard she was carrying were in danger of being thrown out.

'I swear that's the truth before God Almighty,' Julia concluded.

'Yes, all right,' Michael said. 'You can go, but remain outside. I'll want to see all of you again. Tell Aggie to come in but not for a few minutes.'

In the few minutes before she came he fortified himself with whiskey. Then he treated her as he would a prosecution witness, browbeating her until finally she told him everything including which barracks Bert was stationed in. He wanted to smash his fist into her face. To put his hands round her throat and stifle the life out of her. He didn't. Nor as he had planned did he tell her how much he had always loathed her and her bastard but said: 'You can go now. Pack your belongings and leave the house immediately. You'll be given what monies are owing to you, but no reference. You'll never get a job in any decent house in Dublin again. Go from here and pick up your daughter. I shall phone her employer. She too will be dismissed on the spot. And now, send in the others.'

He passed the same sentence on the other servants and of its own volition Cook's bladder dribbled its contents down her legs and on to the rug.

'The same applies to you and Pat, Julia, but because of the children you can stay till the end of the week.'

'Don't you mean because of the horses? You won't pick up a groom and driver from the agency as quick as a cook and maids,' said Pat. 'Thanks for the offer. We'll leave now with the others.'

While Michael had been questioning the servants Nicole had telephoned James, told him about Molly and how she thought Michael would lose his mind. He promised to come round at once.

She waited in the drawing-room for Michael to finish questioning the servants. In the meantime James arrived. He took hold of her hands, pressed them and spoke reassuringly. 'Something can be done. Don't cry, Nicole, it will be

all right, you'll see. Marianne is a sensible girl, she'll be back before you know it.'

Marianne he knew was a giddy, impulsive girl, only too capable of landing herself in trouble. But it was hardly the thing to say to a woman so obviously distressed. What he wanted to do was take her in his arms, hold her close and comfort her. 'Where's Michael?' he asked.

'Still questioning the servants, I suppose, though I'm sure they know as little about it as we do. He shouldn't be much longer.'

He was quite a while. Spending the time in his study, drinking and brooding, furious at the deception that had gone on under his nose. One half of his mind livid with anger that his Marianne would do such a thing to him, the other half filled with fear of what would become of her.

Hearing a commotion outside, Nicole went to the drawing-room window and looked out. 'It's the servants, they're leaving! Carrying their bags and bundles. Look, James, Cook is crying. They're all outside on the pavement, Julia and the children and Pat too. Michael must have dismissed them! He must think they are implicated. I have to stop him. He mustn't send them away. They've nowhere to go except Julia whose husband has family in Stonybatter. Poor Aggie came from the Workhouse and the others are from down the country. I'm going to them. They mustn't be thrown out like so much rubbish.'

Before she reached the door Michael came in. 'What have you done?' she demanded to know.

'Dismissed them.'

'But why, and where can they go?'

'To Hell's gates for all I care.'

Then he told her all.

'A soldier! In the park all this time? I can't believe it. Gone to England with him, my baby. Getting married? I read it in the note, but didn't believe it. What'll we do?

And the servants – Julia, Pat, Aggie. All of them knew and did nothing?'

'Pat wasn't involved and the others only up to a point. I warned you about Aggie and her bastard. They were the ones. Up to their necks in it from beginning to end.'

'I don't understand. Why would they do such a thing? We got on well. They were good servants. They were good people. Why would they help to lead my child astray?'

'Because, as Julia explained, we banished Phyllis from her home. You see, it all comes back to her and her mother.'

'Michael,' James said, 'aren't you rather wasting time? Presumably Aggie told you what regiment this soldier is in? Why aren't you on your way to his barracks, seeing his Commanding Officer, finding out where he lives? They'll bend over backwards to help you find him, and thereby Marianne. I'd say you could have her back in a few days. I'll come with you. Let's go right away.'

'Oh, yes, that's it. Go, Michael, please, at once,' said Nicole.

'No,' he said. 'She's gone. As far as I'm concerned she no longer exists. While I live she'll never set foot in this house again.'

Nicole went hysterical. She screamed and cried. Hurled accusations at him. 'Maybe if you didn't drink so much, didn't create such an atmosphere in the house, hadn't forbidden Phyllis to come and see her mother, none of this would have happened. I don't know you any more. You're not the man I married. Do what James says. I want my daughter back! Do you hear? I want Marianne back!'

James was racked with embarrassment. To see these people he loved in such a scene. To know that pride wouldn't allow Michael to pursue his daughter. He was a tormented man. What had changed him? How could anyone sacrifice those he loved to save his own pride and in so doing break the heart of his wife? Outside the drawing-

room door Fanny and Nell listened while tears ran down their faces.

Nicole came to the end of her tirade and sat on a sofa quietly sobbing. James again tried persuading Michael to go to the barracks. Offered to go himself. Michael told him it was none of his business.

Instead James offered to make some tea for Nicole. Gratefully she accepted his offer. 'Will you be able to find everything?' she asked, dabbing at her eyes. 'Everyone's gone.' And despite her grief she remembered that tonight there would be no food prepared. Not that she wanted food but the girls must be fed. She spoke her thoughts aloud.

'When I've made your tea,' James said, 'I'll go home and bring one of my servants over until you find others. You can contact one of the agencies and get someone on a temporary basis tomorrow. But what about the horses, Michael, who'll stable them?'

'I will,' said Michael. 'I'm not as incompetent as my loving wife thinks.'

Chapter Twenty-three

IF she could have spent all her time alone with Bert, Molly would have been radiantly happy but it was seldom they were alone. It seemed as if always there were people dropping into the cottage to meet 'Bertie's girl from Ireland'. Kind, smiling people who laughed a lot at things Molly didn't understand. Talking after the first introductions and standard questions about her journey and what did she think of Horsham, of family matters, people and places she didn't know.

Only when she and Bert went for walks on to the Downs and meandered through the narrow, and at this time of the year leafy, lanes where from time to time they stopped to kiss and cuddle, or on the rare occasions when the parlour wasn't occupied, was she happy. Then Bert fondled her, each time going a little further. His hands caressing her backside over the stuff of one or other of her outfits; her breasts, her naked breasts. His fingers and lips sending her into a delirium of ecstacy so that her instinct made her want to strip off and present him with her naked body. Bert, when he sensed this, disengaged himself. Told her how much he loved her but that he also respected her. They could wait a little while longer. Soon they would see the priest and arrange to be married.

One evening in the parlour he announced, 'We'll go and see your padre tomorrow. I've found out where it is. The little church, it's called, on Springfield Road. The proper name's Saint John the Evangelist.'

Bert's father made it plain to him that neither he, his

224

mother nor the relations would go to the church to see him and Molly married. 'Don't go to our own often, funerals and that. But never could I go into a Catholic one. Wouldn't seem right somehow. Nothing against Molly, a nice little girl. And after the ceremony we'll do you both proud. Your ma'll lay on a spread.'

His brothers wouldn't attend either, not even when Bert said in that case he wouldn't have a best man. 'Sorry about that, but they do queer things in Catholic churches,' Nelson said. 'They've got statues dripping blood and bones and things.' The others seconded all of Nelson's statements.

'No hard feelings,' Bert said. 'If she wasn't a Holy Roman I don't suppose I'd go into one either.' But go he had to. Get the marriage sorted out. Get the lines off to her father and a letter from her to them asking their forgiveness. Then everything would be sorted out. All forgiven and money sent. He wondered would it be a lump sum or doled out each month? He hoped not the latter. A lump sum he'd like to start up in something . . .

Rolling in it they were. Anyone could see that from the size of the house and where it was. Then another thought struck him. Supposing they made it a condition that she went back to Dublin to live, staying with them and he visiting when he was on furlough? They wouldn't do that. Wouldn't want to admit to having a son-in-law who was a ranker, and worse still a Protestant. In any case he'd put the pressure on Molly. Threaten if she even considered going back to Dublin after they were married she'd have seen the last of him. He had her in the palm of his hand.

The next day they went to Horsham and found 'the little church'. The door was answered by a woman Molly said would be the priest's housekeeper. The priest was old, so was his soutane. Shabby and old-looking, more green than black in places. He smiled welcomingly when they said why they had come and invited them into the parlour. Its smell

reminded her of her convent, a holy smell of flowers and polish and a faint whiff of incense.

While he talked and asked questions Father Dillon took the measure of the couple. The girl very young, good clothes, educated, well mannered. And the arrogant lancer, with a local accent overlaid by a veneer of others picked up in his travels. A well up man wise in the ways of the world. Not what he considered a couple suited to each other.

'So, tell me now,' he asked, 'how come you are being married here and not at home?' His question was addressed to Molly.

'I ran away, Father. I fell in love with Bert and ran away. But I brought my baptismal lines.'

She handed him the certificate. 'Sit down, my child. And you too, sir.' He put on his glasses and read the lines then looked at Molly. 'You're too young. You're only seventeen. I can't marry you without your father's or guardian's consent. Even if you were of age there'd be a lot of questions I'd have to ask first about your intended husband if he isn't a Catholic?'

'I am not,' Bert said in a manner that seemed to make the reply boastful.

'I take it you both want to get married? No doubts, nothing like that?'

'Oh, no, Father, I really love Bert. More than anything in the world I want to marry him.'

May God look down on you, Father Dillon thought. But maybe I'm midsjudging the man. And I've no right to do that when I've only this minute laid eyes on him.

'Bert, has Molly explained anything to you about mixed marriages?'

'She has. She's told me you don't approve of or encourage them but do allow them.'

'That's right, we do allow them providing you fulfil certain conditions. There's promises you'd have to make.'

'She didn't say about promises. What sort of promises?'

'That you'll do nothing to hinder her practising her religion, and that any children born of your union will be brought up as Catholics.'

Bert shrugged and said, 'That sounds fair enough.'

'It needs serious thought,' the priest said.

'If I give my word, I keep it.'

'I'm sure you do.'

'Would you write to my father and ask for permission?' Molly said.

'You wouldn't do it yourself?'

'What proof could I give him that I was marrying in a Catholic church if I wrote?'

'I will then. D'ye want me to let him know where you're staying? By the way, where are you staying?'

'With Bert's family.'

'And what do they think of the runaway match?'

'They won't come to the wedding, that's because they are Protestants. Like us at home not going into Protestant churches. But they're going to give us a wedding breakfast.'

'So they're not against it?'

'No, Father,' Molly said.

'I'll write to your father. You didn't say if you wanted me to let him have your address?'

'I don't think so.'

'Why not, child?'

'I think he might come over and try to make me leave Bert. Go back to Dublin.'

'Then I'll say nothing about where you're staying. I'd like you both to come in a few times during the week and we'll talk things over. The instructions for you, Bert. Make sure you fully understand the promises. And you, Molly, the part you must play in a mixed marriage.'

'I'm going back to barracks the day after tomorrow. I can't come in,' Bert said.

'Would you be willing to see the Catholic padre there?'

'That'd be fine.'

'Where are you stationed?'

'Aldershot.'

'I know the priest there well, a Kerryman like myself, we were in the seminary together. I'll drop him a line. You'll come in to see me, Molly, during the week? One of the days while you're here the letter from your father may come.'

They thanked the priest and took their leave of him after agreeing that Molly would come on Monday and Friday evening.

On the way back to Bert's home Molly asked did he really not mind about the promises? And truthfully he said: 'I don't mind at all.' So long as he married her, got money out of her father, his children could be brought up as Quakers, Jews, Muslims or Holy Romans, it made no difference to him. And if she wanted to go to her church, as long as it didn't interfere with his pleasure or comfort, why should he care? And in any case, what would anyone do if he didn't keep the promises? It was not as if he could be arrested or slung in jail. A load of old rubbish, religion, all of it.

'Have you heard the latest? Molly McCarthy's run away with a soldier.' The news spread like wildfire. In drawing-rooms all over Dublin, in clubs, in barristers' chambers, anywhere and everywhere the McCarthys were known.

During the second week after Molly had run away a letter came in a large envelope. The writing was unfamiliar and there was an English postmark. Michael opened it. Inside was a folded sheet of writing paper and a sealed smaller envelope. Unfolding the notepaper he read the address: Saint John the Evangelist, Roman Catholic Church, Springfield Road, Horsham, West Sussex. Father Dillon had written:

Your daughter and a young man, Herbert Talbot, have

asked me to marry them. They are determined to marry. However your daughter is under age and needs your consent. I am writing to ask you if you will give it?

I know of the circumstances which brought her to England and am sorry for you and your family. Marriages such as theirs I am never happy to celebrate. In the case of Marianne, if you refuse your consent I won't have to. But I must tell you this: they seem determined on marrying. And as the young man is a Protestant they may go to his church. The law of the land would apply there also, but a sympathetic vicar might well seek the permission of his Bishop to perform the ceremony.

It is my advice that you should come here, see your daughter and persuade her to wait for some time before marrying. The man concerned is several years older than her, and I would judge him to be experienced in the ways of the world. It is possible that he is wielding an undue influence on her.

I have made discreet inquiries about his family. They are law-abiding, decent hardworking people: smallholders, butchers, blacksmiths, that sort of thing. Well liked and respected, as is the son involved with your daughter. However, he left here at fifteen to join the army so it is anyone's guess as to how he has behaved since then. And it is not within my power to seek references for his character from the army.

Looking forward to hearing from you.

Yours in Christ,

Seamus Dillon, Parish Priest

Michael put the letter to one side and removed the small envelope from the larger one. It was addressed to him in Molly's writing.

Dearest Papa and Mama,

Please forgive me for what I have done. I am so sorry. As

I write this I am crying. I miss you all so much. Sometimes when I cannot sleep I wish I had never met Bert and that none of this had ever happened. I wish that I was at home in my own room, in my own bed. But try to understand: I love Bert. I know that I am only seventeen, but Mama wasn't much older when she met you, and your courtship wasn't easy. I remember Mama telling me that Grandfather McCarthy didn't want you to marry her. That you had a falling out. But you really loved each other and still do after all the years. I know it will be the same for me and Bert.

Won't you please come to my wedding? If only I could be sure of your reaction I would come home to be married. That is what I would really like. To be married in the University Church on the Green with you and Mama and all my family round me.

If you won't agree to this, please give me your permission to get married here? I know that if you refuse I will surely die. But whatever you decide, I will always love you.

Molly

P.S. Mama, could you pick out some clothes and under-wear? I have almost nothing to wear. And send some tablets of my special soap. The soap in Bert's house is what we use for the laundry at home. My skin is all blotchy. And I'm so sorry for taking the locket from your jewellery box. I know Papa bought it for me when I was born but that I wasn't supposed to have it until I was twenty-one. I wanted it because you had worn it and when I wear it it makes me feel close to you. And your nightgown I took for the same reason, and to bring me luck in my marriage.

The letter hadn't moved Michael but the postscript made him cry. It was the writing of a child, with all a child's innocence, trust and naivety. He spent the next hour remembering her as such. The delight she had given him. The hopes he had cherished for her. Her birth. The fears he had had for her often outweighing the hopes.

He began to toy with the idea of inviting her to come home and bring the man. Trying persuasion as the priest had advised. And if it didn't work, allowing them to marry at home. Perhaps he could buy the fellow out of the army. Set him up in something. At least that way he wouldn't lose her completely. She would be in Ireland where he could ensure that things went well for her. Wasn't that all that mattered in the long run, that she was safe and well?

He had it almost settled in his mind. Was thinking what he would say in reply to her letter. Imagining her face, her smile when she received it. Imagining Nicole's relief that Molly was restored to them, and Fanny's and Nell's reaction.

And then a voice within his head asked. 'Have you lost your senses? Bring her home! Bring him with her! Someone, your own daughter, so callous that she left without a word. So devious that she plotted and planned the whole affair. Sending you and her mother demented. Made you the laughing stock of Dublin. Your daughter running away with a soldier. A common soldier. The scum of the earth as Wellington, whose men they were, described them. Forgive her indeed! Where's your pride, McCarthy?'

He crumpled Molly's letter and tossed it on the fire. Then wrote to the priest, refusing his consent. As he was about to seal the letter he asked himself, Why am I refusing? Let her marry him. Make her bed and lie on it. I never want to see her again. She will never be allowed over this threshold.

Michael's second letter to Father Dillon was brief. He thanked him for writing, for his concern, and gave his consent to the marriage.

Later in the day he told Nicole about the letter that had come from England. 'From a priest no less, asking for my permission that our daughter could marry.'

'You didn't give it, Michael?'

He ignored Nicole's question. 'That wasn't all that was in the envelope. She had enclosed a letter.'

'Molly! You've had a letter from Molly? Oh, thank God. Is she safe and well? Let me have it. Let me read it.'

'I burnt hers and sent my consent.'

'Not even you would do such a thing,' she said, but in her heart she knew this changeling of a husband was capable of such a thing. 'You're a monster,' she shouted when he didn't deny burning the letter. 'You destroyed her letter and gave your permission for her to marry? You're inhuman.'

Tears of rage were rolling down her face. He stood like a statue, unmoved. 'I used to think you loved her more than me. Sometimes I was a little jealous. But you didn't love her, me, not one of us. No one except yourself. You are and always will be a peasant at heart. What concerns you is not that Molly may be about to ruin her life, but that people will know. Already know. You're still the country-man with the closed mind. Don't show. Let no one know our business. Keep it in the family. Don't let anyone point the finger. You poor fool! Don't you know you've been an object of ridicule for years? A drunk. How many briefs d'ye get nowadays?

'I want to know where she is. I want to know what she said.' Her voice rose to a scream. 'Don't stand there looking at me with a sneer on your face. Tell me! She's my child, I have a right to know.'

He remained silent.

'I hate you. You've destroyed this family. I wish you were dead.'

Then he spoke. 'So do I. But while I live, in my presence you, Fanny and Nell will never mention her name. There can be no contact with her for only I know where she is. Maybe she'll write to the parish priest or her school, appealing for them to mediate. Their approaches will be ignored. Her confederates, the servants, are scattered –

where she won't know. And until the day I die, if it means crawling down the stairs, I'll inspect the post each morning. Do you understand?'

Thinking how she wished for the strength to kill him, to have a weapon to do so, Nicole walked to the window and looked out. He followed her and stood close, repeating his question, his voice hoarse with rage. 'Answer me!'

'I understand,' she said, and continued staring into the park. Although it was still summer she saw that the leaves were gradually changing colour. She heard him go from the room, the door slam, and still she stayed gazing down into the park.

Last night Molly had said a decade of the Rosary that her mother or father would answer her letter, tell her to come home and bring Bert. They would love her to be married in Dublin. She finished her beads, asking, 'And please, Blessed Virgin Mary, if they don't, let Papa give his consent and Mama send on my clothes. I can't be married in what I've got. And send the soap, I know I could buy some in Horsham only I haven't any money. Well, I have what Aggie stitched into my stays but I don't want to break into that. If I told him, I'm sure Bert would buy me clothes and soap, but I don't know if he has much money. His family don't seem to have. Or if they do, don't spend it on the things we do at home. So please intercede for me.'

Now, as she neared the Presbytery, she looked hot and slightly dishevelled for her clothes, meant for town living, were looking the worse for her country lifestyle, and her hair, through being washed with the coarse soap, had lost much of its bounce and gloss. She felt sick with nervousness as she waited for her knock to be answered. Knowing it was possible a reply to their letters might have arrived.

'Your father has given his consent. The letter came this morning,' Father Dillon told her after his housekeeper had shown her into the parlour.

'Oh, thank you, thank you so much. Bert will be delighted. Did Papa answer mine?'

'No, but I expect he will soon. Perhaps you should write another and this time give the Talbots' address?'

'Yes,' she said, 'I will. He may have been offended that I didn't give it.'

'Perhaps. Sit down, you look tired.'

Molly smiled. 'I don't sleep that well. The bed's not very comfortable and Annie – Bert's sister – snores. And she's a big girl so I'm a bit cramped.'

'Ah,' said the priest, 'I know all about the aggravation of snoring. I had a brother whose snores shook the rafters. Would you like a glass of lemonade?'

'No, thanks, I'm grand.'

Father Dillon thought, Indeed, you look far from grand. For someone who's just received the news they wanted, your look is one of dejection.

He wasn't happy about this marriage, and he had tried to convey so to her father in his letter. Maybe I should have said so outright instead of only dropping half hints? he thought.

He watched her fidget with her hair and every so often clear her throat and wondered what she had written in the letter home. Did she beg forgiveness, their acceptance of Bert? To go home and be married there? How he wished her father had not given his consent. But he had and so he must continue to talk to her about the Sacrament of Marriage. 'You, Molly, as the Catholic partner must do all in your power, by word and example, to bring Bert into the Catholic Religion. That means no backsliding, no missing Mass, for that wouldn't be much of an example. You must be tolerant and patient. Live your life as a good Catholic. Do you understand and promise all of that?'

'Yes, Father, I do. Thank you.'

'God bless you, child.' He made the sign of the cross then showed her out. He watched her walking away and said to

himself, If you were my daughter I'd be over here this minute and drag you home by the scruff of the neck.

On the morning Molly was to be married Annie gave her a tissue-wrapped parcel. In it were three tablets of scented toilet soap, one pale pink, one cream, and a lavender-coloured one.

'Oh, Annie, you shouldn't! You're so kind. I've been longing for soap. Thank you very much.'

Annie blushed as she went about removing her clothes to the parlour where she would sleep for the two nights Bert was home. 'You're lucky getting our Bert. He's the best-looking and the nicest. I know you'll be happy. I wish it was me.'

'You'll soon find someone,' Molly assured her. 'When we have our house in Aldershot you can visit. You'll probably find a gorgeous handsome man there.'

'D'ye think so?'

'Of course I do.'

All the time she talked she was thinking about the coming night when she and Bert would be in bed. Thinking of his kisses and how he would fondle her breasts, kiss them and her nipples. She wasn't sure what would follow that, but recalling the sensations she experienced when he did those things, was sure whatever it was would be just as wonderful. Probably what Phyllis had whispered about: a man putting his hand up her skirt and touching her private parts. Bert had never attempted anything like that. But once they were married she was sure he would. And she wasn't frightened. It wouldn't be a sin. She was only a little bit sad, she thought, because no one belonging to her would be at the wedding. Sad and disappointed that her mother or father, Fanny and Nell, hadn't written. And surprised most of all that her clothes hadn't been sent on. Bert's mother had sponged and pressed the turquoise suit. It hadn't been a great success but would have to do. She'd

wear the locket and hope no one would notice the stain on her skirt.

When they came back from the church the relations had arrived. Some brought presents and some gave Bert small amounts of money. There were casks of cider and beer and plates of meat, ham and chicken, and bowls of trifle. Everyone was in great humour and wished her and Bert a long and happy life and that all their troubles should be little ones.

As the day went on Bert spent more time drinking and talking to the men. She felt lonely and left out. The women were kind and included her in their conversations. She still found their accents hard to understand and in any case, after laughing and joking about first nights, they tended to talk about relations who lived too far away to come to the wedding.

It was midnight before they went to bed. Bert was very drunk as, with an arm holding her too tightly, he led Molly from the room and the uncles called advice after him.

'I'll have to go down the back,' he said at the bedroom door, and kissed her, forcing open her mouth and his tongue into it. His breath reeked of drink and tobacco. She didn't like the smell but even so became aroused by the passion of the kiss. She hurried to undress and wished there had been a long looking glass to see herself in her mother's nightgown. She was in bed when Bert returned.

'Blow the candle out or we'll have them buggers looking in.' He got in beside her. 'My little wife,' he said. 'Little Molly Malone from Dublin's fair city.'

He got on top of her, reached down in the bed and pulled up her nightdress. With his knee he parted her legs. For a very short time one of his hands stayed between them, groping for something, and when he found what he was looking for he thrust something inside her. And again and again he thrust, and she bit her lip so as not to scream. Quicker and quicker he moved until, with a great shudder,

236

he lay like a dead weight on her and fell asleep, not hearing her moans of agony.

She rolled him off her and his snoring filled the room. She lay in the dark with tears spilling from her eyes and, although she wasn't aware what it was, blood oozing from her torn vagina. Was this, she wondered, how it was supposed to be? Was this how it would always be? And then she wanted to pee. Carefully, in case he should waken and do it again, she got out of bed and from under it pulled out the chamber pot. Her nightdress was wet. She lifted it and even in the dark, by the feel and the smell, a faint smell like iron, knew the wetness was blood. Was it the curse come early? Forgetting her urge to pee, she groped her way round the room to the drawer where her underwear was and took the first thing that came to hand which was a camisole. It hurt to walk. Down there it hurt and throbbed. She felt as if she was on fire. The curse wasn't like that. She went to the chamber pot and squatted to pee, which at first wouldn't come and when it did burnt and stung, making her want to cry out. Holy Mary Mother of God, she silently prayed, don't let me. Annie's just down the stairs, I'd waken her. But most of all she was afraid of wakening Bert.

She replaced the pot, and folding the camisole, put it between her legs, holding it in position until she was in the bed where she lay as close to the edge and as far away from her husband as she safely could.

Chapter Twenty-four

FOR a year after Molly left Nicole appeared to have lost her mind. She took little interest in her appearance and daily walked the streets of Dublin searching for Aggie and Phyllis. They knew the name of the man Molly had run away with, knew what he looked like. With his name and description she would go to every barracks in the city, to everyone in the country, seeking him. She could go to England if necessary. Find him. Find Molly. Bring them home.

She went down area steps, knocked at kitchen doors and asked maids and cooks. No one knew Aggie or Phyllis. At the house where Phyllis had been employed there was a sympathetic cook who brought her in, sat her down and gave her a cup of tea.

'The doctor and his family went to America to live and their servants were scattered,' she told Nicole.

Sometimes she forgot to eat, to comb her hair or wash her face. Sometimes she forgot which street she had already been to and called again. Servants, spying on her said, 'It's that poor madwoman, don't open the door. God look down on her, she'll be arrested one of these days or finish up in the asylum.'

During this time when Nicole was doing her obsessive searching it was Fanny who ran the house, engaged the servants. They seldom stayed for long. Objecting to working for a man who roamed the house permanently drunk, mumbling to himself; a woman who left at the crack of dawn and didn't return until late into the night. 'No,'

they would say to each other, 'I'm not staying in this place. I never came across such queer goings on. And on top of everything else taking orders from a frosty-faced bit of a child.'

Fanny saw them come and go and envied them their freedom to do so. Envied Molly wherever she was, and Nell escaping for hours at a time to school. Many times she contemplated running away. Leaving the house that grew dirtier and dustier, the kitchen that smelled of congealed grease and mice, ashes and cinders in grates not properly cleaned. Brass and silver turning black and green.

Often to console herself when servants absconded, when the burden of shopping and cooking became hers and all her coaxing of Nicole to eat had failed, she made plans to go. Find a room in Dublin, run away to England. Otherwise, she told herself, I'll spend the rest of my life here. My matriculation a waste of time. Matriculation with honours in every subject. My hopes of becoming a doctor so many castles in the air. But if I left I could find work, save and pay my own way. In Dublin I'd be accepted in Cecilia Street or there's the Elizabeth Garrett Anderson in London.

And then she would realize that these thoughts were fantasies, never to become reality. For who, if she went, would care for her mother? Nell, at sixteen couldn't be relied on to make her bed, much less anything more responsible. Apart from sitting and holding her mother's hand and crying in sympathy with her over the loss of Molly, Nell was useless. Even her despised father had to have food provided which he seldom ate.

She missed Molly, worried about her, but not every minute of the day. Molly at least had had a choice and took it. Like a bird she had flown and was probably having the time of her life. So Fanny didn't dwell too often on her, didn't shed too many tears.

James was the only visitor these days. Keeping her

239

company when her mother was out roaming the streets, her father shut in his study incoherent with drink. And he gave her heart with his optimistic view that things couldn't get any worse, that one day they would improve. That eventually her father would relent and tell Nicole where it was the priest's letter had come from asking for consent to Molly's marriage. Then Molly would be found, all forgiven, and life return to normal.

One evening when she and James were talking he said, 'Miracles do happen,' looking at this beautiful girl so like her mother when she first came to Dublin. 'Every day miracles happen somewhere in the world.'

And every day, he thought, I pray for one that will restore this family to its former happiness and selfishly ask especially for Nicole's sake that God may intervene.

Seeing her as she had become broke his heart. She had been transformed into a spiritless broken creature, wandering the streets, knocking on doors, sometimes to have them slammed in her face. He had witnessed such a scene accidentally on his way to the Law Library, walking up Mountjoy Square. He saw her in front of him and watched as she made her way down some area steps to the servants' quarters. She had, he guessed, been taken for a beggar or a madwoman and he wanted to run down the steps and rescue her. Pick her up, hail a cab, and take her to his home where he would care for her. But aware of how embarrassed his even recognizing her would make her, he desisted and hurriedly walked on.

One day while wandering the city on her fruitless search Nicole thought of Julia. She remembered Michael telling her Julia had only been involved in Molly's earlier deception, had known nothing about the soldier or the elopement. But supposing she had? The servants lived out of each other's pockets. She might know or remember something that would give a clue. In any case she was Nicole's last hope. There were two places where she could

contact her: at her in-laws' in Stonybatter or the Crowley home in Ballydurkin.

Nicole had eaten nothing since the previous night. She seldom felt hungry any more. Her light head and periods of confusion she didn't connect with lack of food. By the Ballast Office clock she saw that it was a quarter to four as she began the walk along the quays to Stonybatter. There were many shabby, unkempt, thin, distracted-looking women walking along her side of the quays. No one gave them or Nicole a second glance.

She was very tired and her head muzzy so that now and then she stopped by the Liffey wall, pretending an interest in the swans, seagulls and flowing water as she rested for a while.

Then strange things began to happen. In the water she saw Molly. She saw two Mollys. One a little girl, swimming, laughing and waving at her, and one a grown up girl looking as her mother had last seen her. Only now her mouth was open and she screamed as the seagulls swooped to peck at her eyes. 'Mama, Mama,' Nicole heard her cry, 'help me, Mama! Please help me!'

Summoning what little strength she had, Nicole hoisted herself on to the wall and jumped into the Liffey.

When by midnight her mother hadn't come home, Fanny tried rousing her father from a chair in his study where he slept in a drunken stupor. She shook him, called his name, shook him again. He opened his eyes, looked at her blankly. She told him her mother hadn't returned and how late it was. He mumbled something then fell asleep again. Leaving him, she ran to Nell's room and woke her. 'I don't know what to do. She has never stayed away so long. Oh, Nell, I'm so frightened.'

'Ring Uncle James, he'll know,' said Nell as she got out of bed.

'Supposing he's out?'

'We won't know that until we telephone. You make some tea and I'll do it.' Nell, for the first time ever in her life, was in charge. James was in and promised to come at once. Fanny and Nell dressed while they waited for him. 'He'll want a description of what Mama was wearing. Do you remember?' Fanny did and Nell told her to write it down. 'And the turquoise locket – that's very important.'

'You make it sound as if something terrible has happened to her,' Fanny said, and Nell saw that she was trembling. Fanny whom she had always thought so cool, calm and collected. 'Please God nothing has,' she said, putting an arm round her older sister, 'but the more information we give, the easier it will be to find her. She could have lost her memory, be walking round in a daze. It doesn't mean her life is in danger though,' she said, and prayed silently that it wasn't.

When James arrived, first he tried rousing Michael and when that failed, began to ring round the hospitals. The fourth told him that a woman dressed as he described Mrs McCarthy had been admitted that afternoon. There was no identification except the Christian names of a man and a woman on a locket.

'That's her,' James said. 'I'm coming over right away.' There was a pause and then he spoke again. 'No, I am not her husband. He is indisposed. I'm a close family friend, and I'll be bringing her two daughters.'

'Is she dead?' Fanny asked. 'Oh, please God, don't let her be dead. It's all my fault. Sometimes I get so annoyed and impatient with her and wish she would die. I hate her for what she's doing to herself.'

'Your mother isn't dead. Nell, fetch something warm for you both to wear. You mama's fine. We're going straight away to see her. So wipe your eyes and don't blame yourselves. You've been wonderful to her. There's absolutely nothing to reproach yourselves with.'

They set out, hoping that along the way an empty cab

might come, but each one that passed was occupied. 'Never mind,' James said, 'Jervis Street isn't too far, we'll take the short cuts.' They went along the Green and Grafton Street, turned into Dame Street then down into Temple Bar and crossed the Ha'penny Bridge. Up Liffey Street, their pace increased as they neared the hospital in Jervis Street. A nurse greeted James and told the girls they were to come with her while Mr Farrell spoke to the doctor. 'I'll make you some cocoa and afterwards you can see your mother. Come along now,' she said in a brisk authoritative manner. 'You too, Mr Farrell. Dr Mangan's room is on the way.'

There was something familiar about the doctor's face, James thought, as he listened to what he had to say. 'She was very lucky. A young man pulled her out. Went in fully clothed, could have drowned himself. She's fine now, you can see her in a minute. The poor woman. What drove her to it, I wonder?'

'You're not suggesting she attempted suicide?'

'It looks like it.'

'She isn't that sort of person.'

'All sorts of people commit suicide, Mr Farrell.'

'But not Nicole, never Nicole.'

'You think she went in for a swim? Don't I know your face?'

Ignoring the question, James continued with his defence of Nicole. 'There are metal ladders down the walls of the quays. She may have dropped something and foolishly tried to retrieve it. A bag or a purse, perhaps.'

'Possible but unlikely,' Dr Mangan said, still studying James's face intently.

'Weren't there any witnesses?'

'You can be sure the path was thronged, but the Irish, as you know, are never eager to come forward once police are on the scene.'

'What about the man who saved her?'

'He vanished. People know attempted suicide is a crime

though rarely is anyone prosecuted. Who'd want to add more misery to an unfortunate who tried it? I know who you are – James Farrell, we were at Clongowes together. You were friends with Michael McCarthy. I was a few years younger so never had anything to do with you. Just saw you around. The woman – she's a McCarthy.'

'Michael's wife.'

'The French girl?'

'Yes,' said James. 'The French girl.'

'My girls were in school with the one who ran away. Terrible business that. Might have a bearing on what happened?'

'Probably,' James admitted.

'And Michael gone to the dogs. Such a waste. Such a brilliant fellow. What in the name of God happened to him? I worshipped him at school. Where is he now, by the way?'

'Indisposed.'

'A polite way of putting it! Don't worry about the attempted suicide, I'll fix that. She took a notion into her head to feed the swans and went halfway down the ladder to stop the gulls robbing them. The police won't believe it of course but on my say-so they will pretend they do. We'll go and see her now and collect the girls on the way.'

She was asleep in a small room. Like a little child who had been put to bed without its hair being brushed. It lay in snarls on the pillow.

'They'll tidy her up in the morning,' Dr Mangan said softly, so as not to waken her. 'Sleep and feeding is what she needs. We'll keep her in for a day or two. But as you can see, girls, your mama is fine. No need to worry about her. We'll leave her now. Come back tomorrow.'

Outside the ward James thanked him. 'I'm very grateful. You're a brick.'

Dr Mangan shrugged. 'A favour for an old school friend. She'll want minding. See what you can do with her

husband. A runaway daughter is bad enough. Coupled with McCarthy in the state I believe he is permanently in, it is enough to make anyone contemplate suicide.'

To be sure of finding Michael sober, James spent the rest of the night in his study and confronted him the minute he woke. Through the hours while he had waited he recalled what Nicole had endured at the hands of his friend. His beautiful Nicole whom he remembered as a young trusting girl. A child really when she had first met and fell in love with Michael. Looking at the bloated unshaven face of him, snoring in his chair, James entertained murderous thoughts. How could Michael inflict such pain on her? Give permission for Molly to marry, destroy her letter, not reveal to her mother where she was, who or where the priest was who had written asking for his consent to the marriage? The man had to be deranged.

Michael stirred, shifted his position, and presented another view of his face. And seeing it, James saw another Michael. His friend. His champion. He and Nicole in love and happy for a great many years. And he asked himself what had changed him? Brought him to where he was now? Something, though what James didn't know, obviously drove him to drink.

He would do everything possible to make him stop. He hoped that his friend still loved Nicole enough for the shock of her attempted suicide to start him on the road to sobriety.

James watched him waken. Saw his bleary bloodshot eyes look at the clock on the mantelpiece, saw him with difficulty get up from his chair, turn towards the door, and the surly expression on his face as he asked, 'What in the name of God are you doing here? Watching me, spying on me?'

'I've been here all night. I want you to come down to the kitchen with me and drink pints of black coffee. And I don't want you to raise your voice or cause a scene. What I

have to tell you is serious. The girls have also been up half the night, may still be awake, and I don't want them to hear this.' James took hold of his arm. 'Once we're in the basement, I'll tell you.'

'Nicole in hospital! Threw herself into the Liffey! Jesus, Mary and Joseph, where is she? I have to see her.' The news and the strong black coffee had quickly sobered Michael.

'You can't see her until later. She's grand now. Well, as grand as she'll ever be unless you do as I suggest.' James saw a truculent expression replace the surprised, frightened one on Michael's face. He had intended laying down many conditions but knew he would have to go easy in the beginning. No recriminations about having given his consent to the marriage. No demands to know where Molly or the priest were. He would concentrate on the drinking.

James poured more coffee for both of them and then told him the details of what had happened to Nicole. He listened with his head held in his hands, the mug of coffee ignored.

'The Liffey,' he kept repeating. 'Nicole threw herself into the Liffey. Oh, Jesus, James, how will I ever face her? It's like a nightmare.'

He was crying. James had never seen him cry before. 'I'll do anything to make it up to her. Tell me and I'll do it. Are you sure she's all right? You wouldn't lie to me? Oh, James, I'm so sorry. And the girls, poor Fanny and Nell. What have I done to them?'

'Nothing that can't, with time and a tremendous effort on your part, be put right. I know you. I know your strength, your courage, your determination, and know that if you set your mind to it, you'll pull through.

'This afternoon I want you to come to Church Street with me. There's a priest there with great gifts of understanding. Talk to him. Take the Pledge. That will be

246

the beginning of your road back. From there we'll go to the hospital. Jervis Street is only a stone's throw. Will you do that for Nicole's sake, Michael?'

'Willingly, but for how long will I be able to keep it? I've tried before.'

'I know that. Now you'll try again. Maybe you'll break this one too. But you'll keep on trying.'

'I will. Oh, God, I will. To think I drove her to that. I never meant to, James, you've got to believe that. There's things you don't know about me. Terrible things that make me believe I am going mad. Things I could tell no one, not Nicole, not you, my best, my only friend. That's why I drink. But I'll beat them. I will. I won't let them defeat me and destroy my family.

'Shall I tell you? Shall I tell you something I've believed for years? Something that has made me a drunkard. Addled my mind. Stopped me raising a finger to get Molly back. Blinded me to the wrong I've done Fanny. Helped me to push Nicole to the brink of suicide. Will you listen?'

And he told James about Mag Cronin's curse. The story took a long time to relate. Sometimes during it Michael broke down and cried again. When at last it was finished James asked, 'Why did you never confide in me?'

'You'd have thought me mad.'

'Then why tell me now?'

'Because I don't believe in it any more. The truth came to me suddenly. A revelation. An opening of my eyes to the realities of life. I almost lost Nicole, and if I had it would have been my own fault, not the empty words of a madwoman.

'I've had moments in the past when I came to similar conclusions but they lasted no time. This is different. I can feel the change in myself. It's as though an enormous weight has been lifted from me.' Michael lit another cigarette, inhaled deeply before continuing: 'And it's thanks

to you and Almighty God. He has answered my prayers at last. Shown me the way.

'I will go to Nicole in hospital and tell her everything – after we've seen the priest.'

Chapter Twenty-five

AFTER her wedding night Molly made excuses for how Bert had treated her. He had drunk too much; it wouldn't be like that the next time. Nevertheless she was relieved when he decided to return to camp without spending a further night with her. Making excuses that as another get together of the relations was planned, he could easily get too drunk, oversleep and miss the first train out the next morning.

'I don't want that, not to be on a charge, maybe have my pay stopped, not now that I'm a married man.'

His mother, father and brothers agreed he was wise. Molly said nothing, afraid that whatever she said her tone of voice would have revealed her thankfulness that she wouldn't have to endure another punishing experience. Afraid that she would have had to refuse, no matter what the consequence. No one had remarked on how obviously painful she found it to walk, though once or twice she thought Bert's mother was watching each time she had to move about the room.

'That sofa's very hard, so if it's all right with you, I'll come back in the bed?' Annie said. Molly hadn't known what to do with the blood-saturated sheet and had left it on the bed. When Annie saw it, without commenting she left the room and returned with her mother.

'Did you come on during the night, dear?' she asked.

Molly said she hadn't, she wasn't due for another two weeks. 'That's more than there should be, that's a lot of

blood. Were you hurt? Down there – are you torn? Don't be shy with me, love, I only want to help.'

Blushing, not able to meet the woman's eyes, she admitted that she thought so. 'It hurts when I walk and pass water, and I'm still bleeding when I pass water.'

'Men,' Mrs Talbot said. 'Some are like wild things, especially if they've been drinking and my Bert's a big man. In the heat of the moment they've little consideration. Don't think so bad of him. You'll get better and learn a trick or two. Annie, fetch a clean sheet then bring in the bath and put water on to boil.'

Annie brought the sheet and then dragged in a tin bath. While she removed the soiled sheet, Mrs Talbot talked. 'You'll have to sit in the bath and then I'll give you a greasy ointment. It'll help you to heal. And afterwards, you know when you and Bert are ... well, you know, use it beforehand. It's an age old remedy round here. A few old women make it and pass on the secret to their daughters. Everyone knows the bulk of it is from sheep's wool. The herbs are the secret. Brides with impatient husbands and women on and after the change find it a blessing. I'll get you a supply of it before you go to Aldershot.'

Several cups of salt were tipped into the bath and Molly had to sit in it for an hour with Annie or Mrs Talbot adding hot water from time to time. The salt stung and she cried out.

'That won't last. Salt is the great cure-all. Bear it now like a good girl. You'll feel better tomorrow.'

She did, well enough to walk into Horsham. Intending to see the priest. Tell him about the brutality she had suffered. Tell him how she had felt that Bert was punishing her, not loving her. Tell him she thought she had made a mistake. But as she neared the church her nerve failed. How could she talk to a priest about such things? It had been embarrassing enough admitting to Bert's mother that she had been hurt. And hadn't the priest warned her of the

trials married couples had to go through? Maybe what had happened on her wedding night was just one of the trials.

She turned round and walked back, her mind more concerned with why her mother had not written or sent on her clothes. Mama was so fastidious. She must realize how little underwear, how little of anything, Molly had brought with her.

Bert wouldn't get down for at least a month. She wasn't sorry. Although she missed his presence, her fear of another brutal act was greater. She helped about the house. Pegged out washing, fed the hens, collected eggs, and swept the red-tiled floor. Mrs Talbot wasn't a fussy housekeeper, saying often, 'So long as the beds and clothes are clean and food on the table, there's no rush about floors or windows or such like.' So Molly's afternoons were free. Free to write endless letters to her mother, father, sisters, and ones to the house where Phyllis had worked. And free to watch and wait for the post by which a reply never came.

Some nights she cried herself to sleep after thinking of the predicament in which she had landed herself. Some nights she made her mind up to take the money from her stays and run back to Dublin. Throw herself on her father's mercy, and as she had in her first letter and every one since, beg forgiveness.

At other times she told herself that she had only been here a short while. That when next Bert came it would be different. That really she loved him.

Every day Michael fought his battle against drink. It began as soon as he woke with a throbbing head, a dry mouth, and throughout his body a trembling sensation. He felt as wretched as if he had filled himself with alcohol the previous night and knew from long experience that the only instant cure was 'a hair of the dog'. There were mornings when he succumbed to the temptation but they were few for always to the forefront of his mind was

Nicole's attempted suicide and the fear that if he failed to keep the Pledge she might try a second time and succeed.

But as days then weeks and months passed so did his withdrawal symptoms and craving for drink diminish. Though never so completely that, passing a public house on the way to his chambers, the waft of porter released into the morning air did not fill him again with a longing for whiskey, brandy, wine, porter . . . anything would do. And he carried on a dialogue in his mind: 'A small whiskey, just the one, would put me right. I have the willpower to stop after one.' But he kept on walking. Having come far enough along the road of almost complete abstinence to know that what he told himself wasn't the truth.

Since dismissing the servants he had got rid of his beautiful pair of matched bays. Dublin was a compact city, the majority of places within walking distance. His chambers were a pleasant stroll away across the river. He enjoyed walking. Enjoyed the feeling of his health and strength being restored. He enjoyed mingling with the crowds, admiring the houses and buildings which for so long he had become oblivious to.

He no longer took briefs but was called on for opinions. Those of his colleagues who had liked and admired him rallied round, pleased to see his recovery.

Thoughts of Molly were seldom far from his mind. He questioned how he had handled the affair. Blamed himself. Doubted too his ban on Fanny's studying medicine. They were complex issues with which he was not yet ready to come to terms. In Molly's case his emotions swung from grief, pity and anger to bouts of rage that she had run away with a soldier. She whom he had adored. With Fanny it was different. Had she been less forceful, coaxed or pleaded her case, perhaps it could have been resolved. But Fanny was unlike either of his other daughters. Except for a couple of days after Nicole had come home from the hospital and she

had scarcely left her mother's side, Fanny was too self-contained for his liking.

But once Nicole was up and about her concern for her mother seemed to have evaporated. She spent her days either out walking or in her room, poring over textbooks. Being polite when she encountered him, a cold politeness that made him want to strike her for the satisfaction of getting a response. Nell, to whom he had never paid such attention, had turned up trumps. Practical and reliable, she it was who suggested that if they were ever again to have a decent, hardworking staff the house must first be thoroughly cleaned. 'For who,' she said, taking him and Nicole on a tour of the house, 'would want to work here?' Pointing out how months of neglect had left dust, dirt and grease everywhere. 'What we need is to employ a team of daily women to scrub, polish and scour. Pay them well. I'll supervise. And when the house looks like it used to, then we'll get permanent staff.' She was right. It had worked and once again there was a cook, two maids and a young girl who helped wherever she was required.

But what pleased Michael most of all was the change in Nicole. Her appetite restored. Looking lovely again. The affection and encouragement she gave him, though as yet he still slept in a separate room. But time and his complete conquering of his liking for drink would also see that come right.

The fear of the curse still haunted him. He had told the priest in Church Street of it in confession. The priest told him such things did not exist outside of the mind.

'You see it all round you. The fear of ploughing a field in which there is a rath. The dread of bringing the May into the house, throwing salt over your shoulder, never leaving by a door other than the one you entered a building by. Fear of black cats, black dogs. Hundreds and thousands of superstitions, so many I couldn't remember them all. The majority of people couldn't if you asked them.

'Your family has been most unfortunate. So are many more. Call it what you like: Fate, an accident, God's will with a purpose behind it. One that we may not be able to understand, but his will nonetheless. And that, as a Catholic, you must believe. To say put the whole thing out of your mind is easier said than done. But with Faith in God and constant prayer, you will succeed.'

Michael went to daily Mass, he received Communion more often than was obligatory, and he prayed. In the morning, at night, and many times during the course of his walks through the city. He seldom passed a church without going in and lighting a candle, or in some a votive lamp. And like his battle against drink, he came to believe the priest's words that with the help of God he could also win this one.

Each day Nicole wondered and hoped that it might be the one on which Michael spoke about Molly. Told her where the letters had come from so they could begin a search to find her. He didn't, and all too well aware of his struggle to remain sober, she never raised the subject, though not a day passed when Molly didn't occupy her thoughts.

They began to entertain once the house was in order. Small dinner parties to which James was always invited. As their closest friend he often came long before the appointed time. Sometimes Michael hadn't yet come back from a visit to a church where he was doing a Novena or visiting the priest in Church Street. Then Nicole would talk to James of her fears that all might not be going well with her daughter. 'I know she chose to run away. That it was a selfish thing to do. That she didn't consider the anguish it would cause the family. But that was her nature. Unthinking, impetuous, foolishly romantic. Making decisions without any thought for the consequences. I try to keep her in a separate compartment of my mind so that my grief and sorrow aren't

consuming every part of me, for that would be unfair to Fanny and Nell. They need me too.

'Poor Fanny with her dashed hopes. Friends she went to school with already in their first year of medicine. She doesn't complain, but I know what she is thinking. And though the hullabaloo has died down Nell is still affected by it. She gets fewer invitations to visit other girls' homes. People are afraid that, being Molly's sister, she might have a bad influence.' But now that she had met Dick she had hopes for her happiness.

James gave her sympathy and encouragement. Complimenting her on how well she was coping. How she was the mainstay of Michael's recovery and that soon he was bound to relent, tell her what she needed to know, and then Molly could be found. Helped if she was in difficulties. Perhaps she wasn't. She could have made the right choice and be happy with her Lancer. Eventually they could make their peace, be reunited.

As time passed and no news came from Molly's parents, Bert's hopes of a cushy little business faded. When he came to Horsham to see her, the first question he asked was if they had written? Then had she written, and was she pregnant? She came to dread his visits, knowing his reaction when she answered his questions. Told him she had written many times to everyone in Dublin, even to the address where Phyllis had worked, but got no replies. He taunted her. 'A lot they cared about you. Catholics: I thought they were supposed to be full of charity? Maybe you were only a maid after all, like your friend. Just another skivvy only better dressed. What proof did I have that your father was a barrister or that you lived in that posh house?'

Her instinct was to ask, 'Was that why you married me? I thought you loved me.' She didn't, having learned the hard way. Bert was an expert at hitting her where his blows left no marks. In the stomach with his balled fist, on her breasts,

between her shoulder blades if her back was turned. The first time after a punch landed on her stomach, winding her, he leant close and whispered, 'If you scream, I'll break your neck.' She didn't doubt that he was capable of such an act.

'No one in my family has ever not had a child. You're either a barren bitch or are getting rid of them. Taking the little black pills. Shoving crochet hooks up your cunt or Slippery Elm Bark. I know all the tricks, don't think I don't.'

She kept silent and thanked God she had never conceived. How could she have love for a child of Bert's? She might just as well lie down in the road and open her legs to the first passing man. Even he might treat her with more gentleness. And there was another reason she thanked God for not becoming pregnant. One day she would leave Bert.

As yet it was only a hazy idea, begging many questions. What would she do for money? Where would she go? How would she escape from Horsham without Annie or his mother noticing and talking her out of it? His mother and Annie who were so kind in their rough and ready way. Annie who, when Molly was undressing, had noticed the bruising. Comforted her. Told her lots of men beat their wives. Sometimes the women didn't mind. It was, some said, a proof of love. And in any case, what could you do about it? He was your husband. He could do anything he liked to you.

Bert's mother rubbed another homemade salve over the bruised flesh, making excuses for him. He didn't know his own strength. Always was quick-tempered, but kind and good behind it all. He was probably jealous wondering what she got up to when he was back in barracks. She told Molly things would be better when she got a place in Aldershot. 'Twasn't natural for a young couple to be separated so.

Soon after the Boers declared war on England in

October 1899 his brothers joined the army. After their basic training they were sent to South Africa where Molly hoped and prayed Bert would finish up too. Be killed. Then her way out would be clear. But months went by and he was still in Aldershot and they were still waiting to be allocated a quarter.

Molly never grew to like Horsham. She missed Dublin. Missed the city to walk through: its lovely shops, the cafes where she went for coffee with her mother and sisters. She longed for good, pretty clothes, underwear, toiletries. She believed her skin was destroyed, and certainly her hands became rough and chapped. Cracks appeared in them after she had washed clothes in soda. Annie and her mother smeared them with lard or one of their homemade salves.

Bert came home on leave and for occasional weekends. She was never sorry to see him go, relieved that her body was her own until the next time. Free from his accusations of procured abortions and his latest threat of seeing her priest, telling him she was getting rid of his children and drawing his attention to her never going to Mass.

It wasn't a conscious decision to miss Mass. One Sunday Molly slept late and after that didn't go again. While the priest who had married her was still alive she felt guilty, remembering his kindness and the promise she had made as the Catholic partner to set a good example. Now she felt nothing, all her thoughts and energy focused on how she could safely leave her husband.

Bert was eventually allocated a married quarter. Immediately Molly heard, the rape, the beatings, seldom getting all or even a share of her fourpence a day married allowance, were wiped from her memory, romantic dreams taking their place. Bert really did love her. In the heat of the moment he was hasty. Drink made him so. Made him do and say all the bad things.

But once they had their own home, all that would change. He would be kind, loving and tender. Living in barracks was terrible. Sleeping above the stables – imagine the smell! – in a bed only six inches from the next one. And the bucket or vat, an enormous utensil anyway, in the barrack room where the men peed. Your food served in the same room, brought by the orderly on duty in big tins or pails, dished out, and having to eat it sitting on your bed. Was it any wonder he came to Horsham in bad humour?

All that would change. Molly would cook him delicious meals. Never say or do anything to aggravate him. Never disagree with him. Look after his clothes, pamper him. They would be blissfully happy. In Aldershot there would be plenty to do. Places to see, and shops, lots of interesting shops. And women of her own age to make friends with. Wives of men Bert knew. They could invite them in for supper and cards. She would also look after her appearance more. Buy olive oil to massage into her scalp and in no time her hair would be as glossy as ever it was. And she'd buy cream to rub into her hands and face, and keep her nails as they used to be. Bert would be proud of her.

Molly took a cab from Victoria to Waterloo, nervous and excited, afraid she would miss her train. Afraid she would get on the wrong one. Wondering how she looked. Would Bert like what she was wearing? Her turquoise suit and matching hat under a tan secondhand coat. It was, she thought, a most becoming coat, but warm and hadn't cost much. She would take it off when the train stopped at Aldershot.

On the right train but terrified of missing the station, she made a nuisance of herself in the carriage, enquiring frequently if Aldershot was the next station. Until an elderly man, out of either kindness or exasperation, said, 'I'll tell you as we approach it.'

And when he did she was up, lowering the strap, letting

down the window and craning out. Bert was there in all his glory and her heart leaped. My husband! My handsome husband! He's so gorgeous. Taller, broader, better-looking than any other man on the platform.

Bert greeted her with apparent pleasure, kissing and embracing her discreetly. Asking how her journey had been.

'It was sunny earlier on, but the rain has started so we'll get a cab,' he said, taking her arm and bag. She carried the small valise. Leant close to him, telling herself over and over, I'm here. We're together. Soon we'll be in our own home. She was as happy and hopeful as on the day she had received his note asking to meet her.

The cab's window steamed up. Molly wiped it with her handkerchief and looked out. Aldershot wasn't as she had imagined. Soldiers, soldiers everywhere. Some wearing the unfamiliar khaki, the colour of uniforms worn in the Boer War. Only small shops. Nothing interesting. It seemed a dull and dismal town, lacking such charm as even Horsham had. A sense of foreboding filled her. Had she made a mistake in coming here? It lasted no more than a few seconds, banished from her mind by Bert's presence.

'This here,' he said, as the cab turned into a long road, 'is Queen's Avenue.' She saw young leafless trees along either side of the Avenue. 'What sort of trees are they?' she asked.

'Horse chestnuts. In years to come they'll be a sight worth seeing. And that,' he pointed out a building, 'is the Louise Margaret Hospital. For women's complaints and babies.' She imagined having a baby, a son for Bert. How proud he would be.

They passed barrack blocks, including Bert's. Others being built. Large green open spaces. More barracks with large squares fronting them where squads of soldiers were drilling. And all along the Avenue more soldiers, mounted Lancers and artillery men.

But no shops, for women, children, or anything that promised interest or pleasure.

As she was mulling over what little Aldershot seemed to offer, Bert said, 'This is it, North Camp,' and the cabby turned into an opening displaying a small square with washing lines strung from poles, and rearing behind them a three-storey redbrick building with iron-railed walkways along the length of each level.

'We're on the first floor,' Bert said as he paid off the cab driver, 'number nine. This way.' She followed him up a flight of stone steps and along the verandah, where the noise of screaming children, screaming women threatening dire punishments, and the loud swearing of men sounded from many of the flats they passed.

The steps in front of some doors were etched sharply in the fading light from applications of whitestone. Others were encrusted with mud and filth. Papers, ash and cinders lay about them. 'There's always the sluts,' Bert said, avoiding the debris. 'They'll clean up in a day or two in case of an inspection, or the bloke will be on a charge.'

Treading her way as carefully as he, Molly said, 'Inspection! Do the army inspect your home?'

'They're not your homes. Nothing is yours in the army. They inspect when they like. Have to. Only way to keep some buggers clean. It's the same in barracks. Miss Nightingale started it. More blokes died in the Crimea from dirt, lice and no sanitation than bullets and shells. Very keen now on cleanliness, the army is, in barracks and married quarters.'

Molly thought, as they arrived at number nine, what a dreadful thing it was that strangers could come and inspect your home.

'Here we are then,' Bert announced, unlocking and flinging open the door which led straight from the verandah into a room. Brown linoleum covered the floor, highly polished, reminding her of a hospital ward. The one

window was curtained with dark green serge so narrow she knew that when the hangings were drawn they would be without a single fold. The walls were of bare redbrick. Her heart sank.

She looked round the room, saw a small range, a kitchen table and two chairs. Another two wooden chairs with arms stood either side of the fireplace. There were presses in the alcoves, an assortment of enormous fire tools in the fender. And she noticed the doors, five of them in such a small room, and wondered where they led. One, she felt sure, must open into a sitting-room or parlour.

'I'll make us a cup of tea,' Bert said, adjusting the range's dampers, removing a round iron lid and covering the revealed surface where the fire was visible with a huge kettle which had been on the hob. 'You'll find tea and sugar in the ration box.' Molly looked blankly at him. 'There, on the table. But take your things off first. The bedroom's through there.' He pointed to one of the doors.

Its floor was covered with the same brown linoleum and its walls were of the same redbrick. Two single iron beds were made up with rough brown blankets. There was an alcove with hooks screwed into the wall and further along the wall another door. Into the parlour, she thought. She laid her hat on a bed, hung her coat on a hook and tried the door. It didn't budge. She must ask Bert where it led. Coming back into the living-room cum kitchen she explored what lay behind the remaining doors after giving Bert the tea and sugar. A lavatory, a coalhouse and a scullery in which was a larder.

She began to unpack the ration box. It was oblong, painted dark green, and divided into different sections. One held a number of paper bags: tea, sugar, flour, porridge oats, tapioca, lentils, dried peas, butter beans, and a bag as big as any of the others, white pepper. Even with her limited experience of dry goods she judged the amount to be

enormous for a condiment. Four ounces, sure to be. Enough to last for ages.

In other sections she found a coarse-grained loaf, three tins, two without labels, a huge bar of household soap, a blood-stained paper in which was wrapped a thick wedge of purply-brown ox liver. The sight of it made her want to retch. She swallowed hard, controlled the feeling, and unpacked a block of salt and an assortment of root vegetables.

'Won't be a jiffy now,' Bert called from the range where the kettle had started to sing. 'The teapot and crockery are in the right-hand press.' The teapot, like all the utensils she had noticed, was of more than generous proportions, and the crockery thick and plain white. Even in Bert's home there had been a few china cups; here she had expected to find similar if not better.

'You're very quiet,' he said, bringing the teapot to the boiling kettle, spooning in tea and filling it. 'Well, what d'ye think of the place?'

She was tired, hungry, disappointed, her guard down. Her ability to lie momentarily deserted her. 'I thought we'd have got a house,' she said, immediately wishing the words back.

'A house?' he shouted. 'You thought we'd have got a house? You ungrateful cow! You fucking Irish bitch! Houses are for Senior NCOs. For Warrant Officers.'

She tried to make amends. Apologizing, pleading. 'I don't mean it's not nice. What I mean was, well, you know.'

She ducked as the pot of scalding tea flew towards her. In her romantic daydreams she had forgotten reality. His temper. The size of his fists. The hurt they inflicted. She shook with fear as he came near. He caught hold of her by the shoulders, his fingers digging into them, shaking her so that she felt dizzy and saw stars dance before her eyes. And all the while he shouted abuse.

'Every time I came to Horsham it was, "When will we get a quarter?" I haunted the Company Office, begging, pleading compassionate grounds. You didn't get on with my family. You didn't have a bed to sleep in. That you might be expecting. The aggravation I caused with my constant complaints. How the single blokes took it out on me. "Fucking married pads", they call us. Jealous of the allowance and quarters while they pig it in barracks. And the married ones with more points than me still waiting, threatening what they'd do if I jumped them in the line.

'And you thought you'd get a house! Thought because your father's a barrister the army'd make an exception! Is he, I wonder? What proof did I ever have? I met you in a stinking cellar with your mate and her mother. A pair of whores. Probably running a brothel. Your father's been in a great hurry sending you anything. Could be the fucking gardener, for all I know.' His lips were full of spit and his blue eyes glared like a wild animal's.

He let go of her and she fell into the spreading pool of tea. He kicked her in the ribs. 'Well, this is what you've got and you'd better keep it clean. None of your Irish pig sties here. I'll inspect it every day. One crumb on the floor, one speck of dust . . . The range better be blackleaded and the step done, otherwise I'll make pulp of you.' He emphasized his threat with another kick.

Holy Mary, Mother of God, don't let me scream. He'll kill me if I scream. She dug her nails into her palms and her teeth into her bottom lip.

'What you should've had was how it was not that long ago,' Bert shouted. 'You and me and the other married couples bedding down behind a curtain at one end of the barrack room. All of us fucking our wives cheered on by the men. And the next day the women off to the washhouse to do the laundry. Not just their husband's, for the other soldiers as well.'

His gleaming black foot found her ribs, her back, again

and again. Each kick accompanied by another obscenity. Molly fainted and he left her there, unconscious in her new home.

After coming to she crawled to the bedroom and dragged herself on to a bed where mercifully she passed out. When she woke it was dark and she heard the sound of music. A trumpet, she thought, a beautiful heartbreaking air, so poignant that she began to cry with loneliness and grief, recalling her home, her parents, and longing to be once more in the safety and security she had always taken for granted.

She fell asleep until woken by a brisk urgent bugle call. Her body had stiffened during the night so that it was with great difficulty she got up. Bert's bed hadn't been slept in, nor was there any sign of him in the kitchen. She splashed cold water on her face and attempted to brush her hair. It hurt too much to raise her arms and she abandoned the attempt. She sat as she was, barefooted, half-dressed, and didn't care if every officer in the camp came to inspect her home. A knock on the door made her think that perhaps they had. Unsteadily making her way to open it, she hoped they had. Surely they would help? Take pity on her. Take her away before Bert returned.

The biggest woman she had ever seen stood outside. A woman she judged to be almost six foot tall who, except for her large breasts, could have been a man so powerfully was she built. 'I'm Cora,' she said. 'From next door. I heard the ructions last night and knew you were being done over. Can I come in?'

Molly nodded her head, too dazed to query or question. 'I haven't come to nose. Only to see if you're all right.' Cora came closer and inspected Molly's face. 'A crafty sod, doesn't leave any marks. Where did he hit you?'

'My ribs. Kicks. I feel so sick. I want a cup of tea and to go back to bed. Only I'm afraid in case he comes back. You talk like a Dubliner?'

'From Liverpool. You know what they say – Liverpool's the capital of Ireland. Me dad's a lascar and me mam from Mayo. One of the queenly women of the West of Ireland. From her I get the build and height and from him the kinky black hair. The physog's a mixture of the two of them. Has he duffed you up before?'

'Lots of times, but never so that it shows.'

'And I suppose you think it'll change? For God's sake, sit down before you collapse.'

Cora helped her into one of the arm chairs. 'They never change. I'm forty years of age. Been a soldier's wife for twenty. Not that it's only soldiers. Men! And I've never known a wife beater change except mine. The first time he tried it I split him, ten stitches in his head. Couldn't let on his wife did it. Be a laughing stock in front of his mates. But you're not big enough, not strong enough. What'll you do?'

'What can I do? Where would I live? Money, where would I get it?'

'You'd be better off on the streets. I'm serious – he'll get worse. They get a taste for it. He'll make a punch bag of you. And God help you if you have a child. He could kill you. Let me see your ribs.'

Carefully Cora lowered Molly's shift from her shoulders and rolled it down. 'Sweet suffering Jesus! You poor child. The lousy bastard. Haven't you any brothers that'd kick the head offa him? Lift the shift down. Have you anything to go round your shoulders?'

'I haven't a shawl, there's a towel on the bed.'

Cora brought it. 'There now,' she said, draping it round Molly. 'Save pulling you about. I've got strapping inside and an ointment for bruising. Them ribs will go black and blue.' While she talked she was regulating the dampers, increasing the draw on the fire. 'Stay where you are.' She put the kettle over the fire. 'I'll go back inside, get the stuff

and then make you a cup of tea. Now don't move from there.'

She was back in no time, made the tea, punched two holes in the condensed milk tin and with a knife hacked between the holes until there was enough space to spoon out the thick sticky substance. 'Drink that and then I'll see to your ribs.'

Her big square hands gently spread the ointment over Molly then bound the strapping round her. 'Now you get into bed and sleep. Later on I'll make you a bit of toast and jam. And I'll watch for your fella coming home for his dinner. Let on I took you to the hospital. Tell him I heard you screaming with the pain. Say the hospital strapped you up.

'The mention of the hospital'll put the shite crossways in him! Not that the military, no more than the police, will interfere between husband and wife. All the same, he'll know the army, being what they are, will have a record. He'll think so anyway. And if next time the injury is more serious, then they'd have to act. Mightn't benefit you but he'll lay off you for the time being.'

Cora found a nightdress, slipped it over Molly's head and helped her to the bedroom, promising to come and see her later in the afternoon. Bert, when he came at dinnertime, was very solicitous. Enquiring if he could get her anything, another blanket, pillow, water, whatever she wanted. She wanted nothing, only to sleep. He agreed sleep was the best thing. Then questioned her anxiously as to what she had said at the hospital. 'How did you say it happened?'

'That I fell down the steps.'

'Nothing about me?'

She shook her head, wishing he would go away. Let her go back to sleep.

'Good girl. Never tell anyone in authority your business. And her next door, the half black, half man?'

'The same story.'

'You stay in bed as long as you like. D'ye want anything? I'll get whatever you need. Just say the word. Nothing at all? Then I'll let you sleep.'

When he wasn't there Cora came and made food for her. Brought laudanum, warning her to take it only if the pain was desperate. 'Otherwise you get a liking for it.'

Molly's ribs healed but her fear of Bert increased, making anything she said to him stilted and unnatural, always watching her words in case one would annoy or offend him.

He gave her no money and she dared not ask. She made do with the rations. Some weeks there was dried fish instead of meat, sometimes meaty bones. Always butter beans, dried peas and lentils with which she made soup. Occasionally her craving for fresh milk and butter became overpowering and she used some of Aggie's money to buy small quantities. Cora took her to the canteen where most things could be bought and told her the prices weren't too bad. She also took her to the washhouse. Told her about the other wives.

'All sorts,' she said. 'Tough cows, split you as ready as look at you; pissy-arsed drunkards, any man's for a bottle of Red Biddy; romantic fools; good-natured; kind; dishonest. All sorts, same as you find anywhere. Poor cows the majority of them.'

'You've been to the washhouse,' Bert said when he saw damp clothes drying before the range. 'You can earn money there. Soldiers pay fourpence a day for their washing to be done.'

'I might,' said Molly, 'I'll think about it.'

She told Cora that Bert had suggested she did soldiers' washing. 'You mustn't! Never. Not if you starved. Some of those blokes have the clap and crabs. My fella got a dose of them and so did I.

'I've got a better remedy,' said Cora. 'I don't let him near me. Not any more. He can stick it up anyone he fancies but

not up me. At my time of life I'm not risking a dose of the clap and visits to the Lock Hospital. Tommy, my eldest, is leaving school soon and going back to Liverpool to live with me ma and da. He wants to go to sea like his grandfather. The other three will soon be old enough to work then we'll all clear out. Leave him on his arse. Finish up with the Chelsea Pensioners, he will.'

'But what'll you do for money?' Molly asked.

'Plenty of work in Liverpool. Go back to what I know, being a barmaid. I won't be sorry to say goodbye to the army.'

They saw each other every day, in the mornings or after dinner, and gossiped. Cora told Molly about her sister in London. 'Our Verna is as big as me. That's where the resemblance ends. Only natural, seeing as how she's only my half-sister. Me ma was married twice, so Verna's as white as you. She's got two girls. One mad about the stage. Gets bit parts now and then.'

'That's what I always wanted to do, go on the stage, and look where I finished up!'

'You're still young enough to do anything so long as you take my advice and leave him.'

On another day when they were having a gossip, Cora told her she could expect a visit from the Regimental Sergeant Major's wife and the wife of the C.O.

'The two together?'

'Separate occasions. The new wives are always visited. It's their way of welcoming you to the Regiment. It makes me sick, the guff about "the Regiment". Of course the men swallow it. I suppose they have to otherwise how would they go out and let theirselves be killed? Some of the wives do too. Boast about their Regiment being better than another. A family affair. All my eye! If your husband died or was killed you'd be out in the street in no time. Great family feeling that is. I'll be interested to hear what you think of your visitors when they come.'

But before they did, an appalling realization dawned on Molly. She was pregnant. If she had a baby she was tied to Bert for life. And even if she lost it, he would believe she had done so deliberately. She wandered round the flat in a distraught state grateful only for the fact that, assuming she had her period, he hadn't touched her for the last two nights. But sometimes, without having intercourse, he would lie on top of her and satisfy himself that way. Maybe he would tonight. He'd notice then that she wasn't wearing the thick rag.

When she could bear her own company no longer she went to Cora, asking, 'What am I going to do?'

'Nothing for the time being. That is, unless you want to make sure you're not carrying?'

'I don't know what you mean?'

'You could get rid of it.'

'But that's a mortal sin!' said Molly, looking aghast.

'It's a sin not to want it too. Maybe you'll be lucky and lose it.'

'He wouldn't believe it was natural, he'd kill me. Or beat me so badly I'd be as good as dead.'

'Have you said anything to him about missing?'

'No, but he's bound to notice that I'm not bleeding.' And she told Cora how he lay on top of her.

'Put your rag on then. He doesn't inspect it, surely to God?'

'He spares me that.'

'Then wear it, and again next month if you don't come on. It'll give you a breathing space. You might change your mind about trying to shift it.'

Molly shook her head. 'No, I could never do that. I couldn't kill a baby, but God forgive me, I'd be glad to lose it naturally. How do women get rid of them?'

'Different ways. Pills, gin, jumping off tables, crochet hooks, knitting needles, squirting carbolic soap suds inside you. The first lot don't always work. The needles, soap suds

and Slippery Elm do. Some do those things theirself, and then there are women who will do it for you for a few bob.'

'Slippery Elm, what's that?'

'A small twig with the bark stripped off it. Slides inside you easy. Mind you, with that, the needles and crochet hooks, you can bleed to death. They puncture the womb.'

'Oh my God, don't tell me any more! The women must be mad.' Molly covered her face with her hands.

'Desperate more than mad. Feeling like you do about a pregnancy. Not married or else a bastard of a husband, already a houseful of children. Or else a child that's not their husband's and no way of passing it off because he's been foreign.'

'And are some of them Catholics?'

'Some are. But Hell seems a lot further in the future than a child that's going to make its appearance in a few months.'

Molly took Cora's advice and wore the rag and prayed for the missed period to be a false alarm, and if it wasn't for God to let her lose the child. Just before her next one was expected Bert was called to the Company Office where the adjutant told him a phone call had come from a hospital in Horsham where his mother had suffered a stroke and died.

He was given a week's compassionate leave. Molly was sorry that Mrs Talbot had died without their having met again but at the same time hoped Bert wouldn't expect her to accompany him to Horsham. He didn't. 'I'd like to have you there. I'll get a travel warrant but I'd have to fork out cash for you, which I haven't got.'

Molly pretended disappointment while secretly relieved that she would have a week without him. He went down to Sussex that evening and she rejoiced in her freedom.

The next morning she woke with low back ache. It had been a false alarm. She was going to start. The pain moved to her belly and every so often she went to the lavatory, hoping to see signs of blood. Coming out from one visit she

heard a knock on the front door, opened it, and stared uncomprehendingly at a well-dressed woman who smiled and introduced herself as Mrs Heywood, the Colonel's wife.

'I was miles away,' Molly said, realizing she had kept the woman outside longer than good manners decreed. 'Please come in.'

'I heard that your husband's mother died so I wasn't sure if you would be in. But as I was visiting other wives, I thought I'd knock. It's very remiss of me to have left it so long. I should have come before to welcome you to the Regiment.'

'That's very kind of you,' Molly said, smiling and displaying her dimples. 'Please sit down. And would you like some tea? I'm afraid I've only got condensed milk which is vile.'

What a charming girl. So pretty and poised. Immaculate too despite her shabby clothes. What was she doing in another ranks' quarter? Edward had mentioned Talbot marrying a girl from Dublin. Many soldiers did. But she'd never come across one like Mrs Talbot. Of course, he was a handsome brute.

While pursuing these thoughts Mrs Heywood refused the tea and continued to apologize for the unexpectedness of her visit. The pain in Molly's belly worsened: a pain she had never experienced before.

The Colonel's wife said, 'I called to welcome you, as I said, and ask how you are settling in? If you like Aldershot? And to give you these.' She held forward a small basket with apples in it. 'My father lives in Farnham. His apple trees are very fruitful.'

'Thank you very much.' Molly put the fruit in a crockery basin. 'I'm getting used to married quarters but can't say the same about Aldershot. It's very dull after Dublin.' She gave back the basket.

'Ah, yes. Dublin is lively. I enjoyed living there. Did you live in the city?'

'Fitzwilliam Square.'

'Delightful houses. Are your parents still there?'

'Oh, yes,' Molly replied, but wouldn't be drawn further.

'When the weather improves there are some pleasant walks. It's pretty along the Basingstoke Canal. And of course you are lucky – your husband is such an excellent horseman, wonderful on ceremonial parades and that sort of thing, we like to keep him at home. So you won't be separated.'

The pain in Molly's belly worsened and she felt sick. One of her longed-for avenues of escape was that Bert would be sent overseas.

'Well, dear, I really must go. Now remember, you are part of the Regiment. We are like a family and help is always at hand should you need it.'

Molly thanked her for the visit and showed her out then ran to the lavatory to see if she had started. She hadn't. She went to Cora's. 'I keep thinking I'm about to come on. I've terrible pains, not like the usual ones.'

'That happens sometimes after you've missed a month. I saw you had a visitor. What do you think of her?'

'She was nice. She brought me apples and bad news. Bert, she said, is such a good horseman he's not likely to be sent foreign. When I heard that my pain got worse!'

'Mrs Heywood brings apples to all the wives. She's a good sort. You look a bit grey in the face. Maybe you're having a miss.'

'What'll I do if I am? He'll kill me. Oh my God!'

'If you are losing it, it'll be over and done with before he comes back unless you lie up. Keep on the go. You'll be all right, I'll see to you.'

'Oh, Cora, what am I going to do? I can't go on living like this.'

'Let's have a cup of tea first. Pull your chair nearer the

range.' While she was making the tea, and when they were drinking it, Cora talked. 'I've been thinking about you. I've heard all this before: "I can't stand my old man, I'm going to run away." For all sorts of reason they soldier on. But in your case it's different. I know you mean it.

'I've laid awake, thinking about you. Worrying in case you do away with yourself. I think I've found the answer, and I think it's a good idea and one you should follow. Especially with what Mrs Heywood told you. No going overseas, and field exercises not until next year. He'll stick to you like a leech.

'D'ye remember I told you I have a sister in London, our Verna? She's great. Lives in Soho over a cafe. They run it. Her husband's a lovely fella. A cockney, works in Covent Garden. The thing is, there's a warren of rooms over the cafe. You could go to her.'

'Could I really? But what would I do for money? I've got enough for the fare and a few pounds over. But afterwards, to pay rent and keep, what would I do for that?'

Molly doubled forward with a sudden pain.

'Another pair of hands is always welcome in Verna's. Someone she could trust a Godsend. In any case, it would be a beginning. You could look round for something else to do once you got used to London. Didn't you tell me you could sing and dance? Christmas is coming and they take on extras for the pantomimes. But the main thing is, you'd be shut of him. And he'd never find you. What d'ye say?'

'It's like an answer to my prayers. A fairy tale come true. Never having to sleep with him again. Never to be afraid when I hear him at the door. Could it really happen? Would you write to your sister?'

'I have. Sounding her out, like. You'd be very welcome. And if you go I'll give you a letter to take with you.'

'I'll go. If I don't do it now I'll finish up like the women you told me about. Always threatening, never doing

273

anything, and finishing up battered and broken in spirit as well as body.'

'Good girl. Now go back indoors. Pull and haul the presses and beds about. Go up and down the steps. Keep on the go. If you've a threatened miss, you'll lose it and no mortal sin. And if it's your period coming on, it won't do you a bit of harm. Make the flow easier.'

In the middle of the night Molly woke in dreadful pain and knocked on the connecting door. During the few minutes while she waited for Cora blood began to flow from her. Bright red blood, so that she knew it wasn't her period starting.

'You're losing it,' said Cora. 'I've bundles of newspapers, I'll go back for them.' She brought them and a few pieces of old sheets which she put on the mattress. 'Get into bed. With the help of God it'll soon be over.'

'Oh my God, if this is a miscarriage, what must it be like having a baby?' Molly asked.

'Worse but not much,' Cora said. 'A miss is painful, very, but doesn't last as long.'

When, within a couple of hours, the tiny foetus was expelled, Molly cried with a mixture of guilt and relief. Cora was busy wrapping what had come away in newspaper. 'I never wanted it, God forgive me, but I didn't kill it, did I?' Molly sobbed.

'Of course you didn't. Don't get that idea into your head. Keep reminding yourself how your life would have been if the child had lived. And another thing – it probably wouldn't have been right. If you lose them naturally it's because they weren't right in the first place.'

'Is that the truth?'

'I think so. It's the belief anyway. You'll bleed for a while yet but in a day or two it'll peter out.' She used some of the sheeting to pad Molly, removed the blood-soaked newspapers from the mattress. 'I'll burn this lot in my place

while everyone's out.' She gave Molly a clean nightdress, rearranged the bed and told her to get in.

'Stay there for today and you can get up in the morning. And the day after you'll be well enough to go.' She collected the bedding and papers. 'I'll be back in a few minutes and make you a bit of toast and a cup of tea.'

As Cora had forecast, Molly felt better the next day. She was well enough to pack her few belongings. So few that they fitted into the valise she had brought from Ireland.

When they were bidding each other goodbye, Cora, with an arm round Molly, said, 'Verna will write and tell me you've arrived and give me all the news. Don't you, on the off chance that the letter might fall into his hands and give the game away. I'll send all the news to Verna.'

'I doubt if he'd care.'

'Don't be so sure. He'll lose the married allowance for one thing once it gets about that you're gone, and the quarter as well. He won't relish going back to barracks.'

'You're right,' said Molly, 'on those counts you're right.'

'From now on you look on the bright side. Another couple of months and it'll be 1903. A new year and a new and better life for you. I'll be up if it's only for a day. Maybe not until Easter, but when I do you'll be looking like a new woman. Drink that tea and eat a bit of the mashed potato. Billy'll be home in a few minutes from school and I'll send him for a cab.'

Molly was on tenterhooks while she waited to be gone. Terrified that every step she heard on the verandah might be Bert returning from Horsham. Not relaxing until the train from Aldershot was well on its way to London. Then she again became nervous at the enormity of what she was undertaking. Going to Cora's sister. Someone she had never set eyes on. Practically penniless, destitute really. If only, she thought, I had the fare, I'd go back to Dublin. Throw myself on the mercy of Mama and Papa. I should never have broken into Aggie's money. 'Keep it for a rainy

day,' she had said. Well, this was a rainy day indeed and Molly had only her fare and ten shillings to her name.

Then her natural optimism took over and she counted her blessings. She was away from Bert. In Soho he would never find her. Verna would be as kind and welcoming as Cora. For the time being she could help out in the cafe to pay for her bed and board, but who knew what else might lie in store for her? There were many theatres in London. One of Verna's daughters was an actress. She could show Molly the ropes. She started the journey in high spirits.

Chapter Twenty-six

EACH time the train stopped at a station and Molly saw soldiers about to come aboard her stomach lurched, imagining that Bert might be one of them even though there was never a Lancer amongst them. He's so sly he could be wearing a different uniform, even mufti, she told herself. But eventually her fears subsided. He was in Horsham. How could he follow her when he didn't even know she had left?

At Waterloo she took a cab to Soho, and as it drove across Waterloo Bridge was amazed at how wide the river was. Twice, she guessed, maybe three times wider than the Liffey. The pavements were thronged with people. She saw shops and theatres, and so many fine buildings. London was wonderful. Already she loved it. Knew she would be happy living in it.

Verna was expecting her. She was as tall as Cora, and as big, but her skin was pale and freckled and her long gingerish hair up in a bun. But she spoke like Cora and warmly welcomed Molly. Her daughters, Maisie and Maria, were every bit as welcoming and Molly immediately felt at home.

'You'll meet Harry when he gets up. He works in Covent Garden as a porter. Out at the crack of dawn. First thing he does when he comes in is to go to bed.' Little was seen of him. But when he was about he was always cheerful and Molly felt welcomed by him as well.

She loved London. She loved the crowds, the sights, the smells and sounds. The narrow streets of Soho, its small

squares and foreign faces, like none she had ever seen in Dublin.

The cafe was a modest affair serving only snacks, tea and coffee. But it seldom lacked customers, mostly regulars on first name terms with Verna and the girls. In no time this also applied to Molly.

Verna was generous with time off. Molly, Maisie and Maria shared the morning shift while Verna slept late. In the afternoons she took over with one of the girls helping. The two off duty were free to do what they liked, so that Molly learned the way to Covent Garden, Leicester Square, Shaftesbury Avenue, Piccadilly Circus, and how to get to the river.

Maria pointed out famous landmarks, reminding her of the walks long ago in Dublin with James. As formerly, she wasn't particularly interested in buildings, monuments, old churches or statues, but on her walks with Maisie, who seemed to know every theatre in London, she bubbled with excitement.

On one of their walks Maisie talked about the approaching pantomime season. Knowing that Molly could sing and dance, she said, 'You might get a part. They take on lots of extras for crowd scenes. Mostly children. But you're not very tall and you're skinny, though not so bad as you were when you first came. You might get taken on.'

'How? What would I have to do?'

'Be outside the theatre at the crack of dawn. Hundreds turn up, mothers with their children mostly. Some of them there from the night before. Then it's the luck of the draw. The stage manager goes through the crowd picking this one and that. Pretty ones, cheeky-looking ones. They're a rough crowd, especially the mothers. Scratch your eyes out they would. You look very young for your age. I think you'd have a chance . . .'

'But how will I know when and where to go?' asked Molly.

'Leave that to me. I'm in the business myself when I can get the work.'

Cora wrote to Molly telling her that Bert had come, politely in the beginning, asking if she knew where his wife was:

> Of course I lied like a trooper. Let on to be surprised and said how it just showed what people were made of. Her running off without a word to me that was so good to her!
>
> He seemed to swallow this but was back the next night, and the next, drunk, hammering on the door. And what he didn't call me! A black bitch. A half man. Another fucking Catholic. I felt sorry for my fella who wanted to send him arse over the verandah, but he's only half Bert's size.
>
> But I settled his hash. I was at his door first thing in the morning and told him if he ever came near my place again, I'd be up to the barracks and report him. He hasn't been near since.
>
> You're well rid of the blackguard. I'll come up when I can.

Sometimes Molly had nightmares in which she dreamed of Aldershot and Bert. She was back in the quarter, listening in dread for him coming home. Cowering as she waited while his key turned in the door. Shaking with fear, her heart thudding as she anticipated the massive fists pounding the soft parts of her body, and when she'd fall to the floor his big boots, which in her dream became enormous, kicking her in the ribs.

But always in the dream the door wouldn't open. Then he'd start trying to break it down. She would hear the first crack, the splintering of the wood. At that point she would waken, sweating, trembling. Hear the soft snoring and snuffling of Maisie and Maria who shared the room. See the little lamp that burned day and night before the statue of the Sacred Heart. And realize she had escaped, she was safe.

★

Maisie told her that the following week they would be auditioning for extras for the pantomime season. Looking at Molly, who was beginning to put on the weight she had lost in Aldershot, she said, 'You'll want to do something about your bust. Your face could pass for fourteen but not them. Bind them as flat as you can.'

The night before the audition Maisie and Verna wound a wide strap of torn sheeting twice around Molly's breasts, securing it with safety pins. They had her put on her bodice and blouse surveying her from the front and sides, the two of them laughing and Molly complaining that she couldn't breathe.

'You're talking, aren't you? Then you're able to breathe. Pa'll call you when he's going to the Garden, that'll give you plenty of time.'

She didn't need the call, having been awake all night, her mind a whirl of excited thoughts. There was a chance, a real chance, for her to go on a real stage. Appear in a pantomime at Drury Lane. She might get the part of Principal Boy. Earn a lot of money. Buy beautiful clothes. Have her own apartment.

On and on went her daydreaming until Verna's husband Harry, not wanting to waken his daughter, came quietly into the room.

'Christ!' he exclaimed. 'You didn't half give me a fright. Lying there with your eyes wide open. Like a bloody corpse, and someone forgot to put the pennies on his peepers! There's a pot of tea in the kitchen. Know your way to the Lane?'

Molly whispered that she did.

'Good luck then,' Harry said, and tiptoed out.

Molly heard the noise before she turned the corner. Crying children, laughter, swearing, the voices of women threatening to maim for life Flo, Mabel, Bill or Mary if they didn't

stop whingeing, stay where they were and do what they were told.

'You bleedin' little sod! You kick my Tom again and I'll break your neck,' one woman screamed at someone else's child for a change.

Hesitantly Molly edged closer to the milling crowd and stood on its edge. No one took any notice of her. But as the sky lightened she saw that the crowd was mostly children above whom she towered. She was as tall or taller than most of the adults.

As the light improved she saw that women were staring at her, and she felt embarrassed and angry that Maisie had convinced her she could pass for a child.

Three women standing near her huddled closer, talking to each other, stopping now and then to turn and look at her. One of them asked, 'Who have you brought?' The voice was challenging; it and the stare reminded Molly of women outside Dublin tenements. Army wives in the washhouse. She turned and ran away. Stumbling and crying through the streets, saying over and over to herself, 'What a fool I am. What a poor deluded fool. Fame and fortune, luncheons and bliss in the afternoon! As if I didn't know all about that bliss and what it can lead to.'

Chapter Twenty-seven

VERNA and the girls consoled her, Maisie admitting that she had been wrong. 'I'd forgotten what vicious cows the women are and that you're not as tough as me.'

'That's you all over, our Maisie. Molly's gorgeous and don't look her age. Even so, she'd never pass for a child. You haven't the sense you were born with!' her sister scolded.

'You shut up! I was only trying to help. If you were that sure, why didn't you say something before Molly went?'

'As if you'd have listened,' Maria retorted.

The sisters continued arguing until their mother intervened. 'Stop it, both of you, and get back in the cafe. Molly, love, you've been up half the night. Go and lie down. Look on the bright side. Another year's just round the corner. Something else will turn up.'

'That's right, Moll. In the New Year you can try The Chapel on the Green,' Maisie said.

'The chapel?' Molly looked puzzled. 'You mean like chapels at home?'

Maisie laughed. 'No, it's a music hall in Islington. Sam Collins sings Irish songs there, he's famous for them. Me and Sam get on great. You'll get work there, honest to God.'

Halfway through 1903 she did, as The Irish Colleen, sometimes singing sad laments, songs about old mothers or sweethearts left behind in Ireland. Tears streamed down the faces of the audience who were mostly Irish and mostly

drunk. On other nights her songs were jolly and humorous, making good-natured fun of her fellow countrymen and women, who rocked with laughter. She was one of their own. Allowed to poke fun. They clapped and clapped and stamped their feet, shouting, 'Molly, Molly, Molly, oh!'

She looked out at the sea of faces, thrilled that she had captivated them, given so much pleasure.

Never in her life had she known such happiness. From the first day she was hired and went behind the scenes, into the props room, she felt at home. She saw masks, some grotesque, hanging on walls. Painted backdrops of country scenes, sea shores, rooms. Costumes that from stalls or gallery glittered like gold and silver; stage jewellery that shone like precious stones. In one part of her mind she knew it was all fake, tawdry even, but in her heart it was magic.

For the audience the magic began when they entered the auditorium. For her when she entered by the door the actors used and breathed in the smells. Paint, dust, fabrics old and new, greasepaint, face powder, tobacco smoke, strong colognes, lavender, sweat, alcohol, and lingering traces of scent from the rows of costumes. It set her up. Whatever her humour when she arrived, and sometimes it was bad from late nights, her period, overindulgence the night before in a public house, a whiff of the theatre atmosphere revived her spirits.

Molly had never fully realized how attractive she was. Now, with endless admirers hanging round the stage door, some with flowers, chocolates, invitations to supper, she was left in no doubt that men admired her for more than her singing and dancing.

She accepted the flowers and occasionally the invitations, still wary of men and the way they might treat her. To go to the public house in a crowd was one thing, but to trust her happiness to a man again was something she couldn't envisage. Besides which she had ambitions. She loved The

Chapel on the Green but intended to move on from there. Make her name. Be known all over London. Become rich and famous.

Verna said when Molly began to pay for her board and keep: 'I don't expect you to help in the cafe any more, love. Rest, or now the weather's improving, get some fresh air. There's an electric tram that goes to Clapham. It's nice out there. You could walk to the Common.

'Oh, I nearly forgot, there's a letter for you from Cora.' It was a short note in which she wrote that the visit at Easter was off. Funds were low, but God was good and maybe she'd manage it later on.

Bert had apparently gone back to live in barracks once the army twigged Molly wasn't living in the quarter. Now it would be safe for her to drop her old friend a line. The woman who'd moved in next door wasn't a patch on Molly.

She intended to write and send Cora a little money towards her fare, but somehow she never seemed to find the time. Cora again postponed her visit. She wrote to Verna and occasionally included a note for Molly.

And so time passed, Molly satisfied with her work and making a name for herself. Only now and then overcome with a longing for her family and Dublin.

Chapter Twenty-eight

IN 1903 Michael celebrated his fiftieth birthday with a dinner party. While he and Nicole were dressing for dinner he reminded her, mentioning Molly's name the first time since she had left home, 'She's twenty-four this year.'

'Yes,' she replied, 'I hadn't forgotten.' He didn't detect the bitterness in her voice. Wasn't aware, she believed, just how deep her resentment towards him ran. How long she had waited for him to admit that he hadn't banished Molly completely from his mind.

So engrossed had he been in defeating his addiction to alcohol, re-establishing his position in society and becoming fanatically religious, to her way of thinking, she had almost given up hope he would ever mention Molly again or reach a decision about Fanny's future. She grieved so much for both of them. Her poor lost daughter and Fanny, coming up for twenty-three. Beautiful, intelligent, ambitious – deprived of what she wanted most of all.

There were times when Nicole was tempted to tell her, 'Do as Molly did. Run away. Go to London. Go to medical school there. I will pay your fees. I have my own money.' A French marriage contract had seen to that.

But always when she thought she had summoned up the strength to do so, her courage failed her. Much as she loved and wanted to help her second daughter, she knew she couldn't face the prospect of the consequences. Michael would become again as he had been. She knew she was being selfish. That it was a parent's duty to sacrifice themself

for their child. But despite everything that had happened between her and Michael, she loved him. And so chose him above everyone else. For two years he did not mention Molly again.

They slept together again. In his arms she forgot her grief for Molly and Fanny, and convinced herself that one day it would all come right. One day he would tell her what he knew about Molly's elopement and marriage; one day he would consent to Fanny's wishes.

So why, she asked herself, when the day had apparently come, did she feel so bitter?

He sat on the side of the bed, his face glowing with health and happiness. And she asked herself why she couldn't share fully in what he was experiencing? Sharing . . . that was it. He hadn't confided his fears in her. She resented that. He always followed his own lead. He was doing it now. Suddenly, like a genie released from a bottle, a fairy godmother, he would grant wishes. Magnanimously allow Fanny to do what she had wanted to do for years. Tell his wife what she had had a right to know for years – where Molly was, or had been. He had denied her that. Caused her immense suffering. And now, in a moment of pure self-indulgence, he planned to right all these wrongs. His belief in the curse had been a form of self-indulgence too. He had wallowed in that crazy superstition and in the process marred all their lives. And here he sat, like a spoiled child, planning treats for everyone.

Had it crossed his mind that Molly might be difficult to find? And what such a wild goose chase would do to his wife?

Poor Michael, in so many ways he was like a child.

'Isn't it wonderful, Nicole?' he said, leaning forward and kissing her. 'I love you. It will be all as it was in the beginning, I promise you.'

Fanny's long beautiful face remained impassive when

Michael made his announcement. 'Well, Fan, you've got your wish. The brass plate will go up on the door yet. Françoise McCarthy, M. D. It's May, you'll be all right for the Michaelmas Term in Cecilia Street.'

He sat at the breakfast table the next morning, smiles wreathing his face, gazing at Fanny, thinking how like Nicole she was. The same eyes, the same dark hair, but her face lacked the warmth of expression which lit her mother's.

Nell, who since her father's alcoholic period and Nicole's attempted suicide, was no longer in awe of him, now asked the question he had wanted to come from Fanny. 'What's brought this change about?'

'A miracle, I suppose you could call it. An answer to years of prayer and devotion. D'ye see, I was burned by something terrible.' He told them how he had believed in the power of Mag Cronin's curse. Fanny was afraid to look at Nell in case she giggled and set her off. 'It nearly destroyed me. But it's finished and done with now. I feel a new man. I feel reborn. I've many a thing to put right. The first I've settled — your medical studies have been postponed for far too long, Fanny. Now that's taken care of. Then there's poor Molly. Your mother and I are going to England to bring her home.

'And you, Nell.' He gazed at her. Dependable Nell. No beauty. Short and sturdy, fair-haired and blue-eyed. A faint resemblance to Molly, but faint was all it was. 'There's nothing I can put right for you. You've got all any girl wants. A handsome fiancé from a good prosperous family, Dick's father being one of the wealthiest wine merchants in the city. But I'll buy you a splendid house. And you'll have a wedding that Dublin will talk about for years to come.'

'Thanks very much, Papa, you're so kind. You've always been so kind to me.' The irony was lost on him. He had probably put from his mind his first reaction to Dick when Nell fell in love with him. Forgotten that he had dismissed

him as the son of a shopkeeper; forgotten that he had said, 'That fellow won't comb many grey hairs. He has a dawny look about him.' Nell had never forgotten her father's cruelty nor would she ever forgive him.

Fanny thanked him in her usual detached manner. 'I'll go down and make enquiries about registering.' And Michael thought: She has a cold streak in her. I've never understood her and never will. But she'll make me proud of her, there's no doubt about that. If only she had been a boy! Such a brain was wasted on a woman.

He left the breakfast room feeling deflated, but not for long. Within minutes he was imagining the reunion with Molly. Seeing in his mind's eye her lovely face. His Molly with the golden hair, dimples, and warm loving nature.

Chapter Twenty-nine

DURING the week in May 1905 when her mother and father planned to set out from Dublin to find her, Molly moved into her own flat.

'When can I come and see it?' Maisie wanted to know.

Molly told one of her white lies. 'I've arranged so many things for the first few weeks, I'll have to let you know later.' The fact of the matter was, she'd decided to put Soho and the people who knew her story behind her now.

Maisie gave her a long, hard look. Maria wished her luck and Verna embraced her. 'You've been like a daughter to me. Think of this as your home where you'll always be welcome.'

The girls sat with Nicole while she breakfasted in bed. 'You must be very excited at the prospect of finding Molly?' Nell said.

'Excited, yes, but fearful of not finding her. So much water has flowed under the bridge. My poor foolish impetuous Molly could be anywhere in the world.'

Both girls suspected their mother harboured feelings of resentment that Michael hadn't acted years ago. They talked about it to each other, and their own hostile feelings towards him for causing Nicole so much grief and pain. And, in Fanny's case, for delaying her entry to medical school until she was twenty-three. How all her life he had taken Nell for granted. His contempt for her fiancé and the cruel jibe that he wouldn't live to be an old man, which was at the forefront of her mind this morning.

Each girl longed to criticize him to their mother. Hear her opinion confirming theirs. But they knew, whatever her true feelings might be, loyalty to Michael would keep her silent.

And so it was with great surprise they heard her say, 'I don't understand your father. He knows I haven't been well lately. He knows how tired I am and yet he is behaving like an overexcited child before Christmas. Why do we have to go to England immediately? What difference would it make, delaying the journey for a week or so?' She sighed deeply. 'But always it must be his way. Such power men have over the lives of women.'

'You're really ill, aren't you, Mama?' Fanny asked in concern.

'No, darling, I'm not. A little off colour perhaps. Spring and early summer can have such an effect. Nevertheless, I could do without a boat journey tonight.'

'Please God, it will be a smooth crossing and you'll sleep, and again on the train, so you'll arrive fresh as a daisy in London.'

'Please God it may be so. Nell, I'd gone to bed before you came home last night. How was Dick?'

'Not great. His doctor advises a postponement of our wedding until next year unless there is a marked improvement. Oh, Mama, I'm so frightened he may have consumption!'

'Has that been mentioned? Does his doctor share your fears?'

'He hasn't stated it but Dick is taking such a long time to recover from his pleurisy. Often that's an indication that something more serious ails the lungs.'

'Now, Nell, this is not like you. You're not given to morbid imaginings. You never meet trouble halfway.'

Nell, who was sitting on the bed, moved closer to her mother. Fanny removed the breakfast tray and Nicole put an arm round Nell, drawing her close. 'My poor little baby.

Hush now.' She stroked her hair. 'It will be all right, you'll see. The summer is coming. It will soon have Dick well again.'

'Mama is right, Dick will . . .'

Fanny never finished what she was about to say for the door opened and Michael came into the room, bright and breezy. 'Have you forgotten the day that's in, Miss Françoise McCarthy? You're to put your name down for the medical school today. Off you go and dress in your best. Run along. You too, Nell, while I talk to Mama.' He came to the bed and kissed Nicole.

Outside the two girls exchanged glances.

'I feel heartily sorry for you, Fanny, having to spend so many more years at home.'

'So do I,' she groaned.

'I could murder him sometimes and that's the truth, God forgive me.'

'He would, I'm sure, God is very understanding. You can come with me for the walk. Stop in Mitchell's for coffee.'

'Don't you know he'd be with us that far? Isn't he going to Thomas Cook's? Thanks all the same but I'll stay and help Mama with her packing. You don't think she's really ill, Fan?'

'No, I don't. She's nearly forty-six. I think she's on the change.'

'Really?'

'Why not?'

'I suppose I've never thought of Mama growing old.'

'One of the few certainties in life, Nell.'

Fanny and her father left the house, turned into Merrion Row, along Saint Stephen's Green and past the Shelbourne Hotel where porters were carrying luggage into the lobby: well-used leather cases, dressing boxes, ladies' hat boxes and high rigid ones in which tall hats were carried.

Michael acknowledged salutes from porters who knew him. 'Grand morning, sir,' they said. 'Grand indeed', he replied, and continued what he had been saying. Talking about Molly, Horsham, London. Françoise paid little attention, immersed as she was in her own thoughts.

She could have found her way blindfold to the medical school, for so often since leaving school had she dejectedly walked down Crow Street to stand at its end, gazing across the narrow road where stood the Catholic University School of Medicine. Enviously she had watched the students going in and coming out. Men and women since the latter had been admitted in 1897.

Often as she had watched the women a smile lit her face and to herself she recited a limerick James had taught her:

> A maiden at college named Breeze
> Weighted down by B.A.s and M.D.s
> Collapsed from the strain
> Said her doctor, 'It is plain
> You are killing yourself by degrees

By the time it was written women had triumphed but how hard and long had been their fight! She had read with great admiration of their struggles. Of Elizabeth Blackwell, Elizabeth Garrett Anderson, Sophia Jex-Blake, and many, many more.

'Well,' said Michael as they reached the end of Grafton Street and Thomas Cook, 'this is where we part. Good luck with the registration.' He kissed her cheek. ' 'Bye darling.'

She turned into College Green and continued up Dame Street. There was one thought uppermost in her mind. Once I qualify and am no longer dependent upon him, never again will I allow a man to interfere in my life.

Before travelling to Horsham, Michael and Nicole stayed a

night in London. Their hotel faced Hyde Park. Looking out of the window towards it, Nicole said, 'I wonder if we'll find her?' Not very long afterwards, when she and Michael were getting ready for bed, Molly and a wealthy admirer drove past the hotel on their way to Molly's new flat.

Michael was in an amorous mood. 'Another honeymoon, darling,' he said, raised on one elbow, gazing at Nicole, who lay with her eyes closed.

'It will have to begin tomorrow. Even the following day,' she said.

'But, Nicole, it's a special occasion! A celebration.' He bent and kissed her. 'We must mark it. Please?'

She opened her eyes and looked into his: bright, shining, fanatical. No, that wasn't true, passionate. Yes, that was it. Selfishly passionate. Not so long ago, a few months previously, even though she no longer loved him as she once had, her body would have responded. Now she felt afraid. Something ailed her. Something sinister. She had considered 'the change', but her menopause surely wouldn't cause such bone weariness, such an overwhelming need to sleep? When she returned home a visit to her doctor was imperative.

Michael sat up and became querulous, accusing Nicole in a whining voice of spoiling everything. 'How often in all the years we've been married have I refused you?' she countered.

'That's not the point,' he said. 'Now, of all times, we should be together. Tomorrow we may have Molly back. This is the eve of all our troubles being over, and as I said earlier, should be celebrated.'

She was angry at his blackmail. Wanting to wound him, tell him he was an arrogant fool who not only believed in curses but miracles as well. And surely it would take a miracle to find Molly sitting in Horsham waiting to be rescued? But she curbed her tongue and lied, telling him

she understood how he felt. Tomorrow, after a good night's rest, she wouldn't be so tired. 'Let me kiss you goodnight,' she said.

Like a sulky child he shook his head. After a few minutes she heard him get his rosary beads from their case on his bedside table. She fell asleep to the sound of his murmured prayers.

Nicole saw Horsham as Molly would have seen it and grieved for the disappointment her daughter must have felt. Molly who had loved Dublin, its shops and theatres, its gaiety, the thronged streets pulsing with life. She hoped that Molly's husband had made up for all she had left behind.

'I didn't know them, they married before my time,' said the priest of Saint John the Evangelist.

'But you must know her? She'll be one of your parishioners.'

'We're a small parish and if she came to Mass I would. She doesn't. No one answering her description does. I see,' he said, looking again at the parish register, 'that the husband was a soldier? She's probably living wherever he's stationed. You could ask his people, they're local.'

'You know them?' Michael asked.

'Ah, no. The husband wasn't a Catholic so I'd have no knowledge of the family. Let me get you some tea. You both look tired.'

Michael refused but Nicole accepted. While they waited for the refreshment the priest asked, 'I take it you lost touch with your daughter?'

'We did, Father,' Nicole replied. Wanting to add, Not through Molly's fault. She wrote, I'm sure, many times. No one saw the letters except her father who would have destroyed them.

'It says here in the records that Herbert Talbot was a soldier. By any chance did you know where he was

stationed in Dublin when he met your daughter, Mr McCarthy?'

'We knew nothing about him, Father,' Michael answered, and elaborated on the lie. 'No one did, not her sisters nor the servants.'

Nicole listened, recalling as he spoke James pleading with him to go to Beggars Bush Barracks after Aggie had disclosed her part in the affair and where the Lancer was stationed, and heard again Michael's refusal.

'I'm very sorry for you both but I can't offer any help. Unless you happen to know where your daughter lived in Horsham, I'm afraid the trail has gone cold. You could maybe ask in the town, in the public houses.'

Michael knew the Talbots' address. He had opened Molly's second letter in which she included it. Without admitting this to Nicole, he couldn't divulge it. He'd pretend to take the priest's advice and go through the motions of asking in a public house. Women didn't go into them, his deception would go unnoticed.

'Ah, the tea. Thank you, Mrs Brodie.' The priest introduced Nicole and Michael to his housekeeper. As the woman was about to leave he suddenly remembered that she had worked for the old priest.

'Mrs Brodie, I don't suppose you'd remember a young Irish girl and a soldier coming in to be married, about six years ago?'

'Indeed I do, Father. A lovely little girl. No more than a child.' The housekeeper's long thin sallow face, that had appeared cranky-looking, became pleasantly animated. Nicole's heart leaped in her breast with joy and hope. Tears filled her eyes. Maybe after all it wasn't a wild goose chase. Maybe they would find Molly.

'I remember the pair of them. Sure, Father, I can see you've got the records out. Didn't you notice my name? Wasn't I one of the witnesses to the marriage? How did you not notice it?'

The priest scratched his head, a habit of his when embarrassed. 'To tell you the truth, I don't know,' he said, smiling apologetically at Nicole and Michael. 'But go on, Mrs Brodie. D'ye have any other information about the two in question?'

'They were the handsomest couple I ever saw in my life. But 'twas a sad wedding. Not a soul attending it. And she crying, though at the same time beaming at him. A fine big fella. A Lancer he was.'

'Did you know where he lived?'

'I did, Father. I made it my business to find out. He was away most of the time in Aldershot, stationed there. She used to come to Mass for a while. But I never got to know her.'

Nicole could contain herself no longer, sobbing and questioning Mrs Brodie at the same time. 'Have you seen her lately?'

'Not this long time.'

'Her husband's family, are they still here?'

Please God, let them be. They'll know where Molly is. I'll forgive Michael. I'll be a good wife to him. Only let me find her, please God, Nicole prayed in her mind.

'The father and mother died and everyone else went away. There's a young couple in the cottage now.'

Michael reached for Nicole's hand and squeezed it. The priest thanked Mrs Brodie and Nicole said, 'I want to go there. I want to see where she lived. The address, Michael, we need the address.' Mrs Brodie gave it. And though it was embedded in his memory, Michael wrote it down.

'This was where you let her come to live,' Nicole said later as they stood before the cottage. 'Our child. A little girl. You could have prevented it. I hate you! I'll hate you for the rest of my life. You and your curse. If such a thing existed then you *deserved* to be cursed.'

She turned away and began walking back to the town.

'Wait for me,' he called after her. 'Tomorrow we'll go to

Aldershot. We'll find her, I know we will.' But they didn't. A soldier directed them to the Lancers' barracks where a brusque adjutant told them that Private Trooper Herbert Talbot was serving overseas. His wife had left him before his posting. He could give them no more information.

'Could you at least tell us where our daughter lived in Aldershot?' Nicole asked, outstaring the arrogant young man.

He looked away, shuffled some papers on his desk, then regretting his ill manners and feeling sorry for this pretty woman who was obviously distressed, said, 'North Camp, a little way up the road. I'll have someone show you the road.'

Standing outside the squalid quarters, seeing the slatternly women, hearing their raucous voices, Nicole was filled with pity for the price Molly had paid for a brief love affair. And with a terrible sense of despair, realized she might never see her again. Never know if she was sick or in want.

While she stood thinking these thoughts, too tired and dispirited to care that Michael moved amongst a group of women, asking if they had known a Mrs Talbot, Molly was delighting in her new flat. Going from room to room, smelling roses, eating the chocolates a rich admirer had sent as a welcoming gift.

Chapter Thirty

BOARDING the steamer in Holyhead, Nicole collapsed. Michael had a doctor called before the ship sailed. He diagnosed exhaustion, prescribed a mild sedative, a light diet on the journey, and further medical advice when they arrived in Dublin.

'Not a trace of her,' Nicole told the girls as she lay in bed waiting for her doctor. 'They separated. Other than that, nothing.'

'Don't cry, Mama. You didn't really believe you'd find her,' said Fanny.

'Not really, but I hoped we might.' She dabbed her eyes and smiled a wan smile.

'I could murder Papa for raising your expectations. He's strutting around downstairs outlining his next campaign aloud. His enquiries to the War Ministry. Not even noticing when I left the drawing-room. Talking to himself,' Nell said, criticizing for the first time ever her father to her mother.

'Sometimes I think he's losing his mind,' said Fanny.

The same thought had occurred to Nicole, but loyalty to Michael prevented her from agreeing. Instead she asked how Fanny had got on at the medical school. 'Did everything go well?'

'Yes, no problems. Except my age. The majority of students will be years younger.'

'And the school objects to that?'

'Not at all, Mama – that's all in my mind.'

'You'll overcome it. You'll be so engrossed in your

studies you'll . . .' The remainder of her reassuring advice was cut short by the arrival of the doctor.

The girls left the bedroom. 'What have you been up to, Nicole, you look worn out?' He sat on the side of the bed and she thought how he had aged since their first meeting when she was expecting Molly. Twenty-four years was a long time. No doubt he saw the same changes in her.

He asked about her symptoms, made appropriate comments, then began the physical examinations.

'Well, Nicole, there's nothing serious wrong with you except that you're pregnant − about three months. Congratulations! Wait till Michael hears. A great morale booster for a man past his prime. November, I'd say.'

She had thought of cancer, heart trouble, kidney trouble, a host of diseases, but never that she might be pregnant.

A baby at her age? She knew it wasn't uncommon, nevertheless she was shocked. She didn't want a baby. A grandchild, yes. She was too old. Might never live to see her child reared. He had made a mistake.

'I can't be! I've never missed.'

'That happens now and then. My mother had a kitchen maid who never suspected until the child was almost born. She blamed the pains on sour gooseberries. A genuine case. She had a husband, no need to hide her condition.

'You'll get used to the idea in a few weeks. You must remember the other babies? The nausea and sleepiness during the first few months? You'll feel grand soon. Michael was pacing the drawing-room like an expectant father when I came up. Will I break the news that he is?'

'You might as well,' Nicole said, sitting up, already feeling better now that she knew she didn't have a life-threatening disease.

Dick's health also improved dramatically. Plans for a September wedding were resumed. Nicole, recovered from the discomforts of early pregnancy, took charge. Invitation

lists were drawn up, hymns chosen, caterers engaged. The University Church on Saint Stephen's Green booked for the third Saturday in September, and Nell's wedding dress, ready for several months, was tried on to ensure the fit was still right.

In the middle of August Dick haemorrhaged from his lungs. Tuberculosis was confirmed and he was advised to enter a sanatorium in Switzerland. Nell was devastated. Disappointed at the cancellation of the wedding, terrified at the threat to Dick's life, and filled with hatred for her father who had prophesied such ill fortune.

Fanny went to medical school and the following month Nicole gave birth to a son: a small, delicate baby whose fragile hold on life had to be guarded night and day. Two nurses were brought in for his round-the-clock care. He was wrapped in cotton wool. Nicole's milk was expressed and fed to him by pipette. A daily teaspoon of whiskey was also prescribed.

So slender was his hold on life that immediately after being born he was baptized and given the name Rory. His cry was weak and undemanding, like the mewing of a kitten. So unlike the lusty bawling of her other infants, Nicole thought. Convinced that he wouldn't survive, she steeled herself not to let him into her heart, though in sleep she dreamed she held him in her arms and greedily he sucked her breasts. When after six months the dream became a reality she fell in love with him.

The prayers, votive lamps and candles that had been said and lit for his survival were now intoned and burned in thanksgiving that they had. Michael spent hours gazing at him, declaring him to be the image of the McCarthys, and planning his future. He was adored by his sisters and for Nell a comfort and distraction from thoughts of Dick in his Swiss sanatorium.

Molly now became the focus of Nicole's anxiety. In her dreams she saw her in a street, called to her, ran after her,

but always failed to lessen the distance between them. In other dreams her daughter appeared thin and haggard, alone, always alone, with the look of pain and poverty about her.

It wasn't fair to burden Nell with her grief and worry. God knows, Nicole would tell herself, the poor child has enough of her own. Nor did she confide in Fanny who was wrapped up in her studies, beginning a new life for which she had waited so long. And as for Michael, to him she couldn't broach the subject without bitterness and accusations so anxiety and grief must be kept to herself.

Rory grew fat, round and rosy. He was a McCarthy and looked like Molly as an infant. He had her golden hair and dimples. Everyone adored him. And he rewarded their cooing, tickling, comic faces and baby talk with beaming smiles.

Nell adored him so much that she took over many of his nurse's duties. She was a middle-aged woman, devoted to Rory. Nicole, fearing that she might come to resent Nell for usurping many of her roles, explained to her about Dick.

'Nell suffered a terrible blow last year. Her wedding was arranged, everything set, and a short time before it her fiancé became seriously ill and the wedding had to be cancelled.'

'The poor girl! And him, too. Did he recover?'

'No, he's in a sanatorium in Switzerland. I'm telling you all of this so you'll make allowances for Nell. I know her interference is annoying, but I think she gains great comfort from the attention she lavishes on Rory.'

'Well, indeed I will. I was annoyed, you're right there, but never again. Is he making any progress?'

'So they say. His letters are cheerful.' Nicole shrugged. 'But who can tell with consumption?'

'It's a curse of God, a scourge, so it is. I'll remember him, and her too, in my prayers.'

Fanny drove herself hard, often studying until late at night, forgoing whist and bridge which was just becoming popular, only relaxing her arduous routine to attend meetings of the Suffrage Society. She was a great admirer of Mrs Pankhurst and her daughters, Sylvia and Christabel, and had fumed with rage when in 1905 the Women's Enfranchisement Bill was talked out in the Commons by Henry Labouchère. She could imagine him as a man like her father, blathering for hour after hour. Objecting to women getting the vote on the fatuous grounds that they could not be soldiers. On and on he would have spouted, until the time allotted for the Bill's reading ran out. Men! she fumed, and renewed again her vow that once her father's financial support was no longer necessary, never again would a man hold sway over her life.

Her father still attempted it. Only last week he had commented on her outfit, standing before her decked in his own motoring clothes. He had dismissed the chauffeur once he learned to drive and now sported a bowler hat and long motoring coat of heavy, loudly checked wool, suitable for use in cars with hoods.

He'd looked her up and down. 'I don't understand you, Fanny. Your clothes are so severe. All the young women are wearing pretty things, becoming coats and skirts, charming wide-brimmed hats trimmed with feathers and wide ribbon bows. Where are your trimmings? Your clothes are plain to the point of dowdiness. You don't carry a parasol. It's glorious weather. A time for finery. You're young and beautiful. Why hide your light under a bushel?'

Behind his back Nell rolled her eyes upwards, her way of silently showing what she thought of her father's opinions. Nicole, also out of view, put a finger across her lips.

Ignoring her mother's signal, Fanny retorted contemptuously, 'I'm studying to be a doctor, not trying to catch a man!'

Chapter Thirty-one

1914

LATELY Nicole's friends and daughters were constantly telling her how well she looked. 'It's Rory,' she'd say. 'When I was expecting him Michael forecast the baby would bring us a new lease of life. He has too, I've never felt better.' She didn't add, 'Physically that is.' Didn't burden them with the grief she had suffered for Nell's tragedy . . .

For six years Nell had waited. Writing letters to Dick, and visiting him. Welcoming him home on two occasions, only to have him suffer a relapse, be hospitalized in Dublin and then sent back to the sanatorium. She had made several trips to Switzerland, returning from the majority downcast by how little if at all he had improved. But in the spring of 1911 it was a different story. She was jubilant. A new treatment was being used. By early summer, the clinic's professor had assured her, Dick would be fit and well.

'It's a miracle, Mama! All our prayers have been answered. At last we'll be married.'

Nicole ostensibly shared her delight. Didn't undermine it by asking the question uppermost in her mind: 'Did the professor say he was cured?'

Neither did Fanny, though like Nicole she also had her doubts. 'Poor Dick, he may well be a hopeless case. Perhaps they decided at the clinic there's no more they can do for him, so why not a little lie? Let him come home, marry. Let them have a taste of happiness, however brief.'

'But surely they wouldn't do such a thing? The dishonesty of it, and so unethical,' Nicole protested.

'More humane and honest than continuing to charge enormous fees and have him die a lonely death surrounded by strangers. It can happen very suddenly – a massive haemorrhage. No time for relatives or Nell to get there.'

'Darling, are you quite sure? I know you're almost qualified and have been on the wards for years, have experience with tubercular patients, but all the same, I find it hard to believe.'

'I'm sorry. I shouldn't jump to conclusions. Doctors never should. But as they say, "A little knowledge is a dangerous thing." And that is all I have as yet. Only the years bring wisdom. I haven't seen Dick, spoken to the professor, or heard what the treatment is. I'm ignoring everything I've been taught, and it's unforgiveable of me, Mama. I'll be very happy to be proved wrong.'

'I know you meant well. We must put our faith in God and the professor and give Nell a fairy tale wedding.'

Nicole's mind became easier as pleasanter thoughts filtered through. Rory was to wear a suit of cream satin as a page boy. 'I'm a boy,' he had said. 'Boys don't wear satin.' Six years old and already wanting to prove his masculinity! But Nell – she was sure he loved Nell more than her – had coaxed and calmed him down. Promised him the most marvellous present, one he could choose for himself, and all was well.

She thought of poor, romantic, greedy Molly who didn't know Nell was to be married, and Fanny almost qualified now. She began to think about Horsham and Aldershot then forced herself to put them from her mind. To concentrate on other things. On the appointment Fanny was bound to get in Saint Vincent's as a houseman.

Fanny had changed in the last six months, swinging between moods of gaiety and what sometimes seemed like despair. One day being demonstratively affectionate, as she

had been this evening, and the next silent and brooding. The strain of her final year probably. But lately Nicole had found herself thinking that the same mood swings affected women in love. Was there a man in Fanny's life?

There was. His name was Peter Corrigan, the senior registrar in one of the hospitals where Fanny had gained practical experience on the wards.

At first she'd found him arrogant and overbearing. But as time passed, she realized she was falling in love with him and he with her. He was in his early-thirties, tall, fair and good-looking. He was also married.

Dick came home from Switzerland. Any lingering fears of Nicole's were allayed. He looked the picture of health. His cheeks weren't flushed with the fever of consumption but slightly tanned, and he had regained the weight which on his last visit they had all observed he'd lost.

When Nell, remarking on his lovely colour while stroking his face, asked, 'How can you be so beautifully brown after living in snowy mountains?' he told her, 'Up there the sun shines brilliantly. Part of the new treatment was exposure to it.'

The caterers were engaged, invitations sent out, and the church booked for the second Saturday in June. Nicole's dressmaker fashioned her gown in double layers of turquoise voile patterned with shadowy flowers in pale pink. It had a low belt and floating panels. Her hat was wide brimmed and draped with the same material as her dress. Her shoes were elegant, toes long and pointed, a double strap across the insteps, and had high heels. They were of a deeper shade of turquoise, dyed to match the lockets she and Fanny wore.

'That's more like it,' Michael said admiringly when he saw Fanny dressed for the wedding, in an outfit soft and feminine like her mother's, differing only in colour. It was

pink predominantly with a shadowy flower pattern in turquoise. He kissed her and Nicole. 'I don't know which of you is the most beautiful.'

At that moment Nell came down the stairs in her cream satin wedding dress and veil of Brussels lace. A gasp of admiration greeted her. Michael stepped forward and, taking her hand, said, 'The title is yours. You're the fairest of them all.'

The wide hall was crowded, the servants having come up to see the send off. Roses adorned every surface available, pale pink like Nell's bouquet, dozens and dozens of them, filling the air with their scent.

Rory, completely at ease in his satin page boy suit, bobbed amongst his parents, sisters, and close friends invited to see Nell before she left, in and out, ignoring his nurse's good-natured scolding, telling everyone Nell and Dick were buying him a steam engine. First thing in the morning, before they went on their honeymoon, they were taking him to choose it.

The two carriages arrived, hired from Waller's in Denzil Street, and drawn by silver-grey horses. Nell's was beribboned and flowers lay along the folds of the hood which did not need to be raised on the warm June day.

The other vehicle carried Nicole, Rory, and a friend of Nell's who was to be her bridesmaid, Fanny having refused the honour. 'I'm too old,' she'd protested.

'Only a year more than me. Please?' Nell coaxed.

'But you're the bride. That makes all the difference. I know that many in our circle consider me an oddity. Studying medicine! A lady doctor! Not quite respectable! Usually I don't care, I'm rather proud of being outside the herd. But not on your wedding day, there I'd be judged an old maid.'

Nicole, listening to Fanny, thought: Not long ago you wouldn't have cared about any of their opinions. And she

wondered again if there was a man in Fanny's life. A man she loved who maybe didn't return that love.

The church was like a flower show, the clothes worn by the women like exhibits in a fashion parade. At the appointed time Nell arrived on the arm of her father. The organ accompanied a soloist who sang Gounod's 'Ave Maria' from *Faust*. Everyone was present except Dick, his best man and parents.

Heads leant close together and the women whispered, 'They've been delayed. They live a long way out. On a day like this the coast road will be congested.' Speculation rustled through the chapel like wind through a field of grain.

The organ played the *Intermezzo* from *Cavalleria Rusticana*. The music finished. The priest spoke to the bridal party, suggesting they should sit down. They did so. Rory sat on his father's lap, reminding him that tomorrow he was having a steam engine.

From the vestry door to the side of the altar the sacristan approached the priest who sat at the opposite side reading his breviary, raising his eyes now and then to look at the church's open doors where two ushers waited. The man genuflected before the altar then on soundless feet moved to the priest, bent and spoke. The silence in the church was palpable.

The priest rose, went to the seat where the bride sat with her family. 'I'd like you all to come into the vestry.'

There was a buzz like that of bees. Feeling threatened, Rory began to cry. His nurse told him, 'I've something lovely to show you. It's outside. Come with me for a minute.'

One by one, with anxious faces and sick hollow feelings in their stomachs, the family followed each other into the vestry.

'Nell,' said the priest, 'there's no easy way to tell you this . . .'

Fanny and Nicole exchanged fearful glances. Michael asked, 'Was there an accident? Are they all right? Is it just a delay?'

'A terrible, terrible tragedy. Nell . . .' The priest stood close to her, took her hand in his. 'Nell,' he repeated, 'as they were about to leave the house Dick suffered a massive haemorrhage and died.'

The bridesmaid screamed. For a split second Michael thought he saw the face he had never seen in Ballydurkin and heard her mocking cackle. He blessed himself quickly and the vision vanished.

Many a time afterwards Nell related how she had felt nothing as the priest spoke. Neither shock nor grief. Only a sense of numbness, and very cold. There was the sound of someone sobbing, the priest's voice, but all distanced from her. As if she was in a dream where she could see and hear but not recognize the surrounding faces nor understand what they said.

Her memories were of being put to bed, wrapped in blankets, and the doctor with his finger on her pulse, saying, 'She's in severe shock. No alcohol. Weak, sweet tea, warmth and quiet.' And from somewhere in the house the loud wail of Rory, lamenting that now he'd never get his steam engine 'cos Uncle Dick had gone to Heaven where there were angels but no trains.

She moved through the cycles of grief. Anger with God. Why him? Why did you let it happen? He was young and kind. Good-living. He believed in you. He never harmed anyone. We loved each other. Why?

She moved on to the 'if only' stage. If only we'd married two years before that. If only we'd ignored the doctor's advice in the beginning . . .

Her next phase was one of self-pity. I was never meant to marry. I'm plain and dumpy, not worthy of a husband. Not worthy of a man as handsome as Dick.

And finally she came to terms with her loss.

Through all the phases of her grief she had talked of them with Nicole, who listened and consoled her, grieved for the terrible tragedy she had suffered, felt it unlikely that now, in 1914, with Nell entering her thirties she would get another chance. And if ever anyone was cut out to be a wife and mother it was her.

She would think to herself how unfortunate her daughters had been. Nell doomed to a reluctant spinsterhood. Molly, God alone knew where. Fanny unexpectedly turning down a houseman's job in Vincent's and going to the Elizabeth Garrett Anderson Hospital in London where she'd worked for two years. Two years during which Nicole had worried constantly about her, believing the leaving of Dublin was to do with a man, one she loved and who had rejected her.

Chapter Thirty-two

FANNY went to the Elizabeth Garrett Anderson Hospital in London instead of the Dublin one to gain experience that might not be available in Ireland. In the future she hoped to specialize in obstetrics and gynaecology. The London Hospital admitted only women and so was ideal.

But there was another reason, a more pressing one. She and Peter Corrigan were desperately in love – a love which he argued demanded her giving herself completely to him. 'I don't understand you. An advocate of freedom for women, the vote, birth control, free love. And with me you behave like a silly schoolgirl! For God's sake, you're a woman. I'm not going to make you pregnant. But I can't take much more of this. It's degrading. It's disgusting. Like any little ninny holding out for a ring before the final surrender. I'm married. In our case there can never be a ring.'

She loved all the things about him that she despised in other men. His dominance, arrogance, conviction of always being right, dismissiveness of all views and opinions other than his own. He was godlike, she would think. He reminded her of her father when she was a little girl and had adored him from afar.

What she felt for Peter made nonsense of all her previous beliefs and vows never to allow a man power over her life. And yet she couldn't cross the final hurdle. It wasn't fear of pregnancy nor the hope of marriage. She, Peter and his wife were Catholics. Divorce was forbidden. Was it, she wondered, the Catholic Church's teaching on fornication,

on remaining chaste before mariage? All those ambiguous talks from the nuns after the girls had reached puberty. Had they had so much influence? Perhaps, she admitted. Well, anyway to a certain extent for she no longer thought of herself as truly chaste. She couldn't, in all honesty, having delightfully experienced the whole gamut of sexual fore-play, exploration, even orgasm, only drawing the line at penetration.

And now Peter was demanding all or nothing at all. Mocking her stance as a new liberated woman. And as he had said: 'A doctor, for Christ's sake!'

She spent a lonely first six months in London, working endless hours on the wards, in the theatre, anywhere her services were required. And endless hours turning over in her mind the question of whether she make the final commitment. Realising how much she missed him, how she yearned for his kiss, his touch, the scent of his body. After the six lonely months she wrote and invited him over.

She moved out of the doctors' residence into a small flat on the Euston Road near the hospital, and after their first lovemaking knew she was his for ever. That she could die for him. Kill for him.

She returned to Dublin where sympathetic friends lent flats occasionally. Otherwise it was making love wherever the opportunity presented itself. On both of their parts it required many deceptions, Fanny telling her mother of bridge clubs, late duties at the hospital and her Women's Suffrage meetings.

Peter couldn't use bridge as an excuse. His wife was a first-class player and knew he was mediocre. Nor could he use any of Fanny's other ploys. His had to centre around medicine, and he lived in fear that, knowing most of the medical fraternity, she might stumble across the truth that no such meeting had been held on such and such a night.

In empty buildings, on beaches in the dark, in secluded sand dunes during daylight, and pine-strewn forests, they

made love, each as insatiable as the other. Over and over again he proclaimed his love for her. And when she asked a question which had been tormenting her with jealousy, he told her that, since they became lovers, he had not had intercourse with his wife. 'I think she was relieved. She always seemed to treat it as a duty, a thing to be endured rather than enjoyed.'

'Not like me,' Fanny said, naked in his arms in the bed of a friend.

'Not like you, my madly passionate woman.'

Nicole noticed that the nipple of her left breast was inverted. The same thing had happened after Rory was born and Nicole remembered the nurse tut-tutting and tweaking it out to clamp on the pump. She tried to do the same thing but it didn't budge. Assuming it was not important, she gave it no further thought. From time to time as she dressed or undressed she saw the distorted nipple. Part of old age, she would think. It probably happened to lots of women. But it wasn't the sort of thing to gossip about. At least she was spared Michael's queries and comments. They no longer made love now.

He had retired, from everything you could say except planning Rory's future and religion. Rory would study law. Rory would reach heights he never had. Michael had converted his study into a lookalike chapel. It lacked only a priest, tabernacle and confession boxes. An altar, statues of saints on wooden pedestals, the Stations of the Cross, holy water font and enough chairs to seat a dozen furnished the room. His latest acquisition was a genuine church candle-stand with a place for the unused candles and brass fixture complete with slot for coppers to pay for them. Never less than half a dozen burned at a time.

She found it an eerie place. Nell and Fanny joked that perhaps Papa was thinking of taking Holy Orders. When they first said this Nicole pondered the truth of it. The

Catholic Church didn't encourage but allowed it, though she had never known of a husband with a living wife who had. The common belief was that, in such a case, the wife entered a convent. Maybe he was contemplating Holy Orders? Maybe that was the reason for his celibacy?

Whenever Nicole thought of Michael becoming a priest she told herself, Not if it depends on my becoming a nun, he won't. I'm enjoying life. Rory is a healthy boy, God bless and spare him, Fanny thriving and Nell making the best of things. I want to live, not be buried alive in a convent.

There was time now for her to stand and stare at beautiful buildings, visit the National Gallery, stroll through Saint Stephen's Green, read books she had intended reading for years. She had unlimited leisure and she loved it.

Only if she suggested a visit to the Zoological Gardens was Rory eager to accompany her. He preferred playing in the park facing the house after school. There, while his nurse sat knitting and gossiping, he romped with the grandchildren of couples who came to live in the Square when Nicole and Michael moved in.

On 4 August 1914 war was declared. In London and Dublin men responded to the sound of the drum and Lord Kitchener pointing from a poster, its caption reading: 'Your country needs you'. Young men seeking adventure left their office stools and ledgers; tailors laid down their shears, took tape measures from round their necks; shop walkers hung up their shiny frock coats, mechanics their oil-soaked overalls.

From public schools, universities, hospital wards, from all classes and all walks of life, they went to defend the Empire, Belgium, and other small nations being overrun by the murderous Hun. From nagging wives, pregnant sweethearts, boredom, lack of opportunity, work and money,

they chose to go. In any case everyone said it would all be over by Christmas.

In his chapel, mortifying his body by kneeling for hours on arthritic knees, Michael prayed for them. Prayed for Molly, Fanny and Nell, Nicole and Rory. Prayed for the dead, for anyone he could remember, even Aggie and Phyllis.

Fervently he implored God never to let down his guard and allow the spectre of Mag Cronin to enter his mind. And never forgot another plea: that his investments would prosper.

Nicole's left breast became inflamed and she found a lump under her arm. She bathed the inflammation with a solution of boracic powder and treated the lump with hot fomentations. She considered visiting her doctor then decided to wait until after Christmas. Eventually Nell went with her.

I've known her for more than thirty years, delivered her babies. Have been intrigued by and a little in love with her, thought her doctor. Now she sat in front of him, still beautiful, smiling, waiting for his diagnosis. He didn't ask why she hadn't come sooner or scold her for not doing so. It would serve only to alarm her and in her case would have availed her nothing. Her cancer was of a pernicious type, in both breasts, and had spread to the liver. She would live three to six months.

'Well,' she asked, 'is it serious?'

'No,' he lied, 'but unpleasant. A severe inflammation, painful in the weeks ahead while it runs its course. You may get more lumps under the other arm, in your neck. They're glands, doing their job defending your body. I'll prescribe something to help them. The medicine will make you tired, sleepy. It's supposed to. Powerful stuff so don't worry about the weariness. I'll call in and keep an eye on you.'

He prescribed a powerful sedative. The morphia he'd hold back until the pain began.

After Nicole and Nell left he telephoned Saint Vincent's and asked for Dr McCarthy. When Fanny came on the line he said he'd like to see her as soon as possible, a health problem of her mother's he couldn't discuss over the telephone. She arranged to call in the afternoon.

He gave her the news as one doctor to another and then spoke as a friend. Comforting her, offering his handkerchief to dry her eyes, close to tears himself.

'She doesn't suspect?' Fanny asked.

'She's a good actress if she does.'

'Poor Mama, she never has been self-absorbed. Will you tell her? She would want to know.'

'I don't think so. If the prognosis held even the slightest hope, I might. But not in these circumstances. I'll tell your father.'

'You can't! He's not fully in charge of himself. I think he's slightly mad. A case of religious mania. He'll collapse, be more of a burden than a help. There'll be two invalids in the house. And he's bound to tell Mama.'

'He's her husband, Fanny, he has the right to know. You must tell Nell. She'll be very involved.'

'Of course. Nell's a brick. She'll cope. If only I could feel so sure of Papa.'

'He may surprise you. Please arrange for him to come and see me.'

Reluctantly she agreed. Thinking: If it was my patient, I wouldn't tell him. Then she put her objectivity to one side and thought as a daughter. Vulnerable, confused, certain of nothing except that she didn't want her mother to die.

Before leaving the consulting room she telephoned the hospital for permission not to return that day. Something urgent had come up. She was needed at home. When she arrived Nicole was resting. Nell greeted Fanny, put her arms round her and whispered, 'It's cancer, isn't it? I guessed. It is, isn't it?'

'Yes,' Fanny said, clinging to her sister.

'A bad case?'

'One of the worst possible, and it has spread.'

'Oh my God! Poor Mama. I want to scream, to cry, but I can't, for her sake and Rory's. Can they do nothing?'

'Palliative treatment, that's all. You were with her. Do you think she suspects?'

'Not a thing. I'd swear to that. Let's sit in the breakfast room. We won't be disturbed.'

Fanny told her that the doctor insisted their father had the right to know, and how she had objected.

'Mama would handle it better than him. She's the one I think should be told. I wouldn't want to be dying and not know. And I haven't a quarter of her normal courage. She'll have things to say, to arrange, plans for Rory's welfare. Even perhaps a letter for Molly in case she should ever turn up.' Nell began to cry. 'Oh, Fanny, it doesn't seem real, sitting here talking about Mama dying. If you'd seen us this morning! Not a worry in the world. Almost skipping along. Oh, Fanny, isn't life terrible sometimes? Will she live long?'

'Not very – three to six months.'

'Poor Rory, robbed so soon of his mama. We'll have to be very brave,' Nell said, getting up from her chair. 'I'll have to bathe my eyes not to show I've been crying. And you'd better see Papa about going to the doctor. Will you go with him?'

'I suppose I'd better,' Fanny replied. 'We'll say nothing to the servants at present for fear misguided sympathy might alert Mama to how seriously ill she is.'

'Yes, that's a wise precaution. Let's hope Papa will be as sensible.'

To their immense relief, in their mother's presence he behaved as always, though Fanny told Nell how, after hearing the diagnosis and prognosis, he had wept like a child. And when they passed the chapel late in the evening, when Nicole was in bed and the servants in the basement, they heard him sobbing.

For the first month after the cancer was found Nicole continued to look and eat well. Only her increasing tiredness, which she blamed on the sedatives, caused her to complain. 'Though I must admit, it isn't an unpleasant feeling. Like soaking in a warm bath, drowsy, contented. But on the other hand, such a waste of time. I'll be glad when that part of the treatment stops. So far it isn't having the slightest effect on the glands. Too soon probably.'

The girls and Michael steeled their souls to smile, to agree, to contradict her as if everything was normal. The doctor called, examined and reassured her, telling her and whichever of her daughters, usually Nell, was present that the treatment was working, but slowly. Alone with them he confessed that deterioration was progressing rapidly. Soon they must engage a nurse.

Fanny interviewed and engaged two to start at a later date.

The pain began. 'Where is it, Mama?' Fanny asked.

'In my chest, my stomach, my back. I know it sounds ridiculous but it seems to be everywhere.'

'You haven't eaten anything for days. That's what ails you.'

'My stomach feels too queasy. I've nausea all the time now.'

'It's lack of food. When you miss meals your body is deprived of minerals. That causes aches and pains and nausea,' Fanny said, while thinking, the cancer has spread to the bones and lungs.

'Will you get up? You might feel better sitting in a chair. I'll put it by the window. The snow makes the park look so beautiful.'

'I think I'll stay in bed today.'

'Then I'll have lunch sent up on a tray.'

'No, darling. I couldn't eat anything. But I'm very thirsty. Get Cook to squeeze some oranges.'

Fanny pretended to be interested in some children

building a snowman in the park. Non-existent children whose antics she described, afraid to look at mother, not wanting her to see the tears which, on pretext of blowing her nose, Fanny dried.

This was the first day her mother didn't get up. The beginning of the end. You could see it in her face. It was time for the morphia to be prescribed. Continuing with the monologue until she had controlled herself, she then turned back to the bed. Nicole was asleep. She tiptoed from the room, found Nell, told her of the change in their mother and that she would telephone the doctor.

'Let Papa know, he's in the chapel.'

The doctor came almost immediately. Fanny went upstairs ahead of him, her father and Nell to waken her mother. She was awake already. 'Fanny, I'm glad you came. I was about to ring for you and Nell. Papa I will want to speak to alone. Sit down, darling.'

'The doctor's here. He and the others are waiting for me to call them up. Shall I?'

'No, not yet. Well, perhaps Nell.'

When the girls were seated on the bed, Nicole took a hand of each in her's. 'What would I have done without you when Molly left, when I went into the Liffey, and when Rory came? I love you both very much and I don't want you grieving too much when I die.'

'But, Mama,' they said together, 'you're not . . .'

'I know I am. Don't be worried or frightened. I'm not. Of course, given a choice, I'd prefer to live for a long time. Well, long enough to see Rory grow up. That is truly what saddens me.'

'Did you know all the time?' asked Nell.

'No, I didn't. I believed I had an infection, that I'd get better. Then a week ago, maybe when the pain first started or glands came up in other places, suddenly I knew. Something about me changed. I suppose everyone does know when they're dying. Some won't admit it. Or maybe

319

it's an instinct some have lost. Once we must all have had it, like animals. They know, slink away to find a quiet private place.'

Fanny and Nell were crying openly, Nicole as well. 'It would be unnatural if we didn't. Ah, life seems to go so quickly. Yesterday I was a little girl in France, then a young bride in Dublin, a young mother. But really, it was all a long time ago. I'm not young any more. I've had a full, rich life. I've been a lucky woman. I know that Rory will be taken care of, but Papa . . . he's tiresome, I know, but, he wasn't always so.'

A bout of coughing seized her. She let go of the girls' hands and clutched at her ribs. Fanny wiped the sweat from her forehead, the skin under which no flesh seemed to remain so that her fingers felt the skull. Please God, she prayed, don't let her linger. Don't let her suffer.

Nell stood by with a glass of water which she held to her mother's lips. Nicole sipped a little.

'Such a cough and such a pain in my ribs! I think I've cracked them. Could coughing do that, Fanny?'

'I doubt it,' she said. 'You've just strained yourself.' She dabbed cologne on the temples that had always been hollow but never sunken as they were now.

'Shall I let Papa and the doctor come?' Her mother's ribs had probably cracked. The pain must be excruciating. She'd need morphia.

'In a little while. Listen, there's some money of mine. The sum settled on me by my papa.'

Her voice was a hoarse whisper now. They leant close to her.

'Before Rory was born, before Molly went away . . .' She sighed. 'I'm so tired.'

'Don't talk any more,' Nell urged.

'I have to. Lift me higher.' They propped more pillows behind her. 'Rory must have a share.' She had to rest before continuing, 'Advertise for poor Molly.' She closed her eyes.

Michael knocked then opened the door. 'You were so long in calling us, I wondered if anything was wrong?'

Nicole, her eyes open, waved a hand, beckoning them in. A long beautiful hand from which the lacy cuff fell back, exposing her arm. Nell shuddered to see how thin it was. How hadn't she noticed before? Her mother's beautiful rounded olive-skinned arm come to this.

Michael, followed by the doctor, came in. 'You're looking grand,' he said, bending to kiss his wife. She was gasping for breath. 'Tell them, Fanny,' she panted, 'tell them.'

'I shouldn't have underestimated your intelligence,' the doctor said. 'I'll change your medicine. It will ease the pain, make you sleep.' She smiled at him and said something. He couldn't hear and bent closer. She spoke again in laboured whispers. 'Yes,' he said, stroking her hand, 'instinct not intelligence. You're probably right.' Michael made no attempt to control his sobbing. Nicole swallowed the morphia.

'I'll stay until you fall asleep, darling.' They left the room and Michael lay on the bed beside his wife. Later on Nell and Fanny looked in on them. They were sleeping, turned to each other, their father's arm across his wife's waist.

He seldom left her side, eating his meals there, sleeping on Nicole's bed. Fearful that in his absence her breathing would grow shallower and shallower until the last breath passed, barely audible, and she would have slipped away.

During her brief wakeful periods she indicated that she preferred his company to everyone else's. The girls felt hurt at the rebuff, until one day Nell said to Fanny, 'It's hurtful but she knew him long before us. More than thirty years. Imagine that. She was nineteen when they met.'

'I used to feel jealous of them, they were so wrapped up in each other. She loved us. I suppose he did too. But they loved each other more.'

Fanny thought of Peter, how love for him excluded all

else. How in the midst of grieving for her mother, her longing to be with him took precedence over all else. How this minute, if the telephone rang and it was he, wanting to see her, she would find an excuse to go to him. 'Now I think I understand how it was for Mama and Papa. To love someone as they did must be wonderful,' Fanny said, and willed the telephone to ring.

'I do too. Dick and I loved each other deeply. I'll never forget him.'

Once the nurses were installed Fanny had gone back to work. During ward rounds she saw Peter. There was seldom an opportunity to speak unless to answer a question asked about a patient, but notes were left in places where each would find them. Passed, but not too frequently, to a porter with instructions to find Dr Corrigan or McCarthy.

The notes were some comfort while she waited for things to return to normal. Illicit weekends, or making love in places where at any moment they might be discovered. The furtiveness only heightening their excitement. She hated herself for wishing things back to normal, for that meant the death of her mother. She knew it was callous of her and could do nothing about it.

Nicole died on a February evening with the priest, her doctor, Fanny, Nell, Michael and the servants reciting the Prayers for the Dying. Only Rory and his nurse were absent. Michael held one of her hands in his. She breathed her last little breath as the prayers were finishing. Those not family left the room. Each in turn kissed their wife or mother. Nell and Fanny embraced their father. 'We'll leave her now, Papa, for the nurse to see to.'

Tea was sent to the drawing-room where they sat in silence until Nell said, 'Poor little Rory. I'll tell him in the morning. She'll look nicer after being laid out.'

Michael, for the first time in years, craved the oblivion drink would bring and chain smoked instead. For a while

they consoled themselves with cliches. God had taken her out of her suffering . . . She's in Heaven now . . . She had a good life . . . But suddenly Michael said, 'I killed her. I broke her heart, never mind what the doctor writes on the death certificate.'

'Ah, Papa,' Fanny said, 'you did no such thing. Mama had cancer. Lots of women of her age die of the same. You mustn't blame yourself.'

He ignored her. 'I broke her heart the day I wouldn't tell her where Molly was, let her see the letter she had written. God forgive me! In His mercy He may. I believed . . . well, you know what I believed. Possessed I was by the certainty that Mag Cronin had our future in her hands, was playing cat and mouse with me and my family. Going to Beggars Bush Barracks, to Horsham, or the moon itself would have altered nothing. The life I led your poor mother! And I adored her, worshipped her, was mad jealous of her.

'I knew that James was in love with her. Always from the time he first laid eyes on her. Neither of you knew that, did you?' They admitted they hadn't and he continued, 'Poor James, I'll have to write and tell him, he'll be so sorry.

'Thank God I'd sense enough not to accuse her. But there were other ways to vent my spleen, to make her life unpleasant, God forgive me.'

'Poor Papa, don't cry. Will I get more tea? This has gone cold. A sandwich or something? You've eaten nothing all day,' Nell said, and Fanny sat beside Michael on the sofa and put an arm round his shoulders.

Now they saw him clearly, an old man, broken-hearted, nervously puffing cigarettes, his hands shaking, raised veins on their backs. His head was bent, the pink scalp showing through the thinning silver hair. They listened to the story of how he'd met Nicole simply, with no embellishments. A story from their parents' past, when they were young lovers. And they cried along with their father and knew no matter how much in the future he might try their patience,

they would see him now in a different light. With more love and compassion. Remembering a time before they existed when he was young, gallant, and filled with hope for a bright future.

Michael was remembering a special day, the one when this house became theirs. They had made love on a rug left by the previous owner. He'd told Nicole a supposedly true folk tale. He knew she knew he had invented it. Was it that day Molly was conceived or was that when Nicole told him she was pregnant? He couldn't remember. That happened lately.

But clearly he heard his voice, telling her how in the years to come they'd have grand dances in this room. And when they grew too old to dance, they'd sit and watch their grandchildren gliding round the room. And they'd remember this day.

It was a beautiful memory, one he couldn't share with his daughters. It was his and Nicole's.

Chapter Thirty-three

FANNY applauded the 1916 Rising. The courage of such a few brave men and women pitting their puny strength against the British. She hated the majority of her fellow countrymen who laughed and mocked at their efforts. Soulless creatures blind to the ideas they aspired to – until the brutality of what they were fighting against was pushed under their noses by the executions daily of the rebellion's leaders, including James Connolly, already mortally ill, carried out on a chair to be shot.

'How fickle people are,' she said to Peter. 'Last week those that are praying and weeping now were laughing and jeering at the same men. Didn't they know what courage, however foolhardy, they had shown? Didn't the scoffers and jeerers anticipate how it would end?'

'Ah, darling,' he said, 'you take everything so to heart. It was always so. Remember Jesus. And don't forget what a confused and confusing country we live in. The mob were Irish, the majority God-fearing Catholics. Not a group one would have expected to favour the English, but you'll find nine out of ten amongst them would have sons, fathers or brothers fighting in France. Where else in the world would you have such a situation?'

He smoothed her hair. 'You are getting silver streaks, not the odd grey hair. Very attractive.'

'What is described as "distinguished-looking" on a man and "ageing" on a woman,' Fanny said humourlessly.

'Nonsense, you're not old.'

'I'm almost thirty-five – half my allotted life span nearly over.'

'Are you saddened, knowing that if you stay with me you'll never have a child?'

'Consciously, no, but I dream of having babies, losing babies, babies being born looking like you who vanish. Die, I suppose. My body warning me time is running out.'

'It would break my heart, but if you wanted it I would release you. You could still marry and have a family.'

'Never say such a thing, never!' She pounded her fists against his chest. 'I never loved a man before you. Not even a crush on one. If you went out of my life I'd die, kill myself. Kill you.'

He kissed her. 'I love you. I'll never leave you. And when the war is over we'll travel. Go to France and Italy. Have a bed to call our own for more than a night.'

'And what will you tell your wife to explain your absence?'

'We made a pact, remember, not to think about her. It hurts you. She means nothing to me. But we are married, Catholics. That means very little to me but Jane's devout. Now we won't mention her again. And remember, the bed is only available for a few more hours.'

Fanny promised. They made love. Peter fell asleep. And just before she drifted off, into her mind came the thought: Unless she dies, he'll never be mine.

Molly read about the Rising on Easter Monday, 1916. Nostalgically she recalled the streets and buildings mentioned in the articles, thought how brave the Volunteers were, and hoped her family hadn't been harmed during the week's fighting.

Since it looked as though the war would never end, she offered to switch her act from Irish ballads to patriotic songs, and was taken aback and a little worried when the theatre manager gruffly advised her to stick to what she was

good at. Three weeks later he hired a skinny young Cockney girl, all teeth and bones you could cut yourself on, who led the cheering audiences in rousing choruses of 'Pack Up Your Troubles' and 'Goodbye, Dolly Grey'.

The stage door johnnies left fewer invitations and presents for Molly these days. She didn't miss the bouquets or fending off persistent advances in cabs or private dining rooms, but the champagne and chocolates . . . well, Molly missed those until she realized there was no shame in buying them for herself. After all, she was in her thirties now, couldn't expect to be treated like an ingénue all her life. Fat, fair and almost forty – what was wrong with that?

Nevertheless she was uneasily aware that the applause was growing less warm with each passing week, and the manager less and less polite.

To keep her thoughts occupied Nell acted more as a housekeeper than the mistress of the family home. Ordering the supplies, checking the linen, inspecting the laundry, running fingers over furniture and window ledges. She seldom found anything amiss and when she did called no one to account. The self-imposed tasks were ways of keeping busy, of not thinking. Not allowing herself to admit that her life was a miserable one.

Rory, at eleven years old, no longer sought her company.

Fanny was at the hospital during the day, sometimes on night duty, playing bridge, attending meetings. A week could pass and they not see each other. Her father spent his time praying in his chapel or rearranging it. Once he had come to her in a disturbed state asking if he should send for the priest.

'But why, Papa?' she enquired.

'I've never had it blessed. What sort of chapel can it be without being blessed? Maybe it should be consecrated?'

'I don't think so, Papa. Churches are only consecrated

because during Mass the bread and wine becomes the body and blood of Christ. But maybe a blessing. Only since you don't allow the servants in, it would want a good cleaning first. Let me know when that's convenient and once it's spick and span we'll bring the priest.'

That satisfied him, but maybe only for the time being. Bring the priest indeed! He'd judge her father to be losing his mind. And Nell would find it hard to disagree.

Thoughts of her mother were constantly with her. She sometimes expected to open the drawing-room or bedroom door and find her seated before her mirror or looking out of the window. Sometimes she thought she heard her voice calling her name.

She knew that as when mourning Dick only time would change this. Not that you'd forget. You never forgot. But the memories weren't so laden with grief.

The family solicitor, Brian Moynihan, had placed an advertisement in an English newspaper, the *News of the World*, where people who had lost touch with their families and had been left bequests were asked to make contact with the advertiser, usually a solicitor, when they would hear 'something to their advantage'.

'I've placed them before, Nell. Some were answered. But now there's a war on. People on the move.'

'Not women. Not many women on the move surely?'

'Some of them. There are women in the army, and doing nursing. I'm only warning you not to be too disappointed if you don't get an answer in a hurry. How often do you want me to advertise?'

'What d'ye think?' asked Nell.

'Twice this year and then annually for a while. I wouldn't advise it be done indefinitely.'

On the day the manager moved her to the bottom of the bill Molly knew it was only a matter of time. Her money had been cut more than once as her stock with the

audiences fell, and the comfortable flat and smart little maid had long since been dispensed with. She was down to one room in Brixton, near the Hill where the big stars had their grand houses.

'You must have done all right,' one of the chorus girls tried to comfort her. 'All these years on the boards. You must have a bundle saved by now – enough for a nice little business.'

The truth was that greedy, careless Molly had little more than twenty pounds, the exact same sum Aggie had sewn into her corsets before she fled for London.

But when, without looking her in the eye, the stout, red-faced manager told her they'd decided to feature a knife-throwing act instead of her sentimental songs, Molly didn't make a fuss. Late in life she remembered her mother's strictures on how a lady never showed her true feelings – even though her heart was pounding and a high, terrified voice was asking over and over in her head: What'll I do now? Oh, God, what will I do?

She thought back over the years to her arrival in London, a terrified and penniless fugitive from Bert, and the answer was suddenly blindingly obvious. One lovely September day she set off for Soho.

In the park the trees were pretty with their autumn leaves. Molly's spirits rose with each step nearer Saint Anne's Court. She forgot her increased weight, her age, and thought only happy, hopeful thoughts.

Picturing Verna's delighted greeting. Telling her and the girls about the life she'd lived in the theatre, and the way they'd cruelly thrown her over.

Then there'd be tears and Verna saying, 'Never mind, love, things'll work out. You've a bed here, and work if you want it.' Maisie would say, 'No, she doesn't, Ma, she'll get fixed up in the theatre. Maybe not a part straight away, but props or wardrobe.'

Molly sighed with relief as she saw the cafe. It hadn't

changed in all the years – except that inside stood a man she didn't recognize behind the little counter. 'Yes, love, what can I get you?'

'I was looking for Verna.'

'You'll have to look further than here. Packed up years ago. Went back to Liverpool.'

'I never knew that.' Unknown to herself proclaiming the statement as an accusation, she continued speaking in the same manner. 'I came back to live here, to work here. I never expected her to be gone.'

'You a friend then?'

'A very close friend.'

'How come she never told you then?'

'Oh, God! Oh, Jesus, Mary and Joseph, what'll I do now?'

'Try sitting down for a start, otherwise you'll fall arse over tit. You're a big girl, I mightn't be able to pick you up.' He helped her to a chair. 'You have a good cry, and I'll get you cup of coffee.'

'I never wrote. She didn't know where I lived. But when I did give her a thought, it never crossed my mind she wasn't still here.'

He left her to serve a customer. From the tiny kitchen she heard grease spitting as he fried the order. Everything was the same: the smells, the rickety tables, wobbly chairs, yellowing lace curtains over the window. Any minute she expected Verna or the girls to appear. Everything the same . . . everything that didn't matter.

'The bloke next-door takes lodgers if you're looking for somewhere to stay,' the cafe owner said when he rejoined her. 'So do I, but my lot are permanent.'

'How much does he charge?'

'Two bob a night, I think.'

Molly thought wistfully of the smart little flat she'd once been able to afford. Even her last bedsit in Brixton seemed like a haven now she had left it. The man didn't pry and she

didn't volunteer any more information. Instead she asked, 'Why did Verna leave?'

'Her girls cleared off, and then her old man snuffed it. Dropped dead one morning on his way to the Garden.'

Molly took the room in the house next-door. It was a back room, drab and furnished with the bare essentials. The landlord, a tailor, was friendly, smiled and greeted her in an accent that was difficult to understand. But it was a warm greeting. The man who kept the cafe was also friendly. She knew no one else in London but theatre people and they didn't welcome a performer down on her luck. Once she'd been happy in Soho, and felt at home there. So she took the room.

Chapter Thirty-four

THE war was over. The men came back, crippled or blind, shell-shocked, shambling, lost-looking. Those still whole searched for the land fit for heroes they'd been promised, and work if they were lucky.

Michael was sixty-three and looked ten years older. He seldom went out, sold his motor car, wrote numerous letters to James who never replied. Not even to the news that Nicole had died.

Rory, at thirteen, was almost as tall as his father. 'A McCarthy, every inch of him,' Michael said to Nell and Fanny, 'though not in his ways! I was never that distant with my father. When I went down to Clongowes last weekend he hadn't a word to throw to a dog. I thought for a minute he was ashamed of me.'

'Papa, of course he isn't. He's very shy. He's exactly the same with us, isn't he, Fanny?' Nell urged.

She agreed that he was. 'It's his age.'

'What's age got to do with it?'

'He's going through a difficult stage.'

'Ah,' said Michael dismissively, 'that's more of those newfangled ideas. Bad manners is what it is.'

From time to time letters came from the family solicitor informing them that the advertisements for Molly were still being placed in the *News of the World* periodically. Immediately he heard anything he would get in touch.

In the little room above the tailor's Molly slept late into Sundays. When she woke she smelled herrings. Always

there was the same smell. The family ate the fish fried, boiled, soused and pickled. Many times after her twenty pounds was spent hunger drove her to accept the herrings in whatever guise they were offered by the tailor's wife, a thin woman with a straggly bun who had eight children, worked in the shop, and attempted with not much success to learn English.

During the war Molly worked in a munitions factory, but not for long. The foreman pinched her bum and touched her breasts. Told her what a fine woman she was – but sacked her all the same when she couldn't keep pace with the others.

Then the men came back from the war and jobs were like gold. All she had left of any value was her turquoise locket.

'You could come out with me,' Greta, one of the cafe girls, suggested on a night when Molly didn't know where next week's rent would come from.

'You mean . . . ?'

'Yeah, nothing to it. I mean, it's not as if you were a virgin or anything. I know you're posh but you've got to eat.'

'What d'ye have to do?' asked Molly.

'All depends what the bloke wants. Anything out of the ordinary you charge extra.'

'No, I didn't mean like that. How d'ye attract the man in the first place?'

'You just stand there and smile. Seldom have to say anything. They're out looking for it. And know when they've found it.'

'And where would you do it?'

'In a doorway. Down a lane. Wherever you're not likely to bump into a copper.'

'I don't know. I don't think I'd like it,' said Molly.

'Who said anything about bleedin' liking it? It's the money you like.'

'No, I couldn't. I'd rather starve. Throw myself in the river.'

'It's your funeral.'

'I wouldn't mind so much doing it, but out in the open.'

'Suit yourself, I've got work to do. I'll buy you a port and lemon, come on. Eh, hang on. I've got an idea. Would what's his name, Grundy, your landlord, let you take a bloke upstairs?'

Molly laughed. 'I keep telling you, his name's Mr Solomon, not Grundy.'

'That's my joke, I know what the bleeder's called. Would he let you use the room?'

'I think so. He'd be in bed anyway.'

'Then you're made. I know just the bloke for you. He doesn't like fresh air either.'

In the public house Greta bought the port and lemon then left Molly by the bar while she went and spoke to a middle-aged man sitting in a booth.

Molly had found her first client.

And afterwards half-a-crown on the wash stand.

'It's the ideal opportunity. Jane is suffering with her nerves, she's gone home for a couple of weeks. What do you think?'

It was seldom Peter mentioned his wife, seldomer still he used her name, Fanny thought. But of late, as Black and Tans were ambushed, and retaliated with ferocity, the IRA raided police barracks, stole arms, murdered constables, and civilians were shot in crossfire between the warring sides, Jane's nerves had become the topic of many a conversation between Fanny and Peter. One-sided usually, Peter complaining of the demands made on his time and attention by his wife's nervous condition. Fanny would make sympathetic noises while wishing that nerve trouble was a terminal condition. Painless but quick.

'Well?' he prompted.

'Home – you mean to England?' Fanny asked.

'Stop wool gathering, Fan. I thought you'd be jumping for joy with the news.'

'At my age it's undignified.'

'For Christ's sake, will you stop always going on about your age? We can have at least a week, maybe ten days, together.'

'And do what? Spend it cooped up here?' She looked disdainfully round the basement flat. It had changed hands several times since they began using it but so far the tenants had all been unmarried doctors, friends or colleagues of Peter's, waiting to move to better accommodation and willing to assist him in his illicit affair.

In all the years it had never been repainted or thoroughly cleaned, Fanny would think each time she and Peter entered it. The air was permeated with unpleasant smells: mould, stale tobacco, drink, sweat and sex. Many couples used it for illicit meetings. It depressed her, highlighted the hopelessness of her life and its prospects.

The older she grew, the more she became aware that sexual passion, ecstatic though it was, didn't compensate for other needs. Her longing for an open relationship with Peter. To walk through Dublin with him, share a home, be acknowledged as his. To sleep all night with him, wake in the morning beside him. What she wanted was to be his wife.

'Listen, pay attention,' he said. 'We won't stay here. We'll go to France. We both have holidays to come. I'll take Jane over, see her installed in Bournemouth. Then you and I'll meet in London and head for the Continent.'

'But Jane . . . I suppose you'll pretend you're going back to Dublin? She'll be expecting letters, telephone calls.'

'I've taken care of that. Letters written and dated, and arrangements made to have them posted at intervals. No

problem about telephone calls. Her father's an eccentric, wouldn't have one in the house.'

'I can't believe it! I've got to pinch myself. A week, maybe longer. Oh, Peter, I love you so much. I'm sorry for being so miserable and moody.'

'It's your age, my darling. I'll make allowances.'

She began to undress. 'We'll see about my age!'

They embraced, kissed and fell on the bed.

Fanny wore her mother's wedding ring. Between Boulogne and Paris she asked Peter to put it on her finger, waiting until their carriage had emptied. Memories of making the same journey with her mother years ago came back as the train made its way into the Gare du Nord. How excited she, Molly and Nell had been. Then Nell's usual whingeing when she discovered they weren't at Issoudon. That they would stay overnight in Paris and take another train in the morning.

The railway station appeared not to have changed over the years. Dirty, crowded, noisy; huge engines belching steam. The smell of strong cigarettes and the sound of French being spoken. Her mind didn't linger long on reminiscences or observations, her thoughts kept returning to the present. To Peter, head and shoulders taller than the majority of Frenchmen, holding her hand, squeezing it so that the wedding ring hurt her finger. To a week when they wouldn't be parted. A week in which she would be addressed as Madame Corrigan and for that time believe she was his wife.

'You were wrong,' he said as they left the station and walked into the sunshine. 'Last week you said it was the last fine day before winter. Just feel this glorious heat.'

'Ah, but that was Dublin. This is Paris, and Paris is magical. It always welcomes lovers,' Fanny replied.

'My romantic, neurotic, ancient nymphomaniac. God, I love you!'

In honour of Paris, and to please Peter, she had bought new clothes, far less severe than her usual ones. A costume of fine cream woollen cloth, the skirt to mid-calf, its front straight, sides and back with fullness from unstitched pleats. The jacket had raglan sleeves and finished just below her waist where it fastened with a single large button. Anticipating that the weather would be chilly, she had chosen a large fur collar. It was uncomfortably hot as they walked to their hotel, a small one just round the corner from the street facing the railway station. Her large-brimmed hat was trimmed with a grosgrain ribbon the colour of weak coffee. She wasn't used to shoes with such pointed toes, and, crossing the street, grumbled that they pinched.

'A small price to pay for the admiring glances you're attracting,' Peter said.

It was on the tip of her tongue to ask: 'As many as Jane would?' Jane with her Nordic beauty. Fanny had seen her at medical functions and knew she was nicknamed The Ice Maiden by the young doctors.

The question wasn't asked. First because Jane was never discussed unless it was unavoidable, and secondly because she no longer existed. She, Fanny McCarthy, was Mrs Peter Corrigan for the thousands and thousands of minutes ahead of her.

Now remembering their passports, the different names, she panicked. 'A lot of good wearing a wedding ring will do when I'm McCarthy on my passport and you Corrigan!'

'It's France, not a country hotel in Ireland. Quite apart from you maybe qualifying before we married, and therefore quite legitimately having a passport in that name, do you honestly think the hotel will give two hoots? Now relax, and forget about everything except our glorious taste of freedom.'

For a couple of days she did. The weather remained warm and sunny. They explored the city, sat at boulevard

cafes watching Paris pass by. Reading the newspapers. Commenting on the number of Americans there were.

Paris, Peter said, was full of writers, artists and rebels against the restrictive way of life in their home countries. France to them meant artistic freedom, inspiration, European culture, not to mention no Prohibition. 'There's an Irish colony here as well,' he said.

'I hope we don't run into them,' sighed Fanny.

'D'ye know many Irish painters and writers?'

She admitted she didn't.

'Neither do I, so stop worrying.'

But on the third day, browsing through the second-hand book kiosks erected along the banks of the Seine, she clutched Peter's arm and urgently whispered, 'That man who's just passed – I'm sure I know him and that he recognized me.'

'From where?'

'I don't know, but he did, he stared.'

'So would I. You look gorgeous. Paris is full of men who appreciate a beautiful woman.'

Fanny wasn't convinced. The strolling through the streets, the coffee-drinking at pavement cafes, became a nightmare. For in the passing crowd sooner or later there always appeared a face, sometimes a man's, sometimes a woman's, she believed she had met before and who recognized her.

After a row in which Peter said she was guilt-ridden, neurotic, and an Irish Catholic to the core, he relented and agreed they would move on to Bourges the next day.

Rory went back to college for the new term. During the holidays he and Michael had discussed his future. He'd put forward no objection to reading law at university, nor later reading for the Bar, but the day before he was to leave he announced his intention of joining the British Army when he left school.

Michael ranted and raved, came close to striking him, prayed that God would still his hand, then called on Nell. When she came he told her to keep Rory out of his sight and that tomorrow she could see him off alone.

'What's happened, Papa?' she asked.

'He's thrown everything back in my face! Deserted me. My only son. I pinned my hopes on him, and he's going to be a soldier. A British soldier. Every opportunity in front of him. He could become Ireland's leading judge. Take him out of my sight.'

He hurried away from them to his little chapel where he knelt, tears pouring down his face, praying aloud. 'Dear Jesus, it's only a little setback, isn't it? He could change his mind . . .

'Dear Jesus, help me. Don't desert me. You've given me your special grace all these years. With it I banished from my mind the obsession that was destroying me and my family. Sometimes it's been hard and without your help I wouldn't have succeeded. I faltered when I couldn't find Molly. When Dick died, and above all when I lost Nicole. But you were there beside me to comfort and support me and I came through.

'Now and again I remember. I hear that voice from Hell and doubt begins to take hold. Guard and protect me, I implore you. I'll accept the daily grief for the loss of Nicole and Molly. The sadness I see in poor Nell's eyes when she's remembering Dick, being deprived of a husband and children. Fanny's not finding a husband nor advancement in her career. I accept them all as your Will. Don't ever let me doubt that and see in its place a malign influence at work.'

He stayed for a long time, kneeling in silence, until peace descended upon him and he knew God had heard and answered his plea.

Molly built up a steady clientele of middle-aged and elderly

men who crept up the stairs when the tailor and his family were asleep.

Before each one's arrival she fortified herself with gin or port and lemon, often snoozing while the men went about their business. If they noticed, none commented. Thursdays, Fridays and Saturdays were her busy nights. Once the smell of their unwashed bodies, of sweat, drink, onions, jellied eels, and of their occupations – soot, engine oil, plaster dust – would have nauseated her. But lately personal hygiene didn't have as much importance in Molly's life as once it had. She accepted them all. They were her providers, paid her rent, for food and drink, and gave her many laughs as well.

For two months after returning from France Fanny and Peter saw little of each other. This they'd agreed upon as Jane's visit to her home in England hadn't improved her nervous condition. 'I'll spend all my free time making a fuss of her. Not that I think it'll make the slightest difference – but one never knows. She never did like Ireland and now, with this War of Independence, she loathes it.'

'Then why doesn't she leave? Go home to England?'

'She's a good dutiful Catholic wife in some respects. She sees her role as being by my side.'

Inwardly Fanny seethed. What right had Jane to be by his side? She who couldn't possibly love him, who had regarded their lovemaking as something to be endured. Fanny wished her dead. Wished her caught in the crossfire between the Black and Tans and Michael Collins's men. Imagined herself confronting her, telling her she herself was Peter's rightful wife, that there was more to marriage than a certificate. Then she asked herself how was she to endure living the rest of her life in this fashion? The balance of her mind was being affected or why else should she harbour such murderous thoughts about a woman she didn't know?

A woman whose only crime was that she loved her husband.

Their holiday in France had made the situation more fraught. For a week she had lived as his wife. Shared an intimacy that was more than sexual. Experienced for the one and only time in their long relationship what it was like to be married. She couldn't endure it for much longer. One way or another, she had to take charge of her life. There was only one way. In the New Year she would leave Ireland. Go to England or America. Start a new life alone. For though she didn't doubt that Peter loved her, she knew he would never desert his wife. He could and did commit adultery, but nevertheless believed in the Sacrament of Marriage. She found that difficult to understand but as she often told herself, her brand of religion, though nominally the same as Peter's, in practice wasn't.

'You're very pensive. Not having second thoughts on our decision to stay apart for the time being?'

'No, of course not. Come December we'll be back in the flat.'

'I'm afraid not.'

'Don't tell me someone with moral scruples has taken it over?'

Peter laughed. 'Nothing like that. There's a conference in Belfast, I'll be there for the first week of December.'

'I'm sure I'll manage not to fall apart. You'd better go now.'

They had risked this rendezvous in a small hotel outside Dublin. A seaside resort deserted by visitors once the summer was over. Travelling to it on separate trains. Meeting on the shore. Walking on the pebble-strewn beach, buffeted by the wind. No shelter where they might have made love. They embraced and kissed, no one to observe them except seagulls – swooping, crying, as if in sympathy with their predicament.

The hotel lounge was empty. They ate tongue sandwiches and drank hot whiskey. When it was time to go Peter kissed her hurriedly outside the door. 'Until December,' he said as Fanny went for her train.

Chapter Thirty-five

'Ah, Fanny, there you are. I was looking for you. A patient I'd like you to see. But don't rush your coffee.'

He sat opposite her, Dr Massey, doyen of Dublin's medical fraternity. An old man, the oldest still in practice. A benign-looking man, silver haired, bald as if it had been tonsured. Merry eyes and a sweet smile belied his more formidable side. A good, charitable man, he sat in the free clinics twice a week and was revered by the poor of Dublin. And he tolerated no opinion other than his own.

Fanny had some respect for him; for his great age, the excellent doctor he must once have been. But now he was past it. Hadn't moved with the times, was out of touch with modern medicine. Scoffed at new discoveries and treatments and was ruthless with anyone who dared query a diagnosis or prescribe alternative treatment.

'Peter Corrigan's wife Jane has been brought in. You know Jane? You and he worked in Vincent's before you came to us.'

Fanny nodded. 'Yes, only to see though, at balls and medical functions. I believe she's English. Is she seriously ill?'

'Difficult to tell. Always is with the hysterical. That sounds unkind. I don't mean to be unkind but women who have problems with their wombs tend to be slightly unbalanced.

'She and Peter have been most unfortunate. Several

343

miscarriages, the last one only a few months ago, and they wanted children so much.'

The little rest room suddenly felt stifling. Fanny found it difficult to breathe. He wasn't just old, he was in his dotage. Had to be. Peter desperately wanting children? Massey was a senile old fool! How could there have been miscarriages? She had Peter's word for it, he never touched his wife. Not once since they'd fallen in love.

'Are you unwell? You look pale.'

She took several deep breaths, regaining some composure, enough to assure him she wasn't ill, only tired.

'Good. In that case, we'll go along. Jane's rather shy and sensitive by nature. As a woman your presence will put her more at ease.'

'Yes, of course,' Fanny said as they went along to where the private wards were. And before reaching Jane's: 'What did you say ailed her? I'm afraid I've forgotten.'

'According to O'Gorman who sent her in she's complaining of abdominal pain, nausea, and has a slight fever. I think she's on the change. An early one. Nearly forty, still desperately wanting a baby. Unlikely now, I'd say, with her history.'

Fanny fought to be objective. Look dispassionately on this woman. Put from her mind thoughts of miscarriages – recent ones if Dr Massey was to be believed.

But even as she entered the ward memories of the few days spent in Bourges were in her mind. The small hotel, its rooms above the restaurant. The smell of pork and prunes being simmered.

On their last afternoon Peter ran out of cigarettes. The restaurant and bar were closed. He went out to buy them, was gone a long time. So long that Fanny began to worry. Imagining him under the wheels of a cart. Seeing horse's hooves pounding his head, leaving him dead in the street. No means of identification on him. The Gendarmes milling round, their capes swinging, questioning bystanders. Gallic

shrugs. His body taken to the morgue. How would she know? How could she be found?

She ran to the window, opened it and leant out. The sun was shining. Pails of golden, red and bronze autumn flowers, chrysanthemums, stood on the market stalls that edged the square. Across it she saw the thousand-year face of the cathedral rising in its majestic glory. And amongst the people hurrying to escape a sudden shower she saw Peter and was relieved and so delighted she called his name aloud. 'Peter,' she shouted. 'Peter,' she called again. Passers by looked up at the window, saw her waving hand and radiant smile. Wondering who she was, who she was smiling at. Looking about them, they saw the tall man, also smiling radiantly. And in turn they too smiled and went on their way, smiles lingering.

As she followed Dr Massey to Jane's bed, Fanny thought, It was the loveliest day of my life. I'll remember it when I'm an old woman. I'll remember it when I'm dying.

Jane Corrigan's golden hair was loose, silky ropes of it spread on the pillow, and her nightgown was peach satin.

'Jane,' Dr Massey asked, 'how are you feeling? Still in pain?' She nodded.

'This is Dr McCarthy. Françoise.' She barely acknowledged the introduction. Watching her tense face Fanny deduced the reason was pain, not hauteur or rudeness.

'Let's have a look, shall we?' The nurse carefully folded back the sheet to just below Jane's navel. 'Show me where it hurts, dear,' Dr Massey said. Jane placed a hand beneath her left hipbone. Careful not to disturb the sheet, he slipped a hand under it and palpated the area, gradually moving his hand, his fingers gently probing the surface of her belly.

'Relax,' he told her, 'let your stomach go limp. Good, good. Tell me when it hurts.' She winced when his fingers returned to beneath her hipbone. He drew up the sheet.

'Have your bowels opened today?'

The movement of her head could have been interpreted

345

as yes or no, Fanny thought, as could her answer to Dr Massey's next question, 'Any looseness?' She was too ill, in too much discomfort, to answer. Dr Massey looked ruminative, stroked his silky moustache and cleared his throat. Fanny dismissed the appendix as the cause of Jane's malady. Her knees were not drawn up, guarding her abdomen. Another diagnosis occurred to her, a serious condition needing immediate surgery. One that, had Massey not mentioned the miscarriages, she wouldn't have considered. But if Peter had been lying about not having sex, and obviously he had, Jane could have a tubal pregnancy.

During her time in the London Hospital she had twice seen them diagnosed in the nick of time. And once missed. The woman's fallopian tube ruptured and she died from a massive haemorrhage. If Jane Corrigan had an ectopic pregnancy and it wasn't spotted, she could be dead by morning.

No blame would be laid at anyone's door. It was a notoriously difficult condition to diagnose, the symptoms mimicking so many other less serious complaints.

Dr Massey was talking in a fatherly, reassuring voice. 'Nothing to worry about, Jane. An infection. I'd like Dr McCarthy to have a look at you.'

'Rather like a second opinion,' Fanny said, smiling at Jane. Thinking, as she spoke, Second opinion, my eye! That egotistical, senile blunderer doesn't know what such a term means. She rubbed her hands briskly together to warm them before the examination.

'Cold hands, good for pastry,' she said as the nurse again rolled down the sheet. 'But not pleasant for the patient.'

As she palpated she asked questions. 'Mrs Corrigan, besides the pain, have you any other symptoms? Any discharge, loss of blood?'

'I missed a period, but it is starting.'

346

'Ah, yes,' said Dr Massey. 'Irregular bleeding, beginning of the change. I told you that last time I saw you.'

'I think I'm pregnant,' Jane said, turning her head to avoid Fanny's gaze.

So do I, thought Fanny. It's there beneath my fingers. Yours and his. But you'll lose it.

'Well, Fanny?' Dr Massey asked.

'As you said, an infection of the urinary tract.'

If she didn't get out of this room soon, get away from this woman who had Peter's doomed child inside her, she would lose her self-control. Already it was slipping. Her professional self giving way to a jealous, hate-filled, vindictive woman.

Dr Massey was reassuring his patient. He would prescribe some treatment. In a few days she'd be as good as new. 'I'll be in in the morning. Nurse Bermingham will give you something to help you sleep.'

In the corridor he said to Fanny, 'It may be an ovarian cyst. No point in alarming her. No urgency. See how it is tomorrow, eh? Could account for the bleed.'

So could an ectopic pregnancy, Fanny thought, but who am I to question his diagnosis? I could telephone Peter in Belfast. He'd be here in a few hours. He wasn't in awe of Massey. Could get someone from the Rotunda to see his wife.

His wife. A surge of bile came up her gullet, burning it. Why should I care?

Because you're a doctor trained to save life. You took an oath, remember? Because if it is a tubal pregnancy, it will rupture. She's eleven weeks. The time is ripe for rupture. She'll bleed to death internally.

And if she does, a voice other than her conscience whispered, then he'd be free to marry you.

Fanny went to bed, convinced she would be awake all night, and immediately fell asleep. It was later than usual when she came downstairs. Nell was finishing her breakfast

and reading the *Irish Times*. She put down the paper and poured tea for Fanny. Handing it to her, she said, 'There was a telephone call for you earlier.'

'Who was it?'

'He didn't say, didn't leave a message.'

Peter – it must have been him. Fanny felt afraid. He must be back in Dublin. They'd agreed there should be no contact while he was in Belfast. 'I won't be a minute,' she told Nell, 'have to get in touch with the hospital.' With the receiver in her hand, she had second thoughts. She never rang the hospital to enquire about a patient. It was as quick almost to go there.

Enquiring about Jane Corrigan, who wasn't one of her patients, would cause comment especially if . . . She couldn't follow that thought through. Should she try Peter's home number? No, a servant would answer. She replaced the receiver. 'Nell,' she called from the hall, 'don't bother about breakfast. I'm late as it is. I'd better dash off.'

Her diagnosis had been right. Jane Corrigan had died during the night. A nurse found her semi-conscious, bleeding internally. Blame was laid at no one's door. Even Dr Massey spared the usual behind-his-back gibe of burying his mistakes. For everyone agreed, including Fanny, how difficult it was to diagnose a tubal pregnancy.

A letter from Peter which had come in the afternoon post awaited her when she came home:

Dearest Fan,

You will know by now why Jane died and believe the worst of me. Don't judge me too harshly. What occurred between myself and Jane in no way devalued our relationship. I have only ever truly loved you. And though to some it might seem indecent to talk of such a thing now, for us not to would be hypocritical.

When a suitable time has elapsed we will begin a

courtship, become engaged and marry. I love you. I'll always love you.

Peter

Chapter Thirty-six

IN 1923 Rory joined the British Army. Before leaving Dublin he spent a lot of time with Nell, the two of them walking into town, commenting on the number of motor cars, buses and electric trams. But how the hackney cabs were still holding their own.

He liked the cinema: Charlie Chaplin and Buster Keaton were his favourites. Nell had been to see Rudolph Valentino in *The Sheik*. She admitted to having loved it, but not to having fallen a little in love with Valentino. She believed he resembled her dead sweetheart, Dick. Often when she lay in bed, thinking about him, his face and Valentino's would merge, becoming one.

On one of their walks through town they went into the recently opened Metropole Cinema and had tea in the restaurant. Elvery's was close by. After tea they'd go there for cricket flannels and sports equipment for Rory to take with him to England.

She was proud to be seen with this tall, fair, handsome young man. They looked alike, both having the McCarthy cast of features and hair – though hers was fast turning white. People sitting round them, she thought, would assume they were mother and son. And I could have been, too, she said to herself. I was twenty-two when he was born.

'I'm surprised how well the da is taking my leaving after the initial ructions.'

Nell objected to his calling Papa 'the da'. It was

common. But she never commented on it. 'He tries hard to be tolerant nowadays.'

'I think he's slightly mad.'

'The poor man — he wasn't always so. There's been great sadness in his life. Terrible tragedies in his family.'

'I know all that. The drownings, losing the farm. His sisters dying and Molly running away. All part of life. It didn't have to turn him into a religious maniac.'

'Ask the young. They know everything,' she said.

'That's very sarcastic for you.' Rory looked hurt.

'I'm sorry, love.' She covered his hand with one of hers. 'You were so certain, so definite in your opinions of Papa. And you don't know the whole story.'

'What else is there?' he asked sulkily.

She told him about Mag Cronin's curse and how it had obsessed their father fairly late in his life. Made him an alcoholic, driven their mother to attempt suicide, almost destroyed the family. 'He believed in its evil power as you and I believe the sun will rise in the morning.'

'What about Fanny, my mother, you, Molly before she ran away? Did you and they believe in it?'

'Oh, no. Never for a minute. Not then or now. But Papa did and I think it's only his devotion to God, over zealous though you may think it, that keeps him sane.'

'One set of superstitions replacing another?'

'That's a terrible thing to say. Surely you didn't mean that, Rory?'

'I didn't. I was trying to be clever. I'm sorry. But it all suggests to me that he's unstable. Probably always was. Ask yourself, would any normal, right-minded man believe what you've told me?'

'If you put it like that, I suppose not. But not everyone's the same. Things affect one person that wouldn't take a feather out of another.'

'How is he getting on with Peter Corrigan? Does he approve of the engagement?'

'Delighted, but as he said to me, wasn't it a pity they didn't meet sooner? They couldn't, of course. Peter's a widower. His wife died a couple of years ago. Papa was just regretting Fanny didn't marry years ago. She's older than me, forty-one. And he'd love grandchildren. It'll be up to you now.'

'Moll might have children. Do you still advertise for her?'

'Once a year. Poor Molly. She could be dead and we'd never know.

'I suppose we'd better make a move or Elvery's will be shut. Tell me again why it isn't to Sandhurst you're going?'

'Because I'm joining the Royal Artillery. And Gunners go to The Shop.'

'What d'ye mean, the shop?' asked Nell.

'Woolwich, London. That's where I'll do my training and be commissioned from.'

'Now that we've got Independence you could have joined our own army.'

'I want to see the world. Not much chance of that in the Free State Army.'

For the sake of decorum Peter and Fanny waited almost a year before appearing in public together.

While they waited, long passionate love letters went to and fro. Each wrote of the future. They looked forward to an end to their illicit affair – but for all the hole and corner aspect of it, the beaches, forests, dungeonlike flat, they had had wonderful exciting moments which neither would ever forget.

Once in a letter, Fanny queried why they couldn't have carried on with their secret meetings.

'We went undiscovered then, why is it more likely now? Sometimes I want you so much I'm tempted, usually late at night in bed, to get up and go banging on your door, demanding that my needs should be satisfied.'

Peter replied: 'If the dungeon was available perhaps we could risk it. But you know what O'Driscoll is like. He's the most po-faced prig! Not for a million pounds would he lend his flat to anyone. So, my darling, curb your desire. Time is passing and soon we'll be together for always.'

Never since the letter he wrote on the morning Jane died did he again refer to having been found out in his lie. In the beginning the fact that he had lied to her weighed heavily on Fanny's mind, for she was still troubled by why she hadn't trusted her own judgment and somehow alerted someone that Jane was having an ectopic pregnancy.

And then she would soothe her conscience by blaming Peter. The shock of discovering that through all the years of their affair he was having intercourse with his wife had unhinged her. Clouded her judgment. Exaggerated her awe of Dr Massey. That had to be the reason, the only reason. She was a doctor, dedicated to easing suffering, to saving life, not a murderer.

She and Peter would start afresh. The past was done with. She would never upbraid him for his lies. Never mention them. Their courtship would be wonderful, new and fresh, as if they had just met and fallen in love.

A medical ball coincided with the end of his mourning period. He went. So did Fanny. They were already acquainted so it was only natural that he should dance with her, escort her home, leave . . . and then, as Molly's Bert had done years ago, come in through the garden door where Fanny waited to guide him to her bedroom.

He sent her flowers, bought her jewellery and an engagement ring. There was a party and a date was set for their wedding in 1924.

When Peter, Michael, Nell and Fanny bade goodnight to the last of the guests to their engagement party and returned to the dining-room, Michael asked where they intended setting up home.

'Round here somewhere, I suppose,' replied Fanny. 'Two brass plates on our front door.'

'Here, Hume Street or Merrion Square are the only suitable places,' said Michael. Wishing he could buy them a house as a wedding present. But money went nowhere these days.

They talked about houses and localities, then about Ireland and events there in recent years. The ending of the War of Independence, the signing of the treaty, the last of the killings, so they had thought. An Irish Free State which in no time erupted into that most vicious, pitiless civil war, with friend killing friend, families divided. Men who would have died for each other, when their struggle was against England, now dying by one another's hand.

'And poor Mick Collins, our golden boy, gunned down by one of his own. Who'd have thought it?' said Michael.

'Lord have mercy on him, he knew it himself,' said Nell. 'Didn't he say when he signed the Treaty: "I'm signing my own death warrant"?'

Fanny yawned, complained of being jaded, and reminded Peter she was on duty early. It was time he went home and let them go to bed. She saw him to the door where she whispered, 'Walk for ten or fifteen minutes. Nell and Papa aren't used to being up so late, they'll fall asleep in no time. I've left the garden gate open.'

Mr Solomon prayed for someone to order a suit or overcoat. Customers came but not for bespoke garments. Came for alterations, to have trousers reseated, let down or taken up, and poor women brought in the shabby, shiny suits of their sons who were going after a clerical job, to be turned: laborious, painstaking work, turning a suit inside out, completely remaking it, reworking buttonholes and attempting to make the existing ones, now on the wrong side, invisible.

In Leeds he had heard there was more opportunity. He

warned Molly in advance so she could find another room. She found one three streets away. For a while her regulars still came when the public house closed but after a while found another woman closer to hand. Some weeks she had to do it in the open air. Some weeks she only barely made her rent money. Some weeks she longed never to wake up when she went to bed.

Nell saw with sorrow the signs of delapidation about the house. The servants worked hard but not all their assiduous polishing of brass, silver, rosewood and mahogany could hide walls that needed re-papering, ceilings and doors painting, sash windows that required rehanging. In her mother's time maintenance took place regularly. A brief explanation to Michael who, with a dismissive wave of his hand, would say, 'You know what's needed, have it seen to.' Tradesmen and craftsmen were employed, the work done and cheques signed without a quibble. Not so lately. Even the provisions merchant's, the butcher's and coal supplier's accounts, Michael scrutinized. Suggesting that so much meat, such a quantity of groceries and coal, was excessive.

She replanned menus, ordered fewer joints, less cream and fresh coffee. But overall it made little difference. Once, when presenting her accounts, she drew her father's attention to the fact that college fees no longer had to be paid for Rory, nor clothes bought.

'Nor food,' retorted Michael. 'When was the last time he set foot in the house, tell me that?'

'I think he was hurt and offended that none of us went to London to his passing out parade. You know, when he received his commission.'

'Wasn't I laid up with pneumonia? And Fanny as usual in her hospital minding strangers. Only for you I'd have died.'

'I wrote and told him all that. Poor Rory, he's lonely at heart. I tried to take Mama's place, and did to some degree,

but it's never the same. He's made his life in the army, in England. I doubt if we'll see a lot of him in the future.'

'What makes you think so?'

'His letters, if you read between the lines. He's distancing himself from us.'

'He's not the only one. Molly did it completely and Fanny's following in her footsteps. When she's not working, she's out with him.'

Nell didn't comment but felt the same way. For Fanny was like a giddy young girl with her first sweetheart. Though recently Nell had wondered if their romance was as recent as it was made out to be. Several times Fanny talked about events shared by her and Peter, once mentioned a holiday in France, then catching herself on, would hastily change the conversation.

Reflecting on these snippets, Nell would convince herself she had misheard, misinterpreted. Fanny, for all her liberated ideas, would never have had anything to do with a married man.

Nell's existence was a lonely one. She went to daily Mass, belonged to the women's sodality. Walked in Saint Stephen's Green, and sometimes went further afield to Herbert Park. She was stocky rather than stout, and not interested in clothes, choosing them for warmth and comfort rather than to enhance her appearance.

Occasionally she pondered on how different her life might have been if Dick had lived. They would have had children. Instead of traipsing the streets killing time she would have been involved in something worthwhile with a future to look forward to. Not the bleak prospect of old age with no one belonging to her close at hand. Fanny and Peter would almost certainly buy a house in the vicinity. They weren't likely to have a family. Probably both finish up as professors in the medical faculty of one or other of the universities and pursue an active social life. Not much room in it for an old maid like Nell.

Such gloomy thoughts never lingered long in the parks, dispelled by the changing seasons, snowdrops and crocus, buds on the trees, the feeling of spring. Nest-building blackbirds and starlings, robins, sparrows, and chattering, quarrelling starlings. Old men and women with small dogs or walking sticks, wrapped against the cold, or in panama hats, linen dresses and suits enjoying the sunshine. There were babies and children with their nursemaids to observe, and babies minded by children not much older than themselves, some barefoot, some in clothes several sizes too large. Pretty cheeky children, not in awe of the park keeper, ignoring the 'Keep off the grass' signs.

Women's skirts, she noticed, were now worn just below the knee and Nell thought how out of touch with fashion were her own calf-length ones.

On a day when she had found the walk down Grafton Street particularly exhilarating she turned the corner into Nassau Street. A taxi cab stopped outside Jammers. From the cab Peter emerged, and then, assisted by him, one of the most beautiful girls Nell had ever seen. A girl she judged to be not much more than twenty years old. Should she continue on as she had intended? In which case they couldn't miss each other. The girl stood looking up the street while Peter paid the taxi driver. It was uncanny, Nell thought, how strongly the girl resembled Fanny twenty years ago. She felt a great sense of foreboding, turned to a shop window and pretended great interest in the goods displayed until she saw from the corner of her eye Peter and the girl go into the restaurant.

Molly moved again to a room in Lupus Street near Vauxhall Bridge. It was smaller and more dismal than the previous, and divided in the middle by a curtain hanging from floor to ceiling. Behind this flimsy partition another woman slept, ate and plied her trade into the small hours of the morning.

The woman was older than Molly, unfriendly, and drank when she wasn't asleep.

Molly missed the Solomons, even the smell of their herrings. She missed Soho, and all the people she'd known there. Trade was bad. Men, even foolish drunken ones, passed her by for younger, more attractive girls. It was her size, she would think, and smile warmly at the memory of one of her regulars in Soho describing their lovemaking as like falling into a feather bed. The men nowadays didn't seem keen on feather beds. The young girls in their twenties were skinny as boys.

As she grew older and her life more miserable, Molly's thoughts returned more and more to the only happy times she had known. Not, as she would tell herself, that while living through them, she had known them to be happy. But with hindsight they were – until she ran away. That was the beginning of all her misfortune.

She thought despairingly of her life now. Dirty, smelly men, leaving her a florin or half-a-crown. Never able to get their smell out of her room or off her skin. Imagine if her mother knew! Imagine if she saw Molly up against a wall in an alleyway, skirt above her waist and a man she'd never seen before going like the clappers of Hell.

Mother would have begged on the streets rather than do what I do, Molly realized. But how else could I earn the rent and money for a little food? I could maybe become a charwoman – probably earn more money. The truth is, at heart I'm a wanton. A loose woman. Forced to make a choice between my skirt up over my knees or down on them, scrubbing a floor, I'd pick the first any time.

But her life, she decided one day, didn't have to be all bad. Somewhere there might be a man for her – a kind, gentle type. Not young and not rich. A widower, maybe – someone with a home of his own. A man who could take a liking to her, love her a little. If only she had something like

that to look forward to her present way of life might not seem so unbearable.

Her purse was heavy with coins today. Two shillings' worth in ha'pennies, threepenny bits, pennies and farthings. She'd heard one of the girls talking about a fortune teller on the Walworth Road. Didn't fleece you and was good apparently. But Molly didn't fancy the walk in this weather. There was supposed to be another good one up a street on the left-hand side, first turn after Waterloo Bridge. She charged two shillings. Dear for that locality. All the same, it might be worth it.

Half-fearful, half-expectant, she turned into the street where Madame Celeste foretold the future over a barber's shop.

Madame Celeste sat at a table covered by a green chenille cloth. On the table were a pack of cards, a crystal ball, a Coleman's mustard tin and a skull the size of a closed fist. Into its open top Madame was flicking her cigarette ash.

Molly looked to the uncurtained window. She couldn't be sure but it looked as though fog was creeping in through it. She didn't care. She'd have her fortune told and leave quickly.

'I only tell the truth, not what people want to hear,' the fortune teller warned.

Molly nodded her head.

'You're Irish,' said the woman.

'I am.'

'And run out of luck.'

'I have,' Molly admitted, and thought: This woman's not all there.

'You come from a cursed family.'

'Oh, that. That was nonsense,' laughed Molly.

'Was it?' asked the woman, and Molly thought for a minute that her voice had changed, a strong brogue taking the place of her Cockney accent. She dismissed the idea, attributing it to a muzzy head brought about by hunger.

The fortune teller continued to talk. The Irish brogue became more pronounced and the woman's little black eyes grew smaller and more piercing. 'Was it all nonsense? All the tragedies? All the unhappiness in your life and your family's?'

The voice now reminded Molly of those she had heard in Ballydurkin.

She felt uncomfortable and annoyed, believing the woman was jesting with her, imitating an Irish accent.

'Your family will remain cursed until the end of time.' The accent grew stronger, and Molly thought the woman was not only a jokester but a fraud as well.

'Look,' she said, 'I only came to have my fortune told. D'ye think you could do that?'

The fortune teller was swaying in her chair. A bloody good actress though, Molly thought. I wish I had my money back. It's freezing in here. The fog was definitely coming in through the window, little swirls of it hanging inside the panes.

'More tragedies will fall on your family – but it can change. The curse can be lifted. It won't undo your past but it will free someone else's . . . someone who'll become very precious to you. Only I can tell you how . . .'

'How then?' Molly demanded, losing her patience.

'Reparation must be made. A descendant of the man who caused the curse to be laid must marry a descendant of the one who was wronged.'

'Is that all? Is that my fortune?'

The woman regarded her with unseeing eyes. Molly could contain herself no longer. Standing up, she started to shout: 'You bloody old fraud! How dare you make a joke of my voice and tell me such rubbish? I've a good mind to call a policeman and demand my . . .'

Oh, Sacred Heart of Jesus, she's dead! She's not moving! The expression's gone from her eyes. Oh God, I'd better get out of here. I could be accused.

Molly ran from the room and down the stairs into the street and across the bridge. The fog seeped into her, soaking her clothes. She kept hurrying, neither knowing nor caring where.

As she turned into the Strand a hand caught hold of her elbow. A policeman! Her heart almost stopped.

A man's voice said, 'Miss, you'll do yourself an injury. Slow down, for God's sake. Are you all right?'

It wasn't a policeman, even in the fog she could tell that, though from the voice it was definitely a man. 'You should be wearing a hat. Your hair's soaked. You'll get your death of cold. Let me buy you a drink to keep out the chill?'

'Please,' she said. 'Yes, a drink, I'd like a drink.'

He was a widower. His name was Anthony Crampton and he had a house in Finsbury Park. Molly told him certain things about her life. How she had eloped, that her brutal husband was a Lancer and she had run away from him after life in married quarters.

She told him about working in the cafe then on the stage, but pretended that after that she'd worked as a factory hand.

'It closed down,' she said finally. 'My luck's run out. I was going to throw myself in the river when I met you, only I couldn't find the way in this fog.'

'You mustn't talk like that. Where there's life, there's hope. You're a young woman, a fine woman. Where are you living now?'

'That's just it. That's why I wanted to do away with myself. I lost my job last week and I've only money for the rent till Friday. After that I'm out on my ear,' Molly lied.

'You poor girl. Couldn't you ask for time to find another job?'

Molly liked him. He had a kind, tired-looking face, not much hair. His suit was shabby but clean, so were his nails. Everything clean and tidy. He was old, nearly sixty she

guessed, and obviously not rich. But he had a house. He might grow to like her.

'I'm afraid not,' she replied. 'The landlord said if I don't pay the rent on time he'll throw me out. That's why I was going to . . .'

'Don't say it. Can I call you Molly?'

She nodded.

'Right then, Molly, here's what we'll do. That is, if you want to? My house is no palace but it's got plenty of rooms. You can have one until you get on your feet. What d'ye say?'

'Well, I don't know. I mean, I've only just met you.'

'Think of me as a landlord you'd just met. You wouldn't know him either.'

'I suppose so, but maybe I won't get a job. Then what about the rent?'

'I've other tenants. You can keep the place tidy. Sweep the stairs, give the downstairs windows a rub, that sort of thing. And for the time being, forget about the rent. What d'ye say?'

She had angled for such an offer but when it was made, even though she expected there might be another price to pay, was so relieved, so grateful, that tears filled her eyes.

Seeing them he said, 'No need to cry, girl, I'd never refuse anyone shelter. Stay till you've sorted yourself out. Will you do that?'

'I'd be very much obliged. I don't know how to thank you.'

'You can start by calling me Tony. About your things, clothes and that, will you want to go back and get them?'

'No, there's nothing worth going back for. I'll go home with you now.'

'Good. Now I'll get you another whiskey, and maybe a pie?'

'I'd love a pie. I didn't realize how hungry I was.'

She watched him make his way to the counter. A tall,

thin man, not pushing or shoving. A gentle person. The man who could be her redemption.

Chapter Thirty-seven

MOLLY was in Heaven when Tony brought her to his home in Florence Road, Finsbury Park, a shabby three-storey house. On the way there he explained that he had the downstairs rooms and one on the first floor as a bedroom. That there was a small one on the same landing which she could use.

'The others are let out to the lads. Irish labourers. A decent lot. Drink a bit but cause no trouble. Nothing else to do in the evenings, so far from home. They pay their rent and don't bother anyone. They're hardly ever in the place. You'll have no trouble from them.'

She didn't immediately notice dirt embedded in the wooden draining board. A flyblown mirror above the mantelpiece. Congealed grease on the gas cooker and the oilcloth. Or the smells of mice, gas, and innumerable fried meals.

She was aware only of the warmth of the kitchen, its cosiness, and above all a sense of security. Tony made her tea and toast spread with fish paste. He filled two stone jars and took them to the room she'd sleep in, to air the mattress.

Molly drank the tea and stretched her feet to the fire he had revived since they came in and thought maybe he'll let me keep house for him permanently? I'd do it just for the bed and board.

When he came down from the bedroom he sat opposite her. Of an evening, he told her, he didn't come home until after seven. It was up to her how she spent her day. She

might get a bit lonely with no one else in the house, but soon she'd get to know the neighbourhood. People were friendly. Then he said he was tired but for her to stay up as long as she liked. He showed her where the coal was kept, and the food. 'Root round in the morning, you'll soon get the hang of things,' he said, and went to bed.

She stayed down for a while longer, thanking God for her luck. Wondering was the fortune teller dead? Would there be anything in the papers about it? Wondering if like all the men she had known, Tony would be looking for payment in kind. She expected so and that she wouldn't object. He was giving her board and keep, and in any case, though not the handsomest of men, he wasn't repulsive.

She went to bed and fell into a deep dreamless sleep. When she woke there wasn't a sound in the house. Looking at the clock she saw that it was midday and panicked until remembering Tony didn't come home until the evening.

On the table in the kitchen she found fifteen shillings and a note from him, telling her she'd need money for meat and veg. Fifteen shillings! She'd get plenty of meat and veg for that, and enough left over for a pair of knickers, a vest and slip. She kept thinking she was dreaming and any minute would wake up and find herself back in the curtain-divided room with the other woman coughing or screaming abuse.

Before going shopping she had a look round the house. The room next to the kitchen was filled with junk. It was meant, she supposed, to dine in. The parlour was overfurnished with a piano, two whatnots laden with knick-knacks, an inlaid oval table on a pedestal. There was a red plush-covered chaise longue with two matching armchairs, and four other upholstered seats, also in red plush. A black overmantel with mirrors, a long one in its centre, flanked by fluted pillars.

Every surface was covered with dust. On top of the piano were two tortoiseshell frames holding tinted photographs. Molly saw that one was of a man and woman, a young

couple's wedding picture. The bride wore a picture hat and mid-calf white dress flounced round its hem. The man had on a suit, was serious-looking and his hair was wavy. He was staring at the camera with a serious and slightly alarmed expression, but the young woman was smiling, her head turned slightly towards him. She was very pretty, very young, and looked very happy.

The other photograph was of the same woman, alone, in her bridal gown, looking directly at the camera.

Molly replaced it and picked up the other one. It doesn't look a bit like Tony. I'd never recognize him, but I suppose it is him and his wife on their wedding day. You can see she was younger than him. She probably died upstairs in his bed. I wonder if he'll ever tell me about her?

He did after she'd been in the house for three months, during which she was happier than she'd been for years. Each day she shopped on the Holloway Road, cooked stews, sausage and mash, bacon and liver, and with help and advice from Tony, made roast dinners on Sundays.

He worked as a sorter in the Post Office. He had been there since leaving school at fourteen. He'd gone to live in Florence Road just before that and had been there ever since.

'It was a funny thing that, living in Florence Road and marrying a girl with the same name. Flo, I called her, he said on the night he mentioned his wife for the first time.

He wasn't what you'd call a talkative man, Molly thought, sitting in the kitchen eating dinner with him. Three months it's taken to get this far. Not that I mind. And I don't feel lonely when he just sits there, smoking his pipe and reading the paper. It's as if I've known him all my life.

Fanny was surprised to find a letter from Peter when she arrived home from the hospital one day asking her to meet him for dinner that night. Surprised because she hadn't

expected to see him until the weekend. Both of them were studying for further qualifications, sitting examinations before their wedding early the following year. She was also surprised at the hotel he had chosen for their dinner: a small dingy place on the Quays near Island Bridge, noted only for its popularity with cattle dealers.

'It's most peculiar,' she said to Nell as she drank a cup of tea before she went to have a bath and change.

'Perhaps something has come up about the house?'

'In that case, why didn't he just drop in here? Peter's under some sort of strain. Maybe we're being too ambitious cramming in examinations, looking for a house and arranging a wedding?'

'The wedding surely isn't that difficult? It's going to be a quiet affair. As for the exams, I'm not qualified to comment, but the difficulty in finding a house I don't understand. Since the Treaty was signed, more and more families have been going back to England. There's houses in abundance.'

'I've thought the same,' said Fanny, and wondered if she was ageing as quickly as her sister Nell. Nell's only forty-one, twelve months younger than me, but she looks fifty, she thought. She could do more with herself. Her hair, her clothes. Poor Nell, it's easy for me to be critical of her. To forget she has no incentive to keep herself attractive. Alone here, Papa no company. And she's never developed any outside interests. Not even whist. And has never been made love to. Imagine never having known a man.

'Anyway, I'll soon know what the mystery is all about. Now I'm going to soak in a bath as hot as I can bear. If you're still awake when I come in, I'll tell you.'

Nell laughed and said, 'Me? I'll be fast asleep before you two reach the coffee stage.'

Fanny looked at herself in the bathroom's full-length mirror, a recent purchase of hers which Nell had declared

indecent. She'd told Fanny how she always covered it before undressing.

Fanny was pleased with her own reflection. Her waist as narrow as when she was a girl. Her belly flat, her breasts small and firm, their nipples slightly tiptilted. She cupped them in her hands and thought how in a few hours it would be Peter holding them. Of how much she had missed their regular lovemaking since the studying began, and how tonight she would insist that he come back to the house with her.

He met her in the foyer. She touched his face.

'You look so tired. Poor darling, you've been working too hard.' They went into the bar. A waiter brought a menu and asked what they wanted to drink. Peter ordered two sherries. 'Sorry,' he said, 'for not greeting you more effusively. I am tired. How are you?'

'Puzzled,' she said, 'as to why you chose this place? But delighted to be with you anywhere.' He smiled and she thought how much she loved him and how a week without him had seemed an eternity.

Cattle dealers in heavy tweed coats came in, drank whiskey and left to catch trains from the nearby railway station. Peter and Fanny studied the limited menu. The waiter brought their drinks. They ordered then talked about their respective courses, the forthcoming examinations.

Fanny felt uneasy. They were talking like two people who were only slightly acquainted. Labouring at their conversation, uncomfortable gaps of silence. Then, unable to resist, she asked: 'Peter, why here? Why did you pick this Godforsaken hole?'

'I wanted to be in a place where we had never been. Somewhere with no associations. Where we'd never been happy. Where there were no memories. A neutral place.'

'Neutral isn't how I'd describe it. It reeks of cow dung and overcooked beef,' she said in a sardonic voice.

'I'm sorry. I'm so sorry.'

'For what? Are you ill? Has something terrible happened to you?'

'I can't go through with it. I've wanted to – I tried. I was going to write but that would have been cowardly. I owed you the courtesy of telling you.'

'Telling me what, Peter?' she asked, terrified, for she knew what he was about to say.

'I can't marry you, Fanny.'

'Why?'

'There's someone else.'

'Oh, I see.' She was going insane. She was having a nightmare. She wasn't sitting in a room that reeked of inferior food, filled with country voices ordering drinks, talking cattle prices, and another saying, 'I didn't seek it out. It just happened. I tried to fight against it. You have to believe that I wouldn't have chosen to hurt you.'

'Who is she?'

'A girl – a French girl.'

The waiter came and announced, 'Your table is ready, sir.'

'D'ye want to eat, Fanny?'

'And vomit over the table? I thought for a minute I was mad. I'm not. It's you. Do I want to eat? Can you hear what you are saying? Do I want to go into a dining-room and eat with you? It's like a bad play. Masticate my steak, chew it forty times before swallowing. You're a sadist! There's no kind way to tell a woman you're jilting her. But to drag her half-way across the city, to set the scene in such a place, to ask her if she wants to eat when all she wants to do is kill or die! Get me a cab. I want to go home.'

'I'll take you.'

'Not tonight.'

'You can't go alone.'

'Why not? That's my future, isn't it? Order the cab. Don't even see me into it.'

369

She stood in the foyer. He hovered behind her. From the station she heard the whistles signalling a train's departure. Her blood ran cold inside her body as if she was dying. She wasn't. She was filled with hatred, a murderous hatred, and her mind sought ways of venting it. Ways of revenging herself on the man behind her.

And then he dared to touch her, saying her name. Begging her forgiveness. The only man she had ever loved. Would ever love. Would have died for. Had killed for.

She shrugged off his tentative touch and walked out to the waiting cab.

Driving home, she forced herself to look at the river. The buildings along the quays. The people passing. Deliberately blocking from her mind what had happened. Controlling herself until she got inside the house and called at the top of her voice, 'Nell, where are you, Nell?' Then she sat on the stairs, crying bitterly.

Nell came down in a faded pink flannel wrapper, her greying fair hair hanging in two plaits over her shoulders. 'Oh, Fan, my love. What ails you?'

Fanny turned, and putting her arms round her sister's legs, buried her face in the pink flannel, sobbing. 'He threw me over. Peter threw me over. Jilted me. Oh, Nell, what am I going to do? He isn't going to marry me. I sat and listened to him as if I didn't care. Answered him as if I didn't care. But I did! Oh, God, how I did!' Her crying was so loud that Michael heard and came out of his chapel to see what the disturbance was.

'Fan,' he said, 'you're crying. You never cry. Only when something terrible's happened. When your mama died . . .'

She rose from the stairs, walked the few steps down to where he stood.

'You!' she said. 'You thwarted me, mocked me, stood in my way. Let me grow old before I could do what I wanted. Tonight a man jilted me. Peter threw me over for someone else. He isn't going to marry me.

'I hate you! I always will. You destroyed my life. If you'd let me go to medical school years ago I'd never have met him. But I'll have my revenge! I'll have my revenge on both of you. Him I'll sue for breach of promise, and you will learn what sort of a daughter you reared.'

'Don't, Fanny. Don't sue. Accept it with dignity. You're still young. Still beautiful. I've been there. I've heard the cases. The woman is shamed. *You'll* be shamed. You'll win but they'll crucify you. He'll only lose money. You'll lose everything.'

'Is it me or you you're considering, Papa? Your daughter's dirty linen being washed in public.'

Michael came towards her, his hands outstretched. 'Please, Fanny, for your own sake, don't sue.'

She moved back from him. 'Don't you dare touch me! I hate you, don't you understand? I loathe you. Have done for years. Away back to your chapel and pray for your salvation!'

Michael lowered his arms, turned and shuffled away. Nell and Fanny were about to go into the parlour when they heard the noise coming from the chapel.

'My God,' said Nell, 'it sounds as if he's smashing things. We'd better go and see.'

'Do if you want to. I'm staying put. That he may smash it up. That in the process he may drop dead.'

Nell went down the passage and was back quickly. 'Fan, you've got to come! He's going crazy.'

'He has been for years. I'm going to bed.'

'No, you've got to come. He's got an axe . . .'

Reluctantly Fanny followed Nell. Some of the servants were coming up the basement stairs, asking could they help? Fanny thanked them and said no. If they needed assistance they'd call. Before they reached the chapel they heard their father's voice, screaming obscenities, and the crashing of objects.

Oblivious to Nell and Fanny standing by the door,

Michael swung the axe above his head and smashed it into the face of Saint Anthony.

The statue shattered and fell in large plaster chunks to the floor. 'I trusted in all of you. Bastards, liars, cheats, deluders! I believed in you. I believed you were interceding for me. And as for *you!*' he bellowed, raising the axe again and moving through the rubble and broken chairs, the over-turned candlestand tapers. He approached the biggest statue, the Sacred Heart. 'You, that I put my trust in to protect my family, to protect me! You're no better than the rest. I'll finish you off! And what's more, I'll finish *her* as well. She's here. I can feel her. I can smell her. She's never left us, but I'll find her. I'll finish her off . . .'

The axe hit the head of the statue. Nell made the sign of the cross and exclaimed: 'God between us and all harm!'

'I'm going to telephone the doctor. Lock the door. Leave him. He's a raving lunatic. He'd plant the axe in your head, not knowing you from a plaster statue,' Fanny said.

The new young doctor came, son of the man who had delivered Nicole's babies, attended her when she was dying. Cautiously he unlocked the chapel door. Michael sat in the middle of the destruction, looking at them with wild inhuman eyes. Froth rimmed his lips. He groped for the axe among the debris, found it, and began to rise to his feet.

The doctor shut and locked the door. 'I'll call an ambulance. He'll have to be shifted.'

'To where?' asked Nell.

'Grangegorman, Nell. I'm sorry. It's terrible for you, but he'll have to be restrained. His poor brain has snapped.'

'Long, long ago,' said Fanny.

The ambulance came and two attendants. The door was cautiously undone. Michael sat amongst the debris, but on seeing the men attempted to rise, to pick up the axe. They rushed him and in seconds had his arms pinioned, then put on the straitjacket.

Nell sobbed as he was led out of the house. Fanny put an arm round her.

'Poor Papa, taken out like a wild beast! How long will he have to stay in the Asylum?'

'For a long time, Nell, I'm afraid.'

'Is there anything either of you want?' the young doctor asked. 'Something to make you sleep? I've a few things in the bag.'

Fanny thanked him and said no.

'I'll phone you tomorrow, Fan, and tell you what I find out.' He bade them goodnight and went.

Slowly they made their way into the parlour where Fanny poured two whiskeys and insisted Nell must drink one. 'You've had a terrible experience. Take the drink like a dose of medicine, it'll do you good.'

They sat side by side. 'Thank God,' said Nell, 'Mama didn't live to witness it. D'ye think he's insane, Fan?'

'Without a doubt, God help him. Maybe I drove him over the edge. I said some terrible things.'

'You didn't mean them. You were that upset. Did you hear him on about "her"? Blaming our misfortunes on "her"?'

'I know,' said Fanny. 'Blaming her for Peter jilting me. For me suing him for breach of promise.'

Nell fanned the dying fire with the bellows. 'I don't know what to say to you about Peter. It doesn't seem real, nothing about this horrible night does.'

She threw a log on the rekindled flames and sat beside Fanny, who said, 'Earlier I too found it unreal. Now I know it's not. Strange how your mind works. While dealing with one dreadful event it can confront and consider another. Even while watching Papa being strapped into that jacket, I was seeing Peter's face. That horrible hotel. The smell of it. Him saying in one breath how he loved someone else and with the next asking if I wanted to eat.'

'What will you do?'

'Go to the hospital in the morning. Study for my exams. Prepare myself for the next few days when word will have got around and I'll be pitied, laughed at behind my back, receive genuine and false sympathy.

'I'll work like a Trojan. Make my name, not as the woman Peter Corrigan jilted but as the best gynaecologist in Dublin. I'll sue him and donate the compensation for my lost youth to charity. Don't worry about me, Nell. I'll survive. But tonight, and for many nights, I'll cry myself to sleep.'

PART FOUR

Chapter Thirty-eight

1930

THE beautiful house into which Michael and Nicole had moved, where their children were born, Nicole died, and from which Michael as a crazed old man had been taken to an asylum, was now set out in flats.

A year after being committed to spend the rest of his life in Grangegorman Michael died. Rory, who had travelled no further than Wiltshire and South Wales in the British Army, came home for the funeral. And after it heard the family solicitor read his father's will and tell him, Fanny and Nell that thirteen hundred pounds, ten shillings and fourpence was all the capital left between them.

'Poor Michael, he wouldn't be told,' the old man said. 'He'd got it into his head he had a flair for investments and threw good money after bad. Then last year the Wall Street Crash finished him completely. Thank God there's still the house. I know there's a lot needs doing to it but it would still fetch a good price. And there's the money your mother left to Molly. You could apply to have her presumed dead. It would then come to the three of you. But my advice at the moment is to go home and think the whole sad business over. I'll help and advise in any way I can.'

'There's not much left of what I inherited from Mama. Army life's expensive, geared for those of independent means, so Mama's money has been used to supplement a first lieutenant's meagre pay. But what there is you're welcome to,' Rory offered his sisters.

Fanny and Nell said they wouldn't dream of taking a penny.

'I think it mightn't be such a bad idea to go for having Molly presumed dead. She probably is. And whether she is or not, I don't think she deserves it,' he said.

'Ah, Rory, it was what Mama wanted. Molly's money must never be touched.'

'It will in the future if we don't apply for it, go to the Crown, or now, I suppose, the Irish Free State.'

'We'll manage, Rory,' Fanny said. 'The medical fraternity can't keep me outside the pale for ever.'

'Don't be too sure,' said Rory. 'Medicine, law, the Church – Anglican, Catholic, whatever – are laws unto themselves. Did you suspect you'd be ostracized when you began the case against Peter?'

'I don't know. But then I was so full of hate and bitterness I couldn't think beyond revenge. Now I realize such an outcome was what poor Papa was warning me against on that last dreadful night. Not entirely his horror of our lives being exposed to the public.

'And, of course, once I'd filed the petition the signs were plain to see. The invitations to social functions that didn't arrive. Being excluded from hospital gossip. All that sort of thing. But my anger and what I believed was a sense of justice kept me going. I also had faith in my exam results and the appointments I'd worked so hard to get.

'As you know, I won my case, got costs and compensation, but not the appointment, not even the renewal of my contract for the job I was doing.'

'It was monstrous,' said Nell. 'I wouldn't have believed people could behave like that.'

'I tried to rise above it,' said Fanny, 'decided to go into private practice.'

'The brass plate,' said Rory.

'Yes, the brass plate went up on the wall by the front

door, and I waited for patients who never came. I should throw it out. One of these days I will.'

'How did you manage, moneywise, I mean?'

'Some savings, those for the trousseau that never was. Mama's money, Nell's miracles of thrift. We had to let some of the servants go. And I did stints in my old hospital in London.'

'She was a fool,' interjected Nell. 'She could have had a permanent post in London, but wouldn't leave me. As if I was a child!'

'You know that's not the whole truth. I love Dublin and didn't want to leave. And I kept thinking it was a nine-day wonder. That one day I'd be invited back, all forgotten and forgiven.'

'And Peter, what became of him?' asked Rory.

'He had the grace to leave the country, he and his young bride. I believe they're in Australia.'

'I wish I could be of more help,' Rory sighed. 'I'm not much use as the man of the family.'

'You keep writing and visiting,' said Nell, 'that's such a comfort.'

'I have to report back tomorrow but let me know what you decide. And don't forget, what little I have is yours.'

They decided, with advice from the solicitor and estimates from builders, to convert the house into flats. They kept only the ground floor for their own use, regretting the loss of the beautiful double drawing-rooms above. But the solicitor pointed out those rooms would command a high rent.

The builder put in a dumb waiter which carried refuse from the top flats to the basement where the caretaker and his wife, living rent free, carried it to the ash bins, cleaned, kept the garden tidy, changed electric light bulbs beyond Fanny and Nell's reach.

They budgeted to afford membership of the Royal

Dublin Society, went to concerts, and used the Society's library. They didn't attend the Dog or Horse show, because Nell wasn't interested in either horses or dogs and Fanny wished to avoid being snubbed by past colleagues for whom the shows were events they never missed.

Long periods of time passed without Fanny's dwelling on the past. Then something – a song, a piece of music, passing a restaurant where she and Peter had frequently dined – brought memories flooding back. How much she had loved him! Believed they would grow old together. Now it seemed her sister would be the only companion of her old age.

'You get used to anything,' Nell said one morning at breakfast. 'In the beginning I hated having strangers in the house, didn't you?'

Fanny looked up from an article she was reading in the *Irish Times*, one that infuriated her. It told how in London women civil servants had voted that compulsory retirement of women who married should be implemented. 'Not really,' she replied truthfully, 'I hadn't noticed the change.'

'That's because if you haven't your nose stuck in a book, it's in a newspaper. The same as when you were a little girl,' Nell said, smiling affectionately.

Fanny debated with herself whether or not she would tell Nell about the London civil servants but decided not to. Her reply would be: 'I think they're right. Think of all the millions of men out of work.' The one thing she was incapable of – thinking. God, she was so boring. She read the *Evening Herald*, women's magazines and light romances. Had vetoed the wireless as an extravagance. What, if anything, Fanny wondered, went on in Nell's mind?

Then she took herself to task for harbouring such unpleasant thoughts. Nell applied her mind to the running of the house. Managing the money, cooking, baking, preserving. Writing regularly to Rory.

He had attended a staff officers' course at Sandhurst which he'd passed with flying colours and was awarded his majority. Nell was jubilant when she heard.

'Rory, a major! Imagine that, and he only thirty.'

Yes, it would be a poor lookout for them both if Nell kept her nose buried in books and newspapers. All in all, for two old maids they got on well. Fanny looked across the table at her sister serenely glancing through a copy of *Tit-Bits* and said to herself: You've fared better than me. Your man died loving you. Your memories of him are all beautiful ones.

Nell was not discontent with her life. By now she had grown used to the tenants. 'Very respectable men and women' was how she described them. An ex-soldier, Captain Robbins, with beautiful manners. A retired concert pianist who lived in the drawing-rooms. A terrible tragedy, Nell always thought, on the rare occasions she and the woman met. She seemed to have lost all but the most rudimentary use of her hands. It probably accounted for her unfriendliness. Two elderly sisters had the two floors of smaller rooms above. Once a month they invited Nell to take tea with them.

On her first visit she'd found it strange to sit drinking tea in what had been her parents' bedroom, remembering how Mama's dressing table had always stood between the windows. Which way the bed had faced. All the memories. The happy and the sad times. But as the room took on the aura of its new occupants Nell came to enjoy her visits.

Fanny never went to tea with the Misses Browne; never, except for a curt nod, acknowledged them. Acted as if Captain Robbins was non-existent and avoided when possible all contact with the pianist. Often Nell criticized her behaviour. 'I was the one who hated letting the rooms at first. You didn't mind, you said. Now you are so resentful! Treat the tenants so rudely!'

'Only the pianist. Silly bitch! Exudes the impression that living in rented accommodation is beneath her. As if she'd played in London, Paris, Vienna, when everyone knows Belfast was the furthest she got! The Misses Browne on the other hand are too obsequious. And military men never appealed to me.'

In April 1936 a letter came from Rory:

Dear Sisters,
I am engaged to be married. I know I should have told you sooner about Angharad, my Welsh fiancée, and I apologize. I've known her for a couple of years. We met in Senneybridge when I was there at practice camp. Her father farms in the area. Angharad was one of a party invited to a dance in the mess. We corresponded occasionally and met in London, but it's only recently that there was talk of marriage though I'd always hoped one day she would be my wife. Then it seemed as if there was all the time in the world before us.

But with the way events are taking shape now, it seems only a matter of time before we'll be at war with Germany. It wasn't how I wanted to see the world. I had visions of beautiful hill stations in India, shooting tigers, meeting rajahs, long leasurely cruises on P & O liners. All the stuff I'd read about. Alas, if there is a war, the reality will be very different.

And so I mustered my courage and popped the question. We both feel that we should live before we might die. This sounds morbid and dramatic. I'll probably never go further afield than Larkhill, spend the war on Salisbury Plain. Anyway, we plan a quiet wedding in June but before that I'll bring your future sister-in-law to meet you. First week in May for a few days.

Fondest love,
Rory

Fanny, at Nell's insistence, had read the letter aloud. By the time she finished, Nell was crying.

'Why are you crying? Aren't you happy for him?'

'Of course I am,' said Nell. 'Very happy.' And the crying turned to sobbing. 'Only it'll never be the same again. He'll never be ours again.'

Fanny came round the table, bent and put an arm round her. 'Of course he will. I know you reared him after Mama died. I know he was closer to you than me. That you thought of him as a son more than a brother. And I know the old saying: "Your daughter's your daughter all your life, but your son's only yours till he takes a wife . . ." But it doesn't have to be like that. You'll see, it will be fine. They'll visit us and we'll go and see them. And just think of when they have children.'

'Yes, you're right. I'm sure she's a lovely girl. And God knows I wouldn't want him finishing up a crusty old bachelor. We won't be here for ever. I'm glad he'll have someone to take care of him.'

Her crying subsided. She dried her eyes. 'Fanny,' she asked, 'is he right, is there going to be a war?'

'All the signs point that way. But, Nell, if there is, be glad that Rory will be married long beforehand. He'll have known years of happiness. And we can still hope that the signs may be wrong.'

'I'll pray that they are. I'm a silly old woman, a jealous old woman. I'm going to write and congratulate Rory. But first we must talk about how we'll put them up.'

'You and I could move out of our rooms, let Rory have yours and the girl mine. I wonder how you pronounce her name?'

'An-har-ad. The g's silent, I believe.'

'Listen, give her my room. I'll tidy it up. And put Rory in the basement where he usually sleeps. You've been puffing a bit lately, you can do without climbing stairs.'

'I must admit I wasn't relishing the prospect. Are you sure he won't mind?'

'Why should he? After all, they'll only be here for a few days.'

'Only a few days,' Nell said, then her face crumpled and tears filled her eyes.

'Now what ails you?' asked Fanny, her voice tinged with impatience.

'Why didn't he ask us to the wedding? We're his only relatives.'

'I would guess – a guess that's all it is, so don't get hysterical again – that she's not a Catholic. Or, maybe he's considering our straitened circumstances, his pauper sisters, and is too stingy to pay our fares. Does that suit you better?'

'Why are you being so horrible to me?'

'You drive me to it. Rory's over thirty, a major in the army. When will you realize that his business is his own? Now can we stop behaving like two cantankerous old women?'

'Or like we were as children.'

'Exactly,' said Fanny.

'I'll write the letter.'

'And I'll go and start tidying my sty of a bedroom.'

They smiled at each other.

Angharad reminded Fanny and Nell of their mother. She was diminutive by the side of Rory. And had the most beautiful brown eyes either of them had ever seen. Alone with the sisters, she told them she and Rory were being married in a Register Office.

'We feel that will offend fewer people. My father is a devout Methodist and I know you're Catholic. It will be a very quiet affair. No reception. Rory and I will have dinner afterwards with our bridesmaid and best man.'

'A very sensible arrangement,' Fanny said, and out of politeness Nell nodded her head as if she agreed.

But when she and Fanny were alone, later in the evening, she wept for the mortal sin she believed Rory would commit, and reminisced about when he was confirmed.

But mostly she talked about his christening. How she was his godmother, responsible for his spiritual welfare, and wondered where she had gone wrong.

Fanny didn't attempt to offer consolation or explanation, not until she felt that Nell had talked herself out. Then she asked: 'Despite the mortal sin and all that, d'ye like Angharad?'

'I think she's lovely. Beautiful and sweet-natured. I'm sure she'll be a good wife to Rory. I don't blame her in the slightest, she isn't the Catholic. Just imagine, he's the first one to marry out of the faith in the McCarthys. I'll pray for them both.'

'Angharad's an only child,' said Fanny. 'Farming stock as well. Sheep. Rory forgot to mention in his letter that she is a teacher. Or rather was. When she's married that will have come to an end. Isn't that appalling?'

Nell didn't agree as Fanny knew she wouldn't. 'Married women have husbands to keep them. It's their duty to stay home and make way for single girls and young men.'

Fanny complained of being tired. 'You're not,' said Nell. 'I'm boring you. I know the signs. You'll go to your room and read until the small hours.'

'Probably,' said Fanny.

Chapter Thirty-nine

As time passed Molly became more fond of Tony. She had settled into the neighbourhood, made acquaintances rather than friends, and could banter as well as the next one with shopkeepers and the fruit and vegetable stallholders. Tony was kind and considerate. The lodgers, except for a raucous bout of Irish songs when they came in from the public houses, which soon ceased as one after another fell into a drunken sleep, caused no trouble.

With Tony's guidance Molly could now cook a Sunday dinner, shepherd's pie and toad in the hole – dishes she had never eaten at home and only occasionally in Soho. Once or twice a week he took her to the cinema and in fine weather they walked on Hampstead Heath. But not once had he ever tried to kiss her, and she found herself longing for a man's arms around her. A kiss on her lips. But most of all to sleep in a bed with one and make love. Not just any man. It was Tony she had grown to love, but either he didn't fancy her or maybe was past it. She decided the time had come to try him out.

One night when he had already gone to bed she wrapped a scarf round her head and, after putting on her nightdress, went to his bedroom door, pretending to be in agony with ear ache and asking if he knew if there was any olive oil in the house? After knocking she had to wait a few minutes before he came to the door and was surprised to see that he had put on his trousers. She had expected him to be in his long drawers.

He was very sympathetic, telling her he used to suffer

with his ears and knew what the pain was like, and that Flo always kept a bottle of olive oil for ear trouble. Molly knew that, knew where it was in an Oxo tin, but played dumb.

'Come down to the kitchen. It'll be warmer and we can have a cup of tea after I've seen to your ear,' Tony said.

He threw a few sticks on the still smouldering fire and they caught. Molly moaned, groaned and grimaced with her supposed pain. Tony found the small bottle of oil and a dusty piece of wadding. 'I don't suppose the dust will matter,' he said as he put the bottle to warm by the hob. 'Not as if it was a cut, like.' He put the kettle on then asked if she'd like a drop of whiskey. 'The best painkiller of all.'

'Only a little,' she said, and winced convincingly. They drank the whiskey. 'I feel better already,' said Molly.

'You'll feel better still once the warm oil goes in,' Tony said as he tested the heat of the bottle and then, to be certain, poured a drop into the palm of his hand. 'That's it. Just right. You'd be better standing up.'

She stood and leant close to him, the weight of one breast against him. 'You'll have to bend your head to the side and lift your hair out of the way.' She detected a tremor in his voice and leant more heavily on him. The warm oil went in, trickling down, and he plugged her ear with the dusty wadding. He put down the bottle and as she was about to lower her head, said, 'Don't, not yet,' and kissed her neck. 'I've wanted to do that for a long time. I watch you sometimes when you put your hair up. A woman's neck is beautiful.' He let down her hair and turned her to face him. 'And this I've wanted too since the very first night.' He kissed her mouth. 'It's the whiskey – not that made me want to kiss you, but it gives a bloke a bit of courage. I hope you don't mind?'

'Ah, Tony,' she said, 'I don't mind.' And she put her arms round him and kissed him.

'Steady on, girl,' he said. 'Let me get me breath.' They both laughed, then had another whiskey, turned off the gas

under the kettle, and arm in arm went up to bed. Where Molly found Tony a gentle, considerate and satisfying lover.

Her life was now complete. Several times a week they made love. It left her feeling cherished, precious. That's a word I've seldom used, she thought one night before falling asleep. But now and then it keeps popping into my mind.

When Chamberlain came back from Munich with the promise of peace, Tony said, 'Pull the other one, guv.'

'Don't you believe him?' Molly asked.

'No,' he said, 'I never believe politicians. Playing for time, that's what they're doing.'

'You mean, there'll be a war?'

'There'll be a war. But don't you start worrying. Thank God I'm too old to go. And there's nothing much round here for bombing. Poor buggers living near the docks may not be so lucky. That's how it goes. Not much say over our lives, we haven't. Make the best of things, eh?'

Before 3 September 1939, when war was declared on Germany by Great Britain, preparations had got underway. Children from what were considered the areas most likely to be bombed were evacuated to the safety of the country. Gas masks were issued and air raid shelters allocated to some of the population. Other people in less vulnerable areas were advised on how to build their own.

In Ireland similar precautions were followed. Nell's greatest fear was that Rory would be one of the first to be sent into action. Fanny reassured her that wasn't likely.

'How d'ye know for certain?'

'I don't. But it's highly unlikely. He's a senior instructor of gunnery. Far more valuable training hundreds of others in how to use the guns.'

'D'ye really think so? You're not just saying it to allay my fears?'

'I really believe what I'm saying. As we used to say when we were children: as true as God.'

War was declared. In England food was rationed, and gradually whatever wasn't rationed became scarce. Went 'under the counter'. In Ireland tea was severely rationed, to two ounces per person per week. Clothes, too, had to be bought on coupons. Flour changed from white to grey and produced a dark heavy coarse bread on which every stomach ailment was blamed. Anyone coming home from England was begged to bring in a white loaf. A thriving black market sprung up, selling many things, but especially tea at £1 a quarter.

In May 1941 the bombing campaign started in earnest. Thousands of civilians were killed and amongst them was Molly's Tony. 'I begged him,' she cried after the police had brought the news. 'I begged and pleaded with him not to go down the East End. D'ye think he'd listen? Not him.'

'Moll,' he said, 'Alf's dying. He was my mate. We started in the Post Office together. He's got cancer. D'ye think I'm going to let Hitler stop me seeing Alf?'

Never had she thought it possible to miss anyone so much as she missed Tony. He was, she had come to realize, the only man she had ever loved. But, as she told herself, life had to go on. So she swept the stairs and cleaned the house and joined queues wherever she saw one formed, and took whatever was available when and if she reached the counter. As often as not the shopkeeper or stallholder would call out that whatever it was he'd had was all gone. And away went the women in search of another queue.

Tony had left her his savings, Molly took over the rentbook for the house and the lodgers paid their rent regularly. She was managing quite well except at night when she went to bed and cried herself to sleep.

One morning she joined a queue, got to the top, and the woman wrapped two onions in a sheet of newspaper. Which was unusual these days, paper like everything else being scarce. In the kitchen she unpacked the onions, put them away and smoothed the sheet of paper. She'd later

have a gander to see if there was anything interesting in it then cut it into squares for the outside lavatory the lodgers used.

This evening she glanced quickly over the sheet of paper. Not finding much to read, she folded it in two and was about to fold it in four when below the crease she saw her own name: 'Marianne McCarthy, sometimes known as Molly.'

She took the paper to the window in case her eyes were playing tricks on her. But, no, there it was. Her name, the address where she had lived in Dublin, and a message asking her to contact a firm of Dublin solicitors. A firm called Moynihan & Son. She couldn't remember if that had been the family solicitor's name. She didn't think she had ever known it. But it was definitely her they were looking for.

She left the house in the care of a neighbour, taking only a few knick-knacks, little presents Tony had bought her, and the photographs of him and Flo. As the boat sailed into the harbour she noticed that the name had changed. Not Kingstown any more. An Irish name: Dun Laoghaire.

I should be excited coming back, she thought, and all I am is frightened. I should have written to that solicitor first. I'm probably on a fool's errand. Probably not a soul I know in the city. And Mama and Papa would hardly still be alive. Nell and Fanny long since married. Living God knows where. What possessed me to plan on going to the house first?

She continued thinking along these lines, sitting on the hard narrow seat of the train taking her to Westland Row station. Strangers would live in the house now, she supposed. I'm tidy-looking enough, but even so. Spent all my coupons on mourning. Cheap-looking. Not what a visitor would wear to the square. A maid would answer the door. Take one look at her and let on whoever lived in the house now was not at home. She'd find out nothing about her family.

As the train pulled into the station, which looked almost exactly as she remembered it, she took heart. Moynihan, the solicitor, would know about the family. He'd know for sure.

Dublin wasn't London. Even so the motor car had reached it, she noticed, though there weren't many and some had balloon-like contraptions fixed on their roofs. Something to do with the shortage of petrol, she supposed. And the old-fashioned horse and cabs were still plentiful.

She took one, and riding in it up Lincoln Place was delighted at how little had changed. Going through Merrion Square, seeing the Natural History Museum, she recalled James and their Sunday afternoon outings. And everywhere there were bicycles.

She was almost there. Then the cab turned into the square. How tall and thick the trees had grown. Scenes of herself, Phyllis and Bert flashed before her eyes. And totally unconnected with these memories another one: the fortune teller's voice talking about a curse and a marriage.

The cab stopped outside the door. Her hands were sweating as she paid the cabby. And only as he drove off did she regret not having asked him to wait. If she wasn't received he could have taken her to a cheap hotel or the solicitor's office. The shabbiness of the house shocked her. Paint was flaking from the railings and had cracked on the beautiful front door. She looked down into the basement area. Once you would have seen gleaming kitchen windows; servants bustling about. Now net curtains covered them and there was no sign of life.

Climbing the front steps on swollen feet and aching legs, she rang the bell, the big brass one set in the wall to the right of the door. And while waiting noticed three smaller bells, one above the other on the left-hand side of the door, metal frames with cards below each one. Her heart lurched. Their beautiful home set out in flats!

She rang the bell again. An untidy woman in a skirt and

short-sleeved maroon hand knitted jumper, felt slippers and no stockings, opened the door. Seeing into the hall, Molly almost cried with joy. It was, though shabbier, the hall as she remembered it. Red carpet, the big Waterford vase of tulips, the Beleek bowl, Mason jug, and on the walls Malton's prints of Georgian Dublin scenes.

'Yes?' asked the woman.

'I'm looking for the McCarthy family. Do they live here?'

'They do, ma'am. Have you come about the flat?'

'I haven't,' she said, and just then a stout grey-haired woman came out of the parlour and asked, 'What is it, Mary?'

'A woman asking for the McCarthys.'

The little dumpy woman came towards the door. They stared at each other. Nell saw a grey-haired woman dressed all in black. A very stout woman with something familiar about her face, but what it was for a minute she couldn't recall. The woman on the doorstep smiled and dimples appeared in her cheeks. And at the same time the stoutness seemed to evaporate and in Nell's mind Molly's transformation was complete.

Nell spoke first. 'It isn't. It can't be. Not after all these years. But, please God, let it be. Let it be you, Molly. Oh, Molly, Molly, Molly, is it really you?'

They went to each other with outstretched arms, tears pouring down their cheeks. And in minutes, seconds perhaps, they saw each other with unchanged faces, two girls again in their parents' house. Mary went away quietly, leaving them embracing, crying and laughing.

There was so much to say. So much to tell. So much heartbreaking news for Nell to impart and so many lies and evasions for Molly.

In the parlour she looked at photographs, mostly of Rory whom she hadn't known existed. One of Fanny when she

qualified. So much catching up to do! Forty years of catching up.

The news of Fanny's disappointed hopes upset Molly most of all and she cried bitterly, lamenting aloud how she had wished all of it on her clever little sister. Nell consoled her.

'Hush now, that was long ago, when you were a child.' And she turned the conversation to more mundane things: Molly's inheritance and the need to ring Moynihan, their solicitor.

Later in the day, when Fanny came home, she was put out to find a stranger ensconced in the parlour drinking tea with Nell: a grossly fat old woman with a frizzy grey perm. Judging her to be one of the women Nell knew from her sodality, she prepared to leave the room as soon as she could without appearing downright rude.

'Don't you recognize her?' asked Nell.

'No, but then you know I'm no good with faces.'

'Look closely,' urged Nell.

She did, stared, and the sagging jowls began to vanish as did the many hairy chins and grossly overweight body. 'It can't be! Oh my God, it is! Oh, Molly, Molly!'

And Fanny, who made a virtue of her undemonstrativeness, broke down and cried as if her heart would break. 'Oh, Molly, I was sure you died long ago. Why didn't you come before?' She hugged and kissed her. 'You should have come. But never mind, you have now. And you'll stay, won't you?'

'If you'll have me.'

'As if you had to ask! Isn't it your home, too?'

While Nell cooked dinner, Molly told Fanny an edited version of her life since leaving Bert, and during the meal listened to Fanny talk about her past. And then the conversation turned to Molly's inheritance.

Fanny said, 'Mama left each of us three thousand pounds,

but of course with the interest yours has accumulated over the years, it will be more.'

Nell decided on the sleeping arrangements. There were two beds in her room. Molly would have one of them. 'You know the chatterboxes we always were. We'll probably talk all night.'

Rory and Angharad's son, Sean, was born in Tidworth Military Hospital in September 1943. The following year he was brought to Dublin to meet his aunts. They fell in love with him, each vying with the other to hold, kiss and play with him.

'Wasn't it a pity Papa didn't live to see him?' they each in turn said at some time during the visit. Fanny said how delighted she was that he had inherited Angharad's beautiful eyes, and how unusual it was to see such brown eyes and blond hair.

Rory informed them they were to be Sean's guardians. Fanny didn't think it a wise choice. 'God forbidding you shouldn't live to see him reared, but we'll be pushing eighty by the time he is.'

'Then may God spare you for there's no one else we'd want.'

'What about his godparents?' Nell asked. 'They'd be more suitable.'

'He wasn't christened. He'll choose for himself when he grows up.'

'Ah, well,' said Molly, 'God is good, we'll put our trust in Him.'

Rory congratulated Fanny on having finally found a post in Dublin. 'I suppose the war has changed people's attitudes?'

'That and the old fogeys dying off. It's not much of a post but I love being back.'

'Gynaecology?'

'Lungs,' replied Fanny, 'that dreadful scourge tuberculosis. I help in a clinic. Had I been younger, I'd have joined the Royal Army Medical Corps. The only good ever to come out of a war is the leaps forward in medicine and surgery it brings.'

Nell asked if he'd noticed how the house had been improved?

'All Molly's doing. Spent her money on it.'

'Mama's money,' she said. 'She loved this house. To what better purpose could I have put it?'

'So, all in all, things are going well for you three?' Rory said.

'All except the gas rationing,' complained Fanny.

'I didn't know about that.'

'Oh, yes. It's on to cook your breakfast, goes off, then comes on in time for making lunch. Haven't you heard about the Glimmer Man?'

'Tell me?'

'Well, when the gas is turned off some is left in the pipes. Enough to boil a kettle if you sleep late. So there you are, the kettle singing, and there's a knock on the door. The Glimmer Man. And then – prosecution.'

'You're joking, Fan?'

'I am not.'

'It's true,' said Molly. 'So don't sleep late, or else sleep very late – till almost lunch.'

In 1950 Molly and Nell, walking through Grafton Street, stopped to look in Brown Thomas's window where Molly exclaimed: 'Such gorgeous clothes! The New Look. Imagine being able to wear such creations. Look at the fullness of that skirt, and the little jacket. Imagine having a waist small enough to wear that.'

'Imagine having the money. Shedding, in our case, eight or nine stone, not to mention fifty years!'

Molly laughed. 'No harm in wishing.'

'None at all,' said Nell. 'Now how about some of Bewley's fresh cream pastries? Those we can afford, and our figures can't get worse.'

They linked arms and crossed the street to the cafe where they ate many luscious pastries and indulged in one of their favourite pastimes, backbiting Fanny. How serious she was. Her taste in music and books.

'She makes me feel stupid,' Nell said.

'Me too. She always did. But she had her good points.'

'I don't remember any.'

'She wasn't a telltale.'

Nell bridled. 'Are you saying I was?'

'You were. You told Mama or Papa or both that Aggie and Phyllis lent the books.'

'I did not!' Nell said indignantly.

'You did, Nell, I remember. You were always getting me into trouble.' Then Molly laughed. 'Listen to us. As if we were still children. I'm sorry.'

Nell smiled. 'I don't mind. I like it. We're such great company for each other. I'm so glad you came home.'

'So am I,' said Molly.

Rory had never been in action. Never seen the world. At forty-five he resigned his commission, encouraged to do so by Angharad who wanted to go back to Wales. Wanted Sean educated there.

They bought a house in the Uplands, Swansea, a lovely three-storey house with a view over the bay. Sean went to prep school and Rory to work for Dupont in Pontypool. They were wealthy now. Angharad had inherited her father's money and in the event of her and Rory dying before Sean grew up, had made a will settling a large sum of money on Molly, Nell and Fanny whom they frequently visited in Dublin. There they found endless amusement in listening to Nell and Molly squabbling like two little girls and making it up as quickly as little children do.

The three sisters vied with each other for Sean's affection. He bestowed it on Fanny, which pleased his parents who admired her and knew she was outside Molly and Nell's charmed circle.

Once they drove down to Ballydurkin where Rory told Sean the McCarthys had farmed and his aunties used to spend holidays when they were children. On another occasion they took him to France, drove to Issoudon and found the farm, still being worked.

He wasn't interested in either place.

Rory made excuses. 'He's only seven, too much to expect of him. But he will be later.'

At sixteen he began asking questions about his ancestry and planning return visits in the future to Ireland and France. 'On my own, when I'm in University perhaps,' he informed them.

Chapter Forty

'I THANK God every morning when I wake up, for letting me see another day and the gift of health,' said Nell, sitting on the edge of her bed, struggling to pull up her elastic stockings. 'We've all been blessed with good health. There's times when I feel like a sixteen year old.'

'When?' asked Molly, struggling to raise her head from the pillow, still a ton weight from last night's extra glass of port.

'What d'ye mean, when?'

'Just that. When d'ye feel like a sixteen year old? Most mornings your groans and moans wake me up. "My knees are crippling me." "My back's stiff as board." "I can't bend to put on my stockings." You're just feeling like a sixteen year old because you're in good humour about the television.'

'You're right, I am. I can't wait! It'll be like having the pictures in your own parlour. Television has to be magic. How else could you see what's happening miles away at that very same minute?'

'I don't know, ask Fanny. She'll explain it. Blind you with science,' Molly said.

'Isn't it a pity she's not in the clinic any more? She'll be putting in her say about what we should watch. News, lectures and all the serious stuff.'

'We'll have to put up with it. It's bought between us so she has a right to her say. I suppose I'd better get up. Are you going to Mass?'

'Why? Are you thinking of coming?'

'I'm not.'

'You should, Moll, and confession too. You told me it's been so long since you've been, you can't remember when it was. Supposing you died in the night, not in a state of grace?'

'Sudden death, sudden mercy. That's what the nuns taught us.'

'I don't know what the world's coming to! You, Fanny, Rory and Sean all lapsed. No, not Sean, God look down on him. Sure he was never christened. You don't know how I wòrry and pray for all your souls.'

'You're always telling me, and keep me awake half the night praying out loud! Hurry up now or you'll be late. And don't forget to bring back the paper. The day doesn't go right for me if I don't read my stars.'

Rory wrote to say Sean had excelled in his 'A' levels, three As in Chemistry, Physics and Biology, and had been accepted by Swansea University. He'd start in October. Rory and Angharad were taking their car to France and motoring down to Provence.

'He should have come to Trinity,' Nell said, after reading the letter. 'He could have stayed with us.'

'They probably don't do the course he wants there,' Fanny said.

'A place like Trinity would do every course. It's a University, isn't it?'

Fanny didn't bother to argue.

In September a distraught Sean rang to say his parents had been in a head on collision driving through France. Both had died instantly. Molly, Nell and Fanny were at first so shocked by the news they were unable to cry, but when they did they wept for hours. Nell sobbed and recalled Rory as a baby, a small boy, a young man. How she had loved him. But most of all was consumed by the terrible

fear that his death being so sudden, he wouldn't have had time to say an Act of Contrition.

Molly kept reminding her of how good-living in all respects except the practice of his religion Rory had been. God wasn't unmerciful. He died for the sinners of this world.

But in the long run it was Fanny who sent for the priest who, after sympathizing with them, closeted himself with Nell for more than an hour. She didn't tell them all he had said to her, only that they should try for Sean's salvation. That when he came next to Dublin the priest would have a word with him.

Whatever else he had said to Nell had consoled her and her grieving for her brother wasn't so distraught. Sean strongly advised them against coming to the funeral. The weather could turn suddenly cold and much as he would have loved them to be there, they were far too precious to him to undertake the journey.

Fanny convinced Molly and Nell he was right. 'We are all pushing on for eighty. Prey to the frailties of old age. Broken femurs in particular. And remember, he's not twenty-one yet, we're still his guardians. At least let us keep on our feet a bit longer.'

After the death of his parents Sean made frequent trips to see his aunts. His tall frame was filling out, his once pretty face becoming that of a handsome man. His hair had a curl to it, his skin slightly pitted by an adolescent attack of chicken pox. Only the wondrous dark eyes of his mother hadn't altered.

His aunts adored him and as they had when he was a baby, vied for his attention and affection. Which he gave unstintingly, though Fanny was his favourite. Molly and Nell he found tedious after a few days. They fussed, fêted and fed him. How they fed him! Enormous breakfasts: two eggs, three rashers, four sausages, black and white puddings,

mushrooms, tomatoes and fried bread. They'd ignore his protests that he couldn't eat so much, Nell dismissing them as nonsense and Molly telling him he was still growing. He hoped not, being six foot three already.

He came to call on his way to Baltimore in West Cork on a field trip to Loch Eyne during his second year in University. 'Don't keep treating me as if I'm to produce foie gras,' he said when once again he was faced with enormous meals. 'I've got to be fit for my diving.'

'Diving where?' asked Nell. 'What d'ye want to be doing that for?'

'Loch Eyne, studying the unique flora and fauna. I'm doing Marine Biology. Studying flora and fauna is part of the course.'

'What has that to do with curtailing your food? I don't understand,' Nell said. She looked quite crestfallen and Sean, because he loved her, forced down a second helping of sausage.

She and Molly found fault only with his clothes, though never to his face.

'Young men in my day wore proper clothes. Only working men had trousers that weren't flannel, linen, that sort of thing. What stuff is in his trousers?' Nell said.

'Denim, I think they call it. Years ago, you'd see overalls made from it,' said Molly.

Fanny, who kept abreast of the times, said nothing.

Sean escorted them to the cinema to see love stories or weepy films, watched them gorge on fresh cream cakes, and pretended interest in their rambling memories of their childhood.

When he went out with Fanny, he would without malice describe his outings with Nell and Molly. Fanny smoked and offered him cigarettes. They went to hotel bars and cocktail lounges. And she understood when he talked about his course.

He listened with interest when she talked about her own youth. The battle with her father to study medicine. 'How did you finally win it?' he asked her one evening, while they sat in the Shelbourne's Horseshoe Bar drinking whiskey.

'I'm never really sure. I think he had some sort of divine revelation. He'd believed there was a curse on the family, you see. According to him it was lifted, or God showed him in some way it had never existed. It's such a long time ago I can't really remember. Except that soon afterwards I was dispatched to register in the University School of Medicine. I was twenty-eight, hardly a fresh-faced student. And he had the gall to expect gratitude!'

'Sounds to me as if he was ga-ga.'

'Not then, perhaps. He was later. He died in an asylum for the insane.'

'I never knew that.'

'You wouldn't. It's something your Aunt Nell doesn't talk about.'

Bridgid Cronin came to Ireland at the end of her second year in University. She spent time in Dublin, in the National Library and Public Record Office, bought books with information on how to trace your ancestors, discovered nothing and decided she'd go to the source – to West Cork – Ballydurkin, the place in which her ancestor had been born.

From Cork she caught a bus to Ballydurkin, a battered old bus that shook and bounced her on the slatted seat. Other passengers at first smiled shyly at the pretty young American girl who wore golden bracelets and fine soft leather shoes. The woman sitting next to her said, ' 'Tis a grand day, thanks be to God.'

Bridgid said it was and remarked on how beautifully green everything was.

'Isn't it the same in America?'

'In the spring, but not like this.'

'I had a brother who went to New York a long time ago. Lord have mercy on him, he died. Are you going far?'

'To Ballydurkin.'

'I've heard tell of it.'

A woman across the aisle leaned over and told Bridgid the bus only went to Bandon. The one beside the woman said she thought the bus to Ballydurkin only went on Mondays and Fridays. Then asked, 'Have you people there?'

Soon it seemed to Bridgid that everyone in the bus was offering information about the bus service, all of it conflicting. She was offered sandwiches and sweets, advice on where to stay if there wasn't a bus, where she could hire a car. She was listening to the advice and answering questions at the same time. Giving them her name, saying where she lived in America, and why she was visiting Ballydurkin.

'Cronin is a well-known West Cork name. You'll pass many a shop with it over the door.'

She was excited, thinking, These are my people. Her people. She'd have spoken like them. Soft, lovely voices. The questions so easily put, so politely you didn't realize you were being questioned.

But not one of them was going to Ballydurkin or knew anyone living there. Though many assured her their mothers or grandmothers, God be good to them, would surely have known.

From Bandon a taxi took Bridgid five miles along a narrow road. Talking to the driver, she discovered that there were only three families living now in Ballydurkin.

'What happened to the others?'

'They started leaving a long time ago. I never remember many there. They've been leaving for a hundred years or more.'

'Did you ever hear of a Cronin there?'

'Is it Andy or Pat you'd be wanting? I knew them both

well. I went to school with them. Two cousins, but they're gone. Poor Andy to his long rest and Pat to Coventry or maybe Birmingham. Were they belonging to you?'

'I think so,' said Bridgid, sick with disappointment.

'You should have come in May. Pat was over then with the wife. They come every year. They've still got the house. You could come back again.'

'Next year?' asked Bridgid.

' 'Twould have to be. Only the one visit, Pat makes. Will I go on so?'

'Yes, do. I'd like to see the house.'

'Yerra,' said the taxi driver, 'sure it's only a house, nothing much to see at all.'

He was right, there was nothing much to see. No thatched cottage but a little one-storey house, a window each side of the door, faced in flat grey concrete.

She got out, opened the gate and walked up to the cottage. The driver followed her. 'Pat was the great gardener. He does a bit when he comes over, but you have to be at a garden every day.' They walked round the back. Behind the house was a low roofless stone building, with what must have been a doorway and to one side a glassless window about a foot square.

'What was that for?' asked Bridgid.

'Before his father's time the family would have lived in it.'

She ran her hand over the stones by the door, conjuring up an image of a young girl. Imagining her walking across the fields that backed on to the house. Going to meet her lover. A lover who must have deserted her.

She asked the taximan would the people living in the two other houses they'd passed talk to her? Know anything more about the Cronins?

'Mary-Ellen's stone deaf and Maggie Hurley, her neighbour, is ninety if she's a day. You'd be better, miss, to go

back to Bandon. I might be able to get you Pat's address. You could write to him.'

'That would be great. Let's go.' Her enthusiasm had returned. She'd write. Ask Pat if she could visit. She'd go to Birmingham or Coventry. On the way back in the taxi, she remembered the church. The book on how to trace your ancestors had stressed the importance of parish records.

She asked the driver, 'Where's the church? I didn't see it.'

'You wouldn't. It was burned down thirty or more years ago.'

'And never rebuilt?'

' 'Twasn't worth it. By then there wasn't enough left to fill two pews. Them that was heard Mass in the next parish.'

'And the parish records?'

'They'd have gone up in the fire.'

Bridgid gave him a good tip and invited him for a drink in the hotel where she would stay the night. He asked several people in the bar if they knew Pat's address. No one did but many hazarded a guess, again all conflicting.

They talked to her about America. Many had worked there before the war. None regretted coming home. Money wasn't everything, they said. She bought them a round of drinks.

The barman talked to her about Pat and Andy Cronin. Telling her they were blow-ins, explaining the term when she looked puzzled. Newcomers. They might still be relations but their family came from another village.

She asked him about the tumbledown stone cottage. 'Could my great-grandmother have lived in that? She left Ireland in 1850.'

'She could, surely. They were living in the self-same cottages till the eighties or near enough. Though come to think of it, I've heard tell all that land up there belonged to

a family called McCarthy. But sure the Cronins could have been tenants of theirs. But Pat Cronin's your man. Knows all about the place, and maybe he's related.'

After dinner the taxi driver came back to tell her he hadn't found anyone who knew Pat's address or would admit to knowing it. 'D'ye see how it is? There's them that are suspicious. You say you're trying to find out about a woman long dead, and sure no harm can come to her. But giving Pat's address to a stranger is another thing.

'But you could write Pat a letter and give it to me for posting. That way I'd have no trouble finding his address.'

'Okay, I'll do that.'

'And while you're down here, miss, see a bit of the place. There's a grand lake I'll run you out to tomorrow. Only a bit up the road. Them students come from all over the place, diving into it and bringing up their plants and queer creatures.'

' 'Tis beautiful all right,' said the barman.

Bridgid sat on a sun-warmed rock looking at the green hills, the expanse of the lake, the black masked figures going down and coming up. She remembered the Lake Isle of Innisfree and heard lakewater lapping. And saw a figure wading towards her rock. His mask was raised and he asked with an engaging smile: 'Okay if I sit here?'

They introduced themselves and shared her lunch, provided by the hotel: a crab salad, cold chicken, fruit and home made bread. Sean threw the sandwiches made by the students' hostel into the lake.

She told him of her plans to return the following year. They exchanged addresses and telephone numbers and promised to keep in touch, which they did. During the Christmas holidays he flew to Chicago and spent a week in her home.

'So far,' she told him, 'no news of Pat Cronin.'

'The Irish!' he said. 'Don't push things. You'll hear.

Come to Dublin for Easter and meet my aunts. They're dotes. You'll fall in love with them.' As I have with you. The last bit he kept to himself but planned to say it before he went back.

And when he did, to his immense relief and delight, she said, 'I think I did with you even before you took off your mask. Walking out of the sea, you looked like a god and I knew you'd be the most gorgeous man I'd ever met.'

Chapter Forty-one

THERE was great speculation about Sean's visit to America and the girl he casually mentioned in his letters.

'He must be very interested in her, not to have come here for Christmas,' Molly said in the New Year.

'I wonder where they met?' Nell said.

'Probably at University.'

'Wouldn't you think he'd have told us her name?' Fanny, who wouldn't admit to being as curious as her sisters, and disappointed that Sean hadn't dropped a line to her as he sometimes did under the pretext of its being an impersonal note about marine biology, scoffed at Nell's and Molly's probing and questioning.

'There you go as usual, making a mountain out of a molehill. You're like a pair of old hens who've lost their chicks.'

Nell and Molly ignored her and continued pondering aloud.

'I wonder if she's a Catholic?'

'His mother wasn't,' Molly said. 'But she was nice.'

'She was, but if she'd been one of us, Sean would have been a Catholic.'

Bridgid, in the run up to her degree, and not having heard from Pat Cronin, postponed her visit at Easter but hoped to come in the summer.

I realize I may never hear from Pat Cronin. For all I know

the taxi driver never forwarded the letter but I'm coming back. Okay, so I'd like to dig into my past, but I'm more interested in my future. And that is you. So I'll be over and look forward to meeting your aunts. Only hope they'll like me.

I love you,
Bridgid

Even Fanny displayed enthusiasm when it was announced that President Kennedy was to visit Ireland and agreed that she would face any crowd to catch a glimpse of him.

On the day, a fine June one, Molly and Nell went to have their hair done. A few years after Molly's arrival, Nell had admitted she was beginning to find dressing her hair wearisome. The washing and drying, the hundred strokes of the brush, and then arranging it into a bun. Hairpins vanishing and her arms raised above her head, feeling like a ton weight.

'Have it cut and permed,' Molly had advised. 'You won't regret it. Look at mine. It's a bit frizzy because I can't be bothered setting it. But I can wash it as often as I like, run a comb through it and it's tidy. You're behind the times, Nell. It's only the young boys and girls who wear their hair long now.'

They envied Fanny's effortless elegance, able to wear clothes she'd had for years, and her eyes like her mother's, not faded or rheumy, and her shiny bun of hair. But they had each other and knew that Fanny must often be very lonely for all her concerts, the exhibitions she went to, her books, journals and newspapers.

On the day of the President's visit they rested after lunch, left the house at four o'clock, walked leisurely to the Sherbourne for afternoon tea. The room to which Uncle James used to take them and were comforted by how little if at all it had changed when so much about them had.

After tea, walking very slowly, they made their way to

O'Connell Street. On his way in from the airport he would come this way. The street was thronged but not uncomfortably so. 'Not,' said Nell, 'as it was during the Eucharistic Congress.' The crowd was in great humour, as it waited to welcome the first Catholic President of America, back in his people's country as the world's most powerful man.

And then the cars were spotted at the top of the street and the cheering began. The presidential car came alongside the sisters. Molly gasped at what she perceived as a bronze god. The late-afternoon sun shone on his hair and skin.

Nell was convinced he had smiled at her, waved to her, and said she had never seen such perfect teeth. Even Fanny admitted he was a handsome man.

Eventually Bridgid heard from Pat Cronin. The letter from Ballydurkin had followed him round England. His wife had died and his job now involved travelling from place to place. But he would be in Ballydurkin for the month of July and would be delighted to meet her then and tell her anything he knew about the Cronin family history.

She wrote to Sean and arranged a time to telephone him at home in Swansea. After midnight her call came through. They compared their degrees, congratulated each other, spoke of their love and longing to be together again. Then they arranged she would fly in on 5 July.

'I'll meet you in London.'

'And then we'll go to Dublin.'

'No, you'll come to Swansea. We'll play house. Pretend we're married. Just me and you alone here.'

'That'll be fantastic.'

'We'll spend a week here, then Dublin, then Ballydurkin. Might be best for you to go down there on your own.'

'We'll see,' she said.

They spent the rest of the call saying how much they loved each other and how they would be counting the days, not many now, until they were together again.

★

'Bridgid Cronin, that's Irish enough. She's bound to be a Catholic,' Nell said after reading Sean's letter. 'And they're getting engaged.' Then she launched into a long discussion of what needed doing to the house. The sleeping arrangements. 'I couldn't put that girl in the basement. I wonder where she'll stay in Swansea?'

Fanny and Molly exchanged knowing looks.

They took to Bridgid immediately for not only was she beautiful but friendly and warm-hearted, and for Fanny she had the added attraction of brains.

The engagement party was a family affair. While the toasts were being drunk, Molly took the turquoise locket from her neck and gave it to Bridgid. 'My father, Lord have mercy on him, bought it for me when I was born. I've worn it every day of my life since,' she lied, not quite up to explaining how she had stolen it the day before she ran away from home. 'We all had one bought when we were born, and Papa bought one for Mama also.'

Conversation then became general, and during it Bridgid mentioned her trip to Ballydurkin.

'Ballydurkin?' Fanny asked. 'Our family came from there.'

'You never told me that, Sean,' Bridgid exclaimed.

'I've only been there once. I'd have been six, maybe seven. I never gave it a thought. Dublin and Swansea are the places I connect with my family.'

'Men,' said Bridgid. 'Never trust them to pass on the family history.'

'Is that why you're going down – to trace your family?'

'Yes. I've been down once already, without success. But this time there's a man home from England. He may be a relation. We've been in touch.'

'That sounds promising. Molly, Nell's fallen asleep,' Fanny said.

'Too much wine, she's not used to it.' Molly yawned. 'I'll be dropping off myself in a minute.'

'Are you going down as well?' Fanny asked Sean.

'Not to Ballydurkin. We'll go to Baltimore. I want to do some diving while Bridgid meets her longlost relations.'

'One day at the most should see that through then we'll do a bit more touring.'

'You both look very tired. Help me take Nell downstairs then you and Bridgid go to bed while Fanny and I clear up.'

'I'll help,' said Bridgid.

'No, you won't,' said Fanny. 'We know where everything goes. It won't take us a jiffy.'

'Poor old Nell. She hates the basement. I was surprised she agreed so readily to the sleeping arrangements,' Molly said as she stacked plates.

'It only seems like yesterday I was volunteering to sleep there when Rory brought Angharad over.'

'Old age, Fan, it takes us in many ways.'

'D'ye think she suspects they've been living together in Swansea?'

'Not for a minute. She hasn't had our experience.'

'No,' agreed Fanny. 'I'm glad we confessed some of our past to each other. It was more trusting of you. Mine you could have read about in the papers that reported the breach of promise case. D'ye still think about Tony?'

'All the time. And since Sean and Bridgid came, not just the settled domestic Tony. Seeing those two so obviously in love reminds me of what it was like. Watching them go upstairs just now with arms round each other made me envious. Is that terrible?'

'Very natural. I felt that way too. Remembering what being in love was like.'

'And as I told you, to begin with I wasn't. I seduced Tony to secure a home and finished up adoring him.'

'You were the luckiest of us. You had everything.'

'Everything is right!' said Molly. 'One day I may tell you just what everything was. But now we'll have a whiskey while we wash up, and then the basement.'

Chapter Forty-two

AFTER Sean and Bridgid left for Baltimore Nell seemed very depressed. Fanny and Molly assumed she was missing them. But when they suggested this to her she said it wasn't that. 'Not that I don't miss them, of course I do. It was something I read. Something about the Kennedy family. The papers and magazines have been full of articles about them. Did you know they are supposed to be cursed?'

'Rubbish!' said Fanny. 'Absolute rubbish. Millionaires, handsome men and women, and one of them President of America. How can they be cursed?'

'Two of them were killed in air crashes and one girl is mentally defective.'

'Well, thousands and thousands of men were killed in air crashes during the war. In any case, why should a curse on the Kennedys concern us?'

'Bridgid's name is Cronin. It reminded me of the story, I suppose, and now I'm worried about them. They're so precious. I love them so much. Supposing it is true that Mag Cronin's curse is real? I mean, that there is such a thing. I think we should warn them.'

'Oh, no, Nell, we must never mention it. I'm sure they'd just laugh, but you can't be certain. Some people are more susceptible than others. You just might implant a horrible idea in one or both of their minds,' said Molly.

'Well, I'm warning you, if I discover that you ever breathe a word about Mag Cronin or her so-called curse,

I'll never talk to you again.' Fanny was angrier than Molly ever remembered seeing her.

'I expected you to take that line. After all, you're the logical one in the family, the scientist. But I thought you'd understand, Molly. Reading your stars every day, telling me about the fortune tellers in London.'

'That's different. I don't believe any of it. Stars, fortune tellers . . . Well, I do for a minute, if it's what I want to happen, good things, happy events. Otherwise I dismiss them. And as for Mag Cronin – well, so far as I was concerned it was just another of Catti's stories.'

'But was it?' Nell persisted. 'We did have terrible ill luck in our family.'

'So do millions of people, all over the world. Every day. The Japanese in Hiroshima and Nagasaki, Jews in the concentration camps, passengers on the *Titanic*. Were they all cursed?'

'Trust you to preach and lecture, Fanny. I only thought it might be a precaution. Put them on their guard.'

'Someone should put a guard on your silly old tongue!' said Fanny, and left the room.

'Don't cry, Nell, I know you meant well. Let's say no more about it. I'll make a cup of tea then you have a little rest and tomorrow your precious pair will be back.'

That word again, 'precious'. Why was it niggling in her brain? Molly wondered after Nell went to lie down.

All the excitement, drinking more wine than she was used to, sleeping in the basement, had upset Nell's sytem. Just as well she didn't know what was going on upstairs. That would have convinced her the McCarthy family were firmly in the Devil's hands!

The young lovers arrived back, skins tanned, radiant-looking, full of high spirits and information. 'You tell them, Sean,' Bridgid urged, looking at him with adoration in her eyes.

'The McCarthys,' he said, 'are not a family to be proud of. At least not my great-great-grandfather, because he put Bridgid's great-great-grandmother out of her cottage and sent himself and herself . . . isn't that how the man from England described them?'

' 'Twas so,' said Bridgid, doing a poor imitation of an Irish accent.

'. . . put himself and herself into the Workhouse. But she, Mag Cronin, before she went, put a curse on our family that exists to the present day.'

'How did the man from England, as you call him, come by his information?' asked Fanny.

'Passed down the generations by word of mouth. Actually, Aunt Fanny, he was a nice guy. I changed my mind and popped over to Ballydurkin for an afternoon.'

'He was real cute,' Bridgid said. 'I spent the morning with him and after Sean came we had a good time in the public house. He doesn't believe in curses. And as for the eviction, there were thousands all over the country every day of the week. Wait'll I tell my folks! That Pat Cronin could make a fortune in the States. What an actor. What a story teller.'

Nell asked if they'd had lunch. Sean said no, but they were going into town to change their tickets. 'We're flying out a few days early. We're going to get married.'

The three sisters congratulated, kissed and hugged them, and then cried. Fanny left the parlour and came back with a bottle of champagne. 'It was to celebrate your return, it's been in the fridge for hours. Now we'll drink to your wedding and future happiness.'

After they'd left for town Nell became gloomy. Fanny made a moue at Molly, a signal to ignore Nell. But she looked so sad, so unhappy, Molly had to offer some comfort. She knelt beside her, telling her not to worry. Everything would be all right.

'How can you say that? How can you know for certain?'

'I just do. I have a feeling. And how can you be so positive in your opinion?'

Nell looked very old, bewildered, lost. Why can't I remember what's niggling in my mind. Precious . . . what was precious? Molly thought.

What is precious? What have I got that is? Sean, that's it! I love him more than anything in the world. He's someone precious to me. A wedding . . . That's it! That's what she said.

She stood up. 'Fanny, come here. Listen. I know it won't mean anything to you, but listen all the same. And you, Nell. If there ever was such a thing as the curse, it's finished. Well, almost.

'A long time ago I went to a fortune teller . . .' She described the place, the woman, the skull on the table, the woman's voice changing to an Irish accent. Even Fanny was listening intently now.

Molly described the fog, how it appeared to be coming in at the window.

'She was going into a trance,' said Nell, suddenly alert. 'It wasn't fog, it was ectoplasm.'

'Where did you learn of such things?' asked Fanny.

'From the television. She was a medium, a spirit had entered her body. From the brogue it had to be an Irish one. Sometimes they're red Indian guides.'

'Whatever it was, she rambled on and on. Then she collapsed. I got frightened and ran out.'

'She was in a trance,' Nell stated confidently. 'But what did she ramble on about?'

'Oh, yes, of course. That's what I started to tell you. About Mag Cronin's curse. And how it could be lifted for ever.' And she told them, freeing Nell's mind from worry at last.

'You wouldn't make that up, Molly? You wouldn't invent all that just to try and comfort me?' said Nell.

'Of course I wouldn't! This is far too important,' Molly protested.

'Oh, thank God, they're safe!' cried Nell. 'They'll marry and be free of the curse. I'll be there. I'll see them be married then I can die happy. I'm going to fly to America. Will you come with me, Molly? Come to America for the wedding?'

'I'd love to. Will you, Fanny?'

'You're both out of your mind. But at least if I went I'd be able to give you first aid if you collapsed. On one condition only, though.'

'What's that?' asked Nell.

'That you never mention any of this nonsense to Sean or Bridgid.'

'There's no need to. Her relation told them about the curse. You heard their reaction. But he knew the truth. Thank God it will soon be a thing of the past,' sighed Nell.

In a cafe in Grafton Street, Sean and Bridgid sat holding hands and gazing into each other's eyes. 'I think you should know you're holding the hand of a very special person,' Bridgid teased.

'I know it well.'

'You don't! I'm not who you think I am. My great-grandmother didn't have a child from your great-great-grandfather.'

'But I heard Pat Cronin tell you so?'

'Ah, that's because you weren't family. The secret could only be divulged to one who was. That, he said, was drummed into everyone who was told the truth. It has passed down from Bridgid Cronin's Cousin Patty. Whispered into her ear by Bridgid herself.'

'So what's the secret? And so much for Pat Cronin and his disbeliefs!'

'The parish priest was the culprit. "He had his way," to quote Pat, "and threatened the girl with eternal damnation

if she named him." And in any case, as Pat said, in those days who'd have believed her? So, Sean McCarthy, you treat me special. I'm blessed.'

'Every day of my life!'

'Isn't that a great story? I can't wait to tell it at home – my home, I mean, not your aunts'. Well, Fanny maybe. But not Nell. I think it would break her heart.'

'I think so too,' said Sean.

also available from
THE ORION PUBLISHING GROUP

☐ **The Girl from Penvarris**
£4.99
ROSEMARY AITKEN
0 75280 342 5

☐ **The Girl from the Back Streets** £4.99
JOYCE BELL
1 85797 418 2

☐ **Silk Town** £5.99
JOYCE BELL
0 75280 405 7

☐ **Dreams of Other Days** £5.99
ELAINE CROWLEY
0 75280 403 0

☐ **The Ways of Women** £5.99
ELAINE CROWLEY
1 85797 438 7

☐ **Goodbye Sweetheart** £5.99
LILIAN HARRY
1 85797 812 9

☐ **The Girls They Left Behind** £4.99
LILIAN HARRY
0 75280 333 6

☐ **The Shadow of Wings** £5.99
JUNE KNOX-MAWER
0 75280 332 8

☐ **Lights Out Liverpool** £5.99
MAUREEN LEE
0 75280 402 2

☐ **Stepping Stones** £5.99
MAUREEN LEE
1 85797 528 6

☐ **A Bridge in Time** £4.99
ELISABETH McNEILL
1 85797 406 9

☐ **Wild Heritage** £5.99
ELISABETH McNEILL
0 75280 287 9

☐ **The Poacher's Daughter** £5.99
MARY NICHOLS
0 75280 183 X

☐ **The Stubble Field** £4.99
MARY NICHOLS
1 85797 423 9

☐ **Old Father Thames** £4.99
SALLY SPENCER
0 75280 313 1

☐ **A Picnic in Eden** £5.99
SALLY SPENCER
0 75280 621 1

☐ **Salt of the Earth** £4.99
SALLY SPENCER
1 85797 146 9

☐ **Up Our Street** £4.99
SALLY SPENCER
1 85797 870 6

☐ **My Little Oyster Girl** £4.99
KIRSTY WHITE
1 85797 097 7

☐ **Tia's Story** £4.99
KIRSTY WHITE
1 85797 491 3

All Orion/Phoenix titles are available at your local bookshop or from the following address:

Littlehampton Book Services
Cash Sales Department L
14 Eldon Way, Lineside Industrial Estate
Littlehampton
West Sussex BN17 7HE

telephone 01903 721596, *facsimile* 01903 730914

Payment can either be made by credit card (Visa and Mastercard accepted) or by sending a cheque or postal order made payable to *Littlehampton Book Services*.
DO NOT SEND CASH OR CURRENCY.

Please add the following to cover postage and packing

UK and BFPO:
£1.50 for the first book, and 50P for each additional book to a maximum of £3.50

Overseas and Eire:
£2.50 for the first book plus £1.00 for the second book and 50p for each additional book ordered

- -

BLOCK CAPITALS PLEASE

name of cardholder .... *delivery address*
.... *(if different from cardholder)*
address of cardholder ....
....
....
....
postcode .... *postcode* ....

☐ I enclose my remittance for £............................

☐ please debit my Mastercard/Visa (delete as appropriate)

card number ⬚⬚⬚⬚⬚⬚⬚⬚⬚⬚⬚⬚⬚⬚⬚⬚

expiry date ⬚⬚⬚⬚

signature ....

prices and availability are subject to change without notice